Seven Archangels:
Perdition's Heirs

Seven Archangels: Perdition's Heirs

Jane Lebak

Philangelus Press
Boston, MA USA

Cover art by Charlotte Volnek
Editing by Michaela DeToma

Dedication

Angelic Special Ops isn't technically law enforcement, but it's close enough that I'd consider it "counterterrorism." I've known a few individuals who've worked both law enforcement and counterterrorism. They have my respect for their bravery and their willingness to sacrifice for the well-being of total strangers.

For that reason, I'm dedicating Perdition's Heirs *to Chris and Christine, two of my favorite law enforcement officers.*
Thank you for your service.

About the Nine Choirs

You've likely heard of the nine choirs of angels, but here's the refresher cheat sheet.

The trillion or so angels whom God created are organized in nine categories. Humans call them choirs for the same reason cows are "herds" and crows are "a murder" and executives are "a meeting." That is to say, English makes no sense. Angels can sing, but they don't always. We also call these groups "orders."

The choirs each have a rank, and from most powerful to least powerful, they go like this:
1. Seraphim
2. Cherubim
3. Thrones
4. Dominions
5. Virtues
6. Powers
7. Principalities
8. Archangels
9. Angels

Don't worry about memorizing that. There won't be a test.

Because human language is imprecise, humans tend to lump all of those together as "angels" even if they're not from the choir of Angels. When it's capitalized, you're referring to the choir. When it's lowercase, you're referring to any of the beings who were formed directly by God before the creation of the universe, spiritual but not physical. (Humans are made differently and don't turn into angels after death.)

Angels who rebelled with Satan are now demons, but they've retained their choir status as well as all the abilities and tendencies that come with each choir.

In general, if it matters what choir the angel is, they'll tell you. Cherubim, for example, are God's academics. The Seraphim are the fiery ones, emotional and generous. Most guardian angels are chosen from the lowest two choirs. Over time, the middle three choirs have gravitated toward defense and guidance, and that's where you'll find Special Ops.

Welcome to a world you've never seen, the world of unconventional spiritual warfare.

Chapter One

Cosmiel made himself nothing at all.

"Ye watchers and ye holy ones," goes the hymn, and for this moment, Cosmiel was both. With his angelic body discorporated, he staked out a sleeping human's bedroom as a watcher, waiting for the enemy's approach. Like a security camera, he didn't analyze. Instead, he quieted his soul into a stillness as absolute as the Void at the edge of Creation.

Existence was the primary good that God had created for angels. Sometimes Cosmiel's job required him to set aside that good.

With his whole team reduced to nothing but their own awareness, Cosmiel could no longer detect any other angels from Special Ops. As far as anyone was concerned, all four of them existed only in the memory of the lone guardian angel who sat exposed alongside his sleeping charge.

Then, an intrusion.

After centuries of discipline, Cosmiel didn't respond. Be aware of the intrusion, but allow the intruder to penetrate. Be—or only barely be. Take note of the encroaching evil. Don't interfere.

Not yet.

The guardian had secured this room with a shield constructed of willpower and authority. His Guard should have repelled anything that didn't have explicit permission to enter, and yet for three weeks this demon had been slipping through. Every night, it afflicted the human with nightmares. Every night, it drove the man closer to despair.

The guardian angel couldn't detect the demon until it struck, and afterward, the demon evaporated to escape capture. A contingent of Michael's soldiers hadn't had any better effect, and with every repeated nightmare, the human lost courage. Exhaustion and fear plagued his waking hours, then resurged during the sleeping ones. This wasn't an ordinary attack.

An unusual attack required an unusual defense. Enter Special Ops.

Experts at covert operations, reconnaissance, and improvisation on the fly, Special Ops inherited the jobs no other angels knew how to handle—or perhaps didn't even recognize as challenges needing to be handled. In a case like this, where an army couldn't keep out the intruder and the ministering angels couldn't resolve the damage, Special Ops stepped in to observe, assess, and then act.

Tonight was Cosmiel's favorite, the "act" part.

As before, although the man's guardian angel sat in watchful prayer, he hadn't detected the intrusion. To Cosmiel, that meant as far as the Guard was concerned, the demon had authority to enter. Intriguing.

The Guard thinned out until the demon slipped through. Cosmiel had once seen someone push a needle through a balloon without popping it, and in effect, this was what the demon had done: fortified the Guard all around itself, then reached through with the merest tendril of itself. Also, it was acting from a tremendous distance.

Cosmiel signaled one of the operatives, who vanished in silence from the stakeout. He'd trace the demon to wherever it had holed up to make its strike.

The demon coiled into the sleeping man's heart like a corkscrew. Wait.

Wait.

The demon readied its power, but just before it struck, Cosmiel burst back into reality, grasping the demon's tendril and choking off the energy.

The demon howled in pain and tried to rip itself from the man's heart, but another operative burst into the room to secure him, and a third filled the room with lances of light in every direction.

Struggling to keep a hold on the demon, Cosmiel called to the operative he'd sent away. "Sophiel! Do you have him on that end?"

In his mind, Cosmiel heard, *Working on it.*

The light lances were a Special Ops invention—not quite a Guard, not quite an angelic sword. They shot through the room from a dozen directions to pin the demon in place, but the demon was half here, half wherever it was striking from. With its energy trapped mid-discharge, both halves were screaming.

From Sophiel, *I've got him.* Following that rushed a sensation of dread, disgust, and understanding.

That sounded like a mystery solved.

The man's guardian angel knelt through his human charge, wings spread protectively against a midnight pierced with spikes of light. He kept projecting gratitude and fear, but their work wasn't ended.

Cosmiel called to Sophiel, "We need the demon in one place. Bring the rest of him here."

Negative. He's anchored to a human soul at this location.

Blast it, of course it wouldn't be easy. But then again, if it were easy, no one would have activated Special Ops.

Cosmiel signaled the other two, and they unpinned enough lances to move the demon while keeping him paralyzed. Cosmiel said to the guardian, "I need you with me." An operative remained to guard the sleeper while they put the demon back together in one place.

The demon hadn't been bilocating, which was fortunate. If the demon had actually split himself into two locations, Sophiel wouldn't have been able to backtrack to the second self. Instead, the demon had stretched himself out from thousands of miles away.

Cosmiel reached through his connection to Sophiel to identify the second location, then wrapped the demon in his blue-purple wings. With a solid grasp on their enemy, Cosmiel untethered them from the plane of Creation and twisted the universe around until the demon was all in one place—and they were there with him.

Angels couldn't typically do that, but Special Ops wasn't a squad of typical angels. They'd reappeared in a narrow street in daylight, surrounded by crowded apartments. Humans rushed past on the sidewalks, passing through without sensing the angels at all, but their guardians noticed and paid attention.

The demon's eyes projected hatred, but he was secured too tightly to speak. Sophiel finished chaining him so they could remove the lances, then moved everyone out of the road and into an alcove with some privacy. At that point, a second guardian angel joined them. Now the team had everything they needed to get this resolved: one demon awash in hatred, two guardians projecting cautious hope, and three Special Ops officers with silver-black uniforms and far too much experience battling evil.

His black eyes alight, Sophiel turned to the first guardian. "This demon is a vengeance demon. He's anchored into a human who not only hates your charge, but as far as I can tell has just cause in doing so."

Cosmiel flinched. "That 'just cause' being why the demon can penetrate the Guard?"

The guardian raised his wings. "But my Guard was strong. Michael's soldiers tried breaking it, and none of them could."

Sophiel shook his head. "Guards can't keep out a demon who has the authority to be there."

The guardian's eyes widened. "How did it get authority?"

With one jade-toned wing, Sophiel gestured to the second guardian. "The demon is anchored to his charge, a young man in one of the apartments across the street."

The new guardian added, "My charge was abandoned at conception. His mother was a woman your charge solicited for sex."

The first guardian angel flinched. "Given the location..." They were halfway across the world from where they'd been five minutes ago. "I can guess who she is. He promised her cash, then abandoned her without paying. He bragged about it afterward with his friends, that feeding her and keeping her off the street for five days was her payment."

Fury boiled up in Cosmiel's throat. Those were sins that cry out to God for vengeance.

Eyes tight, Sophiel looked aside. "I would never ask a guardian angel to divulge details about his charge's state of soul, but this demon's presence indicates the young man harbors anger against his progenitor. Because of the severity of the crime, the demon can act against your charge as well."

Trembling, the guardian covered himself with his wings.

Sophiel extended a wing to the guardian. "No one's blaming you for your charge's decisions. You're there to protect their ability to make good choices, but humans have free will."

Cosmiel added, "I would venture to guess your charge's nightmares never touched on the woman he used. The demon wanted to torture your charge while making sure he would never try to make it right."

Grief-stricken, the guardian angel raised his face. "My charge did ask God for forgiveness. Years ago."

Sophiel murmured, "Cheap grace."

Both guardian angels looked shocked. Special Ops angels tended to have their own vocabulary. It was rather blunt.

Cosmiel added, "After a crime this severe, it's not sufficient to ask forgiveness while doing nothing toward making it right. Asking is necessary, but even after God forgives, there's an ongoing temporal wrong to be addressed." Cosmiel stepped closer to the guardian and lowered his voice. "Your charge must have derailed this woman's life. She must already have been in poverty, and the pregnancy would have put her in even graver financial hardship. He isn't aware of his offspring's existence, so he's never provided for him. Serious crimes like these leave gouges in the soul that provide easy anchors for demons. A vengeance demon gets one hand in one human's crime, and the other hand in another human's wound. Using those, he's pulling them together."

Wide-eyed, the man's guardian raised his wings. "How can my

charge make good on the temporal evil? He doesn't know his son exists. I didn't even know!"

"Your charge has to bring it to prayer and work out with God what to do toward evening the scales." When the guardian angel looked overwhelmed, Cosmiel added, "God never requires a one-for-one repayment. Your charge can't undo all the suffering endured by the woman he discarded, let alone by his son. But he does need to make a start."

The guardian's shoulders dropped. "I'll bring her to mind and encourage him to pray for her."

Sophiel said, "Charity to others sometimes helps the process. Once your charge is praying for her, God may start identifying smaller penances for him, and those actions will begin to change your charge's heart. Together, he and God will work it out."

The son's guardian said, "What about my charge's anger? I've been struggling for years, but I'm not making any headway."

Some of the green faded from Sophiel's wings. "Anger is difficult to overcome as long as the injustice is ongoing."

Cosmiel yanked the demon to its feet. "Bring in the ministering angels for advice. You both may make progress now that we're getting rid of the attacker. Do whatever you can to prevent another vengeance demon from getting a grip, and pray together when possible. If it happens again, you both know what's at play."

Cosmiel dismissed both guardians, then trussed up the demon in tighter chains.

Sophiel and Cosmiel exchanged glances. Where to leave their captive? Cosmiel mused, "Oh, so many choices."

They carried the enemy combatant to the starless edge of Creation, the empty space where Sheol used to hang. The carapace of Hell dwarfed them in the deep stillness.

Sophiel anchored the demon's chains into Hell's outer wall. *That human man's soul—what a mess.*

Cosmiel replied, *They don't send us the neat and pretty assignments.*

Granted, but even assuming the guardian angel can evoke the woman to that man's mind—? How can he begin to make amends?

The man had been living alone, pushed incrementally toward despair. He'd already felt some guilt over what his younger self had done, so maybe now he might start taking steps by donating to charities against human trafficking, or maybe just being more conscious of injustice. Maybe by the time Christ separated the sheep and the goats, He would look that man in the eyes and say, "I was naked, and you clothed me."

Sophiel added, *And the son? He'll live his entire life in the shadow of one young man's evil impulse.*

Cosmiel replied, *I don't have answers. The rest is up to God and both those men. Only grace can stop that kind of evil from persisting to the next generation.*

Cosmiel turned his back on the demon and gazed into the Void. So still. So cold. As Creation thinned away to nothing, that emptiness also carried the promise of peace. No questions about tactics or appropriate use of force or how best to address the damage left in the wake of souls who never took it on themselves to care about the most vulnerable.

At his side, Sophiel projected, *When was the last time you got a breather?*

Instead of flinching, Cosmiel chuckled.

Sophiel's voice changed to a tease. *Two of the Cherubim created a puzzle for you. Six dimensions, three riddles to solve, and a precise order they have to be solved in or else the whole thing locks up in a permanent paradox.*

Cosmiel's eyes gleamed. He had five similar puzzles already, but he hadn't made the time to do them. Not in decades. Still... A puzzle with a paradox lock sounded enticing.

Sophiel brushed a wing against him. *Well?*

Cosmiel replied, *I need to check out things on the home front,* and he flashed back to Heaven.

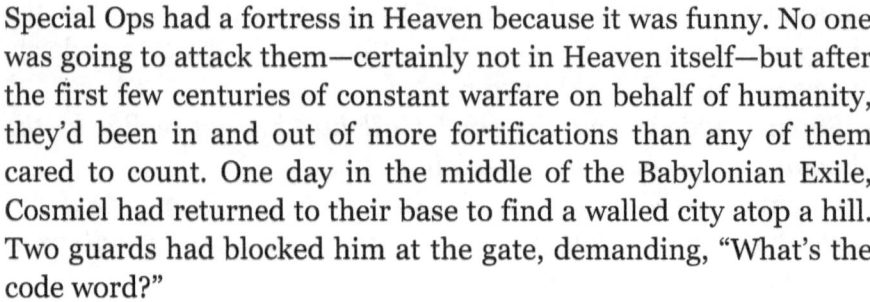

Special Ops had a fortress in Heaven because it was funny. No one was going to attack them—certainly not in Heaven itself—but after the first few centuries of constant warfare on behalf of humanity, they'd been in and out of more fortifications than any of them cared to count. One day in the middle of the Babylonian Exile, Cosmiel had returned to their base to find a walled city atop a hill. Two guards had blocked him at the gate, demanding, "What's the code word?"

Cosmiel had said, "The code word is, *I'm Cosmiel, chief of the choir of Powers, the angel in charge of the entire Special Ops division and therefore your boss, so let me inside,*" which both guards were inclined to agree was, in fact, the correct code. For the next half hour, Cosmiel had explored their beautiful fortress with its doubled walls and high watchtowers, amazed by the entire structure. Eventually he'd called over his second in command because this structure had Sophiel's fingerprints all over it.

Sophiel had appeared, jade feathers fluffed. "What do you think?"

He'd looked too pleased for Cosmiel to say anything other than, "Great job, but consult me next time."

He and Sophiel had worked together for so long that Sophiel hadn't needed to ask, but come on. Even if he knew the boss would love it, he ought to have cleared a change that big ahead of time.

The fortress had kept pace with modern developments. Eighty years ago, one of the team leads had added coiled double razor wire atop the walls, which led to debate: isn't barbed wire for cattle? It looked awesome, though, so it stayed.

New recruits all had the same final exam: break into the fortress. No operative had passed the test in two centuries, but they all scored high points for versatility and style, a good thing considering how often operatives would have to sneak into places angels shouldn't be allowed to go—or blast back out of them again. After each test, Sophiel would patch whatever had seemed like a security weakness in preparation for the next class's literal "entrance exam".

Today, Cosmiel started by checking in with whatever team leads were at headquarters. A school in Greece was dealing with a demonic infestation they couldn't shake. An engineering firm was being deluded by a technological breakthrough without considering its eventual application. A corrupt government (wow, hadn't heard that one before) was playing right into Satan's agenda.

At every stop, Sophiel remained by Cosmiel's side, taking notes and analyzing each case from multiple directions. As a Virtue, his best asset was his creativity. Well, his love of chaos—but the net effect was creativity, and in this job, he could leverage it all.

Afterward, Cosmiel stretched his four wings. What next?

Sophiel murmured, "If you recall, there was a puzzle in your office, and a whole lot of unused leave time."

Before Cosmiel could demur, a Dominion's voice broke into his mind. Auriel, another of his chief operatives, and the one spearheading their most complex case. *It's time. We're going in, and we need you.*

Chapter Two

An operative in a silver-black uniform appeared before Cosmiel. "Anna's approaching in the elevator."

Cosmiel signaled his team in the hospital hallway, and they took positions around, above, and beneath a room walled off by evil. Next, Cosmiel extended his senses until he felt the woman drawing nearer, but he still couldn't sense anything from inside the barricade. They'd tried and failed to break in. That left exactly one route inside, and one chance to take it.

A guardian angel with drab wings and dark eyes stood at Cosmiel's side, wordless. He was the only one not in uniform.

Alongside him, a smaller angel shook her head. Auriel's wings, eyes, and hair were all a beige-gold color, but the sparkle was gone from her eyes. She sent privately to Cosmiel, *With the Guard this strong—any attempt to save our target is a very long shot.*

It wasn't even a long shot. It was an impossible shot. Still, every human ought to have a final chance to ask forgiveness and receive mercy.

Every human soul. Even Linus Ellington.

Anna Ellington paused at the nurses' station. She was a trim, blonde women in her late thirties, all business in her blazer and skirt and heels. She asked a few questions, and then one of the nurses accompanied her down the hall.

Anna's guardian flashed to Cosmiel, feathers flared, never taking his sky-blue eyes off his charge. "Do you still want to do this?"

"Just like we practiced, Turmiel." Cosmiel reached for the guardian's hand. "All you need is my permission."

Shuddering with revulsion, the guardian angel accepted Cosmiel's touch and possessed him.

Cosmiel had done this so often in his Special Ops work that he actually relaxed as his soul got absorbed into Turmiel's. Demons possessed other souls all the time, but even though demons had invented possession, it wasn't an ability limited to demons—and it wasn't limited to possessing humans. Special Ops had long since decoded how one angel could take authority over another angel, although to most angels, the idea was repellent. Why anyone would want to do it remained a mystery.

Well, this was why: sometimes only specific angels had authority to enter a forbidden location. For example, the guardian angel of a human in his final hour had absolute permission to enter that space. Likewise, the guardian of the granddaughter who was about to enter that room. If those two guardian angels each took possession of another angel, they could "smuggle" two Special Ops defenders through the demons' Guard.

The drab angel was Geron, Linus Ellington's guardian. Geron reached for Auriel, who similarly relaxed her will so Geron could take command of her. Auriel's subtle body discorporated, and as she was absorbed into her possessor, now four angels were effectively two.

Turmiel hated it. Cosmiel could feel every bit of Turmiel's revulsion swirling through the guardian like sewage through a river, and Turmiel prayed continuously for strength to bear it long enough to smuggle his cargo inside. Cosmiel wanted to reassure him again that this was an acceptable use of possession, but while being possessed, he couldn't do much. That was the point of possession: for the time being, he was just another aspect of Turmiel.

The nurse stopped at the door, and Anna walked into the room alone except for the angels who passed through with her.

Turmiel recoiled as they crossed the threshold. The space was foggy with evil, a hot darkness centering on the bed at the far wall.

Turmiel, it's okay. Without a will of his own, Cosmiel couldn't steady him. Turmiel's aversion swept through his human charge, and Anna hesitated at the entrance.

"Grandfather?" Anna's voice sounded thin. "I'm here. It's Anna."

Demons charged her. Turmiel called his sword to his hand, and he pulled from Cosmiel's strength to defend her. "Back. You have no authority over her."

Grinning, one of the demons tugged an invisible thread. As if drawn by a fishing line, Anna followed it toward the bedside. She reached for her grandfather's hand but then stopped short of holding it.

To Anna, the room wasn't choked with smog. Anna's human eyes would see a clean hospital room illuminated by fluorescent lighting and a wall-to-wall window overlooking midtown Manhattan. She'd glance at the monitors, note the tray with untouched food, wrinkle her nose at the antiseptic smell, and eventually grow exhausted by the dry air and the monitors' low-level buzz.

Without sensing the demons, Anna would focus on the tall man laid flat, his sharp features all the sharper against his withering body. One week ago he'd been upright and acting as the power behind the throne—or rather, the power behind the CEO's office. Illness and death were taking him in a matter of days. Anna's face contorted as she attempted to disguise her grief, but Linus wasn't even looking at her.

Radiating anguish, Geron approached his human charge through the throng of demons. The fallen angels lashed out at him, but their weapons made no contact. They had authority over the human, but not over the guardian.

Turmiel gazed into the man's soul, and although Turmiel cringed, it was exactly as Cosmiel expected. While a soul like Anna's was flexible, strong, and translucent, her grandfather's was friable like rags, and brittle. What remained was opaque, and even with a guardian's more intimate perception, Geron most likely couldn't see into it either.

Turmiel swallowed hard. Making sure the demons wouldn't overhear, he projected directly into Geron's heart, *I'm so sorry.*

With the light gone from his eyes, Geron reached for Linus. *I knew they'd be eating away at him, but not like this.*

God's grace could heal this soul in a heartbeat, but selfish choices and the resulting justifications cut deep channels. By reinforcing those choices every hour for decades, a soul could, one bit at a time, corrode its own ability to ask for the mercy that could save it. In thousands of years, Cosmiel had seen souls rescued from this state exactly twice.

Oh, but the relief when those two had asked. The shock, followed by the joy, followed by even more relief and laughter. Even for souls in a worse state than this, God was always reaching out. When those two had reached back...?

The demons snickered while Geron sat with his charge for the first time in six decades. Some guardian angels got barred from their charges because of the humans' hardened sin, but in this case, Geron had been forced away by a contract. An acknowledged deal with the devil.

Turmiel didn't dare stop concentrating on Anna. The room was thick with fallen angels—mocking, snickering, leering, but also calling to the woman. *This is it. This is where it ends, and there's nothing more. At least your grandfather lived a life of comfort. That man had power. Snap his fingers, and he'd get anything he wanted. Anything at all.*

Cosmiel couldn't silence them. He couldn't keep Anna's heart from hearing them, and he couldn't shield Geron from their mockery, either. He should have taken steps in advance to protect the old man's guardian. He'd slipped, and Geron had to endure it now.

A demon tugged again at an invisible thread, and Anna edged nearer. "Sid and Forrest can't come today." Her grandfather wouldn't live until either of her brothers could arrive. "Sid's got a screen test for a role he really wants, and Forrest has a campaign fundraiser. But I can stay."

Her grandfather breathed, "Contract."

Turmiel's feathers flared.

"It's okay, Grandfather." Anna's voice went soft. "You trained me to keep everything under control at Pilaster. I've been the CEO for five years, and I'll keep taking care of the contracts. Everyone sends their best."

Cosmiel felt Turmiel's internal flinch at the lie. No one had sent their best. Although he'd founded a Fortune 500 company, Linus hadn't been well-liked.

Linus breathed, "Sign. Contract."

"Of course." Anna wrapped her arms around her waist. "I've got all the contracts under control."

In a room crammed tight with fallen angels, Anna sat without touching a dying man whose soul was shriveling like a love letter tucked between the logs of a fire. He lay with open eyes, breathing lighter and lighter as he stared at the ceiling. This hour was his last chance, and Cosmiel's job was to shield him so he might accept it.

Turmiel kept asking himself whether now was the right time to end the possession, so Cosmiel tensed like a nocked arrow at full extension. Turmiel wanted it to be soon. Wanted it now, in fact. In possession of Auriel, Geron was consumed with anything he could do to assist Linus's soul, except he couldn't touch anything that wasn't rotted through.

Raising his wings, Geron turned to Turmiel. "Now."

Turmiel cast out Cosmiel with enough force that he burst back into full control with his sword in his hand. At his back, Auriel did the same.

A powerful demon took form between them and the hospital bed, sparks in her wine-dark eyes as she manifested her sword. Satrinah, one of Satan's top Cherubim. Cosmiel had expected her to come. On Linus's contract with Hell, the countersignature was hers.

Cosmiel thrust himself in between Satrinah and Auriel, wings spread to protect his fellow operative. Auriel darted toward Linus, trying to get enough of a grip to work on his soul. Cosmiel couldn't shield her from all sides, though. There were so many demons, and he couldn't break the Guard on the room to give his forces access.

The minor demons didn't even have to be here. This demonic throng was a show of power, a chance to gloat at God's loyal angels during a condemned man's final minutes. Even if Hell had done nothing, Linus would still have been lost.

No. Not yet lost. Linus was a lost *cause*, not yet a lost *case*.

While Auriel worked on Linus's soul, Geron prayed for her success. Satrinah only smirked, not even trying to stop them. She had complete authority here. The best Cosmiel could do was to defend Auriel as she went deep into Linus's soul.

Auriel was begging God for Linus Ellington to have one clear minute, even one clear second when he could ask for mercy. She pleaded for Linus to receive the grace of rejecting decades of commitment to the luxury and power for which he'd traded eternity. She'd be broaching Linus's heart from every angle, pushing and challenging and reframing and plucking at all the invisible attachments he'd formed. *Anna. Sid. Forrest.* Over and over, she'd invoke every one of those connections. The strongest ones, though, the ones that bound tightest, would be connections that didn't lead to contrition. Admiration. Comfort. Control.

Auriel made some headway with the comfort because Hell would be uncomfortable, but then Satrinah's purple eyes pierced the opaque shielding of Linus's heart. She spoke in crisp tones. "Remember your loyalty. You never yield in the face of hard work. You honor your commitments."

Cosmiel tried to drive Satrinah away, but he couldn't. *Bravery shouldn't be a vice.* But that's what demons could do once they had control over a man. They spun vice into virtue and virtue into vague intentions.

Satrinah's words startled Auriel into changing tactics. Wings outstretched, she grasped Linus's lesser attachments. Demons worked with these threads all the time, tangling them to make knots, chains, nets—but because Linus Ellington's bonds were formed by sin and the attachment to sin, Auriel struggled to hold them.

She didn't need to hold them as much as to use them, though.

Auriel sent a burst of vibration along the one to Anna, like a note in a minor key. Tears filled Anna's eyes. Auriel sent bursts along all the rest of them as well—listening, testing, re-testing.

Satrinah flared with light, and energy shot back up the connection to Auriel, slamming her into the wall. Geron dove to cover her, but Auriel only leaped back onto the bed.

Satrinah bared her teeth. "Do that again. Let's find out what happens."

Cosmiel pushed up against Satrinah. "Are you scared of her? Why not try that trick on me?"

She gave an unsubtle roll of her eyes. "With your track record? You never stood a chance in the first place."

The demons hooted, but Cosmiel's wings raised. If he didn't stand a chance, that meant Auriel did.

Linus had mere heartbeats until the end. Cosmiel had operated with Auriel often enough to recognize that she'd dropped to her fallback position. Even so, Geron was still attempting to breathe love into any part of Linus's soul he could reach. Like all guardians facing a loss in the final hour, he struggled to revive even one sensation of joy where seeds of grace could extend a shoot toward the light. If Linus made a single impulse toward love, God could dispel this cloud of accusers.

Cosmiel held the line, but the demons weren't swamping him. Even Satrinah backed off, analyzing Auriel's technique. Cosmiel blasted energy at the Cherub, but Satrinah deflected it without effort.

With a shout, Auriel got a good grip on the soul. Geron breathed into Linus with all the love he hadn't been able to offer his charge in six decades.

The man's soul flexed, reached, and then withdrew into itself.

The soul crumbled and collapsed, and with that, all was lost.

Geron collapsed over Linus, wings limp, face in his hands. Then came the call. The final hour had ended in the moment of death.

The demons surged, but Cosmiel flared with energy to hold them back. "Geron, do you want me to take him?"

Geron's head snapped up. "No. I'm doing my job right to the

end."

The guardian angel wrapped around his charge's soul, then slipped between soul and body like a blade sharp enough to shear the electrons off an atom. A twist, and the soul was out, cradled in Geron's hands.

Most human souls had a shape, but Linus's didn't. After decades of rot, it was formless. Its attention was fixed not on the angels, but on the demons. On one specific demon.

Satrinah stepped forward, and Linus's soul lurched toward her. "Hand him over. He's mine."

Without releasing his charge's soul, Geron flashed from the room to God's judgment hall.

The hospital monitors counted down to zero. Anna pushed the nurse call button.

Cosmiel blew outward, detonating the Guards surrounding the room so his team could clear the area.

Standing with folded arms as Special Ops drove out the minor demons, Satrinah remained at the bedside. Auriel knelt through Linus's corpse, face in her hands. Satrinah raised her six wings and towered over her. "Given what you've learned, I suggest you surrender now. Our outcome is assured either way."

Cosmiel got between them. "Leave my operative alone."

"By now that man's judgment will be complete. I can claim my prize." Satrinah turned toward Anna, and Turmiel raised his sword. She waved him down. "I mean you no harm. But do be warned, that poor guardian's present condition is your future."

Cosmiel stepped between Satrinah and Anna, wings spread. "Aren't you supposed to be collecting your prize? There's nothing here for you."

Satrinah snickered. "Oh, little Power, there are three somethings —and I intend to collect."

Chapter Three

Cosmiel suggested Auriel and Turmiel take an hour to gather themselves before he debriefed them. Auriel wouldn't do it, of course. With a Dominion's sensitive spirit and protective nature, she would engage in the sweetest possible disobedience by joining Geron and offering whatever comfort she could.

Cosmiel went back through the Special Ops fortress to check on every operative currently available. Two of them looked strained, and he ordered them to take time off, at least long enough to attend four divine liturgies—and not consecutively.

Theirs was unrelenting work. One of the Special Ops requirements was that every member have a hobby absorbing enough to stop time in their hearts. Something like puzzle paradoxes. Furloughs were non-negotiable, and if three operatives agreed, they could furlough their own superior officer. Before allowing an operative's return, Sophiel required a detailed write-up of how they'd relaxed. That sounded like a joke, but Sophiel had been known to kick his own operatives back out if they hadn't decompressed enough.

When everyone was in a good place, Cosmiel retired to his private office, Guarded the walls, and crumpled in the corner with his face in his hands.

Father, that man's soul.... With all four wings tight to his body, Cosmiel shuddered. That man's soul, and the guardian's grief, and the mockery of the demons who were *laughing,* who thought it was *funny* that a human creation breathed forth from pure love was charred and ruined—who dared think it hilarious that the guardian angel who'd loved him and nurtured him was stroking that soul with a broken heart— *God, I can't—*

He should have prevented Geron from hearing the demons. It was a ridiculous oversight. Silencing their mockery was the least anyone could do for a guardian angel in that position.

Auriel had handled it well. She was an expert at working under high pressure, and after fifteen centuries, no demon could say anything that would distract her, let alone break her spirit. Cosmiel had never seen an angel able to focus like Auriel, and that included the entire choir of Thrones.

Geron, though.... For the demons to torture him with their words was beyond cruel. They already had the human. What did it benefit them to harm the angel?

Cosmiel extended his heart to God, and grace seeped in. Slowly he unclenched his heart, relaxing his wings until the blue-purple cocoon opened. The rest of his tension melted like water. The Linus Ellington case had been a brutal assignment. From the start, there'd been no hope of success. That was why Cosmiel had taken it.

Sophiel would have headed in there. Any of their team could have slipped into that hospital room, but it wasn't fair to thrust them into a fight with the certitude of defeat.

You're looking out for them well, God reassured him. *They love you as their leader.*

Cosmiel went deeper in prayer until he couldn't even produce words, could only hold out to God the sharp ache that swelled every time he remembered Geron's drab wings and Turmiel's disgusted fear.

Then he went one level further until he was totally absorbed in God, contemplating without analyzing. Accepted. Sustained. Fed. God flowed through Cosmiel, and Cosmiel let that current align all parts of him until the rough edges smoothed away.

When God settled him back in himself, he got to his feet. The hour was up. Back into the battle.

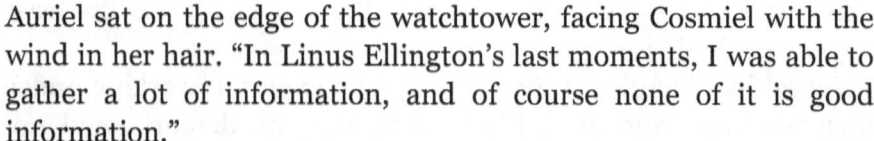

Auriel sat on the edge of the watchtower, facing Cosmiel with the wind in her hair. "In Linus Ellington's last moments, I was able to gather a lot of information, and of course none of it is good information."

Sophiel adjusted his sword belt. "Lay it out, then."

The fortress had war rooms. They could gather in any one of them to have a sedate discussion. Or they could find places for themselves in the light and the wind, Heaven in motion all around. With a failed assignment at their backs and a tougher one before them, this meeting belonged in the open air.

Cosmiel glanced over the gathering. In addition to the Special Ops contingent, he'd invited Michael as head of the army and four guardian angels, Geron and Turmiel among them.

Tingling with the residue of Auriel's power, Geron looked sad, but not distraught. (Cosmiel was right: she had gone to him.) Maybe Geron had spent the last hour in prayer much as Cosmiel had, and maybe that would be enough to support him for as long as he needed to be here.

Even so, Geron deserved a soothing period of silence in the hands of God, not a debriefing. Cosmiel said to Geron, "We won't keep you long. You've already given us most of what we need to know."

Auriel added, "I told you this already, but I wanted to say it again in front of everyone else: you were fantastic. I was impressed by how you kept breathing love into Linus's soul, and he did respond to you."

Geron couldn't raise his eyes. "I suspected how far gone he was."

Cosmiel braced himself. "I'm sorry I didn't silence the demons. You didn't need to hear them."

Wings tight, Geron nodded without meeting Cosmiel's eyes.

Michael said to Auriel, "What information were you able to get?"

Auriel tucked her knees against her chest. "Linus's contract tied him to Satrinah, since she was the countersigner, and the bonds between him and her were strong like elevator cables. Geron reported there was some slack in that bondage during the initial aftermath of his signing, but over the years she'd tightened him up until she had absolute control—and with his full consent. While Geron was able to win Linus the opportunity to make a free choice, Linus chose to remain with Satrinah rather than to reject the contract."

Michael sighed. "I never understand why humans resort to this."

Auriel raised her wings. "Likely for the same reason any soul rejects God and joins up with Satan—or why Satrinah herself is effectively contracted out to Asmodeus and Moloch. The humans enter a bad bargain because it gives them a momentary advantage, and they remain with it because their demonic sponsors keep them comfortable enough to deter second thoughts."

Geron said, "Linus's company was failing, and he felt humiliated. He'd prayed for help, but help never arrived in a form he would accept. Satrinah, on the other hand, teased him along a trail of breadcrumbs that kept rewarding him with small successes. When he was on the brink of bankruptcy, she made the promises he wanted to hear, and they closed the deal. For the next sixty years, she held up her end of the bargain, and for all his flaws, Linus was a loyal man. He held up his."

Michael shook his head.

Auriel put her arm around Geron's shoulder. "You don't have to stay for this. You've done enough."

Geron squared his shoulders, but he didn't raise his head. He was projecting willingness to help, but behind that emotion lay deep, deep sorrow.

Cosmiel said, "We'll come back to you for any questions we can't answer."

Geron glanced again at Auriel, then flashed away.

The angels stood in silence a moment. *God, please.* Geron was just gutted. *Please, give him comfort.*

In a soft voice, Auriel said, "Now we face the next step. I was able to confirm that Satrinah's contract is transferrable down to the fourth generation."

Fear spiked through all three other guardians. Turmiel, who'd seen Linus's soul right at the end, exclaimed, "How can his agreement affect them?"

Auriel said, "If you recall, in his last minutes, I was vibrating all his emotional connections. You felt how I was able to affect Anna, and you also saw how the demons were able to tug that thread to draw her near to him."

Turmiel exclaimed, "But his contract doesn't give them a special hold over her soul!"

In a low voice, Cosmiel said, "Auriel is our best expert on intergenerational evil, and the existence of intergenerational curses is established in the Bible."

Turmiel fell silent, but his eyes were dark.

Auriel said, "Linus's children are dead, but because the three grandchildren were raised by him and his wife, they're now his heirs. His most obvious tie is to Anna because he and she worked together, but he also had very strong ties to the two grandsons, and those ties are reciprocated. All three siblings have materially benefitted from the agreement between Linus and Satrinah, which further strengthens their ties. That would be the case in any demonic agreement, but the wording of the agreement itself gives Satrinah a claim on all three. When Linus died, Satrinah assumed control over those connections. The enemy's next move will be to approach all three grandchildren to renew the agreement."

Cosmiel leaned against the battlement. "We're fortunate in one regard: Satrinah can only approach each grandchild once. If they refuse the deal, her claim is broken. She can't force them to reject her over and over again. Likewise, any of them who accept her agreement would be bound by the terms of the original contract, and we as outsiders wouldn't have authority to take action to rescind it."

The guardian angels were all silent. Watching, Michael looked sad.

Auriel added, "The grace of God can break any and every

contract, but the first effect of the contract is to prevent the actions of sanctifying grace. The demon who signed the contract in effect assumes the place of God to give whatever gifts it wants, meaning that demon becomes the sole service provider. As we saw with Linus, this creates a bond that's nearly unbreakable. For the purposes of this assignment, we have to consider each human's decision to be one-and-done."

Michael said, "What form should we expect this contract to take?"

In broad daylight, talking about her speciality, Auriel sparkled gold. "Descendant contracts follow the same form as the originating contract. In this case, it's likely to offer an exchange of services, closed with a verbal or a signed agreement, and sealed with a token."

Turmiel cocked his head. "What kind of token? And why?"

Auriel's was a horrible area of knowledge to specialize in, but she took so much pride in her work. Ten years ago, Cosmiel had been on an assignment where he'd overheard a mortician, two pathologists, and a surgical nurse eating at a buffet. They'd had a similarly enthusiastic conversation, and only at the end of it, with all four guardian angels snickering, had Cosmiel realized that every neighboring table had cleared right out.

Auriel picked up speed as she explained. "A token can be any physical object the human chooses, but in general it represents a sacrifice. In American culture, contracted human souls don't sacrifice living things, but they do offer something of high value to themselves in exchange for whatever the demon is offering. I've seen tokens of every sort, from money to books to table linens to property. The demon may or may not take the item from the possession of the contracting human, but it does have to be a physical item."

Turmiel frowned. "Why physical?"

"Our enemies can't do anything truly creative." Auriel shrugged. "That's the best I can come up with. Human souls are most comfortable relating to the material world. That's why there's going to be a final resurrection that reunites them with their physical forms—because they don't *have* a body as much as it's a part of them."

Cosmiel prompted, "And the token—?"

"I'm getting to that." She side-eyed him. "Because of their physicality, humans feel best interacting with the preternatural or the supernatural partially through their senses. That's why they create beautiful churches and worship with music. It's why they gather in shared spaces and raise their hands or hug one another or kneel during prayer: they instinctively want to pray with their bodies. Jesus came to them in a body. Moreover, when you look at how God reaches out to them at pivotal moments, it in two parts, with form and with matter."

Cosmiel reassured Michael, "Bear with her," and Michael raised his hands.

Auriel said, "In baptism, you have the words of baptism but also the pouring of water. The words are the form and the water is the matter. In communion, you have the words and the intention, but you also have the bread and the cup. Christ built those things into the system because humans need the physical. So you'll have people praying over other people...accompanied by the laying on of hands, or anointing with oil, or breathing on them."

Turmiel wove his fingers together. "You're saying agreeing to the contract is the form, and the token is the matter?"

Auriel pointed at him. "Correct. The demons cannot make the contract without a token, and the token is always chosen and provided by the contracting human."

Cosmiel added, "Destroying the token doesn't break the contract."

Auriel faced all three guardians. "The more important the token the human offers, the harder it is to get them to break the agreement afterward. If you end up in that position, encourage your charge to hold back when selecting a token. It might give us breathing room later on."

Cosmiel offered silent thanks that parents no longer sacrificed their own children.

Michael turned to the three guardians. "I don't need to tell you how serious this is. All three of you will have whatever backup you want. I've already stationed a security detail around each of your charges, as well as around the spouses and children."

Auriel ran a hand through her short hair. "Thank you. That will give us a few days to shore up our position. Satrinah knows she's allowed one chance to make the offer. She can't approach for the first few days because that's a contractual blackout time, but once she's got everything ready, it's a guarantee she'll move in."

Frowning, Cosmiel said to Michael, "This operation ought to be in Special Ops jurisdiction."

Wings raised, Michael nodded. "Absolutely. But given what you're up against, you can use additional resources. I'm placing those at your disposal."

Sophiel flexed his wings. "It's unfortunate in cases like these that greater numbers don't necessarily lead to better outcomes. With the whole army in that hospital room, we still would have lost Linus Ellington. Our enemies herd in their forces, but the majority of the demons do nothing other than harass us and clutter the place up."

Cosmiel folded his arms. "Since the balance is decided in one soul, by the one soul, our key to victory lies in choosing the correct players for the correct roles. As I said before, Auriel is our best expert on intergenerational evil. She has to be involved as we go forward."

Michael raised his hands. "No objection. But Auriel, if you ever require a legion of angels with swords, you'll have them."

Again her eyes sparkled. "I appreciate the offer."

Cosmiel said, "I'll be heading up this defense myself." Before Sophiel could object, he raised a hand. "This case is our top priority, and I need someone in charge of everything else. You're the one."

Sophiel's black eyes managed to darken, but he didn't object.

Cosmiel turned to the guardian angels of Anna and her two brothers. "I'll be meeting with each of you to assess Satrinah's most likely avenue of approach, and then we'll fine-tune our defense."

Turmiel's hands clenched. "We can beat this, right? All three of us have been shoring up our charges against a potential contract offer ever since we were assigned, so that's got to help somewhat. Won't it?"

The note in his voice was heartbreaking. His charge Anna was in the greatest danger. She'd likely be approached first, and when she gave in, Satrinah would have that much more leverage against the remaining two.

Turmiel's voice deepened, a challenge. "Satrinah insulted your track record. In a case like this, what is your success rate? Auriel may be the best expert at intergenerational evil, but what about you?"

One of the other two guardians spoke up for the first time. "It's going to be a fight. I told you as much, but we have to stick it through to the end, the same way Geron did."

Cosmiel met the speaker's gaze, fighting a deep, deep dread. Jezaryah was the guardian of the middle brother, Forrest.

Also, until he'd been called up as a guardian angel, Jezaryah had worked for Special Ops. He knew the odds.

He knew there was no hope.

Chapter Four

Jezaryah perched atop the Chicago to DC flight, a bitter wind searing through him while Forrest dozed in business class beneath.

Jezaryah tilted back his head to see the stars. There was no need to protect the plane because with this much on the line, Satrinah wasn't going to let anything happen to Forrest. If a minor demon so much as caused turbulence requiring the seat belt sign to go on, she'd boil him in the Lake of Fire.

Of course, the angelic bodyguards Michael had assigned would be thinking Jezaryah was on the roof watching for problems, so he monitored the hum of the engines and the flow of the air. In reality, he wanted privacy. He wanted to pray, except when he reached out for God, he had no words.

Well, one word. *Forrest.*

A presence joined him on the roof. Cosmiel.

They rode in silence, Jezaryah struggling to come up with any prayer other than his charge's name. He wasn't ready for this. For the planned fight, yes, but not for the reality. He'd recognized it was coming ever since the minute he'd been assigned, but he'd kept hoping. Forrest's parents had died in a helicopter accident before they'd had to face the decision. Everyone called it a tragedy —even to the point of claiming the Ellington family was cursed— but Jezaryah had deemed their deaths a blessing. A blessing for them, that was. Not for their children. Their deaths had put their children into the crosshairs.

Cosmiel said, "Thank you for defending me back there."

Jezaryah stared at the rivets securing the skin of the plane. "I didn't realize Forrest was hopeless."

The wind and the engines roared while a gaping hole filled his heart.

Cosmiel said, "There's always hope."

"You always take the hopeless cases." Jezaryah couldn't look at his former commanding officer—and future commanding officer. "Yes, I'm a little sensitive about your track record because it bothers me how taking the hardest assignments gives you the worst outcomes. Then you took on this. I hadn't realized it was that dire."

Cosmiel said, "You have better insight into Forrest than I do."

That was a non-assurance of the very highest caliber, and Jezaryah closed his eyes. "I felt it. When Auriel struck the bond from his grandfather to him, a vibration sounded off within Forrest."

Cosmiel said, "The worst sound you ever heard."

"Forrest didn't recognize it. He doesn't believe in intuition, doesn't hold with inspiration, doesn't..." Forrest believed in almost nothing, not even his own campaign advisors. "But even without recognizing it, he responded spiritually. The attachment is anchored in his core."

Cosmiel shook his head. "Still, there's hope."

"Satrinah will have any number of leverage points with Forrest." Jezaryah fought to stay clinical. How would he have reported to Sophiel back when he was just another operative? If he'd been asked to analyze the situation without any attachment to the human target, what would have seemed most significant? Not his memories of Forrest as a gangly boy. Not his endless struggle to show Forrest a more accepting aspect of the world. "Forrest is running for re-election, and he's wrapped up in fundraising and campaign stops. He's hunting for anything that will give him a point in the polls."

Cosmiel sighed. "The timing's unfortunate."

"You mean, why did Linus live long enough to die during an election year?" Jezaryah snorted. "Ask Satrinah. She didn't leave his death date to chance."

Demons couldn't kill without permission. Linus Ellington had given Satrinah every permission she could have needed. Toward the end, Jezaryah often wondered if Linus's soul didn't reach out to Satrinah's in welcome whenever she visited. The contract had deprived Linus of contact from his own guardian angel, and one thing Jezaryah hadn't expected about guardianship was how much the human souls loved the touch of angels—specifically, their own guardian angels.

He hadn't expected how much he'd love the touch of his charge's soul.

Geron had decades to make peace with the inevitable, except he'd maintained hope. Now Linus had gone where he'd chosen to go, and Geron was still here.

The obvious advice should be not to hope. To keep his plans as practical as possible, to assess the same way Jezaryah would have assessed while with Special Ops, and to set his efforts wherever they'd be most assured of fruition. An iron-cold mind would counsel against love in the hopes of not having one's heart broken.

Instead, when Cosmiel had refused to give Sophiel this assignment, Jezaryah's emotions had crashed because it meant devastation.

Even at this altitude, the frigid air couldn't affect either angel. The hair and feathers of their subtle bodies caught the wind, but that same wind passed through them as it curved along the body of the plane.

"I'm going to do everything I can." Cosmiel sounded subdued. "I will review each of those leverage points with you. We'll consider every possible defense, and between the two of us, we can devise the best strategy for Forrest."

Not a way to win. Just the best strategy.

"I understand." Jezaryah turned to Cosmiel and extended a wingtip. "We'll give it our best effort and pray he responds to God's grace."

I just wish there were hope, Jezaryah prayed.

There's always hope, God replied. *Even in the last seconds, Geron didn't lose hope, and neither will you.*

Chapter Five

Anna met Forrest outside the funeral home with a hug so tight it squeezed away the loneliness.

"Thank you for being with him at the end," Forrest said, but it didn't matter what he was saying. Her brother was here, and for a moment, Anna had an ally. "I wish I could have been with you."

"You didn't have a choice." Unwilling to step out of his embrace, Anna rested her head on his shoulder. "I explained to him. He wasn't really alert at the end, but he was peaceful when he died."

Forrest let her go, and she hugged his wife too. Julia embraced her quickly, saying, "I'm sorry for your loss." Then Forrest held the door for them to enter.

The funeral home smelled of lilies and sterility. Anna wanted to hang back like she always had as a child, but nowadays she was in charge. She'd made the arrangements, paid the bills, and overseen the preparations. Her grandfather had once been Pilaster Group's CEO, and for the last five years she'd been CEO, so the thing to do was stride into that room like she owned it. Which, considering the amount she'd written on that check, she ought to.

They'd opened all the viewing room partitions to create one immense gathering space, and well-wishers had filled it with floral arrangements. On racks, on tables, and stacked in rows, flowers dominated. Grandma would have loved this. Cecilia Ellington had always adored flowers, and at Grandma's funeral, four open-air flower cars had followed the hearse, all those ribbons waving in the wind.

Anna should have brought Grandma flowers sooner, though. Like every time she'd come home from college.

At the very front was Grandfather's casket and a kneeler. Anna remembered the drill. She knelt, hands folded. She ought to have bowed her head, but instead she studied her grandfather's face.

He looked stern. She kept trying to read his expression to anticipate what might have made him angry.

Sign that contract.

She smiled at his voice in her head. That was vintage Grandfather. Even after he'd stepped down as Pilaster's CEO, he'd been at her back, demanding compliance, issuing directives, machine-gunning advice. Grandfather was an ace businessman. He'd known exactly which failing companies to snap up for a song. Then, given a few touches—an adjustment here and a reorg there, plus a financial infusion—suddenly his new acquisitions would be thriving at the world's center stage.

The final thing he'd asked her to do was sign a contract, but he'd been so weak. Who even knew which contract he was thinking about?

Anna stood as Forrest's wife joined her. Folding her arms, Julia leaned on one leg. "He looks intense."

"It doesn't surprise me. He always got what he wanted." Anna sighed. "Have you heard an updated arrival time for Sid?"

Julia dusted some lint off her sleeve. "Sid shows when he shows, and you'll be happy about it."

During the four hours of tonight's viewing, Anna shook hundreds of hands and thanked CEOs and lawyers and accountants and reporters for their condolences. She reassured everyone that Linus had been at peace in his final hours, and they promised that now he was with her grandmother.

Anna took a break to get a drink from the lobby's water cooler. Would Grandma really be with him now? Someone once said there's no marriage in Heaven, so maybe Grandma had met Grandpa at the Pearly Gates and thanked him for coming, and then returned to the largest flower garden in the history of the universe. Grandpa would then march himself right over to God's C-suite and demand an appointment from whichever angel functioned as God's administrative assistant.

Sign the contract.

Yes, Grandfather, she thought. *Your company is in good hands. You trained me for decades to do this.*

"Babe!"

Anna spun as Sid rushed up to her. "You made it!"

"Of course I made it." He squeezed her, and she settled into his arms. He was here. They were all here now, and that was what mattered. "This is a zoo! You'd never have noticed if I hadn't shown. I could have told you I'd been, and you'd never have been able to prove I hadn't."

"Please. You've never been anywhere without everyone noticing you. Oh, but your flowers arrived, and so did your agent's." She looked him up and down. Sid was even more dazzled up than usual. Had he stopped for a haircut and a spa visit on the ride from the airport? "We've also gotten quite a few arrangements from your Hollywood friends."

"I knew I could count on them." Sid put his arm over her shoulder. "You holding up? You're the one who spent the most time with him."

Anna nodded. "I'll be fine. He was himself right up to the end. The very last thing he did was tell me to sign a contract."

Sid hesitated. "Okay, that's odd, because when I walked in here, I heard him in my head, clear as day. *Sid, you better sign that contract.*"

Wide-eyed, Anna said, "Wow."

"Yeah. The old man had plenty of opinions, didn't he? Well, he'd better get me a contract to sign. I'm in contention for a role that will make my entire career."

Anna chucked his shoulder. "Are you listening to yourself? They're going to snap you up."

Sid looked momentarily worried. "You have no idea how competitive things are when the money is good."

Forrest stepped out of the viewing room. "Hey! I thought I felt a rush of wind as your ego entered the building!"

Sid pointed at him. "Not my fault it throws sparks whenever it brushes against your greatness."

Anna waved a hand. "Wow, it sure is getting self-important in here."

Her brothers laughed. They looked great together in suits and ties, a pair of Ellingtons with the world before them.

Forrest said, "Look, this thing is going on until nine o'clock. Afterward, Julia's heading back to the apartment, but let's just us find a place and get some food because we're not going to be able to talk here with a thousand people walking in and out."

Anna put her arm in Sid's. "That sounds like a great idea. Plus, we have to do this all over again tomorrow, and then the funeral. Better to have everything on the table ahead of time."

Sid grinned down at her. "There's my CEO talking."

She wrinkled her nose, and they walked back into the viewing room.

As she stepped inside, she heard it again. *Sign the contract.*

At a nearby bar and grill, Sid ordered a full meal because he hadn't eaten since lunch at LAX. Anna ordered some soup, and Forrest poked at a salad. The food was nothing special, and neither was the decor. The place's only recommendation was it was two doors down from the funeral home, and it was still open at ten o'clock.

Anna said, "The estate lawyer wants to talk to you two, and she needs letters affirming that you're not going to contest the will. Once you've got that out of the way, Lisa can start the rest of the process."

Sid rolled his eyes. "Probate takes forever."

Forrest said, "Maybe that's the contract I keep feeling like he's harassing me about."

Anna put down her spoon and stared at him. Sid said, "Wait,

you too?"

Forrest looked from one to the other. "Hang on, what?"

Anna closed her eyes. "This just got really weird. The last thing Grandfather said to me was about a contract, so I figured that's why it kept ringing in my head."

"Bells are hollow. You've got a pretty good brain in yours." Forrest frowned. "What's going on?"

Sid waved a hand. "Nothing's going on. Grandfather always stressed about flying with a contract for anything you did. Remember when I asked him for an advance on my allowance so I could buy a car, and he made me sign a contract for it?" He shook a finger in Forrest's face. "You don't sign a contract until you've vetted it, boy. You know what you're getting out of it. You be aware of exactly what conditions invalidate it, and you hold up your end of the bargain because that's what you agreed to."

Anna laughed. "That's his voice."

Forrest huffed. "Sure, except all three of us shouldn't still be hearing it, on account of he's dead."

Anna shrugged. "It's one of the things about him that we're all holding onto."

Grandfather hadn't been the most affectionate man. He hadn't even treated Grandma with warmth. But Anna wasn't so innocent in that regard, either.

Forrest said, "Regardless, let's meet with Lisa and sign whatever legal thing she says will get the ball rolling. Sid, you've seen the will, right?"

Sid nodded. "No surprises, Anna the executive is the executor, and otherwise it's all a three-way split. There's some stuff I want as mementos, too, if that's okay."

"You mean like his pocket watch?" Anna dug in her shoulder bag until she came up with a palm-sized box wrapped in paper. "I knew you'd want that."

Sid's eyes widened. "Awesome! Thank you!"

Forrest chuckled. "You're getting a jump start on looting the estate, Sid."

"Hush, you." Anna handed him a longer box. "I didn't forget

you."

Forrest put a hand over his heart. "Well, that's a first. Wait, is that his fountain pen?"

"The very same. Also this," and she passed him a book.

Sid exclaimed, "No fair! I wanted that!"

Forrest's eyes were huge. "*Where the Red Fern Grows*? Where did you find this?"

Sid said, "Anna, you should have kept it. How many times did you read that to us after Mom and Dad died?"

Forrest was shaking his head. "No, you don't understand. Grandfather told me he'd thrown it away. I asked him for it years ago."

"It was on one of the high shelves, so maybe one of the cleaning staff put it there?" Anna shrugged. "I began sorting through his stuff once he got sick."

Sid nodded. "Makes sense. No need to drag out the process."

Anna leaned back in her chair. "Any idea what other mementos you want?"

Sid pursed his lips. "That painting in the sitting room, the one with the horses. Also, if neither of you wants his piano, I'd love that moved over to my place. Appraise the piano and take that and the shipping out of my portion of the estate money."

Forrest said, "Remember that cigar box he always kept on the desk?"

Anna said, "Oh, right," and pulled that out of her messenger bag to hand across the table. "Yes, I remember it. Although I nearly forgot it."

Sid laughed. "Oh, for crying out loud! Remember how you used to go into his office every week and pay part of your allowance back into that stupid box?"

Forrest's brow furrowed, and he deepened his voice. "It's an investment, boy!"

"Well, now it's Grandfather's last campaign donation." Anna rested her chin on her hands. "And for me, he already gave me the clock and that antique French desk last year."

Sid snorted. "That desk is bigger than some apartments. Did you even want it?"

She waved him down. "No, but he insisted. Forrest, you'll need something more. Otherwise it's really unfair, like you got forgotten."

Forrest snorted. "How would that be any different? But if you can find them, I want Grandma's engagement and wedding rings. I also want to go through his books because there are a bunch more he told me he threw away that I would love to keep."

"Done. We can meet at his place tomorrow and get the mementos sorted out." Anna smiled. "Maybe once the paperwork is in motion, we won't hear him badgering us about the contract."

Chapter Six

Auriel flexed her wings as she settled herself in Anna's dark living room. The apartment was amazing, and Auriel made note in case she ever wanted to re-design her own quarters in Heaven. That fantastic grandfather clock, for one thing. The fish tank along the side wall. The floor-to-ceiling bookshelves. The only thing it needed was a few dozen plants. Well, a few dozen *more* plants.

Except, of course, if Anna signed away her soul, then Auriel's own home would be a reminder of tragedy, and how could she enjoy it?

Auriel gestured to the Archangel soldiers positioned around them. They cleared the room of minor demons, then sealed the Guard. Time to begin her work.

Facing the three guardian angels, Auriel said, "We'll need tactics for getting Linus's grandchildren through the funeral. Satrinah can't approach them directly for a little longer, but as we heard tonight, they're already getting indirect advances."

Sid's guardian, Indri, ran her fingers through her wingtips. "I know Exodus 20:5 said iniquity would visit to the fourth generation, but intergenerational evil never seemed real until I walked into this assignment. Their parents dying, Linus's other son dying, Cecilia's early death, the jokes about the family being cursed...except it's true, and they made their own curse."

Pacing by the windows, Turmiel shed even more frustration than Auriel felt. "I don't understand why we can't cut off those invitations at the source. Michael offered as many soldiers as we wanted. Why can't we attack Satrinah to stop her from sending them?"

Before Auriel could speak, Jezaryah projected a cloud of calm. "This isn't a case where the army can intervene."

Turmiel spun at him, sky-blue eyes piercing the dark. "Why not? You've been telling us all along what won't work, but you've never said what will."

Jezaryah was leaning against the grandfather clock that made the only audible sound in the apartment. In the two-a.m. darkness, his eyes gleamed with a dim haze. "There are no guarantees on the positive side. I can guarantee on the negative side that deploying a million soldiers into Hell will have no effect on Anna's situation."

Auriel said, "Anna has a bond with her grandfather because she grew up admiring him and learning from him. He knew how to push her buttons, as Americans say, because he was the one who installed those buttons. His expectations, his beliefs, his approval —"

Turmiel waved a hand. "I know all that."

"Then you know Satrinah has ahold of every one of those mechanisms, and that's what she's using to prepare Anna, Forrest, and Sid. They're at the end of a long fishing line, and she's reeling in each of them because just as they're attached to Linus, Linus was attached to Satrinah."

Wings tense, Turmiel folded his arms.

Indri glanced at the fish tank. "Thought experiment. Let's say you had Michael send in an invasion force to seize Satrinah. Then what?"

Auriel glanced at the soldiers, but they didn't seem upset that she thought they'd be unhelpful.

Turmiel added, "Add in Moloch and Asmodeus, too, since those are Satrinah's bonded Seraphim."

Jezaryah nodded. "Okay, pretend we've seized all three. We can imprison them separately in Heaven, and we can Guard the chambers. Then Satrinah sends her impulses through those same attachments unimpeded because we can't Guard out love or grief or unspoken expectation."

Auriel said, "Two thousand years ago, Belior showed us how those attachments could escape even Sheol. That's how the demons were able to conjure the dead—through impenetrable walls and across planes of existence, they were able to manipulate human attachments. Love is stronger than death."

Turmiel opened his hands. "Then knock all three unconscious."

Jezaryah said, "At which point, the next demon in the chain of command can seize Linus's soul and start manipulating the Ellington siblings." He stepped closer. "I'm just as scared as you are, but the battle has to be waged here, on their home territory, in their souls. Our charges are the ones who have to win it."

The clock ticked past the hour, but a setting on the antique clock silenced the Westminster chimes during the night hours. Auriel knew that was not to wake the sleepers, but it always seemed rather like an attempt to silence the passage of time. Like an assault from their enemies, though, time just kept coming.

Indri shook her head, wings tight to her body. "The enemy has too much leverage."

Auriel stepped up alongside and put a wing around her. "We've planned for years, and you've all been doing your best to limit their power. One thing the siblings have is each other. Also, they had their grandmother's influence and prayers."

Turmiel's feathers flexed. "For all the good that did."

Auriel's hand clenched. Of course Cecilia's prayers had been answered to good effect. It was just that Turmiel wouldn't accept anything other than a complete wall of protection around Anna.

Nor should he. He was a good guardian, and his instincts screamed at him to guard.

Jezaryah leaned against the wall, wings raised. "I'm sorry, but I can't let that stand. Cecilia intervened for her grandchildren at great personal expense. She planted seeds."

Before Turmiel could reply, Auriel interjected, "The best points of defense are in the hearts of your charges. Moreover, the best generals in the war to save them are you three. You know what motivates them, and you know what they each want most in the world."

Turmiel huffed. "Anna wants the company to succeed. Satrinah has decades of experience making that happen."

"Anna wants other things too. Understand them all because Anna's hidden wants and hidden needs are the best way to combat her overt desires. After hundreds of years of defending against demonic snares, I can promise you our enemies have blind spots." Auriel stepped toward Turmiel. "They view the world through a lens you would find very confining. Forrest, for example, wants to win the election—but he has desires he hasn't admitted even to himself. Those are the hedgerows where Jezaryah is going to make his defense. You and Indri will do the same." She turned to the Archangel who was maintaining a Guard over the room. "Do we have a sterile space right now?"

The Archangel projected an affirmative.

"Double it." After a second soldier added his strength to the Guard, Auriel turned to Turmiel. "Let's get one more defense set up tonight."

With a third Guard sealing Anna's bedroom, Auriel crouched over the sleeping woman and rested her fingers on either side of her temples. "She's in a nice deep sleep, so let's get to work." She gestured to Turmiel, who shimmered in the light of Anna's clock. "I'm going to ask you to burrow as deep into her spirit as you can, and then you're going to lay down a protection that may help once the contract offer comes in."

Indri was paying close attention, and even though Jezaryah knew this technique, so was he.

Turmiel discorporated, and shortly she felt him signal that he was in.

"Do you have a good feel for her soul?" When Turmiel projected assent, Auriel continued, "Find that little spot of desire where money and success are. As you're running over the surface of her soul, it should feel like a dimple."

Turmiel replied, *I do this on the regular, feeling for temptations and anger.*

Auriel nodded. "What you're searching out now is more subtle. Since greed is the most common avenue of a pact with the enemy, that's where you're going to mount a defense."

It's not here.

"Keep checking."

I trust you that it's there, but I'm not finding anything.

Auriel frowned. "Can I ride along in your mind to guide the process?"

She detected his nonverbal assent, and momentarily she was absorbed in his senses, taking a slow sweep over the surface of Anna's soul.

A non-guardian shouldn't have this kind of access to a human soul, and Auriel would do her best to forget all the details afterward. At the point when Anna eventually entered Heaven, assuming she did, then all her sins would be forgiven and her soul would be pristine. It would be terrible for a stranger to remember her faults when God Himself had set them aside.

Even so, Anna's soul was remarkably healthy. Turmiel had prepared for this day, and Anna in general was a conscientious person. That wouldn't get someone into Heaven on its own, but it also gave Anna an advantage.

Turmiel sensed Auriel's approval and rejected it because his work wasn't complete, not until the day Anna stood before God.

"There," Auriel breathed, and Turmiel backtracked. "Do you feel that slight impression there? That's her attachment to wealth and comfort."

With all the streams of human desire in and out, it was no wonder Turmiel had trouble finding it. The surface of Anna's soul was rippled with channels of love, graces, gifts, decisions, desires, and talents. As was the case with many people born into wealth, a lot of them funneled right through greed and comfort.

Even so, that dimple wasn't nearly as deep as Auriel had anticipated. In some souls, it had the same shape and function as a black hole. Anna's was more like a belly button.

"Can we let Indri feel this too, so she knows what to look for with Sid?" When Turmiel agreed, Auriel extended her senses to

Indri. After Indri's eyes lit up with recognition, Auriel released her and returned her attention to Anna. "Here's where you're going to mount your defense. I want you to form a very tiny Guard and nestle it into the channels right here." She indicated an area just inside the dimple.

Turmiel gave a hesitant, *I guess?,* but then he had trouble forming a spherical Guard with nothing to brace it.

Jezaryah said, "Remember when they blew bubbles as children? It will be like that, but stronger."

More like a balloon. Wait, I've done it. He projected surprise. *It's in there, but it's fragile.*

"Great. Into the center of that Guard, I want you to insert a thought that will stop Anna in her tracks. Something that will make her reconsider whether she wants this thing she's being offered."

The Archangels surrounding the room were staring in curiosity. They shouldn't be. Soldiers needed to watch the outside of the thing they protected because that's where the attacks come from. On the other hand, none of what Auriel was doing was standard angelic warfare. Angelic soldiers mounted their defense outside the humans in order to keep the humans free to make their own choices. What Auriel had Turmiel doing now was a defense for someone whose perimeter had been breached, and the goal was to block the shot from going into her heart.

Turmiel sent, *What kind of thought would that be? Unless...*

Ah, the "unless" moment. That was always a victory. Auriel would have made suggestions if Turmiel hadn't interrupted himself, but in her experience, the guardian came up with the best solutions. Turmiel would understand Anna's motivations, dreams, hopes, and secret pride. He'd observed her hidden weaknesses. He knew what fears would hobble her ability to commit to a decision.

He mused, *I'm not sure which one to use, though.*

"You're going to make three of them," Auriel said. "If there's one realization that's more devastating than the others, tuck that one right down in the center of the dimple."

Turmiel projected darkness into the already-darkened room.

How devastating is too devastating?

Auriel said, "We're fighting for her soul. If you have a last ditch line of defense, something you'd shout at her right as she's putting the pen to the paper, tuck that in at the bottom."

Turmiel vibrated with pain. Yes, Auriel had just asked a guardian angel to identify the thing that would gut his charge, then leave it armed in her heart. Such an instruction went against a guardian angel's every instinct. It was demonic—literally. This was a demon trick, modified for angelic use. Demons usually fired these thoughts into a human heart on the tips of flaming arrows. A guardian could get right past the human's defenses and plant it like a land mine.

Demons also meant such thoughts for harm. Auriel meant them for interruption, like a bucket of cold water to startle someone mid-panic.

It was awful, and it was necessary. Turmiel got to work. Auriel withdrew.

Indri had gone pale. "How could such a thing help?"

Although he looked nauseated, Jezaryah touched a wingtip to Indri's. "Humans instinctively recoil against making a deal with the devil, so right at the end there needs to be a push from the demon to make them commit. Usually the push comes through a flaming arrow attack. If the demonic attack hits the mark, it will break the Guard bubble. That will release the trapped thought, and the human will second-guess themselves. They'll wonder whether the deal is worth the cost."

Auriel glanced at Anna, still asleep. "Our goal is always to unchain them enough that they can make a free choice. The demons aren't playing fair, so our help at its best will level the playing field."

Indri gave a nervous laugh. "Then why not fill their hearts with fifty little bubbles?"

Auriel sighed. "Humans quickly get accustomed to uncomfortable thoughts. After three, there's no benefit. Moreover, after three— Three times might be impulsive, but at four, they're making a choice. As always, we can't violate their free will. Cannot.

If they keep putting themselves in the position where they need a last ditch defense to save themselves, they have in effect made a decision."

Indri huddled around herself. "I understand."

Auriel said, "Do you know what a flaming arrow attack is?"

She realized then that Turmiel was paying attention to their conversation rather than finishing the bubbles. It didn't matter. He didn't need to install all three at the same time.

Indri said, "Is a flaming arrow when a demon shoots an evil thought into the human's mind from a far distance?"

Jezaryah added, "Sometimes not even from the plane of creation."

Auriel said, "I just wanted to be sure. Special Ops has its own vocabulary, and I don't always remember which terms are in the vernacular."

Indri shook her head. "I've deflected those. They seem to come out of nowhere."

"This one will have one purpose: getting them to commit. The enemy will make the thing they're offering seem like everything in the world, and life without it will seem meaningless."

Indri shuddered. "All right. Three tiny Guards, three defenses."

Turmiel coalesced before Auriel. "I haven't placed the third yet. What if it's irrational?"

Auriel gave a hard nod. "Absolutely. A small or flippant consideration can do the job as well as an earth-shattering one."

Turmiel rubbed his chin. "Then I know what I'll do for my third defense."

Nodding, Indri said, "I'll head back and set them up for Sid as well. It's a reverse booby-trap, isn't it?" When Auriel nodded, Indri added, "If the spherical Guards are like bubbles, and we're inserting a thought into them, that makes them thought bubbles."

Turmiel groaned, and Jezaryah's eyes flashed. "Cosmiel's going to be mad he didn't think of that himself."

"Cosmiel? Sophiel's not going to be able to look any of us in the face for months." Auriel grinned. "Indri, henceforth, they shall be called thought bubbles."

Indri brightened up. "Glad to be of assistance. Would you mind coming by later, to make sure I did them right?"

Jezaryah stood. "I'll head back too. I dislike leaving Forrest alone for so long, even with a security detail."

Auriel said, "I'll come with you."

Auriel and Jezaryah hadn't worked together often. Like Sophiel, Auriel engaged in high-level functions and oversaw complex operations that lasted for decades. Jezaryah had operated within the active teams, someone who took orders from someone who took orders from her. They'd never talked about anything other than business.

She shivered. *God, this is so hard for him.* Jezaryah had accepted his assignment to Forrest without question, but if he'd asked Auriel's opinion, would she have urged him to step aside? Or would she have said, "It's going to hurt, but you're this soul's best chance"?

Jezaryah flashed into Forrest and Julia's bedroom, immediately laying a hand on his charge's head and crouching face to face, eye to eye. Tension rolled off the angel, and Auriel bowed her head, again reaching for God. Archangel soldiers had the room defended, but tension sparkled through them all. Even Julia's guardian Yaron seemed unnerved.

Jezaryah raised his head. "Incoming."

Auriel's sword was in her hand before she could sense the intruder, and she flashed to the center of the bed with her armor on. The Archangel soldiers had the room Guarded, but even so, the Guard shimmered, and Satrinah stepped right through their defenses.

"Leave." Jezaryah didn't have his sword drawn, but he was armored. "It isn't your time."

"I'm performing a walk-through on my property before taking

occupancy." Satrinah raised her eyebrows as one of the Archangels moved for her, and she flashed a defensive perimeter around herself. "My intentions aren't toward the woman. Forrest can have her, but I will have Forrest."

As Satrinah stepped closer, Auriel extended her senses into Jezaryah's, and the guardian allowed it. She reached through Jezaryah's heart into his bond with Forrest, and in there she found the attachment to Satrinah—or rather, the attachment to his grandfather that Satrinah was using for access.

Satrinah whipped around to face Auriel. "Are you attempting to break my hold? I trust you'll discover my attachment is quite firm."

Although it was difficult to wrench her attention away from Satrinah, Auriel pushed as much of herself as she could into Forrest. Her energy coursed through the bond anchoring the man to the demon: the unspoken expectations, the longings, the thought processes ingrained by years of parenting and pseudo-parenting. The vulnerabilities. The anchor—she needed to find the anchor because there would be the most likely arena for their final battle. With both man and demon in the same place, she had a chance of identifying it.

Could Armageddon be waged solely within one soul? Yes, because for this soul, that one war was the only Armageddon that mattered.

Auriel strummed every one of those attachments like a harpist running her hands along several octaves at once. Half of them didn't respond the way they would in a healthy soul. The other half were a minor key that set her soul on end because of how firmly they were cemented in wrongness, and also—

Pain exploded through her. Auriel blinked past the shock to find Satrinah standing over her, wings spread, eyes blazing. "Don't vandalize my property."

One of the Archangels tackled Satrinah away from her, but Auriel couldn't focus. Jezaryah got between Satrinah and Forrest, and that was the last thing Auriel saw before a soldier flashed her away.

She struggled. "I need to be in there!"

The soldier wouldn't let go. "She'll overpower you if you go back."

Satrinah shouldn't have been able to overpower Auriel to begin with. Auriel had been working inside a human soul with the authority of that soul's guardian angel. Satrinah shouldn't have had the authority to touch her in there. Except that she had.

Auriel collapsed to her knees, arms wrapped around her waist. They were in Heaven. The soldier had brought her back behind the gates to a place Satrinah wouldn't be able to follow—unless, of course, Satrinah could.

Cosmiel appeared, wings flared. "How did this happen?" he demanded of the soldier.

Auriel struggled to raise her head, fought to find words. Her mind rang with the aftershocks of Satrinah's strike, and nothing came out of her. Not an explanation. Not even prayer.

Chapter Seven

Anna rang the doorbell to Eric's apartment even though she had a key. His new wife opened the door with a smile, and then both boys were around Anna's legs. "Mommy! You've got to see! Look what I made!"

Gavin had a cat mask, courtesy of kindergarten, sparkling so much that Anna wondered if Pilaster Group's next acquisition should be a glitter factory. "Impressive!" She glanced at Eric's wife. "I'm sorry for your apartment."

Sharon raised her eyebrows. "In half an hour, you get to be sorry for your apartment."

Anna offered, "Gavin could leave the mask here to play with it," and Sharon laughed. Gavin pouted: No, his mask must come with him so he could be a cat. Anna yielded. Her apartment would become the new glitter factory, and her housekeeper Yolanda would resign herself to endless vacuuming—and hopefully not just resign.

This should have been Anna's parenting week, but when Eric and Sharon had offered to keep the boys so she could deal with the funeral, she'd gratefully accepted.

The boys (well, one boy and one cat) walked the two blocks back home with her. Halfway there, of course, Ryan wanted to be carried, so Anna hefted him onto her hip. She was still wearing black from this morning's funeral. Eric had attended out of respect for her grandfather, but it would have been long and pointless to take the boys. Maybe Gavin would have understood, but not Ryan. Eric had brought them last night to the wake, and that had been enough goodbye for a kindergartener and a preschooler.

The insulation went both ways: Grandfather hadn't been involved with Anna's sons because he said children weren't interesting until they reached school age.

In her apartment, the boys ran right to the grandfather clock in the foyer. Anna exclaimed, "Wait! Let me get my coat off!"

Yolanda came to hang up the boys' castoff jackets, then took Anna's coat. "Snacks in the kitchen for good boys," she called. No, that wouldn't distract them. The boys knew the routine. As soon as they began her parenting time, Mommy let them wind the clock.

After unlocking the glass cabinet with a brass key, Anna let Ryan stop the pendulum. Then she fetched a chair so Gavin could insert the gear key and wind the first counterweight, then the second. She had to help Ryan with the third counterweight. Anna always restarted the pendulum herself because she didn't want to shatter the glass. "Gentle" wasn't an age-appropriate expectation for a three-year-old and a five-year-old.

With the clock rewound and the cabinet re-locked, one boy and one glitter-cat trooped into the kitchen to get snacks. Anna made her way to the living room windows overlooking Fifth Avenue.

The world echoed now that Grandfather was gone. He'd loomed over Anna's whole life, at the back of every decision she ever made. So many people had delivered lovely speeches, but none of them had encapsulated the complete sense of him, like the way it felt to stand at these windows watching a storm front on the approach from New Jersey. Light above, darkness below, thick clouds at the divider, and the promise of wind against the skyscrapers.

Yolanda drew near. "If you don't mind, my mother asked me to give this to you."

Puzzled, Anna turned to find Yolanda handing her a folded teal cloth, like a small blanket. Anna unfurled it to find a half-circle of lace, wider than her arm-span. "Oh my gosh," she breathed.

She held the shawl at arm's length, admiring the interlocking layers of leaves and the razor-like ups and downs of the border.

"This is beautiful!"

"When she heard your grandfather was dying, she got right to knitting you a prayer shawl. I hope you don't mind."

"Mind?" Anna wrapped it around her shoulders. Its gentle weight reminded her of Forrest's hug when he'd met her at the funeral home door. "Why would I mind? This must have taken her hours!" She tucked it closer around her shoulders before having a disturbing thought. "What makes it a prayer shawl? Am I supposed to pray while wearing it?"

Anna hadn't prayed in years. Not since Grandma died, and even then she'd felt too guilty to say much.

Yolanda shook her head. "Mom's the one who did the prayer. While she makes the shawl, she prays for whoever is going to receive it. Then she gives it to someone who's in a bad way. Not that you're in a bad way, but she knew you'd be sad."

Anna tightened the lace around herself, remembering how scared she'd been stepping into Grandfather's hospital room. Only then, once she'd gotten inside, instead of dread she'd sensed that little tug toward him. It had felt better to go to him than to stay away. He'd spoken those words to her, "Contract. Sign it," and it had been a comfort. In his last minutes, Grandfather was the same man he'd always been. He was always about business and numbers and obligation.

Maybe prayer did have something to it. Yolanda's mother had been praying for Anna at the same time she'd been at the hospital, and that would have worked some good if the universe had any fairness in it after all.

"I appreciate it." Anna smiled. "She's really talented."

Ryan called from the kitchen. Yolanda laughed as she turned to go back to them, saying, "My mother will tell you it's not talent. She'll tell you it's that when you do anything for forty years, it gets to be a part of you."

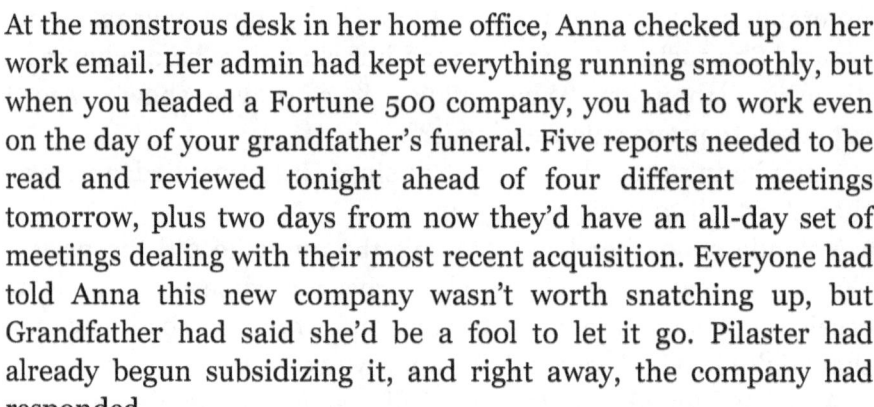

At the monstrous desk in her home office, Anna checked up on her work email. Her admin had kept everything running smoothly, but when you headed a Fortune 500 company, you had to work even on the day of your grandfather's funeral. Five reports needed to be read and reviewed tonight ahead of four different meetings tomorrow, plus two days from now they'd have an all-day set of meetings dealing with their most recent acquisition. Everyone had told Anna this new company wasn't worth snatching up, but Grandfather had said she'd be a fool to let it go. Pilaster had already begun subsidizing it, and right away, the company had responded.

Last month, Anna had walked through their new acquisition's central office and raised everyone's salary thirty percent. Underpaid employees never worked to their potential. Their outgoing leadership hated her for that, and her own board of directors was irritated by the cash she was putting into what they considered a sinking ship. Nevertheless, no one would argue with success. Manage this acquisition well, and they'd see she could handle the company without Grandfather pulling the strings.

Oh, and because timing was everything, next week was the regular meeting of the Board of Directors. They'd want reassurance that Anna had a firm hand on the tiller.

Ryan came to the door but stopped because the boys weren't supposed to enter the office. "Mommy! Can we do a board game?"

Anna said, "Sure, just give me a minute." When Ryan didn't leave, she said, "You want to come here?"

He climbed on her lap. "Your big desk is scary."

"It's super big, but don't be scared of it." She hugged him. "Does your teacher have a desk this big?" When Ryan shook his head, Anna added, "When I was your age, Grandfather's desk went on for miles. I thought it was big like a boat"

Gavin-the-glitter-cat turned up in the doorway too, so Anna waved him over. Ryan said, "That's funny. This desk is a boat!"

Anna said, "And a boat is definitely too big to be a desk," which set Ryan into even more giggles.

Gavin's nose wrinkled. "Why didn't you get a smaller desk?"

"I had a smaller desk, but this was your great-grandfather's desk. He had a big job, so he needed a big desk to go with it. Now I have his job, so when he gave me his clock, he also made me take this." She ran her hand over the polished top. "It's from France, and it's two hundred years old."

Gavin's eyes widened. "Wow."

Ryan tried to open a drawer, but it was locked. "Oh, you need a key." Anna set him down so she could fetch the key ring. It jangled as she let them hold it.

Gavin counted fifteen. "But there are only nine drawers."

"Nine drawers, and four lockable compartments inside the drawers. These two tiny keys don't go for anything at all," Anna said.

Ryan giggled. "I like tiny keys!"

Anna stopped herself before saying, "I always felt like a tiny key that would never unlock anything." No need to burden the boys with that kind of thinking. Life would do that all too soon. Right now, let them pretend they were unlocking a sailing ship while micro-glitter rained onto the antique wood.

She matched a key to a drawer, then let Gavin turn the lock. It had pens, scissors, tape, and sticky notes. Nothing worth locking up, but Grandfather always kept everything locked, so Anna did the same. "I'm guessing there used to be a hutch that got separated from it, but all the keys stayed together."

She re-locked the drawer. "Why don't you go ahead and pick the game you want to play. I need to check something on my computer, and then I'll be out."

After the boys left, she logged into her email to make sure her admin had sent all the necessary reports. He had—but also in her inbox she found a SignAgree email from an address she didn't recognize.

Odd. Usually the legal department sent contracts to her redlined and with recommendations. This contract had come to her directly. Intrigued, she clicked it open.

Sign the contract.

She'd been hearing Grandfather's voice less often today. Maybe he was fading out of the world like a storm finally sweeping out to sea.

As she read the document, though, she knew. This was it. This was the contract he'd wanted her to sign.

Chapter Eight

Cosmiel was a feather's breadth from ordering Auriel to stand down for a few days. "I can't risk you getting sidelined. Last night, Satrinah rang you like a bell tower, and you're still not a hundred percent."

Even with her wings paler than champagne—and sitting against the wall because she was still unsteady—Auriel still protested. "It's not me she was able to strike. She was able to strike Forrest, and I was enclosed in him. This was entirely a bad judgment call on my part, but I'm glad it happened. We needed to understand how she plans to lasso them in, and I think I figured it out."

Across the room, Sophiel stood with folded arms, eyes narrow. He had opinions, and usually he blurted them out when the opportunity presented. His uncharacteristic silence couldn't mean anything good.

Cosmiel said, "Maybe I should Guard you into an office to write a report."

"I'll give you my report again right here if you'll accept what I'm saying." Auriel's shoulders dropped. "Satrinah's in there tight, but the reason she *rang my bell tower,* as you're putting it, is I got too close to something she didn't want me to investigate. The more I recreate that whole situation in my mind, the more I'm convinced she thought there was a chance I could unseat her. She had no reason to show up in Forrest's room at all except as a power move."

In a low voice, Sophiel said, "Cherubim don't usually opt for a dominance display. They're much too surgical."

Still trembling, Auriel met Sophiel's eyes. "Granted. If the enemy wanted a dominance display, typically we'd expect Moloch or Asmodeus. Instead it's been all her. This isn't standard procedure for intergenerational evil."

Cosmiel ran a hand through his hair. "Go on."

Auriel's feathers picked up a pearly tone, and she sat taller. "Each of the siblings has something they want. Satrinah has the ability to provide it, but she's observing because her approach has to be perfect. Her caution indicates to me that she believes she doesn't have a lock on all three."

Cosmiel tilted his head. "Which one doesn't she have a lock on?"

Sophiel started. "We're fighting *because* she doesn't have a lock on them."

Cosmiel sighed. "Just speaking among the three of us, none of them has a fighting chance. Intergenerational evil is the most complex operation there is, and it always gets kicked over to Special Ops because no one else wants to touch it. This isn't a fight for soldiers who tally their wins and losses, and it's not an assignment the ministerial corps could handle on the best day of their lives. We're on this case because God loves every soul and wants each of them to have the best chance possible."

Auriel's tone picked up an urgency. "But there is a chance."

Sophiel said, "Granted, our statistics aren't the best, but it's not about statistics."

Cosmiel shook his head. "Since one-third of the angels fell, our base assumption would be that one-third of the siblings will fall. Now factor in that humans have a predisposition toward evil, and these three don't have a codified moral bulwark to sustain them. Given the choice, they're going to seize the short-term payout as opposed to long-term deprivation and hard work."

Sophiel's voice pitched up. "Turmiel's shot at your statistics was uncalled for, and Jezaryah shut him down."

"My statistics aren't the point." The only way to stay in this job was to accept that when you got the hopeless cases no one wanted to take, success wasn't something you encountered very often. Walk into every war as a losing war, and then the occasional win would feel like a victory. A tie was a victory. Even losing by not that bad a margin became a victory.

At first it had stung to see their best efforts undone by humans with free will. Nowadays, Cosmiel had come to expect it. Pull out all the stops so the human in crisis could have a free choice, and once you got them their freedom, most of them freely chose evil.

Sophiel said, "Our statistics aren't the point because, as you keep saying to our operatives, each human soul is of infinite value and not a statistic. Plus, no one else knows how to handle the things we do."

Auriel tucked up her knees against her chest. "Nor will they do the things we do. Michael was horrified by us getting possessed."

"There's nothing wrong with consensual angelic possession, and it works." Enough of this. Cosmiel turned back to Auriel. "You posited that Satrinah believes she doesn't have a lock on all three, since she visited before it's open season. Well, as of tonight, it's open season. She's approached Anna. Talk more about that."

Auriel sat taller against the wall. She really didn't look good, and Cosmiel was pushing her into action against his own better judgment. At the very least, Auriel needed more time to recover, but the enemy wasn't generous. "Satrinah was able to step through the Guard because something about Forrest's soul gives her permission to access him. She was able to access me through Forrest, but she's not the only one he's bonded to, and I don't think she understands that. That was the revelation."

Sophiel's brow furrowed. "She's a Cherub. Cherubim and Seraphim are all about bonds."

"They relate to bonds in a strictly hierarchical way. Cherubim and Seraphim make very strong primaries, weaker secondaries, and hundreds of tertiaries that are so faint as to not count. They're also aware of the bond between a guardian and a charge, which is not only formal but sealed with a unilateral vow on the part of the angel." She looked up. "What demonic Cherubim wouldn't have are bonds they're unaware of, and that's our backdoor into

Forrest's soul."

Cosmiel rubbed his chin. "The presumption being that you found some of these?"

"Dozens, but the primary ones are to Anna and Sid. Also to his wife, of course, but he's tight with his brother and sister."

Sophiel said, "Not just tribal affinity or family loyalty? That's definitely not something demons would reflexively think about."

Cosmiel paced the chamber. "It's not something most angels would think about."

Auriel said, "Special Ops is very much like a brotherhood, so we do think about it. Forrest is protective of the other two. I imagine Anna and Sid feel the same. If we have any leverage at all, that's where it's at, and I'm unconvinced that Satrinah understands the scope of it."

Auriel was exhausted, but she was willing to keep working. Cosmiel ought to order her to stand down. Still, she'd found something that might be an advantage, and no one entered Special Ops because they wanted to take it easy.

Cosmiel turned to Sophiel. "Top Auriel off with your healing energy. If Auriel's correct, I want us back out there tonight."

"When Satan does these, they're called snares." Cosmiel gave a nervous laugh as he met Turmiel's eyes. "When we do the same, we call it a safety net."

Auriel's voice appeared in his head from California. With Sophiel's healing energy in her, she sounded stronger. *We're ready.*

From Sophiel in Bethesda, *We're a go here as well.*

Anna was struggling to read a quarterly report at her desk, and the soldiers were doing everything possible to keep demons from the room. Sophiel had begged for this grace from God, asking every single friend who'd ever asked him to pray for something if they'd pray for this in return. Sophiel kept a roster of such things, plus he'd made connections with all the angels serving the Heavenly Liturgy. That was a lot of prayer. God had granted the request. For an hour, the soldiers could keep the demons away from all three locations.

Turmiel flexed his copper wings. "Anna's been trying to get work done, but she's thinking about that contract. Her biological responses are all topped out. She's uneasy."

Unless the human suggested the contract, they always responded with anxiety in the immediate aftermath. More telling was what happened the next day.

Regardless, Anna had texted Eric five minutes ago, asking if he could stop by. "It affects the boys," she'd added. Eric was a lawyer, and she had a contract to negotiate.

Cosmiel both spoke and projected his voice to the ones at a distance. "Guardians, let's get this started." He reached for all of them with his heart, and then he prayed, *Father, please bless our efforts. Please protect your children. Guide us so we know how best to help them.*

All three guardians had been praying for allies from the time their charges were young. *Send someone into their life to reinforce what we're saying.* God did send allies to them, but how many friends had they retained? All three experienced a certain discomfort with others' detachment from worldly desire, even as they were fascinated by it. As a consequence, they never stayed close to people who would challenge them, let alone push back hard. As each sibling became more powerful, individuals willing to question them became even rarer.

The only one who'd stuck around was their grandmother, and all of them had rejected her before her death.

Because there were three siblings, though? The trio could in effect become their own allies. Their guardians were now naming the most effective deterrents to signing a deal, and then cross-seeding them into the other siblings. When Forrest felt tempted to sign, if he heard his biggest objection coming out of Sid's mouth, that would reinforce any inclination to walk away.

Turmiel took hold of Anna's unease and whispered, "For some things, the price is too high."

Cosmiel projected Anna's anchor thought outward to the others, who reinforced it in their charges.

From Jezaryah's quarter came another projection: *What would other people think if they knew?*

Public shaming could function as a deterrent if they kept all three conscious of their images. Usually doing things for appearances was a spiritual negative, but Special Ops could work it. Turmiel reached for Forrest's anchor thought and connected it to Anna's.

Indri? Cosmiel prompted.

That's cheating, Indri sent for Sid's anchor thought.

These were solid. All three guardians had known their charges were in the crosshairs right from birth, of course, but the deaths of Linus Ellington's immediate heirs had left their charges with no buffer. Their grandfather's lifestyle had in effect programmed them to sign because the foundation of these three humans' lives was wealth spawned from an evil deal.

Interesting that Linus hadn't transferred the deal while he was still alive, though. Cosmiel would have to consider that later.

Each of the guardians contributed common sense responses that each of the siblings could say to the other, and they interlocked them so one thought would flow into the next. *Grandma would freak if she knew.* That came from Indri for Sid.

A snare had to sound close enough to the human's own internal monologue that they accepted the thought as their own. You couldn't change someone's mind by arguing with statements they didn't hold to be true. "Grandpa would never have wanted this" would float off into the ether, never even becoming a conscious thought. For that matter, even using the wrong term for "Grandfather" wouldn't have teeth.

This meant, on occasion, inserting some truly disgusting thoughts. "Murder is a sin" wouldn't even slow down some people, whereas they'd stop in their tracks for, "If I kill my brother, no one will never admire me again." Cosmiel had on occasion waltzed right past the true reason an action was evil and stopped someone with the pettiest of objections, such as, "If I get caught, my mother-in-law will be smug."

None of these thoughts would turn the tide alone, but as always, Special Ops was leveraging any angle that might pry up an opening for grace.

Jezaryah sent, *Grandfather would hate that you couldn't do it alone.*

Watching Turmiel bind that thought into the framework, Cosmiel murmured, "As if any of us can do this alone."

Sophiel replied, *Granted, but their grandfather would hate them for it.*

Turmiel offered, "We will have your back."

Sophiel sent, *Yes, they all need that one. Get that in there deep.*

Jezaryah sent, *Forrest often felt that all they had was each other.*

Indri projected her agreement.

Auriel sent, *Wait, be cautious. Don't unintentionally reinforce that if one falls, they all fall. Reinforce that they'll defend one another, not that they have to stick together.*

Jezaryah's flinch echoed through the group, but Cosmiel said, *Do as she says. They need to feel able to walk away.*

Indri sent, *What about, "We love you no matter what?"*

Cosmiel sent, *Auriel?*

Auriel replied, *Would that be true?*

All three guardians protested.

Auriel added, *After he signed his contract, did Linus love anybody?*

Chapter Nine

Anna met Eric at the door, shifting her weight. "Thank you so much. I know you already gave so much of your time because of my grandfather, but I'm not sure who else to talk to."

Eric unzipped his jacket. "You said it affects the kids, and you sounded rattled. Are they okay?"

"Yeah, they went to bed an hour ago." Anna brought Eric into her office. "When I got back from the funeral, I had a contract that needed a signature, and I opened it thinking it had to do with Pilaster, only it was weird. It talks about Ryan and Gavin."

Eric's eyes widened. "Threatening them?"

"More like, providing for them." Anna opened her laptop and brought up the document. Eyes glued to the screen, Eric settled into the desk chair and started reading.

She slipped into the leather chair opposite to watch for the moment his eyebrows shot up. Eric was doing great for himself since the divorce. Sharon was good for him, and he deserved someone who cared as much as Sharon did. Eric had always complained that Anna was married to her company, but work as important as hers couldn't stay rooted in the nine-to-five hours. Of course she'd needed to leave early, return late, travel, take calls during dinner—that's how business worked. More to the point, that was how Grandfather worked. In the end, Eric had asked if he was more important to Anna than the company, and Anna wouldn't cave to his ultimatum.

That kind of relationship wasn't acceptable to him, but it wasn't her fault, and it wasn't his. The kids needed stability, though, and she wanted them near. Everyone talked about Anna and Eric as having an amicable divorce, but children deserved parents who could work together. She didn't play financial games with the child support, and they didn't play mind games with the co-parenting. She'd pulled strings to get Eric an apartment only a few blocks from hers. She backed up his parenting decisions (and he backed up hers), and she encouraged the boys' relationship with Sharon.

Anna's marriage to Eric was simply a corporate merger that failed. Unfortunate, but sometimes you have to walk away from a bad deal. Eric had.

His eyebrows never shot up. Halfway through the document, without taking his eyes from the screen, Eric said, "Who sent this?"

Anna said, "No one I know. I asked my admin, and it didn't come through him."

"This individual found your private business email and sent you a contract with details about our children, plus details about your grandfather, without giving any hint as to who it could be?"

"I gave the header information to my IT guru, and he couldn't track it down either. I suppose I could take the matter to the FBI."

Eric kept reading. "Do you want to sign this?"

Anna didn't answer.

"I wouldn't advise any of my clients to sign this in a hundred years. There's no exit clause. It's written very favorably toward you, but even that makes me wonder what the other party is getting from the deal." Eric pushed back from the table. "Lay it on me. Do you really believe Linus Ellington signed such an agreement?"

Anna pulled her shawl tighter around her shoulders. She'd worn it while writing Yolanda's mother a thank you note, worn it while eating the dinner Yolanda had prepared for her, worn it while tucking the boys into bed. Gavin had even snuggled up with her under the shawl.

Eric expected an answer. Anna said, "The last thing Grandfather said to me before he died was to sign the contract. I thought it was something for work, so I told him I would."

Eric snorted. "That's hardly binding."

Anna offered a laugh. "Granted, but maybe it means Grandfather did sign a contract like this."

Eric looked back at the wording. "I can't advise you to sign it."

Her voice ticked up. "It specifically provides for the children."

"You're doing a fine job providing for the children right now. You've got an inheritance that will serve as a lovely cushion for them, and that's without considering that I have a job, and so does Sharon. They've got college funds and trust funds. No one's going to pitch our boys out onto the street."

Anna sounded urgent. "People can die. My parents died. If you and I both died, they don't have grandparents to take them in."

"Plenty of people raise children without signing a document like this." Eric bit his lip. "Your grandfather had rock solid business sense. People said it was uncanny, and if this document is to be believed, it actually was." He shook his head, almost talking to himself. "The legal language is current. This agreement would even be adjudicated under the laws of the State of New York, which says something about the State of New York." When that didn't draw a laugh from her, Eric said, "Anna, if you sign this, there's no out. It's more binding than a marriage, and there's no divorce."

She said, "You and I behaved ourselves during the divorce for Gavin and Ryan's sakes. I'd be signing this for their sakes too."

Eric rested his elbows on the desk and rubbed his temples. She'd seen that look too many times. She'd seen it during the divorce mediation when he knew the right thing to do but also knew she could stop playing softball any time she wanted.

There was still a little glitter on the desktop, even after she'd wiped it down. Eric's elbow sparkled, and Anna fought a smile.

He said, "Can I see them?"

The boys shared a bedroom. Anna stayed in her office while Eric went to check on them. When he returned, he said, "Don't sign this right away. Don't sign it without negotiating an exit clause, but don't sign it right away regardless."

She said, "The offer expires in forty-eight hours."

"I'm aware there's an expiration, but it's not tomorrow, so don't sign tonight." He sat back down. "I'm baffled that we're having this conversation. You don't believe in God. You don't believe in Hell. That was your grandmother's gig, and as far as I know, your grandfather didn't believe in it either."

Anna nodded. "He believed in negotiations, contracts, and the free market."

"He scoffed whenever your grandmother brought you to church. He gave you the cold shoulder for six weeks when I wanted our wedding to take place in a church. Why would a man with that outlook sign a contract with someone purporting to be a representative of the supernatural?" Eric shook his head. "This is bait. Someone wants you to sign a deal for your soul so they can publicly shame you and oust you from the company. You do have enemies in upper management, and I remember the flack you caught after becoming CEO because some C-level officers thought you hadn't paid your dues. If you want to provide for Gavin and Ryan, you absolutely cannot sign."

Anna frowned. "I hadn't considered that. Since it's someone who had my private email, it's someone in my inner circle."

"Consider who would want to set you up. Would either of your brothers do that?"

Anna started. "Forrest would never. Could you imagine the nosedive he'd take in the polls if people thought his sister was a devil worshipper?"

Eric folded his arms, and again the micro-glitter caught the light. "Sid's career might get a boost, but I can't see him destroying you to achieve it."

Anna said, "That leaves you, and although you have a motive, I'm not feeling it. For one thing, if this were your idea, you'd have told me to sign."

Eric didn't look hurt. No, he never showed emotion on the job. It was one of the things she admired about him. "Someone has all this information, though. Who benefits from destroying you?" He gestured to her. "I didn't think you were the shawl type."

The leather chair creaked as Anna shifted her weight. "Yolanda's mother made it for me. She said it was a prayer shawl, and I found it comforting."

Eric snorted. "So you get a deal from the devil, and you're wearing a religious garment. Are you sure you're still an atheist?"

As Eric stood to leave, Anna said, "I think I'm actually agnostic."

Eric zipped his jacket. "Well, it sounds to me like you're being asked to commit to a side. Either God exists, or God doesn't exist. Either the devil is real, or the devil is not real. And if they're both in play, you have to decide if anything is more important than your job."

Chapter Ten

Midnight in Anna's apartment. The team's protected time had ended, and the Archangel soldiers could do only so much to dispatch the enemies. Outside the boys' bedroom, Cosmiel had to work in a field thick with fallen angels.

It almost felt better operating this way. Almost. Of course, Cosmiel relished the quiet times, but the heart of conflict was where his team did their best work.

Cosmiel reassured a dispirited Turmiel, "This is a demonic dominance display. It doesn't mean they have more power than before."

Still, the copper color wouldn't return to the guardian's wings. "I can't even talk to her without them making so much noise she can't hear me."

"She can hear you." Cosmiel put his hands on Turmiel's shoulders. "Do you need it quieter so you can get a better sense of her?" When Turmiel nodded, Cosmiel added, "If I do this, you'll be isolated for as long as it lasts."

Turmiel frowned. "Do what?"

"Special Ops trick."

This was the same thing Cosmiel said just before teaching Turmiel how to possess him. Turmiel resisted a moment, and then the blue faded from his eyes. "I need a break. Let's go for it."

Leaving two soldiers beside Anna, Cosmiel brought Turmiel into the boys' bedroom to get most of the process set up ahead of time.

They'd need to return to Anna to finish it off. "You can break out of this whenever you want," he said as he started working with Turmiel's soul. "It'll be easiest for me to get started if you pray."

Turmiel closed his eyes. "Pray for you to succeed?"

"Pray for whatever you want, which I suspect is Anna's salvation. From my perspective, I only need you to lose your self-consciousness."

Cosmiel tugged at Turmiel's soul and began setting up a framework that would give the guardian some auditory shielding. Prayer was not, unfortunately, taking Turmiel's mind off himself, and being aware of himself would muck up the results. Time for a little distraction. "Do you remember when Special Ops first started?"

Turmiel projected that he didn't.

A perfect topic for distracting him, then. "Were you in the military?" A negation. "Oh, the ministerial corps? Then you'll love this story. Before Special Ops existed, I had command of a legion in the army, which was fine—but sometimes interesting cases crossed my path, and of course some problems you can't solve with an army. You likely encountered a lot of problems like that in the ministerial corps, where you wouldn't need soldiers as much as encouragement, prayer, and guidance."

This was a bad line of thought because it would call to mind that Turmiel did want the army to protect Anna—and that the army wasn't helpful right now. *He needs to gear all the way down,* Cosmiel thought to God, and he smiled at himself because of course God knew what needed to happen. "It was the time of the patriarchs. We recognized that Jacob's son Joseph had to be important in God's plans because he'd seen it in his dreams, but of course Satan also realized it, which is why he'd tried to have him killed. Well, after the Potiphar incident, we couldn't get Joseph out of prison. After a year of struggling to break through, I pulled back my soldiers and went onsite myself to observe. Michael wanted to know what I thought I was doing, but a thousand soldiers hadn't made headway. A thousand more soldiers working for another ten years was unlikely to accomplish more."

Turmiel began relaxing. Good. "My forces had already cleared the area of demons, so how had our enemies entrenched their snares so deeply that all our forces couldn't find a means for Joseph to get free?" Turmiel's interest rose, and as he let go of himself, Cosmiel worked faster. "I spent days in prison with Joseph. I interviewed his guardian, listened to the other angels, learned everything I could about Egypt and their government and their laws and customs."

This was a tricky part of the process: Cosmiel was going to manipulate the actual bond between Turmiel and Anna, and since Turmiel was already hypersensitive about threats to her, every touch had to be smooth and careful.

"Joseph's guardian angel gave me access to Joseph's heart, and his soul was filled with baffles and dams. I found that Joseph now hated his childhood dreams, whereas the Egyptians loved dream interpretation. He never participated when they discussed their dreams because he felt so much shame over what he'd done as a boy. In fact, whenever they told their dreams, he was decoding every one of them, and then whenever one of his interpretations came true, he felt even more shame rather than wonder at God's power."

Quick as a lightning flash, Cosmiel inserted four interlocking Guards within Turmiel's soul. That was the key bit. Everything after this should be easier.

"Shame binds them up, so Joseph's guardian and I had to transform that shame into guilt. Shame is unhealthy, whereas guilt —when someone actually did something wrong—is healthy and fitting." Not that either one of those felt good. Cosmiel could all too easily name assignments where he hadn't wanted to present himself to God afterward because of how badly he'd failed, or the eyebrow-raising things he'd done in order to achieve that failure. How well he could remember the inability to raise his eyes, the discomfort of being seen. It was easier sometimes not to check back in. Lately, most of the time. "Joseph had been trained up as the golden child, so now he felt he didn't deserve the love his father had given him. He felt he wasn't enough."

Turmiel was very deep in prayer now, so he wouldn't pick up the resonance in Cosmiel's heart. Joseph wasn't the only one.

"The 'being not enough' sense was shame, so the guardian and I helped Joseph reframe it: that his real problem wasn't in not fulfilling his father's expectations, but rather that he'd been uncompassionate. Here in prison, that could change. His guardian and I helped him feel compassion for himself over his youthful bragging. Now he felt guilt over his *actions* rather than shame over what he *was*. A week later, the baker and the cup-bearer were talking about their dreams, and Joseph interpreted for them. The gift had been his all along, but his shame had prevented him from using it."

Both boys' guardians were also listening, as were the Archangel guards. How odd. This entire story should have been common knowledge, especially to the soldiers, and everyone knew the story of Joseph.

Cosmiel said, "After Joseph started interpreting, the blockages were gone from his soul. Moreover, when I prayed about the situation, the world felt comfortable—like a ship with the sails trimmed properly and the wind in the right quarter. I didn't get that feeling often back then. In the army, it was always one fight after the next after the next."

He could say the same about his current job. Turmiel had lapsed into a meditative state, maybe not even listening, which had been Cosmiel's intention. He placed extra protections on Turmiel's soul so he could escort the guardian back to Anna.

"I spent the next week in prayer. When I emerged from the Heavenly Temple, I asked Michael if I could hand-pick ten angels to form a special unit. Michael thought I'd oversee this unit in addition to my legion, but it made more sense to concentrate on the new group. I recruited Sophiel and nine others, and we began taking missions that required a special touch. Not quite ministerial corps, but not quite army either. God's only stipulation was that my group not be part of the military, so I resigned my commission, and we were on our own."

The early missions were such an *ad hoc* collection of

assignments. Cosmiel got the puzzlers, the Gordian knots, the cleanup jobs no one felt competent to do. Sophiel demonstrated a talent for improvising, deriving techniques specific to the situations they ended up in. They positioned two angels as spies among the demons to learn their plans. Those spies came back familiar with the things demons could do and skilled in how to do them. Cosmiel's operatives began turning all those techniques slantwise to use them for good. For example, what Cosmiel was doing right now.

In fact, wasn't that even what Joseph himself had said? "You meant it for harm, but God meant it for good." If Cosmiel could accomplish even a little of that...? What a way to be more like his Father!

He missed those days. He missed the ridiculous arrogance of taking on every challenge that crossed his path. He missed the innocence of believing he could do it all. Or rather, believing he could do it all without rendering his soul unfit for holier work.

Very quickly, Special Ops had formed a tightly knit team utilizing a combination of stealth and tactics that you didn't get to employ as a soldier. They got not only the trickiest cases, but their team began attracting the trickiest angels. Anyone in the Heavenly Host who liked turning expectations on their heads had at one point or another been considered (or volunteered) for Special Ops.

They operated under conditions of immediate peril, so Cosmiel encouraged his operatives to do things that were unorthodox. Not sinful—but unexpected. Although any one of them would have preferred annihilation to sin, they pirouetted on the line between light and darkness. They developed their own techniques for fighting, for planning, for listening. "Unconventional warfare," Michael called it.

Zadkiel had served with Cosmiel for a while, and later Remiel— which was awkward because both of them outranked him, and yet both had taken direction and done their duty without question. He'd frequently worked with Saraquael, who was a lot of fun and would discuss poetry with Cosmiel between actions. The core group, though, Cosmiel's original ten, were inseparable. They specialized. They taught others, and they learned what it took to sustain newcomers in the midst of the most relentless fight eternity had to offer.

"Bring me to Anna," Cosmiel breathed, and they flashed to a spot alongside her while demonic forces swirled around them. The Archangels kept them covered while Cosmiel settled Turmiel against his charge. Then he reached into Anna and completed the connection.

Turmiel looked up, shocked. Good. Every time Cosmiel did this, the guardian turned to him with the same expression.

Turmiel glanced around the room, then drew close to Anna and stayed close. A moment later, he was deep in her soul, accessing whatever he could of her dreams to shield those sleeping thoughts from demons.

Special Ops had learned to do what the demons did, only to do it with love. Demons could affect the hearing of a person in thrall, making them hear voices. Cosmiel had used that same technique to invert the connection: instead of an angel making Anna hear angelic voices (or more usually, demonic), now the guardian angel could detect only what the human charge could detect—meaning he couldn't hear preternatural voices. The demonic projections would fly right past Turmiel, and he could focus on guarding Anna.

Turmiel couldn't hear other angels, either, but the relief streaming from his soul proved it was worthwhile.

Anna stirred and checked the clock. She got out of bed to look in on the boys, inadvertently admitting demons into the room with them, then went into the living room to look out at the lights of Manhattan.

What was she thinking? The demons were whispering to her soul, but Turmiel would be rallying objections to anything she might find tempting. Demons could put forward arguments, and he'd form the counter-arguments. She had to make a fully informed decision about that contract and consent to it with all her will, but part of Turmiel's authority over her was making sure she had the information she needed.

What was the blockage in Anna's heart?

The paths in her heart dead-ended so often. Cosmiel had tried to trace them but found himself baffled at every turn. She wanted things she didn't want. She valued things she didn't value.

Anna picked up the prayer shawl from the couch, then wrapped herself in it to continue watching the streetlights.

Cosmiel's eyes widened, and he rested a hand on the shawl.

His breath caught. Help had been right here all along, smuggled in by the housekeeper.

Cosmiel sent his power through the shawl from end to end to capture every stitch, every nuance.

Demon eyes watched from all the corners. They'd stopped chattering. They were reporting back to Satrinah even now, but Cosmiel had what he wanted.

He flashed to Auriel, ensconced in their fortress with five books open before her and a sixth in her hand.

Cosmiel spread his palms and created an image of the shawl in light. "Quick, as much as you can—cover me with prayer support."

Auriel gasped, "That's an opening!" before Cosmiel flashed away again.

Chapter Eleven

Cosmiel only just got in front of the Throne of God before Moloch appeared alongside, all six of his Seraph wings aflame.

Moloch shouted toward God's throne, "That woman is ours! He cannot use the prayers of some ignorant bystander to negate a claim as solid as ours."

God's throne stood at the center of the nine choirs, in public view of every resident of Heaven—the place angels presented themselves to God after completing an assignment, and also the public forum where demons came to challenge Him. Cosmiel bowed. "Father most holy, I have no authority to negate your enemy's claim over Anna Ellington's soul, but that wasn't what I was asking."

The demon strode toward Cosmiel, reeking of smoke. Like most Seraphim, he was tall, and he flared his wings to dominate even more space. "What petty request did you have, little Power?"

Archangel soldiers got between them. Moloch peered right into Cosmiel's eyes while fire shot from his own. Cosmiel's sword manifested in its scabbard by reflex, and he fought the urge to run. In a low voice so Moloch would strain to hear it, he said, "I wasn't asking you."

Moloch pushed closer, but the Archangels blocked him. Cosmiel focused on the Throne of God with its clouds and light and...well, God. Cosmiel could barely stand here. For Moloch it must be searing agony, but the top demons hated weakness, so they stepped right into the pain to show how weak they weren't. Moloch was only a little less than the Maskim in power. He and Satrinah stood at the top of Hell's tiers of command, and who was Cosmiel? A Power. A sixth-order angel.

"As valid as Moloch's claim is, Father, yours is still more valid. Jesus died to pay for all human souls. Anna Ellington hasn't abandoned salvation yet, but Satrinah's contract gives her a very tight deadline. Especially because Satrinah's contract is for the duration of eternity, I say two days is insufficient for Anna Ellington to make a fair assessment."

Moloch laughed out loud. "Are you asking for an extension on your homework, little Power?"

That stung. Cosmiel raised his hands, recreating the light image of the shawl with its undulating mesh. "Father, your devoted servant in her compassion knitted this garment for Anna Ellington when she learned about Linus Ellington's final illness."

Moloch shouted, "Why are you wasting my time? That wretched knitter had no knowledge of my claim."

Now was not the time to let the demon distract him. Cosmiel said, "The knitter's ignorance of Anna Ellington's peril renders this garment even more important. Your servant knit for her, stitch by stitch, asking You only for comfort for Anna, for peace, and for a gentle transition. Anna has repeatedly wrapped herself in these prayers."

In Cosmiel's hands, the image of the shawl turned warm. God prompted Cosmiel to continue.

"Father of all generosity, you who made the centuries and willed us to travel through them, I beg you to grant additional time to this child of your creation, whose soul you have purchased and whose salvation you so ardently desire. Two days is an unfitting time to discern an agreement of eternal consequence. The gift of your grace can enable Anna Ellington to make a decision with full knowledge and in full freedom."

Moloch was throwing off enough heat that Cosmiel fought himself not to recoil. "It took the knitter eleven hours to make this shawl. I'm asking for you to grant Anna Ellington eleven additional days."

Moloch snorted. "Thirteen days total? Shouldn't you be afraid of the number thirteen, little Power?"

Cosmiel faced him with a smile. "Not as afraid as you should be."

Shoving the Archangels aside, Moloch lunged toward him, and Cosmiel blocked with his sword. Once, twice, three times. Before Moloch scored a fourth blow, every angel in the vicinity had gotten between to drive Moloch back.

One of the Archangels stopped in place. Her eyes swirled with light as her sword vanished.

She turned to Cosmiel with a smile, and she held out her hand. "Thus says the Lord: I will grant your request. Anna Ellington will have eleven additional days for her decision."

Moloch said, "And as a concession for you caving in to this sniveling loser's plea for more time, I demand rights to that woman's body, her children, and her work."

The Archangel turned toward him, hands down. "Thus says the Lord: over her work, you already have rights. Do as you wish. But you may not harm her body, and you may not harm her children."

Moloch glowered. The Archangel's eyes cleared, and her sword returned to her hand.

Cosmiel forced a smile. "Thirteen days. You've lost her."

Moloch tightened his wings at his back and leaned forward. "Little incompetent Power, thirteen days or thirteen thousand days, that woman is mine. You've failed so often you don't even remember how to succeed."

It wouldn't do to collapse now. Cosmiel tightened his hands, one gripping his sword and the other clutching the teal image of that shawl.

Moloch leered. "Your team props you up, and you fall anyhow. I will have the woman. I will have her brothers. I will have her children. In the end, I will have the world, and what will you have?"

Cosmiel gestured with his sword. "I will have eleven additional days."

Moloch snorted, and then he vanished.

Eleven days. God had given them eleven days.

Cosmiel flashed in front of Auriel, wings shaking, hands still clutching the afterimage of that amazing, wonderful, God-inspired teal shawl.

"You did it! I felt everything lengthen." Auriel guided him to the corner so Cosmiel could sit. He doubled over himself, then tightened his wings to his back.

That raw power. That anger. Cosmiel's soul would still be quivering from the force of even one blow from Moloch's sword. He'd taken three.

How did Michael do this on a regular basis? Michael was just an Archangel, but as an eighth-order angel Michael faced down Satan's top three Seraphim without so much as a flinch. Meanwhile, from two choirs above him, the head of the choir of Powers couldn't deal with one of the lesser Seraphim without help.

Eyes closed, Cosmiel reached for God. Grace flooded into him, and then peace, and after a moment strength tingled back into his limbs.

A moment after that, Auriel had her hands on his head, her wings cupped around them both like a cocoon. Her prayer was tinged with concern and desperation. Cosmiel's fingers still dug into the holes of the lace.

He whispered, "The housekeeper's mother. The knitter. She needs protection."

"Acknowledged." Auriel was silent a moment. "Michael just stationed two extra guards on her."

Moloch was going to blame anyone and everyone he could. A human being had inserted herself into his affairs, and he'd get revenge on her the same way he tried to get revenge for everything else. It was always like this, and Cosmiel couldn't spread his wings wide enough to cover the whole world.

That's why there are so many of you, God replied. *You each take a part.*

God could cover the whole world Himself. It was just that He chose to do it by giving them the privilege of helping one another.

Auriel sat back, wings tucked up. "Eleven days is tremendous. You did that without any time to prepare."

"I thought of asking for one minute for every stitch in the shawl, but I couldn't figure out which was longer." Cosmiel gave an embarrassed laugh. "I hope I chose the right one."

"You're getting your color back. You were translucent when you returned. Was Satrinah that bad?" She hesitated. "No, that was Moloch. His power's all over you."

It would be clinging like smoke. Cosmiel should find a quiet corner of Heaven and purify himself of the stench, but instead he'd let it settle in good and deep. He had other plans for that residue. "It's not about me. Let's plan our next eleven days."

"First thing, we make doubly sure Yolanda's mother is safe." She formed a Guard and spoke into it. "Sophiel, Anna's housekeeper's mother is under threat. Michael's stationed soldiers, but we need you perform a trace on her." Then she flashed the Guarded sphere to Sophiel.

Good call. Sophiel would be able to trace back any evil designs on the woman and request specific help if necessary.

The shawl replica remained warm, a sweet weight that humans should find comforting. Ever since Eden, they liked being covered. They enjoyed the sensation of being held even with no one there to hold them.

As he studied the undulations of the mesh, Cosmiel mused, "It's not just the prayers knitted into the wool. Anna responds to the shawl itself."

Auriel said, "It's the kindness of the gesture. Someone took a significant amount of time to do something for her, think about her, and pray for her. Even though Anna doesn't believe praying has any effect, surely she recognizes the good intentions behind doing so."

Shaking his head, Cosmiel passed the fabric through his hand. "Her connection to this shawl goes deeper than appreciation." He extended it to Auriel.

Wings raised, she held it a moment, then spread it out on the floor before her. Murmuring, "No, it doesn't want to be away from me," she gathered it back into her arms and held it against her heart, then draped it as best she could across her winged shoulders.

"Looks good on you," Cosmiel teased.

Her eyes sparkled gold. "Fashion is my number one concern, specifically human fashion." She was wearing the same silver-black uniform he was, and even off-duty, she tended to stay in it. "This isn't a garment that fits the wearer, but it's fitting for it to be worn, if that makes sense." She spread it over her lap. "I wish I made body heat. It pairs better with warmth. Also, I don't think you recreated the whole thing, so I'll have to study the actual garment."

Stung, Cosmiel said, "I was working quickly."

"That's not a criticism. You scored us eleven days, which may have won Anna her eternity." Auriel was barely paying attention to him as she traced the route of the yarn row by row. "Even so, I need access to the real fabric. I'm used to working with generational evil, but I think what we have here is the opposite."

Cosmiel started. "A generational blessing?"

She looked up. "Yes, and it's a stronger force than you or I considered."

Chapter Twelve

In her office at Pilaster Group, Anna didn't bother taking a seat. Her admin had stacked papers on her desk and brought a coffee, but after a half day off for the funeral, plus the hours planning it and dealing with estate issues, Anna had too much work to catch up on. Her first meeting started at 7:45, and the schedule afterward was wall-to-wall meetings until lunch. Most likely she'd work through that as well.

Yolanda claimed Anna was rail thin because she never stopped to eat. She did eat, of course. You didn't have to stop working in order to chew and swallow, and she knew from experience which meals could be managed one-handed.

She had three minutes until she'd head down the hallway for meeting number one, regarding their newest corporate acquisition. It needed some attention, sure, but Grandfather had never been wrong.

That contract, though.

The SignAgree email sat in her inbox, burning a hole in her heart. She'd need to set an alert on her calendar to make sure she accepted or rejected it before the deadline, although letting the deadline pass was effectively a decline.

Her admin returned to the doorway. "Edwards phoned from the Long Island Railroad. He's ten minutes out."

Anna paged through the folder in her hand. "Tell me when he arrives, and then I'll join the meeting."

Her admin said, "I'm really sorry about Mr. Ellington. He was a great man, and he had such a head for business."

"He did. Thank you." Anna smiled but said nothing else until her admin left the room.

Ten minutes was enough time. She opened her email, brought up the contract to check the deadline before entering it into her calendar, and paused.

The contract had changed. It now gave nearly two weeks to decide, whereas the original had allotted her two days.

This was intriguing. She scanned through the rest of the document for additional changes, like maybe Eric's suggested exit clause, but nothing leaped out at her. At least not until the bottom: failure to sign this agreement permits *what*?

Her heart stuttered. She scrolled back up the document to where Ryan and Gavin were mentioned, but that clause wasn't amended with a threat. Back to the bottom: if she didn't sign, the originating party would hold all prior gifts to Linus Ellington to be null and void, and they would reclaim everything they had contributed. See attachment.

The attachment was new. Anna opened the image and scrolled right to the bottom where she found Linus Ellington's signature.

Grandfather. His stately handwriting was a remnant of times when penmanship was a course of study. Even at the end of his life, when his vision wavered and weakness overtook his limbs, even in those last days he'd had bold handwriting. It was a skill: craftsmanship, swordsmanship, penmanship.

Grandfather's agreement was much shorter than hers, typed on a Smith Corona with its even spacing and characteristic font. It totaled one page. In simple legal language, Linus Ellington offered complete loyalty in exchange for business success.

You didn't even believe in God, she thought. *Why would you entertain such an offer?* Moreover, how would anyone have proposed it? She checked the date against her own knowledge of company history. Back then, Pilaster had still been SavCo Dry Goods. Grandfather hadn't yet married Grandma. The company had been struggling to make payroll.

Grandfather never talked about those days. Anna had heard about them from Grandma, and when Anna once made the mistake of asking Grandfather, he'd erupted in a rage like no other. Anna had felt ungrateful for weeks, slinking about the house afraid even to speak. Grandma too had spent the next weeks shaken.

Grandma was ten years younger than Grandfather, even though she'd died first. It must have been hard on her, losing both her sons at a young age. The tabloids had talked about the Ellington family curse, but whatever curse it was had missed Anna and her brothers.

Unless it hadn't. Unless this contract before her eyes was the source of the curse. Or was the curse the source of the contract? Grandfather's brother had also died young—years before this contract was enacted. Anna's great grandfather had abandoned his family. Her great grandmother had died penniless. Grandfather's sister had ended up confined to bed for five years before dying. One weekend when Grandma had headed out to church, Grandfather had snapped, "I owe nothing to God."

The image had a note attached to it, so Anna clicked. It read, "Original document archived in the French desk, second drawer."

That much she knew was wrong. She'd spent hours working at that desk, and there was no such document.

Anna made a note to check the drawer, then plugged the new date into her calendar. The extension was a relief. She had so much work to do, and the extra days would give her another chance to consult Eric.

Her admin knocked. "Edwards is here."

Anna closed down her computer and carried her stack of folders to the conference room to discuss a less preternatural contract.

At six-twenty, Anna found both her boys chowing down on chicken nuggets in front of the television. They abandoned their show to give her a hug, and she sat with them to watch a talking toucan getting himself into progressively worse trouble until he came up with a zany plan to solve it all at once.

"Life doesn't work this way," Anna said. "What if he hadn't gotten a replacement cake back into the kitchen?"

Gavin said, "He'd be in trouble."

Ryan said, "He'd cry."

Anna nodded. "I would cry too."

Yolanda was putting on her coat. "Your dinner is ready, and Gavin's project is packed to go to kindergarten. The daycare sent notices home about a field trip, and Ryan needs to wear an orange shirt tomorrow for Orange Day." When Anna started to speak, Yolanda raised a hand. "I already checked, and he didn't have one, so we took a field trip to Duane Reede and bought an orange t-shirt."

Ryan tugged Anna's blazer. "It has a baseball on it."

"That sounds like an excellent shirt." Anna lifted him onto her lap. "You're a hero, Yolanda. Orange Day is saved."

Ryan and Gavin sat with her while she had her own meal, more complicated and better-tasting than dinosaur-shaped nuggets. They told her everything that could possibly have happened to two boys in one twelve-hour period. Anna missed them when it was Eric's parenting week, but the apartment certainly was quieter. On the other hand, she didn't mind not getting events like Orange Day sprung on her at the last second.

After dinner, Anna stacked her dishes in the dishwasher for Yolanda to run tomorrow, and then she and the boys played a board game. They weren't sleepy yet, so Anna tucked that beautiful prayer shawl around her neck, and she lifted a photo album down from the shelf.

Gavin got on the couch beside her. "Whose pictures are for tonight?"

Ryan snuggled in on the other side, and Anna paged through. "These were Great Grandma Ellington's pictures. When she died, Great Grandfather Ellington didn't want them in the house anymore, so I took them." The really old photos were square, their colors muted. Had they dulled with time, or had the old photographs always been less vibrant? "This is Great Grandma. Wasn't she stunning?"

Anna favored her mother's side of the family rather than her father's side, so she couldn't lay claim to any of Cecilia Ellington's beauty. Here was Cecilia as a bride, her eyes bright, her smile daring. At her side, Linus Ellington looked commanding. Socialites had accused Cecilia Ellington of marrying upward. They'd also accused her of gold-digging, when the reality was that for as long as Anna could understand, Grandfather had never given Cecilia access to his money. She'd received an allowance every week to provide for the household, accountable for all receipts. Whenever she'd needed to make a public appearance, Linus Ellington had selected a dress or jewelry and hired someone to style her hair and makeup. When Grandma had slipped treats to Anna, Forrest, or Sid, it had been from her own account. Grandfather had been the one to buy them cars or fly them to Aspen with their friends. Grandma had been the one to take them for ice cream, but she'd never gotten any for herself.

Gavin said, "I forgot," and hugged her tight.

Anna squeezed him back. "Forgot what?"

"Daddy said you would be sad." Gavin grasped her tighter. "He said we had to give you lots of hugs, but I forgot to give them to you yesterday."

As if that jolted his memory, Ryan hugged her too. Anna put her arms around them both. "Thank you. All these hugs do make me feel better."

Anna kept paging through, identifying everyone in all the photos for the boys.

Speaking of sadness, most days, Grandma used to seem sad. Had she known about the contract? Which had come first, the marriage or the realization? Had she married for money and then regretted her choice, or had she married for love and only afterward realized what she'd married into?

Anna showed the boys photos of her aunt and uncle, and then

photos of her parents. Then they reached photos of her when she was little. "That's Uncle Forrest, and that's Uncle Sid. I think little Uncle Sid looks a lot like Ryan, don't you?" Her skin prickled. Sid had always been Grandfather's favorite. Grandfather hadn't been interested in Anna, not until she started high school. Not Forrest, either, which would have made her believe Grandfather didn't want anything to do with children. Sid, though? Sid could do no wrong. If Anna got a B, Grandfather would lecture her about working hard so she didn't embarrass the family. If Sid got a B, Grandfather delivered no lectures. No speculation that perhaps Linus Ellington had the world's stupidest grandchildren.

In a way it had been a relief that Grandfather didn't want to see Ryan and Gavin beyond holiday visits. It was a shame that Grandma had already died, though, because based on the photos of her holding the newborns Anna, Sid, and Forrest, Grandma would have been over the moon. Grandma was the one who arranged for each of them to be baptized. Grandma had been the one who brought them to church on Easter and Christmas.

Grandma must have loved her, and Anna's eyes burned because it was entirely undeserved.

The clock struck eight, so she got the boys their baths and their pajamas, then tucked them into their beds.

She should catch up on the rest of her work. With any luck, she could be asleep by midnight.

Instead, wearing that shawl again, she paged back through the photo album.

I'm sorry, Grandma.

Sid had been Grandfather's delight. Grandma had quietly taken Forrest and Anna's side, helping them whenever Grandfather got too stern even though she never countermanded his discipline. Grandfather always bragged that Sid would inherit the company, but during college, Sid had stepped away from business. Numbers and meetings held no interest for him. Grandfather was disgusted, but after his initial blow-up, he'd accepted Sid again, mollified. Forrest had worked for Pilaster until he abandoned it to go into politics. Again, Grandfather had fought strenuously, even asking

Forrest if he thought Anna would be able to steer the company with the slightest degree of competency.

To which Forrest had replied, "Of course."

Grandfather threatened to actively campaign against Forrest, but again, after a couple of days, his resistance evaporated. He connected Forrest with rich supporters and even donated significant campaign funds.

That left Anna, to whom Grandfather had said, "Don't let me down."

At no point had she let him down. When he'd told her to work evenings and weekends, and when he'd demanded she negotiate impossible deals, and when he'd paraded her out at his side, she'd done it. He'd attended her wedding and let her go on a honeymoon, and nine days later she was back to seventy-hour weeks and regular business travel. He promoted her through the ranks and set her up in the C-suite, taught her how to shut down blowhard businessmen twice her age, and eventually stepped back to let her run the show.

Well, run the show with his constant instructions. Refuse this deal. Take that one. Put everything on the table to accomplish this specific goal.

Anna tightened the shawl around her shoulders. She had work to get done.

Even so, she didn't get started. Her first act was to open the second drawer on the left side of the desk.

There was no contract, as she'd known there wouldn't be. She inserted the key into the interior compartment, and nothing was there either except for Grandfather's cell phone, cold and dead.

She removed the cell phone and charger. This desk was Grandfather's, the same as the job was Grandfather's, but now she was at the desk and she was heading the company, and of course nothing fit. She'd always felt small in front of this desk, and now she felt small sitting behind it.

The drawer wouldn't slide all the way out, and she didn't want to damage an antique by forcing it. Instead she ran her fingers over the interior of the locked compartment.

A document wouldn't be that big. She felt upwards along the bottom of the first drawer, but nothing there. She looked beneath the open drawer, but nothing there either. So where was it?

Again she probed the empty locked part of the compartment.

Oh.

She put the key back in the compartment lock and locked it without the top on. When it clicked, she felt some play in the wood, and after a moment of tugging, she was able to lift out the entire compartment.

Beneath that was another lock.

She flipped through the key ring to the tiny keys that had never had a match, and the first one fit. The lock turned, and Anna pushed until a thin board slid backward.

In that slender space lay an envelope yellowed with age.

The room smelled of old air—of time itself. Heart racing, Anna laid the fragile paper on top of the desk. Then, like a thief covering her trail, she replaced the board, re-locking it. She set the compartment in its spot and locked the cell phone back inside. She closed and locked the drawer...and only then opened an envelope that cracked as it moved.

Inside was the same document she'd seen on her screen, complete with her grandfather's familiar signature. Beneath it, and something not included on the digital image, was a more complex version of the Pilaster Group logo, half-drawn and half-burnt onto the paper.

She took a photo of the symbol, half expecting it wouldn't appear on her phone screen. Her skin crawled when it did, but she shut down her instincts. Something had countersigned that document, and it must have a name. Whether it was an entity or a corporation, its identity must be this symbol. She tidied the image in her photo app, then uploaded it to an internet image search.

She'd expected a whole lot of garbage results, and for the most part that's what she got. Lots of runes, many vector drawings, some pictures of daggers for an unknown reason, and an assortment of Celtic knots.

And then amongst the dross, a hand-drawn image that looked

remarkably similar.

Hands trembling, she clicked onto a page full of text written in another language. Her browser momentarily translated it into English, but even the English terms remained impossible to decipher, with multiple interlocking references to ideas she'd never heard of. The sentences sounded like a combination of religion and magic, hardly her areas of expertise. Spirits of the days of the week, emanations, powers, faces...? What was this stuff?

She scrolled until she reached the image, and then she read the paragraphs around it.

The sigil of the genius so-and-so, it said, embodying wisdom, foresight, and austerity.

Anna considered her grandfather. Considered his relationship to his company.

Yes, that works.

The "so-and-so" was a series of letters (Hebrew?) that hadn't translated, so she popped them into a translation program that identified the characters and read them back to her. The computer voice sounded out, *Sah-tree-na.*

Based on the badly translated page, it seemed like "genius" was the singular for "genii," or maybe "jinn." An online dictionary claimed jinn were demons, but another one made them sound like forces of nature.

A sigil seemed like a written sign for a spirit-entity. It carried more than force than a signature. Rather, a sigil to some extent contained the giver's essence and power. There were nuances that Anna couldn't understand through the computer's bungling translation, something about control. If you had a creature's sigil, you could control it—? Or it could control you?

When you had its name, you had its power. That at least seemed a reasonable interpretation. The sigil enabled some kind of transfer. You became more like the sigil you carried.

Grandfather had been a strong person. Had he been strong enough to force an entity to reveal its name so he could take command over it?

This wasn't so bad. This wasn't like selling your soul to the devil at all. These things she couldn't see were geniis—geniuses. They were essences, merely forces of the universe. They had names and strengths, but that's all they were. Hardly malevolent. If they wanted to help, why not let them?

Anna couldn't see electricity or gravity, either, and she relied on those every day.

That one website was the only place the sigil showed up online. If she searched on the entity's untranslated name, she could likely find it in other places, but there wasn't time. Contract or not, she needed to catch up on work.

Sighing, Anna tucked Grandfather's envelope into one of the file folders. Things hadn't gone well today after Edwards arrived, and her senior officers were increasingly antagonistic. Falling behind on work only three days after Grandfather's death wasn't the path to impressing the C-level executives.

Her admin had forwarded several emails in the last two hours, and Anna scanned the subject lines with an exponentially increasing sense of dread.

That merger was going bust. Pilaster was about to have its first disaster with her at the helm, and three of the VPs were calling for her to step down.

Chapter Thirteen

Cosmiel snuck a glance at Turmiel, concerned because Turmiel still hadn't turned his hearing back on. While Anna slept, he looked markedly calmer than before, but his self-isolation had been over twenty-four hours. Giving him the respite must have been exactly what he'd needed, but on the other hand, continuing it was going to impact their ability to coordinate.

Cosmiel went into the boys' room where their guardians sat beside them on the beds. With a nod to them, Cosmiel opened a Guarded bubble and said into it, "Sophiel, put your imagination to work. I need a low-level repulsion field." Then he sealed the Guard and flashed it to wherever Sophiel was.

The guardians were both staring at him. Cosmiel shrugged. "Sophiel is doing field work while I'm here, and I don't want to interrupt him."

With his brow furrowed, Gavin's guardian said, "You can speak into a Guard and hear it later?"

Cosmiel nodded. "We needed a form of asynchronous communication."

Ryan's guardian said, "Oh, like the thought bubbles."

Cosmiel paused. "The what?"

"You know, when Turmiel made spheres with thoughts in them to derail Anna." Gavin's guardian mimicked a sphere with his fingers. "Indri called them thought bubbles, like in comic books."

Cosmiel rolled his eyes at himself. "I should have come up with that."

Gavin's guardian said, "Well, now we can make speech balloons, too."

Cosmiel hid a snicker as he re-entered Anna's room, knowing exactly how both those guardian angels would spend the rest of their downtime before the boys awoke. Time-delaying a message wasn't a difficult thing to do. Just not everybody did it, nor had a reason to.

Eyes closed, Turmiel sat through Anna's sleeping form, his copper feathers shimmering with the glow of his prayer. Wisps of his petitions escaped. Peace. Protection. Pilaster Group. That was an odd direction for him to be interceding, but Turmiel knew Anna best. Perhaps if Anna felt signing the contract was the only way to lead Pilaster, she would sign it.

That wasn't truly consent, was it? That was coercion.

Cosmiel reached for Auriel, who was consulting with Jezaryah. *Turmiel's praying for Pilaster. God gave Moloch permission to harm it. Should I try to divert his efforts?*

Auriel replied, *Is he still self-isolating?*

Yes.

Then how do you intend to do that? She paused. *Let him pray for whatever he wants. God's guiding him, and Turmiel knows Anna better than we do.*

Cosmiel patrolled the edge of the apartment again, reinforcing the Guards that weren't doing much to screen out the demons. For all that Special Ops engaged in "unconventional warfare," they never engaged in psychological warfare. That was solely a tactic of Satan's agents, and filling the field with these leering mockeries of the angels that used to be—that was harsh. Usually it wasn't this bad, but Satrinah had enough of a claim on Anna to get a steady stream of them through. Enough of a claim on all the siblings.

Worse, once the minor demons had reached a certain density, that very density attracted other demons because it meant not doing any work. They'd have a dog-pile during which they egged on one another without any risk of incurring pain. Such fun, a demon party.

Resting a hand on the wall of Anna's bedroom, Cosmiel concentrated harder. Make that mesh finer and maybe some demons would decide it wasn't worth the struggle. As much as minor demons relished harassing people, perseverance was still a virtue. Demons as a rule weren't overflowing in virtue. The higher order demons excelled at self-discipline, but what kept the lower ones at work was fear of reprisal. Distract them or lure them to an easier target, and they'd go. Except Cosmiel had no desire to lure them to an easier target either because that just transferred the burden to someone else.

While he was fine-tuning the Guard, Sophiel appeared alongside the grandfather clock. Cosmiel spun toward him. "You're injured?"

Sophiel's power signature was thready, and his wings were more a spring green than jade. "Not injured. I have what you wanted."

He must have it because the throng of demons in the foyer was turning into smaller throngs of demons in the kitchen and the office. Cosmiel flashed him into the boys' room, and there they shone brighter. "Talk to me."

As Sophiel spoke, he projected bravery as though that would prevent Cosmiel from noticing how unsteady he was. "I've been toying with an idea for years but never had a reason to try it." He opened a hand and produced a disk the size of a sand dollar, marked with his sigil. "If Turmiel can insert this into Anna's heart, it may deter minor demons who haven't been ordered to stay near her."

Ryan's guardian pushed a question into Cosmiel's heart, and Cosmiel pushed it back: yes, he knew Sophiel looked depleted. The guardian acknowledged and said nothing.

"May I?" Cosmiel raised the sigil, surprisingly light for its size. "This took a lot out of you."

"Not that much," said Sophiel, despite his spot-on impersonation of a Virtue in need of a three-hour nap. "A sigil naturally carries our power signatures, so it was just a matter of amplifying its natural resonance." When Cosmiel prompted him, Sophiel added, "I went into the Heavenly Temple and prayed for admittance into God's inner sanctum. When He gave me permission, I formed three sigils in His presence and prayed for them to resound with His holiness. He wouldn't grant that, but He let me infuse them with mine." Both boys' guardians radiated awe, but Sophiel sighed. "That's not enough to deter Satrinah or Moloch, but it's the best I can manage."

Cosmiel would never have been able to do this, for obvious reasons. Sophiel's soul was pure. An angel so single-hearted could shine like a light to other angels. *Thank you for sending me Sophiel,* Cosmiel prayed for the ten thousandth time since they'd begun working together. (That was a rough approximation. A Cherub would have kept count.)

The only wonder was that Cosmiel could even handle an object this holy. Maybe that's why God had declined to infuse it Himself.

Cosmiel said, "Do we put it into Turmiel, or into Anna?"

Beneath his black hair, Sophiel's eyes looked exhausted. "Either would do, but I think Anna."

Together they went into Anna's room and sat praying alongside Turmiel. Sophiel was likely praying for this gambit to work, but Cosmiel prayed for his second in command to regain his strength.

When he felt Turmiel's hand on his, he opened his eyes to see the guardian looking around the room, now clear of demons. He was projecting confusion, and Cosmiel caught himself before sending a response Turmiel wouldn't be able to decode. Instead he gave him a good old American thumbs-up.

Turmiel frowned, and with a moment's concentration he broke the isolation circuit. "How did you do that?"

Handing over his sigil, Sophiel forced a smile. "My job description is waiting for Cosmiel to ask me to do the impossible, then finding a means of achieving it."

Cosmiel explained how Turmiel could use the spiritual disk with its afterglow of holiness. "It won't purify Anna's soul," Cosmiel clarified. "She's the only one who can affect her state of soul."

"Right, but being near a holy object will give the minor demons a spiritual migraine." Turmiel cradled it. "Thank you. This is amazing."

Cosmiel talked him through the process of creating a pocket

within Anna's soul to contain this spiritual treasure. Angels did things like this to themselves on a regular basis, calling forth parts of their own souls to use as swords or keeping bits of other angels contained in themselves. Human souls, fortunately, had the same plasticity, although not the same ability to manifest their souls outside themselves.

Turmiel sighed. "Thank you so much. The demons were wearing me out, and I needed this." The guardian had softened to him, at least. "Can you give one to Indri and Jezaryah too? We should make these for every human. It's a game changer!"

Cosmiel gestured to Sophiel. "He's made two more, but look at him. The cost is too high. He's about to take a few days of enforced time in the Special Ops headquarters."

Sophiel folded his arms. "I'm fine to oversee operations."

"Then you can be fine overseeing operations from headquarters."

Sophiel's eyes narrowed. "The bigger issue is that these sigils degrade quickly. You'll get maybe two days at peak effectiveness, and then another day or two before it's a useless trinket."

Cosmiel side-eyed him. "You say that as though it's shameful that you only worked out two days of doing the impossible."

Turmiel said, "If you're doing impossible things, can you make it so I can meet Anna in a human form?"

Sophiel choked on a laugh, and Cosmiel said, "I don't think that would help. Would you show up and tell her, 'Hey, I'm a stranger, but if the devil offers you a deal, don't take it?'"

Turmiel blew off a deep breath. "I know it wouldn't change the tide, and I know it takes a lot of energy, and of course I'd need God's permission. But I've always wanted to meet Anna on her territory rather than on mine. When she was a kid playing in the park, I wanted so much to push her on the swing. Even if I could just hold a door open for her, that would be amazing."

Sophiel smiled. "I'd love to secure that grace for you. I've heard a lot of stories about one stranger's small effort making an outsized difference in a human's life."

Beaming, Turmiel looked much stronger now than he had last

night. "Well, that's what I want. That and hearing her say my name."

"I'll pray for it." Cosmiel had prayed for a lot of unlikely things. "Speaking of prayer, were you praying for Pilaster Group? Because Moloch has license to act against that however he wants."

Turmiel's copper wings sagged. "Pilaster's been behind everything that's ever happened to Anna. Her grandfather behaved as if he loved it even though he fathered two boys and didn't love them, and then he raised three grandchildren he didn't love. He treated Pilaster's success as more important than personal happiness or any relationship. She accepts that as if it's the way things ought to be."

Sophiel said, "Especially after the way Linus's first engagement ended."

Cosmiel's brow furrowed. "Anna doesn't know about that."

Turmiel shrugged. "She's heard snippets, but I don't know if she ever connected them." The guardian stroked Anna's hair. "It was so much easier back when I thought 'evil visiting the children to the fourth generation' was external to the people themselves. For her, it formed the fabric of her life."

Sophiel said, "Speaking of fabric, the other thing I meant to report was that I've done traces against evil four separate times today on Yolanda's mother, and on Eric, too. We've blocked attempts on her health and his career. The soldiers stationed with them now are former Special Ops. They'll do regular traces themselves, and they can stay for the next year if need be."

Turmiel's eyes darkened. "It's not their fault that Cosmiel got extra days."

Cosmiel didn't bother replying. Demons had no scruples about venting their rage on innocent parties. If a demon got angry, it must be someone else's fault. Not their own fault for choosing Hell over Heaven. Certainly not that. Instead it had to be an elderly knitter's fault for responding to sorrow with compassion and casting on a beautiful pattern.

Not that demons understood beauty, either, except as something to wreck. That was why they'd missed the shawl's importance in the first place. They hadn't considered that the mother of the housekeeper of one of their targets might care enough to spend her time and prayers on a woman she'd never met.

While Sophiel could extend his senses through a human soul to detect evil intentions toward it, aka the "trace," a demon couldn't do the same and detect prayers. If Yolanda had announced to Anna that her mother had cast on a prayer shawl, that would have tipped off their enemies. With it flowing off the needles in silence, they'd had no clue. The prayers had blossomed between Yolanda's mother and God her Father, and no demon could interfere with that communication. Moreover, when God acted...He acted. Demons couldn't detect it until afterward, assuming they ever recognized it at all.

Turmiel said, "Even if they're targeting innocent people, using the prayer shawl connection was a work of genius."

Cosmiel made a mock bow, and Sophiel flicked sparks at him. Laughing, Cosmiel exclaimed, "Are you implying that wasn't a work of genius?"

Turmiel sat up. "Wait—?"

Both Special Ops officers turned to him. Turmiel said, "You're laughing."

Cosmiel laughed again, this time self-conscious.

Turmiel leaned forward. "Does that mean it's not hopeless? Did the extra days turn the tide?"

When Cosmiel had asked the same thing, Auriel had said no. She'd speculated that two weeks was too long for Satrinah to comfortably wait on Anna, and that there wouldn't be more than a twenty-four-hour respite. Then Satrinah would enact her Plan B, throwing the decision to Sid or Forrest and having them lead the way.

"There's always hope," Cosmiel said. Said it by reflex.

Chapter Fourteen

Anna checked messages Saturday morning to find a text from Sid. "I really need to talk to you."

With trembling fingers, she replied, "I'm in the office all day. Is it an emergency?"

Autocorrect repaired her typos and sent the text. Based on the timestamp, Sid had texted right after waking up, half an hour ago while she'd been knee deep in financial reports with two VPs who had come in on their day off to argue with every single suggestion —while simultaneously refusing to give a straightforward answer to any of her questions.

Sid, though? Sid never "really needed to talk" to anyone.

Why would the entities reach out to him too? He's not part of the company. It made sense that whatever had contracted with Linus Ellington to save Pilaster wanted to contract with Anna as well. Sid on the other hand not only had nothing to do with Pilaster but also wanted nothing to do with it. Or was the entity doing as Grandfather had, and punishing Sid for charting his course away from the company?

Halfway through discussions with corporate counsel, Anna got a reply from Sid. "It is, but maybe it can wait?"

"I have to take this, sorry." She was already dialing Sid before she was out of the room. He had his phone in his hands right now, and his schedule was notoriously volatile. As was her own.

Relief flooded her when she heard his hello. "Sid, it's me. What's going on?"

"I had the strangest conversation this morning, and I need to know I'm not losing my mind." Sid sounded breathless. "Sorry, I'm trying to get to somewhere I can talk."

"Are you safe?" She stepped into an empty conference room and shut the door at her back.

"I don't really know...? It was so odd. Okay." He paused for a moment. "I woke up with my phone ringing in my hand, which is already weird because I don't sleep with my phone, and I turn notifications off at night. The call came from Grandfather's number. I was still half asleep, so I latched onto the idea that you might be calling from his phone. Like maybe something was wrong with the estate? So I answered."

Goosebumps prickled up Anna's arms. "That wasn't me. His phone's locked in a drawer."

"Yeah, I figured that out right away. It was a woman, and she started by saying she knew Grandfather back in the day. I was getting ready to tell her off because obviously this was about to turn into a shakedown for money, right? She was going to say she's the daughter of that other woman people claim Grandfather was engaged to, except..."

When Sid fell trailed off, Anna said, "Except she offered you a deal."

His voice went hollow. "How did you know?"

"Because I've been offered a deal, too. It's legit. I've held Grandfather's original contract in my hands."

Sid breathed, "No kidding?"

Lightheaded, Anna leaned on the edge of a credenza with one hand holding the phone and the opposite arm wrapped around her waist.

Sid said, "This woman knew everything about me, and she knows everything I want. I tried to laugh her off, except she kept drawing me up short by telling me more things, and how would she know all this?"

Anna said, "Did she give you a contract? Run it by an attorney."

"Just a verbal offer. She said I have two weeks to think about it."

Anna lowered her voice. "What happens if you sign?"

Sid said, "Everything. I get everything."

Sid already lived in a world of flash and opulence. What did "everything" mean to him?

Anna said, "And what will she do to you if you don't sign?"

"She didn't say anything like that. She only told me I have two weeks to agree, and when I was ready, she'd call again."

That was better than the threats written into Anna's contract. At least if Sid turned his down, he'd be safe. Sid had no children, and no plans for any. "When I get home, I'll check out Grandfather's phone to see if it called you."

That was the most banal response Anna could have made, but she couldn't come up with anything better.

No one had access to her apartment during the daytime other than Yolanda. Yolanda would have information about Sid, of course, and could fill in the blanks about anything she didn't know. Anna loved her brother, but she figured Sid wanted the same things most actors wanted: a long career, name recognition, approval. Money.

For that matter, Yolanda might have been able to fake the contract to Anna, too. But would she?

Except how would Yolanda have planted the original contract in a drawer even Anna didn't know about? Yolanda had no passwords for Anna's computer. She'd have to be working with a hacker who had the skills to break electronic locks.

Anna's stomach tightened. She'd never mistrusted Yolanda in the past eight years, and she wasn't about to start. She entrusted Yolanda with her children, for pity's sake. Compared to that, a locked desk was nothing.

Sid said, "The woman I talked to, has she called Forrest?"

"I haven't talked about it with Forrest, so I have no idea." After contacting Sid, though, either the offering party had already reached Forrest or would do it soon.

"What should I do? Are you going to take it?" Sid snorted a laugh. "Or did you tell them you're taking your two weeks to consult corporate counsel?"

"I did bring it to a lawyer, and he advised me not to sign until closer to the deadline. In response, they extended my deadline." She drummed her fingers against her leg. "Once the offer is revoked, it's off the table."

"She said the same to me." Sid paused. "Wait up. You asked if they threatened me. Did they threaten you?"

Anna said, "They threatened Pilaster. If I don't sign, they'll take back all the benefits they gave Pilaster in the first place."

Sid said, "If you believe them, isn't that everything?"

Given the date on the contract, Pilaster would have been days from bankruptcy. What did they offer to Sid? What did they threaten to take away from Anna? Everything.

"Are you going to sign?" pressed Sid. "Because it sets off my alarms. You agree to partner with them, and they agree not to destroy everything you've built. It's like contracting for the Mafia, but I've seen enough Mafia movies to know how it works out for regular schlubs like you and me. You're never the star of that film. What you need then is a protagonist to show up and shut down the protection racket. What are they really?"

Anna said, "I looked up the signatory on Grandfather's contract. It's a genii or an essence in some Middle Eastern religion. What did she tell you she was?"

Sid sighed. "That's more than I got out of her. I'd just woken up, and the way she shotgunned statements at me, I never thought to ask. That was dumb."

"You're not dumb." Anna glanced at the time. "Don't do anything without talking to me and Forrest, okay? We'll find a time we're all free and talk through a plan of action. We're all in this together."

"That sounds good. I feel a bit calmer knowing this isn't as bonkers as it sounded at seven o'clock in the morning."

"Good. Stay safe."

Anna headed back to her office, her own words ringing in her mind. *Stay safe.* As if any of them knew how to do that against an invisible mover.

Chapter Fifteen

The hardest part of sneaking into Hell was that Satan funneled everyone through one entrance to have better control.

That was also the best part because it gave the angels more options than Satan ever anticipated, and it was all courtesy of the minor demons.

Cosmiel had discorporated to work on the simplest form of transport into Hell. By releasing the entirety of his subtle body, he could exist as nothing more than awareness; he then reduced even that to such a thin presence that he was undetectable. By picking a busy time at the gate, he could spread out like a layer of oil and take half an hour to pass through, one iota of a half-formed thought at a time, until he flowed fully inside.

Getting out again was never a problem. You might get flushed out like a pheasant from the underbrush, and you might end up with a sword blade between your wings, but by that point you'd gotten whatever information you wanted. Stealth wasn't a concern during the escape, so you could blast your way out.

Cosmiel wouldn't have to do that today. He'd prepared a Special Ops tactic in advance, one that paired nicely with "existing as nothing."

Moving a larger force into Hell always required overwhelming the gate guards. That was the second way in, but at the cost of whatever information you wanted. In the past, Michael had provided Cosmiel with soldiers to distract the gate guards, but inevitably afterward came a tight sweep of Hell, and whatever information you wanted ended up triple-locked. Not worth it.

The third way in was faster, more dangerous, and frankly disgusting: pretending to be a demon. Could Cosmiel do it? Yes. Was that his last resort? Also yes. If challenged, you had to sound like you were committing blasphemy, and no matter how much he'd greyed up his soul by using demonic tactics, there were some bridges Cosmiel wouldn't cross.

The fourth way in wasn't Cosmiel's last resort, but it hurt like blazes because it was supposed to hurt like blazes. Gabriel was the one who'd figured out how to do it back at the time Christ died, and afterward, Cosmiel interviewed him in case it would get an operative straight through Hell's walls. It did. It was awful. He'd documented it and then never done it again.

Cosmiel didn't pray while oozing into Hell. He studied one bump at a time, one rock, one grain of dirt out of place. He registered one noise, one voice, one crash, one sharp order. One wisp of smoke. One laugh. He noticed everything in a way that had his heart taking notice of nothing, and in this way, no one took notice of him.

This method didn't hurt. It was a modification of the way angels lost themselves in prayer, only honed to be useful in a very specific way.

Back in the fortress, a still-recovering (and still-annoyed) Sophiel served as Cosmiel's spotter. That was to say, Cosmiel had made a duplicate of himself and left it there. Most angels didn't bilocate on a regular basis, but most angels also didn't sneak into Hell on a regular basis. Cosmiel's other self had most of his essence but very little of his energy, and no awareness passed between the two parts. In the event that Cosmiel got detected, he could fade out this iteration and transfer all his awareness back to the rest of himself in Heaven. Under house arrest until he recovered, Sophiel would babysit the weaker form and assist if necessary.

Once Cosmiel reached Hell's rocky caverns, he located a nook and solidified his subtle body again. Momentarily he was ensconced in a very small space, keeping his thoughts very small to match.

Cosmiel did adapt himself now to seem like a minor demon, bristling against any contact with other demons (that didn't need to be faked) and repulsed by the human souls. That also didn't need to be faked. Cosmiel wanted nothing to do with the humans here. As an angel, he still felt the impulse to help them, but they were beyond help. How many of them had he tried to keep out of this place?

He pushed through the throngs in the main level, moved through caves, and headed away from the Lake of Fire...all the time shutting out the sounds as best he could. He couldn't do for himself what he'd done for Turmiel, but at least these voices weren't directed at him. As with many situations in Special Ops, he'd just have to cope.

Right off Hell's main level lay the lab area, where the chief torment was the impenetrable darkness. Cosmiel slipped into those corridors and finally relaxed a little. Most of the damned stayed out of the lab area because even at full shine, an angel couldn't cast light very far. The humans couldn't do it at all. Here, you moved by feel and by memory.

Cosmiel had infiltrated the lab areas so often that he had the entire thing mapped, and all the maps memorized. He could find Satan's offices in a heartbeat (Satan's C-suite?), but this time Cosmiel avoided the larger caverns that the Maskim and their overlord called home. Instead, he wanted the slightly smaller ones. Specifically, Moloch's.

Satrinah's lab, though... Oh, what a treasure hoard. Who knew what she'd be inventing, experimenting with, or concocting?

Better yet, who knew how the Special Ops team would be able to purify whatever she was inventing in order to wield it for good? Get Sophiel into that room for half an hour and Special Ops would have new weaponry for the next century.

Cosmiel had no way into Satrinah's quarters, though. Only Moloch's, and first he had to locate them. For that, he could use a tactic Sophiel had come up with about a thousand years ago. Had come up with unintentionally, as it turned out.

In an alcove, Cosmiel began by creating a dozen tiny Guards, invisible bubbles encasing nothing at all. They'd burst the instant they touched anything else, and that pop would register in his mind like a pinprick. Cosmiel floated them in pairs in the hallway, almost touching but not quite. If a demon came through while he was working, the Guards' bursting would alert Cosmiel in time to discorporate.

You couldn't ever claim to be "secure" in Hell, but it paid to take precautions.

Next step. Cosmiel reached back for the memory of Moloch's attack. Recreating Moloch's sword strike in his mind, he took note of the power, the fury, the vibrations. He tracked the pattern of the sword blow back through his arm and his soul, and then he took careful measurement of the disturbance in his heart.

A strike that close—that powerful—left the equivalent of fingerprints. Or more accurately, soulprints. Cosmiel's soul would bear for a fleeting time the reverse image of Moloch's power insignia.

This had been Sophiel's discovery. After a reconnaissance mission gone wrong, one of Michael's soldiers had found Sophiel collapsed in the Patagonian desert, jade wings reeking of brimstone. When asked what had happened, Sophiel only breathed, "Keys," before passing out for two days.

Moloch's quarters would be Guarded so as to be accessible only by Moloch, and only by the use of his own power. The strike pattern of Moloch's power on Cosmiel's soul would to some extent have an image of that power. Cosmiel's imprint would fade soon; the stones in Hell had been impressed over and over, and therefore would never fade. If Cosmiel could match the afterimage on the stones with the afterimage on his soul, that functioned like a nameplate on the door.

Even better, once he found those quarters? That imprint gave him the keys to get in.

Cosmiel concentrated on the walls around him. A demon passed through—Belior—disturbing his Guard orbs. Cosmiel pulled back into himself. Then, once more alone, he recreated the orbs and returned to his scans.

Nothing. He blinked out the orbs and relocated for a second try.

On the third attempt, Cosmiel found a cluster of quarters that all bore Moloch's signature. Some of those would belong to his bonded Cherubim. It took a while of tracing and retracing the signatures, but eventually Cosmiel identified one of the chambers as the most likely target. Next, to get in.

Keeping that afterimage of Moloch's signature in his mind, Cosmiel flowed even more of himself into the bilocated portion until all that remained here was his injury. Not Cosmiel's pain or fear, only the resonance of getting struck with a Seraph's anger. It was the equivalent of ringing a bell, then removing the hammer and the bell from the universe but keeping the sound.

Once the aftershock was all that remained, Cosmiel pressed that image into the Guard. It didn't admit him, but it also didn't repel him.

Excellent. He didn't need to get inside. He just needed to be here. He could be the walls, the floor, and the outside. He could be the Guard itself. Because the bottom layer of the outside was simultaneously the top layer of the inside, and because time passed and because the world changed...because of all that, now Cosmiel was in.

Auriel would have had this kind of imprint on her soul after Satrinah's strike, and that information would have been valuable—but Cosmiel wouldn't ask Auriel to do something like this. The risk was too high, and he didn't want her to get hurt. They'd have to be content with searching Moloch's chamber.

Moloch wasn't inside, so Cosmiel shifted the balance of his essence back to this part of himself. Keeping his signature suppressed, Cosmiel took inventory of everything he could, every sensation, every stray impulse. Seraphim output a lot of energy just by existing, and the demonic Seraphim did nothing to suppress it. The room and all its contents were drenched in Moloch's power, to the point that anything Cosmiel probed emitted a faint buzz. The residual energy gave him a headache.

On the plus side, once Moloch returned, he'd never identify Cosmiel's infiltration over his own vibrations.

In darkness thick as tar, Cosmiel scanned for anything that might help. He wanted a sigil, but he could also use a discarded weapon or any part of Moloch's soul that he'd solidified in some other form. A piece of Satrinah would work even better.

On a shelf, Cosmiel encountered...books? A Seraph kept books? Were they his own, or were they Satrinah's overflow storage? They resonated with Moloch's signature, though, so he must have been using them.

In one niche, Cosmiel encountered a trove of antiquities. The motley assortment of jewelry, watches, and other objects were cold to the touch and seemed to have been undisturbed for ages. Old tokens? Sentimental objects? Cosmiel tried to scan them without activating anything. Linus Ellington's token wouldn't be here, but did any of these objects have an attachment to him?

The Guard shivered. Eyes straining in the dark, Cosmiel pressed against the wall. Energy coursed through the Guard as it flowed and bulged, and Moloch entered, followed momentarily by Satrinah.

As Moloch's heat blew through the chamber, Cosmiel struggled to focus himself past anything like fear. He'd need to flow every part of himself back out of Hell except his awareness, but with Moloch so close, and with a Guard between, he wasn't going to do that easily.

Moloch surged with unrefined anger, and those bits of fire stung like a sandstorm.

Satrinah sighed. "Someday Belior will reach the pinnacle of understanding, and in that brief moment of intellectual achievement, he still won't reconcile himself to the fact that I don't want to unseat him."

Moloch growled, "He would sabotage you in a heartbeat if positions were reversed."

"Precisely. You've successfully named the reason I will never reverse our positions." Moloch's energy ebbed, but now Satrinah's power signature was riveting. She must have reached for him through their bond. "All the same, I neither request nor require you to insert yourself between us. Because I continue to take his insults, he believes himself in control of me."

Moloch said, "That's unacceptable."

"It's an acceptable sacrifice from my point of view. I don't need Belior taking any of my assignments away from me just because he's jealous. Likewise, I don't want Asmodeus to fight you."

"It's a matter of pride."

"Not for me." Satrinah gave a low chuckle. "For me, it's a matter of letting them think they've won while I make the right moves, sweep the set, and secure everything I've ever wanted."

Moloch said, "Belior's going to take credit for the Ellingtons."

"He's going to *attempt* to take credit for the Ellingtons, but called on the carpet in front of Lucifer, he'll discover he cannot answer the first question about the Ellingtons. As of now, he has no authority to approach them. I saw to that. If Belior interferes, he's facing censure from our master, who's a much stronger foe. I'll let that happen."

Moloch huffed. "I should be the one protecting you. Not Lucifer."

Satrinah snickered. "Your devotion is noted. Let go of your emotional response."

Moloch's heat surged again, and the wound inside Cosmiel twinged. He needed to diminish more of himself back out of the room, but how long would it take? How long would Moloch stay? Could Cosmiel wait them out? Cosmiel had never passed through a Guard while the owner was inside it.

A rustle of wings meant Satrinah was moving around the chamber. "Analytically speaking, making pacts with families is Belior's art. If he's jealous that we've shown him to be an amateur at the game he created, that should spur him to outdo us. From a strategic perspective, his competitive nature benefits our side, which is why Lucifer provoked him in the first place. Belior when he's jealous is Belior at his best."

Moloch said, "You're too complacent. Once all three siblings are signed, Belior is going to try to take over the contract."

"Perhaps. Except he never managed to part dear Mr. Linus Ellington from us, not any more than our enemies did. Belior thinks our contracts are about trading services. You're the one who realized it's about winning hearts, and for that, I'm delighted."

Again Moloch's power ebbed. Satrinah kept calming him, but she must be getting scorched by an overload of power.

Abruptly Cosmiel realized what she was doing: she *was* powering up, using Moloch like a battery. Angering him, then drawing off his excess fire. By doing this repeatedly, she was super-charging her soul, gaining more strength than she ought to be able to stockpile.

Now that would be a neat technique for Special Ops to attempt, other than the fact that only bonded Cherubim and Seraphim worked this way.

Moloch said, "So, the politician's heart? Have you decided to follow my directions?"

"I still say the politician's heart is ours even without giving him anything. His heart's wound is much more powerful in this regard, but it also makes him slippery."

Moloch said, "Which is why I promise you my approach is best. The woman has something she wants. The actor, he'll take anything. Those two don't require the same kind of special touch."

That special touch—surely they'd elaborate.

Moloch added, "You used Linus to pattern the politician to accept our offer."

"We patterned them all, but the politician won't break the same way. His guardian is an annoyance." Satrinah huffed, and Cosmiel fought a frisson of pride over his fellow operative. He could preen over Jezaryah later. Now he needed to observe.

Satrinah said, "I've concluded that your plan is brilliant. Waiting will break open the politician's heart in a way that ensures he will embrace us. His anger shields him from his unacknowledged pain, and we can use it. The longer we wait, the larger it grows, and the more likely he'll take anything we offer."

Cosmiel struggled not to react.

"After our enemies altered the timetable, you did excellent work to correct. The other two siblings will approach the politician tonight about our offers, and once they've done that, we'll have all the gears turning."

Moloch said, "Two days will make him feel sufficiently abandoned. Once he's inhabiting that emotional space, we barely have to offer anything at all."

Jezaryah needed to know this. He needed to know the demons were turning a crank on the family dynamics. Had Auriel said the demons wouldn't know about the sibling bonds? Well, not only did they know about them, but they had built them and were adjusting them like a thief cracking a safe. His team needed to stop Sid and Anna from calling Forrest.

Cosmiel needed to leave.

"Come to me," Satrinah breathed to Moloch, and in the resulting silence, Cosmiel tried to flow himself out of the room. Let Satrinah keep supercharging herself. Cosmiel had to arrange a defense against a hyper-powerful Cherub, or maybe the Cherub and the Seraph attacking together. If he made the request, Michael would give him the army.

The demons had been quiet too long, and the moment Cosmiel realized this, Moloch speared him with fire.

Cosmiel screamed. Shock, pain, heat—and there wasn't enough of Cosmiel to fight back, but at the same time, there was too much of him to fade away.

"You're right, it's the little Power." Moloch snorted. "I didn't notice him because of how weak he is."

He again blasted Cosmiel, and the pain forced Cosmiel back into his subtle body, pinned against the wall. Moloch's hatred loomed at his front while the Guard seared Cosmiel's back. Struggling to get control, Cosmiel barely registered that Satrinah had gotten alongside to study him.

He needed to warn Auriel.

"He's bilocating." Satrinah huffed. "Most of him is in his other self. Your Guard can't sever the contact."

Moloch said, "How did he get in?"

"I'm investigating." Her power crackled through the Guard like lightning, and Cosmiel gasped as it spiked through his back and wings. "Your Guard is perfect, therefore he entered despite it, not because of it. Since I don't want to explain a perforated Guard to Lucifer, you will keep him here while I oversee the next step of the process."

Behind Cosmiel, Satrinah laced her power through Moloch's, and now the Guard was double-strength.

Moloch said, "I should be the one overseeing that."

"You should be here ensuring our intruder accomplishes exactly nothing for his trouble." She huffed. "Ideally we'd both be present to secure the politician, but I dislike leaving this creature alone."

Moloch said, "Did he get whatever he came for?"

"I won't even hypothesize why he came here, whether for information or vandalism. His pathetic specialists are grasping at anything they can, though, so we need to detain him."

Moloch said, "Soldiers. Two of them, personally loyal to us. Is that sufficient?"

"Two or fifty, since he got in, he likely planned to reverse the mechanism to get back out again." Satrinah hummed. "I do prefer you attend to the politician with me. I assume the bilocation is part of our spy's escape plan, so let's reunite him with himself."

Cosmiel recoiled, but the Guard held.

Moloch's light crackled before him in the thick darkness. Satrinah got right up beside Moloch, probing Cosmiel with her face cast in Moloch's yellow-black light. She wasn't looking at him. She was looking right through—all the way to Heaven.

Her eyes gleamed while her power crawled over his soul like hungry spiders. "There!" And she yanked.

The heavenly parts of Cosmiel slammed into the parts here in Hell. He writhed. How was she doing this? She shouldn't be able to grab the rest of him, not through a Guard—not right through the side of Hell and into the heart of Heaven.

Moloch growled, "Do you have him?"

"I'm working on it." Her eyes bored into Cosmiel's as she hauled him back into himself. "These vermin keep sneaking into places they shouldn't, and it's time we put a stake through the heart of their oh-so-special operations."

Cosmiel couldn't recoil. He couldn't scream. He was being pulled from both directions. The wrenching, the stabbing through his heart—it went on for ages until he could no longer sense time, no longer sense himself—couldn't sense his extremities. He had no idea where all of his soul was, or whether a part of him was even still back in the fortress.

Moloch flexed his wings. "Is that all of him?"

Satrinah fixed Cosmiel again with her will, locking him down even tighter. "Give up, Power! Your cute little friends won't have time or inclination to stage a rescue, given how badly you botched this operation."

Cosmiel couldn't marshal his thoughts to refute her. But the tugging intensified from Heaven.

Satrinah flared with light and shrieked a startled, "Moloch!"

Moloch grabbed Cosmiel by the throat and blasted him with fire.

Unable to scream, Cosmiel took Moloch's strike head-on.

Chapter Sixteen

Fear.

In Special Ops headquarters, Sophiel's head jerked up, and he flashed to Cosmiel's side. "Hey, boss, talk to your spotter. What's happening?"

Wide-eyed, Cosmiel vibrated as if trying to escape himself. "I can't tell."

Terror burst from Cosmiel like a cloud, and Sophiel wrapped his arms around him. "Whatever it is, I've got you."

Sophiel kept a hard grip on Cosmiel for all of a second before something wrenched Cosmiel from his grasp.

"No!" What was that? Sophiel armored up and scrambled to keep ahold of him. "Fight it! Don't let them yank you apart!"

Apart wasn't the problem. Across the gulf, something was pulling him back together.

Sophiel coiled his soul through Cosmiel as hard as he could, but that grip, that pull—it was relentless. Fire and frigidity scorched through him, and every moment, Cosmiel kept discorporating more. This was tug-of-war over a soul, a Virtue who wasn't even at full strength pulling against a Cherub and a Seraph pair who had united their intentions. "Michael!" Sophiel hollered. "Auriel! Now! Priority!"

Operatives flooded the room. Sophiel couldn't spare the concentration to explain, but then Auriel was pouring her energy into him. "Michael, Cosmiel's bilocating. We need to anchor him or they'll pull the rest of him into Hell."

Sophiel could do nothing else, only keep every part of himself engaged. They'd always known something like this could happen. That's why no one entered Hell without a spotter. But now? What should he do now?

Auriel settled into Sophiel's will to let him access her strength. Between the two of them, they might keep what was left of Cosmiel from getting dragged into Hell like prey being tugged down the pharyngeal jaw of a moray eel.

Michael ordered the other operatives to seal off the room. That wouldn't work. A soul couldn't block itself. Cosmiel had authority to be Cosmiel and always would. The angels needed a clamp, not a knife.

Sophiel gasped, "Lances!"

The nearest operative signaled his team to spread out on the perimeter, and they shot light lances from a half dozen directions to pin Cosmiel in place. Immediately the pressure let off, but Sophiel didn't dare relax. The spikes were holding, but they weren't anchored.

Auriel called out, "Think negative pressure, not positive."

Eyes closed, Sophiel tightened his grip. *God, please. Please, I can't keep him here.*

Auriel was projecting orders Sophiel couldn't decipher, but she had her hands on his shoulders. All he needed to do was hang on, hang on, hang on. Behind them, Michael flared an additional Guard around the room, reinforced by Guards from two other Archangels. Except why more Guards? Guards were useless in this —

"Now!" Auriel called, and abruptly the room felt a hundred times bigger—and Cosmiel slammed against Sophiel's chest, safe in his subtle body.

Auriel sprang in front of them both, securing Cosmiel in place with a smaller, tighter framework of lances.

Whatever of Cosmiel was left, that was. He wasn't moving.

Auriel sat on her heels, palms on her knees, head down and wings limp. Relief and fear and grief seeped from her as if she couldn't contain it all, but she'd done it. Whatever she'd ordered, it had worked.

Finally she took a deep breath, raised her wings, and addressed the other operatives. "Thank you. That was record time for setting up lances, and then the negative pressure—you did that perfectly. I wasn't sure I even explained it well."

Michael sounded stunned as he crouched beside Cosmiel's form. "That was the most unusual fight I've ever seen. Is he back?"

Auriel stroked Cosmiel's feathers. Their purple-blue had faded to lavender. "Most of him is still in Hell."

Sophiel pushed to his knees, wings limp, head down. He tried to speak, but nothing emerged. Their enemies were so strong. So strong.

"You did great." Auriel laid a hand on his shoulder. "Did they hurt you?"

No, they hadn't been able to reach past Cosmiel to his spotter. They'd tried. Sophiel struggled to sit up, then overbalanced and had to be steadied by the operative behind him.

Michael said, "Can you explain what exactly I just did?"

Auriel wove her fingers together. "Sophiel was pulling backward on him. That's positive pressure. It occurred to me that if we went the other way around and made space for Cosmiel's soul to flood back toward us, we'd hold him here without effort and might be able to suction the rest of him back out of Hell. Like the way human lungs work, how the chest cavity expands under the lungs and the negative pressure makes air come in, rather than forcing air in."

Nervous, Michael chuckled. "So I...made extra space?"

"You changed the size of the universe, at least inside this one room." She ran a hand through her hair. "Thank you."

Michael touched Cosmiel. "Except he's still out cold."

Sophiel shuddered. Cosmiel was out cold on the other side as well. He'd felt his consciousness go.

He tried again to sit up on his own, and this time he succeeded.

Auriel faced Sophiel. "Did he send you any information?"

Closing his eyes, Sophiel groped inside himself for anything resembling strength. Cosmiel had infiltrated their enemy to get information, and during that desperate fight, Sophiel hadn't tried to access it. Not that there'd been information to access. The part of Cosmiel that had gathered the information was severed from the part Sophiel had been able to hear.

Auriel added, "Do you know how they caught him?"

Sophiel projected no to both questions.

Auriel studied him. "You weren't at full strength yet. You're going to need to rest for a while."

Not what Sophiel wanted to hear, but then again, he was Cosmiel's spotter. He couldn't leave until Cosmiel returned.

Michael stood. "I'll call up a legion of angels. We need to get him out of there."

Projecting a negation, Sophiel ran his fingers through Cosmiel's wings to interlock the barbs on his feathers.

Auriel shook her head. "If you invade, they'll hide him better, and under heavier guard. If we give him time, he'll break out on his own, and he'll come out with even more information than he already has."

Michael frowned. "How much time?"

Auriel shrugged. "Two days? After that, you can do whatever you want, but he won't be in there that long."

Sophiel backed up that statement with a prayer that, please, God, she would be right.

Chapter Seventeen

Auriel returned to Indri, alternating frantic prayers for Cosmiel with desperate prayers for Sid.

Sid had pulled up in front of a restaurant's valet parking, and Indri flagged his attention when he got too close to the curb. She sent to Auriel, *Is Cosmiel going to be okay?*

Auriel wanted to project assurance and realized she had none, so she switched to historical fact. *It's not the first time an infiltration has gone drastically wrong.*

Indri reminded Sid that he needed to bring his phone, then sent to Auriel, *I'm worried.*

Sophiel's eyes, frightened and devastated, burned in Auriel's mind. She sent, *Sid is our primary concern.*

That offer must be tickling Sid's mind as he handed over his keys and a tip to the valet. Auriel had compared Satrinah's approach to a fishing line, but in this case, Satrinah had baited the lure and walked away. Anna's caution to stall was doing little to dispel Sid's ruminations. If anything, Anna's hesitancy had transformed the offer into forbidden fruit.

Demons clung to the walls and leered whenever the angels looked unsettled. Sophiel's sigil had given their team some distance from the minor demons, but not enough to talk without being overheard. Drawing closer to Sid, Indri projected to Auriel, *Sid has two days more than Anna. That's not what you predicted would happen. You said Satrinah would think speed was of the essence.*

We changed the game by winning Anna extra days. I'm having trouble decoding their backup plan. Auriel rested her hands on Sid's shoulders as he flagged down his agent in the restaurant lobby. Sid's soul was cloaked to her. She'd have to use Indri's connection to do a trace on whatever evil was coming his way, except she knew it would all be coming from Satrinah.

This morning's phone call had terrified even Auriel. Sid had "heard" Satrinah in his head even though the phone wasn't making sounds. Using her claim against his soul, she'd claimed his hearing. Then she'd dazzled him with glamour, leaving him unable to consider normal questions like, "What is your name?"

Sid's extra days, though...?

Oh, of course. Sid had gotten extra time to activate his competitiveness. If circumstances required Anna to decide first, Sid would never stand for that. He'd want to beat her to the punch.

As the two men got seated, Auriel reached with her heart all the way from Los Angeles to Washington, DC. *Jezaryah, any approach to Forrest yet?*

No. He sounded unnerved. *I'm on alert, but so far, nothing.*

Auriel sent reassurance.

Jezaryah replied with a blast of frustration. *I'm trying to prepare him for the idea, but he doesn't even suspect it's on the horizon.*

She made no suggestions. After so long in Special Ops, Auriel trusted every operative would function best when given free rein to do as he needed. She'd also learned to trust the guardian angel's instinct, and Jezaryah was both a guardian and an operative. He'd been preparing for this conflict since the day he received the assignment, even though the immensity of the task felt like trying to extinguish a super nova with a water pistol.

Jezaryah added, *Any word about Cosmiel?*

Nothing.

A pause from Jezaryah, then, *I'm surprised he went in. What did he think he'd find?*

Anything at all, Auriel supposed. It didn't make sense to dive into Hell to find hope, but maybe Cosmiel had.

Jezaryah added, *Is he just flailing? Because it's ridiculous if he took himself out of the game for no reason.*

Auriel sent, *He knows what he's doing,* and left it at that.

That was to say, she trusted Cosmiel knew. Maybe he was flailing. Maybe he wanted not to lose the opportunity afforded by those ever-fading vibrations Moloch had left on his soul, that way they knew for sure afterward that they'd tried everything.

Auriel extended her heart toward God. *I shouldn't have specialized in intergenerational evil. Remember how I was standing in a forest in the northern hemisphere, considering botany as a permanent line of work?*

God replied, *As I recall, you had a reason for making the decision you made.*

Yes, my reason being that I could maintain a greenhouse in Heaven but couldn't intervene on behalf of souls from the top of a tree. She sighed. *For all the good I'm doing right now, I might as well have spent the last millennium cultivating petunias.*

While Sid and his agent ordered, Auriel scanned the perimeter like a secret service agent in the wake of a credible threat. Sophiel's sigil was functioning as intended. Demons thronged everywhere except at this table.

Auriel rested her hand on the agent's soul, and a trace on evil intentions toward him turned up nothing noteworthy. Which was in and of itself noteworthy because Auriel would have bet that when Satrinah applied pressure, it would come through the agent. Sid's ego was tied up in his career. Why wouldn't the decision be?

"So, how do you feel about handshake agreements?"

That was Sid, asking his agent. Auriel's wings flared.

The agent snorted. "They're terrible. Handshake agreements worked in another era, but nowadays? They're not worth the paper they're printed on."

Sid prompted, "Some agents work on handshake agreements."

The agent rolled his eyes. "Some agents still have dial-up internet service, too. You and I have a contract, and if you're ever in doubt about what I will do for you, or what you will do for me, you can pull out that contract and read it. If a situation comes up that we never anticipated, we can amend the agreement. If we have a fight we can't solve, we can show that agreement to a judge." After a pause, the agent said, "Is someone making you an offer? Send them to me."

Auriel turned to find Sid waving the agent down. "Relax. I know how things are done. No one in this business would ever approach me directly."

"Well, if this is about an actor just starting up, they're the ones most at risk." The agent leaned forward and gestured with his fork. "If they go in front of a judge, who's the judge going to believe? Some guy who just stepped off a plane from Cincinnati and says a producer screwed him out of a million bucks, or the producer who's been in business twenty years and doesn't seem like he needs a guy from Cincinnati?"

Sid's finger drummed the table. "This is a good point. It's not enforceable."

The agent said, "The issues are the power disparity and what's at stake. If you offer to pay for a friend's lunch in exchange for an in with their makeup artist, a contract is overkill. If the head of a studio asks an unknown writer for his film treatment, never. Put that thing in writing with a signature on it."

Sid's eyes tightened as Indri poured all her misgivings into his heart.

"That makes sense," he said at last. "The differential in power, and what's at stake."

The agent raised his eyebrows. "Care to enlighten me on who's offering an agreement to whom?"

Sid shook his head. "More like, it's all the nebulous, invisible forces out there moving the world, and they're offering everything."

The agent raised a glass. "In that case, a toast to written, crystal-clear contracts."

Chapter Eighteen

Gavin and Ryan were eating meatloaf and roasted potatoes when Anna got home, but even so, they needed to talk to her now, right now, about all the nonsense they'd saved up all day just so she could know about it. Tuning them out, Anna sat at the table while Yolanda washed the roasting pan. "No, not yet," Anna demurred when Yolanda offered to warm up her dinner.

"You look beat." Yolanda sighed. "You hardly took off any time from work, even for the funeral. Now you worked a Saturday, too."

Anna rubbed her temples. She had too many flaming torches to juggle—work and the kids and her offer and now Sid's offer. They'd be talking to Forrest tonight, after the kids were in bed. She could probably tell Yolanda about her obnoxious COs, two of whom wanted her out of the company, but would that generate sympathy? Or would it give Yolanda more information to use against her?

Why would Anna even want Yolanda's sympathy to begin with? She could have the ear of a preternatural power. What was a housekeeper in comparison to that?

Anna just said, "These are the hours I have to keep."

"I'm worried you're working too hard," Yolanda murmured, then said to Gavin, "Eat your carrots."

Gavin wrinkled his nose, but he did pick up one of his baby carrots. By contrast, Ryan had eaten so many carrots that he might have been trying to turn orange. Yolanda encouraged him to drink his milk.

Anna eyed Yolanda sidelong as she returned to the sink. The housekeeper spent more time with the kids than Anna did. Now she—a *housekeeper*—was telling the boys what to eat and how much of it. Was Yolanda trying to vote "no confidence" on Anna's maternal skills the same way the C-suite was trying to impeach her as CEO?

There would be no ouster on the homefront. Anna stood. "Maybe I will have dinner now." When Yolanda moved for the warming oven, she said, "Don't worry, I'll get it."

Yolanda made excellent meatloaf. Grandma had been a pretty good cook, but Grandfather always had the staff prepare something special for him. Either had seemed fine to Anna.

Anna said, "Have you ever gone into my desk drawers?"

Yolanda laughed. "No, ma'am. I don't even like to clean on top of your desk, but this week there was so much glitter!"

Gavin meowed at Anna, triggering Ryan's giggles. Anna's hair stood on end. Why did they have to be so noisy all the time?

Yolanda said, "Is something missing? I haven't let the boys go in there, but they're sneaky little kittens."

Gavin exclaimed, "I am not!", and this time Ryan meowed.

It wasn't right for Yolanda to blame the boys for her own treason. Anna said, "I wasn't accusing anyone of taking anything out of my office. I just wanted to know if you ever went into the desk."

"It's your holy of holies." Yolanda shuddered. "To be honest, that huge desk is creepy."

Fair enough.

After Yolanda left, Anna gave the boys their baths, then suffered through reading them a book before putting them to bed. Even doing that much made them late to sleep. She had only half an hour before Forrest said he'd be available for a call.

When the whispering and giggling continued from the boys' room, Anna walked away so she didn't storm back in and tell them to shut up. Instead, she went to her office and unlocked the second desk drawer, then the first compartment. Grandfather's phone wouldn't power on. She charged it while she read a financial report, and after two minutes it flared to life.

The SIM card was still out of the phone. The last activity was three weeks ago.

She texted Sid, "The phone had a dead battery. It didn't make that call."

Sid replied, "Creepy."

After the boys were finally asleep and no longer crawling all over her, Anna texted Sid to start the video chat.

"Forrest should be on soon." Sid's eyes aimed off to the side of the camera as he fiddled with the call settings. "I kind of led him to believe it was estate stuff."

"It is about our inheritance." Anna glanced at the yellowed envelope alongside her wrist. "We're the heirs to the curse."

Sid huffed. "Ah, those accursed Ellingtons. Do you think Grandma knew?" Then his head picked up. "Forrest! You made it."

Do you think Grandma knew? was the question of the year, wasn't it? Anna couldn't imagine she did. But then again, Grandma was perceptive. Anna couldn't imagine she didn't.

Forrest's smiling image showed up. "Hey! Glad we're all here. Everything okay?"

Anna couldn't place the furniture at his back. "You're in a hotel room?"

He laughed. "Yes, but on my own hotspot, that way I don't have to use their lousy Wi-Fi for twenty bucks a day, nor are any of our deep dark family secrets compromised." Either he was putting on a show or else he had no idea what was coming down the escalator.

Sid sat up. "So they reached out to you too?"

Forrest frowned. "The media?"

Sid said, "Satan."

With a nervous laugh, Forrest said, "Sometimes I feel that way, too."

Anna said, "Sid, hang on. They may not have contacted him yet."

Forrest opened his hands. "Who?"

Sid repeated, "Satan."

Anna fought annoyance. "Not Satan directly."

Sid said, "The devil otherwise known as Satan?"

"That's not what they're calling themselves. Just quit it." She gathered herself. "Forrest, have you been approached about continuing a contract Grandfather signed sixty years ago?"

Forrest's eyes were wide. "Is someone in the media suggesting our family signed a deal with the devil?"

"Forget the media. Sid and I were approached by an entity claiming to have made an agreement with Grandfather at a time when Pilaster was still SavCo. They want each of us as Grandfather's heirs to re-up the agreement. At first, I thought it was only me they wanted because I'm still with the company, but today they reached out to Sid."

Sid said, "It's effectively the same deal. We agree to be cozy and loyal to them, and they smooth out the way in front of us."

Silent, Forrest looked the perfect politician: he wore no readable expression. After a pause, he said, "Go on."

Sid huffed. "You're not campaigning."

"I am, but I'm not campaigning to you right now." With his brows furrowed, Forrest looked a lot like Eric had when he'd been reading the text of the contract. "Who's orchestrating this? I know we have enemies, but this feels over the top for any of them."

Anna lifted the yellowed envelope. "I found the original contract in a locked hidden compartment in Grandfather's desk."

Forrest whistled. "For real?"

"Everyone always talked about Grandfather's business sense being a sixth sense. Turns out, it was." Anna ran her fingers over the desktop and encountered a lingering sparkle of glitter. "Like Sid said, they told Grandfather which road to take and smoothed out the path before him. Toward the end, he told me to do what they were telling him. And remember at the wake?"

Sid added unnecessarily, "We all heard his voice telling us to sign the contract."

Anna said, "His last words to me were an order to sign a contract. No matter how powerful our enemies are, how could they accomplish all that? They called Sid from Grandfather's phone, which had no power and no SIM card. They sent the contract to my private email address that only a few people have."

Looking uncomfortable, Forrest shrugged. "And yet somehow, they haven't figured out how to reach me."

Sid sighed. "That's a pain because we wanted to know what you planned to do."

"I planned to go to a fundraising event tomorrow morning and then another one tomorrow evening." Forrest shook his head. "None of this was on my radar. I guess I'm not important enough."

Sid said, "They could get you elected."

"The American people can get me elected," Forrest shot back. "Look, I get that I'm not as awesome as you are with the looks and the acting career, but cut me a break. I do know how to run for office—and better than that, I know how to staff people who know how to run for office."

Anna said, "Let's back off for a moment and consider, okay? Sid, Forrest. We don't know that they aren't going to approach you."

Forrest snapped, "I don't know why they would."

Sid said, "What are you on about? It took a few days before they reached me, and the deadline they gave me is different from the deadline they gave Anna. We have no idea how the mechanics of talking across dimensions works, and if they're otherworldly, maybe they want to reach you but haven't been able to."

Forrest looked even angrier now. "Anna they know about because she's running the company, and Sid, you were always the favorite one. Me? I'm the spare. They likely don't know I exist."

Sid leaned toward the camera. "That's not my fault."

Anna said, "I'm sure they know you exist."

Forrest glowered. "This is how it always was, wasn't it? It's how Grandfather was when he was alive, and it's how he is now that he's dead. Dump all the burdens on Anna. Indulge Sid in everything he ever wanted. And wait, wasn't there a third one too...? What was his name? Woody?"

Sid folded his arms. "You know I tried to fix that. And Grandma always stood up for you two."

Anna murmured, "For all the good that did."

Sid said, "I didn't say it did any good, but she tried. No, it wasn't fair. I was actually afraid we were going to have to contest the will as a group because Grandfather might have left everything to me, and that would have been ridiculous. But he *did* give us an even split, and I think that says something."

Forrest rolled his eyes. "It says he listened to the advice of legal counsel because otherwise it would have been an easy challenge."

"But Sid, we do appreciate that you would have contested it." Anna raised her hands. "Let's circle back around to the initial question, which is what to do about the contract offers."

Sid shook his head. *"Circle back around?"*

Forrest huffed. "It's corporate-speak. She has to talk that way, the same way I have to look like a politician when you blindside me with a posthumous salvo from our dead grandfather."

This would be a lot easier if everyone would stop taking everything personally. Sid made a simmer-down motion with his hands. "I'm sorry, man. I wouldn't have brought it up if I'd realized they hadn't contacted you yet. It freaked me right out when Grandfather's phone called me this morning, and I wanted to know if you were taking the offer."

"You called Anna for advice, not me." Arms folded, Forrest leaned back in his chair. "If they do contact me, at least now I'm forewarned. What about the both of you? Have you decided what you're going to do?"

Sid said, "I'm thinking of taking it."

Anna said, "I had Eric look over the contract, and he advised waiting until the end of the offer period before signing. The contract has already changed once in the interim." When Forrest sat taller, she said, "They gave me more time, and they threatened me. Well, threatened the company. If I don't re-up, they'll take away whatever they provided in the first place."

Sid said, "Which would be everything."

"I've traced the timeline as best I can. Grandfather was one defaulted payment away from bankruptcy, so yes, withdrawing everything attributable to them would mean destruction. I can't do that." Anna's gaze lowered. "Grandfather dedicated his whole life to the company." She forced herself to look back into the camera. "We employ tens of thousands of people. In addition, there's the supply chain to think of. If Pilaster Group were to fold, it would mean disaster for not only our employees, but a lot of smaller companies too. Everyone downstream would be affected."

Forrest hunched forward, rubbing his temples.

Sid murmured, "I hadn't thought of that."

"My contract also mentioned Gavin and Ryan, that if I signed, they'd be looked after as well."

Forrest raised his head. "Did Grandfather's original contract mention us?"

"We weren't born yet. Grandfather wasn't even married to Grandma." She withdrew the paper from the envelope and unfolded it carefully along the creases. "It specifies that the contract is transferrable to his heirs to the fourth generation, and we're the third generation. The contract offered to me says the same."

Sid added, "That's what the woman said on the phone, but I don't intend to have kids."

Forrest nodded. "In effect, you two are being offered the same deal he had. Does it say anything about eternal hellfire? Because I thought that was the entire point of a deal with the devil."

Sid barked out a laugh. "Are you serious?"

"Yes, I'm serious. Invisible entities are asking you to sign contracts offering preternatural protection and laying claim to our heirs, so is it more logical that we're dealing with an altruistic Rumplestiltskin? Or are these intangible deal-signers laying claim to our immortal souls?"

Sid made a face. "Both scenarios are exactly the same. Fairy tales."

Forrest said, "Then sign anything you like. Fairy tales can't hurt you, but they can't help you, either."

Anna sighed. "Grandfather signed the first deal, and all his life he insisted church was nonsense."

Forrest said, "Then why'd he sign the deal at all? How can someone believe in the devil without believing in God?"

Sid said, "They're not even devils. Anna looked it up, and it's a fairy or a genii or something."

Anna frowned. "It wouldn't have been about belief or faith. After signing the deal, Grandfather would have had proof."

Forrest's shoulders dropped. "So, you plan to sign?"

Anna nodded. "I do. And when you get it, I think you should, too."

Chapter Nineteen

A tingle shot through Cosmiel. A moment after, needles of sensation danced over his wings and then vanished. Nothing for a moment, then sparks in his limbs. He became aware that he had become aware, and then he became further aware of overall discomfort. He remembered everything. He was trapped. He was in Hell.

Long conditioning kept him from reacting in front of his captors, but he decided momentarily that he was, in fact, alone. Alone and chained to a wall. In the dark.

His first action was to give in to the humiliation and guilt of having been captured. Standard operating procedure: make peace with whatever disgust you felt with yourself after your assignment had gone pear-shaped. Once you got that out of your system, you could work with reality rather than avoiding it.

So, then. The second step was prayer. Cosmiel settled deeper into himself and tried to reach for God, but being in Hell, prayer felt clunky. He couldn't detect either God's touch or the sensation of grace, so he'd have to trust that God was filling him with grace on an insensible level. He was awake, after all, so already that was an improvement. Moreover, there would be angels praying for him on the other side, good and holy angels like Sophiel. God would honor their intentions.

Cosmiel resorted to reciting prayers in his head. He picked the midmorning prayer because that was his favorite and thought through all the words, then did five verses of a seasonal hymn.

More focused now, he set about studying what they'd done to him.

First, and most importantly, he wasn't all here. Satrinah had pulled his entire consciousness into this part of himself, but some of Cosmiel remained in Heaven.

Second, either she or Moloch (or both) had restrained him against the wall such that he had no control over his form. His subtle body couldn't discorporate.

Thirdly, the doubled Guard remained at his back, attuned specifically to containing him.

Cosmiel moved to the next part of the checklist. New operatives laughed when he introduced the "oh no checklist," then stopped laughing and said, "Wait, really?" Yes, really.

1. *Make peace with how badly you bollixed it up*
2. *Pray*
3. *Assess exactly how much of a mess you're in*
4. *Come up with a new objective*
5. *Make a plan*
6. *Enact the plan*
7. *Return to the first step as necessary*

Sophiel wanted to call the recovery checklist SHARPER (Shudder, Help?, Assess, Redirect, Plan, Enact, Revisit) but everyone always defaulted to "oh no." Yes, iron sharpens iron, but what really was the first thing you were going to say when you regained consciousness in Hell with chains securing you to the angry stones? Did you say, "I do believe my skills require sharpening"? No. You did not.

Step four. Cosmiel's previous objective had been to return to Heaven with a warning about Forrest. Little chance of being in time for that now. Cosmiel spent a few extra minutes revisiting the first step before proceeding to the fourth step, although he engaged in a little more of step two as well. *God, I have no idea how to salvage any of this. Please.*

A good objective seemed, at least for the time being, to escape. Another objective, ironically, might be not to escape, but to remain and wring extra information from Satrinah and Moloch. The pair had given him quite a bit already, but in theory he might get more.

Potential information wasn't worth it. Cosmiel settled on escape. For one thing, Sophiel would be working out how to free him, too. Getting more information could be the newer new objective if the "escape" objective failed.

The more Cosmiel's mind cleared, the more he could pin down the source of the tingling. Satrinah had fettered him to the wall with chains formed of her own will. She'd infused those chains with energy that periodically zapped him enough to draw his attention without being enough to harm him. Their drawing his attention meant he was never able to pull away from himself long enough to discorporate, which he'd have to do in order to pull his stuck-in-Hell self back into the rest of himself in Heaven.

It was a clever mechanism. He'd have to tell Sophiel about it in case Special Ops could make their own.

After studying each chain in turn, Cosmiel decided each had an individual zap pattern and created a different sensation. Satrinah would have set up that irregularity to prevent him from ever getting into a rhythm that he could tune out.

Next he turned his attention to the Guard at his back. He'd been able to slip through before by matching his pattern to Moloch's energy, but given the difficulty at shutting his thoughts away right now, he'd never get out the same way even if Satrinah's energy weren't doubling the Guard. With hers in addition? And attuned to him specially? Cosmiel was toast.

Worse, Satrinah wanted to figure out how he'd gotten in. She might not be out of the room at all. She might be observing in discorporated silence because once she figured out the mechanism, the demons could compensate for it.

This really could have worked out better. Cosmiel put himself back in step one to flush more shame and humiliation. If (or when) he had to deal with Moloch and Satrinah again, he couldn't afford to hand them that particular weapon.

Cosmiel prayed, *Given my track record, we should have expected this.*

He retreated further into himself, and soon he relaxed. He was going to be fine. In the long run, he'd be out of this prison, and God would have him back in Heaven. He wouldn't be abandoned down here, and the human souls he'd been trying to help wouldn't be helpless either. If he felt humiliated, well, maybe he could use that. If Cosmiel were as bad at his work as Satrinah claimed, then all three Ellingtons were better off with him trapped on a different plane of existence.

Finally, he smiled. There. If he could laugh at a situation, he could get through it.

Also, while praying and laughing at himself, he'd tuned his mind away from the chains, and that proved he could do what he'd needed to do all along. Now he just needed time. *God, please—just enough time.*

At any point, Satrinah might return and draw all Cosmiel's attention. A ticking clock wasn't going to relax him, though.

After Cosmiel managed to lose himself three times, he finally had enough control and energy that he could do something other than fret or pray. *Suggestions?* He was the only angel at the table during this planning meeting, so the resulting silence wasn't a surprise. *Come on, team, put everything on the table. Suggestions?*

Make a Guard, was the first suggestion to come to mind, so Cosmiel focused until he made a tiny sphere like the alert orbs from the hallway. It hovered near his motionless hand, and as he kept track of its faint signature in the darkness, he wondered why anyone on the planning team had thought a little Guard might help.

Oh, but it might. Cosmiel considered Satrinah using Moloch's anger to supersaturate herself with his power. A tiny Guard could still hold things. Deep within Anna's soul were tiny Guards holding ideas. Tiny Guards could hold voices. What should Cosmiel put into his?

I should fill it with my humiliation at getting caught.

Good suggestion, but what if instead he used that humiliation to create something else: frustration. Because frustration was a type of energy, and energy was what he needed. He didn't have Moloch to supercharge him. Cosmiel had only himself, and inadequacy was a resource he had in abundance.

Five minutes later, he'd nestled tiny spheres in every link of the chains on his wrists and ankles. He kept creating new ones, then thought of every humiliating defeat he'd ever endured at the hands of God's enemies. It wasn't hard to come up with those. Statistically speaking, Cosmiel shouldn't even be working for Special Ops, let alone leading it. If Sophiel brought him a performance review with this record, he'd have suggested the operative consider a career in entomology.

How much time had passed? On the one hand, imagine how much more humiliation he could stockpile if Satrinah returned before he was ready to act. On the other hand, Cosmiel would be able to power a Hell-disrupting bomb with his shame if he blew them too soon and nothing happened.

However powerful the blast was, it had to be stronger than Satrinah's will to hold him. What did she want? She wanted information, and she wanted control. Behind that drive was her own baffled rage that Cosmiel had broken into the room in the first place—a rage born of shame that he knew something she didn't. Her shame versus his meant Cosmiel's little bombs should in theory overpower her chains. She wanted to prove herself perfect. Cosmiel, on the other hand, knew himself to be flawed.

After making sure every little sphere was linked to its closest neighbor, Cosmiel breathed out long and steady. If it failed, at least no one would witness it except his two harshest judges: himself and God. *And...go.*

The detonation shredded the chains and dropped him to the floor. Gasping, Cosmiel reeled from the combined force of his own pent-up emotions. Satrinah would have felt that, too. He had thirty seconds.

The chain pieces were no longer zapping. Finally, he could reach for the part of his soul still in Heaven.

As the seconds passed, he delved deep inside to find that image of God in which he was made. God was...and is...and is to come.

Cosmiel released his heart and rejected his tension and unfurled all his expectations because he had better be able to do this now, like right now—

—and from across the divide, he answered.

As if stretching his arm through a very narrow pipe, Cosmiel brushed the fingertips of his own self, a sweet welcome and great need, followed by a voice.

I bet you could use a hand.

Despite the calmness of the verbal projection, Sophiel grasped hard at Cosmiel, and Cosmiel lunged back toward him.

The chamber sparked with hatred and flame. As Moloch flashed into the chamber, Sophiel held open the gap between the Cosmiel in Heaven and the Cosmiel in Hell.

An inferno roiled through the room. Cosmiel covered himself with his wings, but then Sophiel yanked him back through the gulf between Heaven and Hell.

Cosmiel slammed together like two freight cars interlocking, shivering and blinking in the light. In Heaven. Face-down on a cot in the Special Ops headquarters.

Reeling, Cosmiel flexed his feathers and choked, "Thank you."

Sophiel rubbed the space between Cosmiel's wings. "Stay still. It feels like all of you got back."

Cosmiel coughed, then rested with his hands on his knees and his head down between his shoulders. "Forrest? Did Sid and Anna talk to him? If not, we have to stop them."

"Last night. It didn't go how we predicted at all. Jezaryah is horrified."

"Blast. I was going to warn you." Cosmiel tried to sit up, but the room spun. He flared his wings to keep his balance, but he didn't topple to the floor because Sophiel steadied him. "How long was I gone? That wasn't fun."

"They're not running an amusement park." Sophiel trickled healing energy into his soul. The flow stung at first, but over time it would start to feel warm, and then Sophiel would open the spigot. "Stay put for a minute. You're spent, and your soul is in a panic. I can't make the healing take if you're pushing harder than you should."

"You shouldn't be healing me. You got furloughed because you needed healing."

Sophiel dialed up the healing energy. "Hours of spotting someone who's unconscious gave me plenty of time to recuperate. That, and Michael called in one of his healers."

Cosmiel coughed again. "I need to talk to Auriel."

"Please stop moving before I respectfully tie up my commanding officer." Sophiel took a deep breath. "Michael? Cosmiel's back. And he's being unhelpful."

Cosmiel muttered, "You pulled me out just so I could answer to Michael? Put me back."

Sophiel snickered. "You're going to be fine." He created a sphere with a message putting Auriel on notice, and he flashed it to her.

By the time Michael showed up, Cosmiel was able to sit straight and focus his eyes. Sophiel wasn't fooled, of course, and kept the energy flowing while Michael took a seat on the chamber floor.

Michael's first question was, "What did you think you were doing?"

Cosmiel forced a smile. "Looking for anything that could help. I had to try before we lost the opportunity." When Michael frowned, Cosmiel added, "It's hardly the first time I've gone in."

Michael said, "Alone?"

Cosmiel gestured to Sophiel. "I had a spotter."

"But you went alone?"

Cosmiel shrugged. "Doubling the infiltration team doubles the chance of getting caught."

Michael's eyes were wide. "And then you got through a locked Guard?"

"It's not impossible, just...tricky." Cosmiel shook his head. "It's more tricky when the owner of the Guard enters the chamber, discovers you, and then changes the locks."

At his side, Sophiel flinched.

Michael said, "And subsequently beats you incoherent."

Cosmiel gave a weak smile. "It was a calculated risk. Unfortunately, the only actionable information I gathered is stale."

Michael leaned back. "Stale or not, what did you learn?"

Sophiel called out into nothing, "Auriel? Now."

Cosmiel said, "The first thing I learned was that we needed to stop Anna and Sid from talking to Forrest."

Auriel appeared. "That train's left the station."

Cosmiel sighed. "Sophiel said as much. More interestingly, it's not Satrinah driving their strategy. It's Moloch."

Sparks shot from Auriel's eyes, and she dropped to a seat alongside Michael. "How can that be? Usually the Seraph is acting as the cannon, and the Cherub is the one aiming the sights."

"Satrinah is functioning as the face of the operation, but Moloch's the one developing their tactics. He's charging her up with his fire, and then she's the one taking action."

Sophiel murmured, "That's going to change our defense."

"Won't it?" Cosmiel wove his fingers together. "Also, and the worst part, is that under Moloch's direction, Satrinah's using the siblings against each other."

Chapter Twenty

The Board of Directors would meet on Tuesday, so on Sunday Anna ended up at both a business lunch and a business dinner with executives traveling from out of state, plus a magazine interview in between. She ended the dinner early, though, because the boys would be heading back to their father tonight, and she had no intention of missing the handoff. If that man intended to take her children, she was going to send them off in a manner to keep them remembering her the whole time.

Anna strode in to find the kids eating in front of the TV. Yolanda seemed surprised to see her. Why? What snooping had Yolanda planned to do in those extra hours? Or maybe she was planning to conspire with Eric?

Anna stalked right past her into the living room and dropped her jacket onto the wing chair. "I'll get that," she said when Yolanda tried to take her shoulder bag. "You've done enough."

The boys leaped off the couch to hug her. Anna's skin crawled, and she tolerated it as long as she could before stepping away. "Did you go to your music class?"

Gavin pouted. "Ryan was sick, so Yolanda said we couldn't."

Anna glared at her. "You didn't tell me he was sick. He was fine this morning."

"He only had a runny nose, but the guidelines say not to bring them." Yolanda shrugged. "I didn't think it was worth interrupting you at a meeting."

Anna's eyes narrowed. "Don't I have the right to know when my children get sick?"

Startled, Yolanda said, "It looked like something pizza in front of the television would fix, and I'd tell you when you got home."

Right. And next, Yolanda would filter this back to Eric. *Ryan was sick, but Anna had me plunk them in front of the television and not take them to a doctor.*

Anna turned her back on her housekeeper and went into her office where everything looked undisturbed. Anna shouldn't have tipped her off by asking about the desk. She would have to install security cameras to catch that woman in the act.

Gavin came to the door. "Will you read to us before Daddy comes?"

"Not now." Anna opened her email to find more nice-but-not-nice correspondence from several of the department heads. It wouldn't be long now until they tried to unseat her. Whether it was sexism or the fact that they'd always hated her grandfather, she'd never know. They were monstrous, horrible people. She ought to fire every one of them. Clean house.

She sat back and closed her eyes. What were the odds she could get that stipulation into the contract? If the *genius* on the other end of Grandfather's contract would eliminate every one of the executives plotting against her, even without any other preternatural assistance, the company would run so much easier.

Gavin came back to the door. "Mommy? Ryan needs a tissue."

"So get him a tissue!" She looked up. "Honestly, Gavin! I have just one thing I need to do."

Gavin evaporated away from the door again.

She scanned through the emails, paying closer attention to the ones her admin had flagged as important. Frankly, her own admin could be undermining her by failing to forward important emails and then letting her subordinates think her incompetent.

In her position, she couldn't trust anyone. That was the truth, unvarnished and awful. Then to have Sid breathing down her neck, running to her the way he always ran to someone else to make them fix things. It was always that way, Sid whining to

Grandfather about wanting a better car now that he'd wrecked his other car, or wanting Grandfather to pull some strings so he could go to a better university—and the next year asking for a donation to the college so they'd forget about some stunt he'd pulled.

Now Grandfather was dead, so what did Sid do? He wailed for Anna to fix everything. Of course he did.

Ryan showed up in the doorway, nose running.

"Oh, for crying out loud." Anna shut her computer. "Let's get you cleaned up."

Her desk looked to have been left alone, at least. If Yolanda was spying on her, she was smart enough not to move things.

It might be time to get rid of her. Find a new housekeeper. Maybe call the divorce lawyer and get full custody of the boys so she could stop paying child support to Eric just for him to turn around and treat Sharon to new shoes.

She read them a story, and then it was time to wind the clock. "No fingerprints on the brass!" she snapped at Gavin. "This clock is over a hundred years old. Get it to a hundred and one, okay?"

"Sorry, Mommy." Gavin tried to rub it off with the soft cloth, but she snatched it from his hand.

Eric arrived fifteen minutes early, because of course he was going to do that. Did he do that every handoff, stealing a quarter hour of her parenting time?

While the boys were hugging him, she said, "I have the boys until six."

Eric said to Gavin, "Show me the time on the big clock!"

"We just wound it for Mommy," Gavin said, "but don't touch it because you'll make fingerprints and break the clock."

Eric gave Anna a side-eye glance before turning back to the boys. "Are you two finished packing?"

Ryan said, "I need to get my stuffed animals!"

Yolanda came from the kitchen. With Anna listening, Yolanda and Eric weren't going to be able to conspire or even flirt. Anna ordered, "Go make sure the boys bring everything they need."

Yolanda herded the boys into their room. After she was gone, Eric said, "You didn't get back to me about the agreement."

"You told me to wait until the deadline to decide, and then they extended the deadline." She folded her arms. "Is this your doing?"

Eric frowned. "My doing?"

"Your doing. Because I'm sick of the subterfuge. I am a good mother." She stepped closer and dropped her voice. "I have done everything I can for these boys, and you're undermining me."

Eric raised his hands. "I have no idea what you're on about. The last I knew, you had a contract offer of unknown provenance. I advised you to wait. It appears opposing counsel also advised them to wait."

She said, "Am I supposed to believe you're not sabotaging me? That you haven't tried to hack into my computer or otherwise get everyone on your side?"

Eric backed away. "I'm not understanding this at all. What do you think I've done?"

Anna folded her arms. "You're good at acting innocent."

"I'm very good at acting innocent. I'm also good at being innocent." He put his hands in his pockets. "If I'm to defend myself, I need to know the charges against me."

"You're such a lawyer. I don't care about the technicalities. I want to know what you think you're doing."

Ryan ran out holding his stuffed elephant, and Eric said, "Why don't you go back in your room? Mommy and I need to talk for a few minutes."

Looking worried, Ryan retreated. Anna stalked into her office, and Eric followed, shutting the door behind him.

When he faced her, she said, "You're gutting the company I worked so hard for. You were jealous of it from the start, and then you deluded yourself that I chose it over you. Now you're trying to get revenge by destroying my career. You're using Yolanda against me, and I think you're disgusting."

Eric's brow furrowed. "My disgustingness aside, how would I be able to gut your company or destroy your job? I don't even work there."

"You're spearheading a smear campaign against me with the other executives. You want me forced out."

Eric's eyebrows raised. "In the cold light of day, it benefits me to keep you in that job because I don't want your child support recalculated. Also, again from a totally pragmatic perspective, an ex-wife who's working sixty-five hours a week is going to interfere less in my life than one who's unemployed. You've got nothing to substantiate your accusations, which to this point are entirely circumstantial."

"Quit being an attorney for once and try being a father."

Eric studied her. "I've been a father. Right now, you're being paranoid. Are you signing that contract?"

She squared her shoulders. "I probably am."

"As your counsel, I'm going to recommend against it." He stepped toward her, but she didn't retreat. "Why? Because tonight, you are exhibiting a degree of paranoia that I have never seen from you in fifteen years. You're spraying venom that never even came out during divorce proceedings."

"I was playing nice back then." Anna glared at him. "I promise you, I can unleash a legal hell on you that will be painful and expensive, and I will keep us in court every month until both boys turn eighteen."

Eric sighed. "Anna, turn it down."

She folded her arms. "Are you tone-policing me?"

"Turn down the offer. I would rather you quit your job and sleep on my couch for a year than see you this angry and out of sorts with the world."

Her eyes flared. "Are you minimizing me?"

"Minimizing? I'm telling you, this isn't you. This antagonism—this creeping evil—isn't you!" Eric gestured around the office. "Even without a signature on that agreement, it's changing you. You never wanted power for the sake of power. You handled our divorce with the efficiency of a real estate closing and prioritized helping the boys, not going for blood."

Anna exclaimed, "I let you take advantage of me! No one is going to do that to me ever again!"

Eric gave an infuriating stare. "You're turning into your grandfather."

She slammed her fist into the bookshelf. "I should be so lucky! My grandfather was a good man!"

"Your grandfather was a terrible man!" Wild-eyed, Eric was displaying his entire lying self to the world. "Linus Ellington was a financial abuser! He was a nasty piece of work who mistreated your grandmother, unloaded all his burdens on you, pampered Sid like his personal pet, and turned everyone around him against each other. He underpaid his most loyal people and never looked back at the ones he destroyed."

Anna gasped. "You're not being fair!"

"Really? Think about your grandmother for just a minute and ask yourself what she would be saying right about now."

Anna exclaimed, "My grandmother was weak!"

"Linus Ellington conditioned you to believe your one and only loyalty was to *him!* Not to yourself, not to your family, but to him! He pulled the strings, and you danced. He told you to break up your marriage, and you walked away from me. He saddled you with his company, and now you're carrying it uphill on your shoulders."

Anna flung one hand in the air. "I have responsibilities! I'm carving a place in the world where no one will ever dare cross me."

Eric's eyebrows raised. "And that, coming out of your mouth, was the voice of Linus Ellington."

She pointed to the door. "Get out of my home."

Walking into the hall, he said, "Three minutes ago, you were afraid I'd take our children before the stroke of six."

She hurried him out, kissed the boys goodbye, and then turned to Yolanda.

I could fire her. I could wipe that smirk right off her face and have her at the employment agency on her knees at seven o'clock tomorrow morning, begging for work.

Instead, Anna said, "I'll be in my office," and stalked back inside, breathing hard.

How dare he?

How *dare* he? How could he spout that her grandfather was all those things when her grandfather had done nothing all his life but sacrifice for his company? What Eric called "financial abuse" was being a good provider, and there was nothing wrong with that. What Eric called being cold to her grandmother was leadership for the family. Grandfather coddled Sid, sure, but all three grandkids had needed different things, so like a good leader, he treated them the way they needed. Eric wouldn't give Ryan an acetaminophen if Gavin was the one with the headache, would he?

She opened her computer and logged into her email. At the very top was an update to the contract, sent fifteen seconds ago. Had Eric done something from the elevator? Or was this legit because the entity knew how badly Eric was underestimating her?

She opened the document again. The terms were all the same, only stronger. They would serve as watchdogs over her governance of the company. They would subdue her enemies. They would continue the protection to her own children. She just had to follow their directions and give them her loyalty the same way she'd given loyalty to her grandfather.

She said aloud, "It's too bad this contract doesn't stipulate getting rid of the corporate monsters who are trying to unseat me because they can't deal with working for their betters."

In the corner of the screen, an alert flashed. She clicked, and there was a supporting document. In that document were dozens of screenshots.

Her eyes widened as she clicked through them. Some of these text exchanges had come from as late as this afternoon, just after she'd walked out of a meeting about the newest (and failing) acquisition. The CFO and the Vice President of Planning had a conversation insulting her, her voice, and her clothing, and then anticipating getting rid of her soon.

She clicked again and there was a folder of photos, videos, and ten pages of documentation that caught her breath. She could fire both of them for insubordination, but why should she? This was excellent blackmail fodder. The best revenge was forcing people who hated her to continue doing everything she demanded.

Also, she had proof that the CFO was sabotaging the new acquisition. Again, a fireable offense. Or more aptly, an offense that would clamp a pronged leash around his neck for the remaining long, long years of his career.

"Originals provided upon signing," read the watermark across every single image.

Now they were talking. Finally, she had ammunition and someone able to aim the weapon. Eric had been right to delay signing. All those executives who'd only pretended to answer to her when her grandfather still pulled the puppet strings—they would find themselves at the ends of those strings. Only now they'd be chains, and those chains would be tight.

She clicked back to the main document, then opened the signature line. Push her around, would they?

Oh, right, she needed a token to seal the contract. It wouldn't be destroyed, the instructions said, nor did she need to hand it over. It just had to become the symbol of their contract, so it should be important.

She looked around the office, and then the thought popped into her head: none of this was important.

The thought knocked the breath out of her, and she sat back in the chair, eyes closed.

None of this stuff was important. Her grandfather was dead. Her children would sleep tonight in a building two blocks away. Her marriage had crumbled like a stale cracker, and for what? For a posh apartment and a car she seldom drove and two children being raised by their housekeeper and their stepmother? None of this was important. None of it.

She was about to sign away everything for...nothing.

She rubbed her temples, breathing hard.

This was just a terrible day. She'd yelled at Eric, and he'd yelled back at her. They hadn't even yelled when they were divorcing. She'd scolded the boys for getting fingerprints on the clock, and the clock wasn't important. The boys were important.

Her arms ached. She should have been tucking them in tonight. Before they left, she should have said she was sorry for being so short with them on their last night together. The pressure of her job was getting to her, and she was taking it out on her kids.

Eric had once said, "If you die, Pilaster will post the open position before your obituary," and that had stung. But now...

She wasn't making good decisions. She had days until the deadline, so instead of signing, she shut off the computer and went to the living room. On the way out, she wrapped the teal shawl around her shoulders.

Chapter Twenty-One

Turmiel was shaking beneath Auriel's hands as he cleared the remnants of three flaming arrows from Anna's soul. Auriel tried to fill him with calm, but that was useless. They'd come too close to losing Anna.

Auriel said, "How many thought bubbles did they break?"

Turmiel projected an unsteady affirmative: only one. *None of this is important.*

Resting her hands between his wings, she streamed power into him, along with affirmation. He'd known what would interrupt Anna, and how to keep her on an even keel.

At the room's perimeter, Cosmiel paced like a guard with no clear search pattern.

She'd been preparing to call in the boys' guardian angels and start prepping them for the inevitable second front of an intergenerational assault. Instead, Anna had turned back.

Still pale, Turmiel followed Anna from room to room. She was restless, whereas he needed rest. He was so rattled he likely couldn't even pray, so while he kept watch, Auriel tried praying on his behalf. The only prayer she could manage was, *Thank you.*

Trying to draw him out, Auriel ventured, "You've still got two thought bubbles in there, plus the snares we set up."

Turmiel struggled to pull himself together. "I'm not entirely sure they didn't set off the other two. I'd never felt that kind of rage from her. She believed herself entirely in the right. She'd have done anything and justified it."

Anna flipped on the kettle for tea. Yolanda entered the kitchen, and Anna only gave a subdued, "You can go home now."

Yolanda said, "Are you all right being alone?" When Anna seemed surprised, Yolanda added, "I know it must be hard, sending your boys away. If you want someone around, I have other things I can get done."

Anna went to the cabinet to get the herbal tea and the infuser. "Thank you, but I'm fine."

Yolanda smiled at her. "I'm glad to see you're wearing my mother's shawl. She was so pleased to get your thank-you note, and I know it'll make her happy that you're using it."

Yolanda's guardian angel touched Anna's head before leaving, a quick blessing. Anna brewed a pot of chamomile tea with honey and then sat at the table reading a business magazine.

Cosmiel said in a sharp tone, "Interrupt that. She's soft to you right now."

Turmiel met his eyes, irritated and baffled. But just because Anna's guardian needed a rest didn't mean the enemy would give them one. Even without knowing why Cosmiel had said that, Auriel added, "I agree."

Cosmiel gestured around. "She turned back because none of this is important. Now she's reading about trendy colors in office furniture." He shook his head. "Push on that window to eternity. Encourage her to close the magazine and reach for something she might find important."

Throwing sparks of irritation, Turmiel projected sharply that she wasn't about to access an online Bible and study Ecclesiastes. Nevertheless, he reached for Anna's heart to make her restless, and a moment after, she shut the magazine, then carried her tea toward the bedrooms.

Auriel pressed, *You know what she loves. Press on that.*

In front of the boys' room, Anna hesitated, then went inside. Yolanda had straightened up after they'd left, but Ryan's stuffed elephant had been forgotten. Anna propped it against his pillow and texted a photo of it to Eric.

She didn't take up her tea again right away, instead standing in front of the tall shelves loaded with toys, puzzles, and games. Despair clouded her face.

That same despair echoed off Turmiel. *She's thinking she saddled the boys with the same meaningless clutter as her own life.*

Auriel again supplemented his power with hers. She expanded her senses into the Guards around the apartment, but they were holding. It often went this way: once repelled, demonic forces didn't invade again immediately. Either they couldn't or they wouldn't, not with their pride stung. Also, practically speaking, giving a human soul two victories back-to-back would give the human courage to know temptation could be beaten.

With Anna about to turn away from the shelf, Turmiel breathed, "Look."

She hesitated, then lifted a book from a higher shelf. It wasn't bright and simple like the ones on the shelves the boys could reach. The title was, *Where the Red Fern Grows.*

Cosmiel murmured, "Is that a book she loves?"

Turmiel rested his hands on her shoulders. "She used to read it to Sid and Forrest right after their parents died."

Anna opened to the inside cover. Sid had signed it,

> *To my first nephew.*
> *Don't grow up to be like your uncle!*
> *Love, Uncle Sid*

Anna laughed, then opened at random to the middle. She read for a minute, turned the page, then carried the book back to her room with her tea.

Anna got into her bed. She stacked her pillows behind her, kept the tea close to hand, and laid a thick blanket on her lap. Turmiel tucked himself in at her side, arms around her waist and head to her shoulder.

Auriel's heart twinged. This was so hard on the guardians. They had little to fight with, but still they mustered their strength and stood before the teeth of Hell to protect their charges.

Auriel signaled the Archangel security team and gave soft-voiced orders. Turmiel needed a break—but more than that, he needed to be close to Anna.

With the shawl across her shoulders, Anna started to read. Turmiel's tense wings relaxed, and then his face and his grip. He was hearing the words through her mind, and Anna must be remembering reading to her brothers. For tonight, even if for the last time, she was reading to her guardian angel.

Cosmiel visited Indri, who hugged him hard. Surprised, Cosmiel said, "Is Sid okay?"

She breathed, "I was so scared of what would happen with Anna. They had her in hand."

"She broke free. She's safe for now." As safe as she could be with Hell's top seductress resting her hand on the tiller. "The thought bubbles intercepted Satrinah's push at the end, and we've got Anna settled in and doing something to keep her grounded."

For now.

Fighting the memory of Turmiel's eyes, Cosmiel said, "Sid?"

Indri shook her head. "He's obsessing about the offer. They didn't give him a written contract, so instead of focusing on the wording, he's daydreaming about all the things he could get. He's been looking around his apartment today, examining some of his mementos and a number of high-ticket items."

Selecting his token. Cosmiel's wings sagged.

The token didn't even have any value to the demons, Cosmiel thought as he flashed to Jezaryah. The demons might merely believe that if they could get the human to "sacrifice" a beloved or costly object, the human would stick with the agreement because of the sunk cost fallacy. *Well, we wouldn't want to lose what we've already invested,* the contractee would think, never considering how much more they stood to lose if they didn't cut ties.

Forrest was on an endless scroll through a work document,

occasionally highlighting text and making notes. Jezaryah was reading it over his shoulder and didn't turn as he spoke. "I felt the tumult before. Anna passed the test?"

"She stopped on the verge of signing." Again, Cosmiel fought the nausea that had engulfed him the moment Anna had clicked on the signature line, flaming arrows burning in her soul like a candle with three wicks. Turmiel had been shouting at her, tears in his voice.

Jezaryah had witnessed souls like that too often. There was no need to describe the specifics. His wings sagged. "I didn't realize she'd come that close." He flagged a thought in Forrest's mind, and Forrest scrolled back up the page, then highlighted a phrase. "We've got legislation here for school lunches. It's well-intentioned and poorly-written."

"Better than the opposite." Cosmiel folded his arms. "Still no offer?"

"No offer. He's so unsettled." Jezaryah looked away from the screen for the first time, eyes glistening. "I wasn't prepared for this. For everything else, I had an answer, but for this—this silence, this shunning—I have nothing."

Chills crept over Cosmiel. "It would be best if they never approach him for an agreement."

"Neither of us believes that will happen. They're priming him." Jezaryah kept watching the screen. "They've had decades to prepare their approach. They know our methods of defense. I feel as if, with all three siblings, they're walking right around every obstacle we set in front of them."

It was barely a week ago that Jezaryah had looked Cosmiel in the eye and realized it was hopeless because Cosmiel always took the hopeless cases. Except Jezaryah hadn't given up hope.

"They used Anna's anger to get around her better judgment," Cosmiel said. "On a different level, Forrest is angry too. How does he respond to anger?"

Jezaryah rested his hand on Forrest's shoulders and closed his eyes. A moment after, Cosmiel felt the guardian's response: Forrest responded by looking at the source of the injustice to help the victims.

Interesting. Where was the injustice here?

Jezaryah's feathers spread. The injustice was against Forrest himself. Forrest had always been overlooked, underestimated, brushed aside.

Cosmiel flinched.

Exactly, Jezaryah was projecting. From Forrest's perspective, Anna and Sid had been seen, estimated worthy, and invited closer. Forrest was once again the victim of unfairness.

Cosmiel murmured, "Shouldn't that work in our favor?"

Jezaryah shook his head. "That's not how he responds. He responds by proving himself. That's why he's such a standout politician—because every time the news media drags him through the mud, he works harder to prove them wrong. He'll want to convince Satrinah that the underdog was a good bet. He's going to do everything she ever wanted, only he'll do it better."

Cosmiel withdrew from Jezaryah's raw heart. Without any force, he said, "There has to be a way around that."

Jezaryah turned away from Forrest and looked Cosmiel dead in the eye.

"There's always hope." Cosmiel's words were automatic. They sounded as empty as he felt.

Jezaryah's feathers tightened. "I'll keep praying for it, then. Maybe we'll find some."

Chapter Twenty-Two

Five-thirty came too soon every morning, but today Anna woke up fully clothed, with the emotional equivalent of a hangover.

Instead of staggering straight into the shower, she checked her phone. There were already fifteen messages from overnight, but the conversation she clicked on was Sid's.

"It's been a while since I read that book," he'd texted.

Then again, "Yeah, I remember this passage."

She'd been texting him and Forrest photos of their favorite parts as she'd gone through the book in a two-and-a-half hour reading binge. All those times she and the boys had snuck into the same room at night, terrified of getting caught, Sid or Forrest had wanted her to read that one book, over and over again. There had been others too, but this had been the steady favorite.

Now she wondered why. The story was so sad. Was that why Grandfather had seized it the one night he'd caught them reading after lights out? Or was it that Sid had pestered Grandfather to get him a dog just like in the book, and Grandfather hated to say no to Sid—so instead, he got rid of the thing that made Sid want a dog?

Sid had texted in the middle of the night, "Is this paragraph different? This isn't how I remember you reading it to us."

Now, too early in the morning, Anna replied, "I always changed it when I read it to you. I didn't want you to be scared."

Then, feeling like that wasn't enough, she added, "We always had each other's backs. I wanted to think I was looking out for you."

Forrest had texted her as well. "I re-read this on the plane coming home from the funeral. Your book is less dusty."

About the same passage where Sid had called her out, Forrest only said, "I used to get mad at you for changing this, but I guess I know why you did it."

Again, Anna replied, "We always had each other's backs."

The remainder of the texts were all business issues. The chairman of the board was on her about the failing merger. Several documents had been uploaded to one of the private drives. It was a good thing the boys were with Eric. Anna could stay at the office until midnight.

Eric had seen the photo of Ryan's stuffed animal but not replied. Anna tried not to think about their last conversation, nor about the way she'd been so irritated with the boys when they left.

She'd had a lousy day. Eric should understand that and not knee-jerk blame her dead grandfather for her moods. That was worse than blaming her hormones.

In the shower, Anna waited for the heat to soothe her brain. She should have signed last night. It was so pretentious, thinking nothing here was valuable. Grandfather had surrounded her life with valuable things. The very desk she sat at was appraised in the tens of thousands of dollars. That clock in the hallway was valued likewise. She had a Lexus in the garage beneath the building, and a retirement account that could maintain a comfortable lifestyle until age one hundred if she budgeted well and contracted for short stints when she felt like it. Both boys would have their college fully paid (and Eric couldn't touch those funds except to pay for education). For that matter, her shower gel was twenty-five dollars a bottle, and that got washed down the drain.

All these good things traced back to her grandfather's contract. It was that simple. Calling them valueless was ingratitude of the worst caliber.

By six-thirty, she was out the door; by seven o'clock, in the office. The question of the token had stopped her last night, and she didn't have any energy to devote to it today. Every interaction with the chairman was a battle, and now that she knew to look, she picked up signs that yes, the CFO was hooking up with at least two of the department heads.

They're sabotaging me. That thought kept coming through.

She should sign that contract and secure the ammunition she needed to fire every one of these people out of a cannon.

That's cheating, she told herself. *Grandfather would hate that you couldn't do it alone.*

She did have allies, though, didn't she? Her admin seemed loyal. The Chief Operations Officer did seem loyal to her, and he'd been with the company for ages. Anna Ellington had been mentored up into her current status, shaped and formed by several members of the board. *I need more allies,* she thought into the yonder, and then she wondered whom she was thinking it to. Was that a prayer, or was she thinking it out to those shadow figures who were offering her everything if she married her future and her company to them?

Before tomorrow's board of directors meeting, her public relations people needed a quote from her for a press release about the merger. Pilaster's stock prices had plummeted. *Of course, because with Linus Ellington dead, how can his mere granddaughter run the company the way she's been doing for years?*

Everyone wanted an announcement. Something brilliant that they could tell their investors to pump fire into their flagging spirits and increase everyone's dividends. Anna had nothing other than platitudes about holding their founder's vision as they strode bravely into the future.

Founders can't live forever, but her grandfather had done all he could to pass the mantle.

Sign that contract, and the Ellingtons could establish a dynasty. Gavin or Ryan would inherit this chair after her. They could walk to work, coffee in hand, login to a stack of morning reports, and smilingly threaten the CFO's job.

She'd sign the contract before tomorrow's board meeting. Along with the other reports, she'd hand out the evidence about the

CFO's sabotage and multiple affairs. She'd confront the director with the power of Hell at her back, and she'd tighten everyone neatly into their ranks.

Her own sentimentality might have been her undoing. She needed to brave up and get it done.

Sid texted as Anna walked in the door at ten o'clock. "Do you think Grandma knew? I think she'd freak."

Anna found a dinner in the fridge with reheating instructions. The place was clean. Yolanda had left a note: "Eric asked me to bring Ryan's stuffed elephant, so I've taken it to him."

Fighting irritation, Anna told herself that was better than letting Eric into the apartment. Yolanda shuttled the boys' belongings all the time. They had two of almost everything, but you couldn't duplicate the sentimental stuff.

Anna sat on the couch, facing the grandfather clock. She didn't want dinner. Maybe if she walked into tomorrow's meeting like a starving cat, the board of directors would instinctively feel fear and back off.

Hang on a moment. "The sentimental stuff."

The "token" item could stay with her. Anna just had to designate it and touch it, not part with it. The grandfather clock was likely the most expensive item in her direct possession (well, other than some of the jewelry) and it also had sentiment. No one would be surprised if that stayed with her for the rest of her life. Last night in the fog and anger, Anna hadn't really meant everything was *valueless*. Only that in her terrible mood, she lacked sentiment for it.

Of course. That's why she'd reached for a childhood story: she'd been hunting for emotional connection.

Leaving her work bag on the couch, she walked to the clock and stroked the wood. Yolanda had polished the fingerprints off the brass fittings so the whole clock gleamed. The clock was where the boys went immediately on arriving. They wound it again when they left, that way it would keep ticking through all of Eric's parenting time and still be ready for them when they returned to their rightful place with their mother.

Back on the couch, she watched the slow swing of the pendulum and the advancing hands. The minute hand jumped when it ticked forward. Right before sounding the quarter-hourly chimes, the clock gave a subtle click, as of an indrawn breath. It had taken Anna a couple of weeks after moving in with Grandma and Grandfather to figure out the quarter hour based just on the first four tones.

"It seems fitting," Anna murmured. If she wanted sentiment and value, the clock had it to spare. It was a chain link connecting to her past as well as to her future.

Her phone vibrated. Sid again. "We always did have each other's backs, didn't we?"

It was a group text with just her and her brothers. Forrest replied, "It makes sense."

Sid said, "Why didn't we get therapy or something after Mom and Dad died?"

Because "therapy was for crazy people." That was what Grandfather always said. Therapists dug out your secrets and put them in the light. Grandma had visited a grief support group, but she'd gone alone.

When Anna found out, she'd said to Grandma, "How can you do that? He's given you everything." As if a bereaved mother attending a support group were the ultimate betrayal.

Anna hated herself sometimes. Shivering, she tightened the teal shawl around her throat.

Grandma had advocated with Grandfather for the kids to attend a grief support group for orphans. Grandfather had hit the ceiling. "They have everything they could ever need! Why would we send them to talk about how their family is falling apart when they have a family? You say they're orphans as if they're picking up cans in the gutter."

Grandma had said, "But they lost their parents," and Grandfather still forbade it. Instead, Anna had read to the boys at night with a flashlight, and Grandma had ventured out during the days after the driver delivered the children to their private Upper East Side schools. Grandma would walk to Fifth Avenue as though she were going shopping, and then she'd turn in at a nineteenth-century church, head to the basement, and attend a group using her maiden name.

Anna texted to Sid, "You don't remember all that? About Grandma?"

Despite the group rules about confidentiality, some loathsome gossip-salivating widow had snuck a photo of Cecilia Ellington and sold it to the Page Six people. That was exactly the kind of garbage Grandfather had railed against, about making their private business public. Well, now it was public.

Anna had brought him the paper. He'd glared at it as though burning a hole through the page, then stalked from the room.

Forrest said, "Sid may have been too young to remember that."

Anna texted, "She did want us to talk to someone, but it wouldn't have been right."

Sid texted, "What happened?"

Anna frowned. Grandma hadn't left the house afterward. Not for a long time. Afterward, not alone. She'd gone out with the grandchildren. She'd gone with the chauffeur. Grandfather had always grilled Anna afterward: where were you, and who did you see, and what did you talk about? He'd given Grandma a single credit card to pay for everything and then also demanded receipts.

Forrest said, "He yelled at her. He didn't want people nosing around our family. The newspapers already said we were cursed."

Both the Ellington sons had died. The only family left were the grandchildren. Anna texted her brothers, "Grandfather needed to protect us."

Sid texted, "Aren't therapists bound by oaths or something? They can't reveal what happens in their sessions."

Grandfather would have demanded they tell him everything from every session. He'd have needed to know.

Forrest sent, "Yes."

Anna replied, "There are unethical therapists the same way there are unethical support groups."

Forrest replied, "Considering what he'd have paid a therapist, they'd have had no incentive to go rogue. One step out of line, and he'd have stripped their licenses and made sure they never worked again."

She sent, "Grandfather was keeping us safe."

Sid texted, "It sounds like we would have been safe. Instead it was just us. We had to look out for ourselves."

That's what she was doing now. She'd offer the clock and sign the contract. She was looking out for herself and for her sons. One signature would provide for them all.

Sid texted, "So, Grandma. Did she know about the deal?"

Anna's hackles raised because the first thing you learned about texting was never to send anything incriminating. Not to anyone.

Forrest replied, "Wouldn't she have to?"

Anna replied, "Grandfather made lots of deals. She likely didn't know them all."

That should obfuscate it nicely.

Sid input, "This deal was different."

Anna texted, "I doubt she knew about the one in question."

Forrest sent, "She went to church. If she knew, wouldn't she have left?"

Sid replied, "Maybe not. Everyone has a price."

Last night, Eric had said, "That's Linus Ellington's voice coming out of your mouth." Right now, that was Linus Ellington's voice coming out of Sid's text.

Anna walked to the clock and stroked the ornate woodwork. She had work to do. Specifically, one important piece of work. She texted into the chat, "Time for me to go. I need to sign off."

Chapter Twenty-Three

Cosmiel held a shield around Anna, striking back as much of the demonic attack as he could, but it was useless. She was consenting. Demonic intrusions passed through as easily as bullets through a chain link fence.

Turmiel and Auriel were in tight around Anna. Turmiel had ceased the gentle encouragement and was just shouting. Every single thing he could think of to stop her, he was calling it to her. There were no flaming arrows in her heart. The first of the siblings was about to fall.

Turmiel pleaded, "Do you want to lose everything? Do you really want to be like him?"

The snares hadn't worked to keep the siblings supporting each other. If anything, every snare had pulled Anna in harder.

It's backward, Cosmiel prayed, struggling to relieve the pressure of evil. *Why is it that everything we did to defend her only ended up being useful to the enemy?*

It was backward in so many ways. Anna was making the wrong decision for the right reasons. She wanted to protect her sons. She wanted to protect her employees. She wanted to honor her grandfather's legacy. She wanted to make her grandfather proud.

The whole deal was backward, though. The Seraph was in control, not the Cherub. The human had authority to negotiate the contract. The human didn't even seem eager to do it. None of this was working as it should.

God, I don't understand. He didn't need to understand, though. Right now, Cosmiel needed to fight.

Satrinah and Moloch had sealed the apartment so Michael's soldiers couldn't get in. They hadn't driven out the three angels, but no more could enter.

The pressure was hard and hot. Cosmiel retreated closer to Anna as she opened the computer to re-read the document.

It was time. She was only making sure there were no further changes. Cosmiel called, "Did that sentence say that before?"

Auriel seconded it. Turmiel was pushing questions into Anna's mind: *Is that really what it said? Maybe I should print the document to make sure it stays the same. Is there a change log? Should Eric take a look at the revisions?*

God, please, Cosmiel prayed. Turmiel had tears in his eyes, but yes, Anna was looking at the change log. Then, in response to his prompting, this executive, who put an electronic signature on million-dollar contracts on a weekly basis, sent the document to the printer. She'd sign a paper copy, same as Linus Ellington had. For nostalgia. For no traceable record.

Auriel looked to the printer with flames in her eyes. The printer lost its connection to the computer.

Dear Jesus God, Cosmiel begged, *we're buying handfuls of seconds, but that isn't enough.*

Huffing with annoyance, Anna clicked through the driver settings, and the computer was once again talking to the printer. She re-sent the job.

They had less than a minute. The printer spat out one page, then the second. Anna retrieved them.

Turmiel put into her mind, *I should use one of Grandfather's pens.* He was about to lose access to her. She was already opaque to Cosmiel.

As Anna opened the desk drawer, Auriel looked Cosmiel in the eyes and projected, *Haunting.*

No demonic attack was going to affect Anna now, so Cosmiel dropped his protection to take hold of the room air—and made it go still.

Not perfectly still, of course. That would have killed Anna. But he made it still enough that the temperature dropped around her.

Satrinah swept into the room. "Your Guard cracked like a walnut shell." She reached for Anna.

Turmiel smacked her away with his sword, eyes and wings ablaze.

Chuckling, Satrinah folded her arms. "Fine. In honor of your devotion, I will wait thirty seconds.

Anna uncapped Grandfather's pen. Auriel tried to jam the ink, but by now the demons had control of everything. Cosmiel wrapped Turmiel in his wings because the moment Anna signed, he'd be vulnerable.

Anna raised her head.

The air was still around her. Chill.

Please, let the idea that she's not alone make her realize what she's dealing with. Let her at least be frightened.

Unfrightened, Anna rubbed her goose-bumped arms, then reached for the shawl. She draped it around her shoulders...and then stopped like a statue.

Cosmiel tightened his wings around Turmiel. Anna didn't look frightened. She looked...stunned.

A fourth guardian angel stepped into the room, someone Cosmiel hadn't seen for over a decade.

Auriel dove to cover her, a sword in each hand and shining painful light on the demons to back them off. The new arrival advanced before Anna and rested her hands on Anna's head, then breathed over her.

Eloricel, Cecilia's guardian angel.

Anna dropped into her desk chair, her right hand clutching the shawl over her heart. With her eyes closed, she struggled to breathe.

Cosmiel warmed the air around Anna, but he didn't dare step away from Turmiel. Auriel was maintaining a very small space around Eloricel and Anna.

Satrinah flared her wings. "Sign, you little failure. You're not good enough to make it without your grandfather."

Anna breathed, "I'm sorry," and she uncapped the pen.

Satrinah folded her arms. "Doing this saves everything. Do you want to be weak like Grandma? You hated her."

Anna blinked, and out spilled her tears.

Then she set the pen to the side and tented her arms over the document, burying her face in her palms.

Hands on Anna's shoulders, Eloricel whispered into Anna's heart, "She understood. She loved you to the end."

Anna gave in and sobbed, weaving her fingers into the shawl's lacy holes. Cecilia's guardian spread her hands, and between her fingers was a second image of the shawl made of light. She tucked that over Anna too, whispering, "Grandma did her best, but she couldn't save you from him."

Anna's soul became a cloudy mess rather than fully opaque. With his wings tight over Turmiel, Cosmiel requested access.

Like a pearl diver holding a weight, Cosmiel grabbed Anna's grief at the surface and let it drag him all the way down. She wasn't grieving for Linus. She wasn't even grieving for herself or her children. This grief felt like Cecilia's heart. It burned. It kept pulling away from Cosmiel because it didn't want to be known, and Cosmiel gave it rein because the more it ran from him, the further it pulled him into Anna's soul.

There, at the base of all things, he found it. As with Joseph in prison, Cosmiel found Anna's shame. He touched that raw, painful, scared part of Anna that had never made peace with her own treatment of her grandmother.

Into that, he breathed compassion. She'd been young. She was grieving the loss of her parents. She had shouldered responsibility for the emotional well-being of her younger brothers. She had aligned with the most powerful adult in the household because, for their safety, she needed to.

She'd done what a child must to make her brothers safe. When Linus Ellington turned her against her grandmother, she'd followed him because sacrificing a relationship with her grandmother was the price for protecting the younger two.

Forgive her, he thought in Anna's mind, thought it toward the girl who'd stayed up late at night reading to her brothers. He thought it about the girl who tattled on her grandmother to curry favor with her grandfather. He thought it about the girl who'd ignored her grandmother's overtures and adopted her grandfather's mockery.

So small, Cosmiel thought. *That was too much to put on a child.*

Echoing back from Anna was the thought, *I never wanted his company.*

And then, with startled emphasis, *I never wanted his* company.

The shame shattered under Cosmiel's hands, and he awoke from her soul back in himself, still shielding Turmiel. Anna was breathing hard, staring at the contract with tear tracks on her face. But she was angry. Angry—and for once, not angry at herself.

Turmiel said aloud, "He had no right. He had no right to do this to you. You never wanted this!"

Anna said, "I never wanted any of this!"

Satrinah flared Cherub light around the room, and then Moloch was at her side. Satrinah said, "Your children need this!" but Moloch reined her in. Instead he said, "Your grandfather counted on this one little signature. Not signing undoes his whole life's work."

Anna stood, but she was still looking at the pages.

Moloch said, "Not signing means you're a failure after all. Signing is the only way to prove him wrong."

Turmiel urged, "He had no right to do this to you."

Anna closed her eyes, then said, "Linus Ellington was a terrible person. I can't be like him."

She walked the pages to the shredder. The contract went in as paper and emerged as diamonds.

By the time Anna returned to the computer, the demon Guard was down, and Michael had broken through to flush the room of all but Satrinah and Moloch.

Moloch said, "Tomorrow, you lose everything."

Anna moused past "Accept" and "Reject for changes" to click on "Decline contract." After that, the room was clear.

Chapter Twenty-Four

Turmiel needed respite, and he refused to take it. This despite Michael posting an entire legion of angels wherever Moloch might strike back: Eric and Sharon's apartment; especially around the boys; around Anna's closest allies at work; and finally, with both Yolanda and Yolanda's mother. Not to mention multiple soldiers in every room of the apartment and one soldier in every other apartment in the building.

Cosmiel wanted Turmiel to get at least fifteen minutes alone in Heaven, though. After a fight like this, a guardian needed time to pray and decompress.

Turmiel disagreed. "She needs me," was all he said, and then he settled in deeper to sooth Anna's heart. She was scared. She was moving from room to room. She even went through the boys' bookshelves again to find some other childhood favorite, but then she didn't take up anything.

Auriel said to Eloricel, "How did you get past their defenses?"

Cecilia's guardian wrapped her arms around her waist. "When you prayed for allies, Yolanda felt prompted to pray for Anna. She answered that grace by asking her mother to pray for Anna too, and when her mother prayed, it infused the shawl. When Anna touched the shawl, she revived her relationship with her grandmother, and at that point, Yolanda's prayers were enough to get me through."

Cosmiel whispered, "Generational blessing. You suggested that

Yolanda's mother felt like a stand-in for Anna's grandmother."

Auriel kept her voice low. "Cecilia prayed for the grandchildren's protection. For decades, she knew this was coming, and for decades, she prayed. Those graces were waiting, and when Yolanda's mother prayed, her prayer discharged them."

Cosmiel's eyes glowed. "The ultimate generational blessing."

God was amazing. The economy of grace, the interlocked prayers of the saints, the timelessness of love—God was just so amazing in how He provided for them.

Turmiel still had his wings wrapped around Anna, and tears shimmered in his eyes. "I was absolutely wrong about Cecilia having done nothing to help. That generational blessing meant you were able to enter, and your soul feels enough like Cecilia's that Anna responded."

Eloricel shivered. "I was afraid she'd reject me for exactly that reason. But I guess her grandmother's memory counteracted her grandfather's. It gave Anna a clear moment to make her decision."

Anna returned to the living room and stood in front of the family photos. Hands on her shoulders, Turmiel breathed, "Look at them. It's fine."

Anna pulled out her phone instead. Sid and Forrest had continued the chat. After Sid had texted, "Everyone has a price," Forrest had responded, "Based on what I've seen, most people set the price too low."

Anna scrolled through the conversation, glancing up at the framed photos.

Sid: "How do you mean?"

Forrest: "People don't think long-term of what we give versus what we get."

Sid: "You just nailed why I'm never getting married."

Forrest: "You're in Hollywood. Celebrity marriages never last, so that's smart."

Sid: "Not without an iron-clad prenup."

Forrest: "Ask Anna about that. I couldn't believe the document Grandfather expected Eric to sign."

Sid: "Marriage itself is a contract. I give you everything and you give me everything, forever, except what if I'm giving more everything than you are? No thanks."

Forrest: "It hasn't been so bad for me, but I'm sure of Julia."

Sid: "Anna was sure of Eric, too. Grandma must have been sure of Grandfather."

Then, again from Sid: "I really wonder if she knew."

Forrest: "Sometimes I think yes, and sometimes no."

Anna put the phone back in her pocket and selected a photo album from the shelf, opened at random, then replaced it and went two albums further back in time.

Turmiel sat with her, and Eloricel got closer as well.

Cosmiel approached Auriel, but she interrupted before he even began speaking. "Sid and Forrest are going to get hit hard after this."

Cosmiel's inner wings tightened around his body, and he glanced back at the couch.

Auriel said, "I'm sorry, but we don't have the luxury of standing down."

"We're not going to stand down." But over and over and over— the pressure kept hammering them. "When Anna goes to sleep, we need to get Turmiel out of here. Put him in front of the Throne of God or chain him up at the back of the Heavenly Temple to spend time out of the line of fire." He glanced at Auriel. "I suggest you go with him and recharge, too."

She raised her eyebrows at him.

Cosmiel chose to ignore her unstated observation. She was under his command, not he under hers. "Pray for an hour. I'll keep cycling through all three households."

Shaking her head, Auriel said, "Now is not the time for me to bury myself in prayer. You head to Jezaryah, and—"

A brilliant light took form in the room. Turmiel leaped to his feet, sword manifesting in his hand. Cosmiel placed himself between Anna and the brilliance, and then Michael was at Cosmiel's side, wings flared.

Standing before them, arms folded and eyes glittering, was Satan.

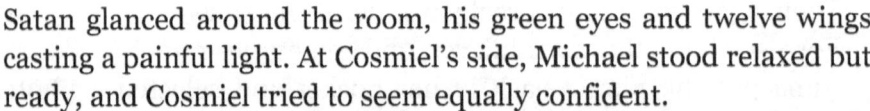

Satan glanced around the room, his green eyes and twelve wings casting a painful light. At Cosmiel's side, Michael stood relaxed but ready, and Cosmiel tried to seem equally confident.

Satan's gaze settled on Cosmiel, and he gave an exaggerated sigh. "Oh, finally. Someone's in charge. It's so difficult when everything's in chaos."

Cosmiel gestured toward Michael. "Actually, that would be him."

Satan shoved his hands in his pockets. "You can lower your weapons. I'm not here to fight, merely to investigate the monkey that had the audacity to refuse my staffers' generous offer."

Michael raised a hand. "You can observe from a distance."

How could Michael speak so calmly? Satan's presence filled the room in a way that overwhelmed Cosmiel's senses. *Steady me,* he prayed.

Satan looked back at Cosmiel. "Satrinah savaged you, didn't she? Her marks are all over your soul."

Cosmiel shrugged. "She did me a favor. My team couldn't have defended Anna nearly as well without Satrinah's information."

"About that, you're going to have to get used to failure. I mean, more used to failure than you already are." Satan's eyes narrowed as he smiled. "Entrusting this deal to my underlings was, as it turned out, an error in judgment. I've corrected it. Henceforth, you'll be dealing with me."

Cosmiel narrowed his eyes. "I don't think it works that way. The original agreement was in Satrinah's name."

"I assure you, it does work this way." Satan flexed the feathers on one of his outermost wings. "The original human was owned by Satrinah, but Satrinah herself is owned by me. I'm not hung up on the technicalities of which service provider administrates the contract day to day, but as of now, my underlings are going to answer to me until new agreements are signed."

Cosmiel forced a smile. "You're out to prove Brooks' Law? Adding more individuals to a failing project only makes it fail slower."

Satan shrugged. "I wasn't aware that had a term, but you would be most familiar with the technical details of failure."

Cosmiel burned inside, but Michael only said, "Thank you for clarifying that the Cherub Satrinah is a wholly-owned subsidiary of the Seraph Lucifer. I would hate to mistakenly attribute to her a defeat that's truthfully yours."

Satan glanced at Michael in surprise. "Do you have any standing to deal with this matter? I don't think so." He looked back at Cosmiel. "As one department head to another, I'll make you an offer. Leave Sid and Forrest to me, and I will leave Anna alone."

Cosmiel opened his hands. "That in no way benefits us, since as it stands, you already have to leave Anna alone."

Satan made a dismissive gesture. "This monkey will swing back to me. She's too enmeshed with her luxuries. Her pride won't withstand what happens at that board meeting tomorrow. I can't take her *life*," he added, irritated, "but I can take everything that makes her life enjoyable. She'll deal with me." He raised his eyebrows. "But I'm willing to hand her over to you if you just stay out of my way with the other two."

Cosmiel furrowed his brow. "I don't see why you'd bother making this offer if our failure is a certain outcome."

"Today I feel generous. It's a failing of mine. Despite cliches about 'working like the devil,' I would much rather do less work on these easy, unfulfilling cases." Satan opened his hands. "So? Her for them?"

"No deal." Cosmiel kept his gaze steely and hoped his voice wouldn't tremble. "No deal between you and us, and no deal between you and them."

"Your loss. But I guess you're used to that." Satan looked back at Michael. "I'm still not sure why you're here."

Failing to look insulted, Michael said, "It will forever be a mystery."

"Your leash-holder does so enjoy His mysteries." Satan held his hands apart, concentrated, and said, "Before I leave, though..."

His eyes flared, and then in between his hands he held a sphere. Inside that sphere was Linus Ellington.

Eloricel gasped. Satan shot fire into the sphere, and Linus Ellington's soul lit up like a plasma globe. Satan concentrated until a blue-green laser shot from the sphere to Anna. He jerked it to the side, and Anna stood from the couch.

Turmiel slashed his sword through the light, but Satan said, "Don't bother. Recall for a moment how this whiff of divine breath in a meat suit conducted himself in life: he controlled her, and she's still under his control." Satan flared power through the sphere again, and other lights beamed from the globe. Two of the strongest went off in the directions of Hollywood and Washington, DC. "Satrinah anchored these well, and they remain fully functional. Death doesn't end love, and neither does it end fear."

Eloricel's eyes glistened with tears. Satan pulled another attachment from the sphere, yanking a demon into the room: Satrinah.

She took her place at Satan's side with a bored arrogance, as if she should have anticipated he'd be showing off right about now. Satan said to Satrinah, "Illuminate me again, how exactly did this tailless monkey outwit you?" Giving her no chance for an answer (though to be fair, she didn't look interested in providing one), Satan lit up the bond between Linus Ellington and the fallen Cherub. "Indulge me by admiring the strength of that! I'm quite in awe of Satrinah's work." He turned back to Cosmiel. "You can't fight this. You took the hand, but you're going to lose the set. Trade with me. Anna's security in exchange for standing down, otherwise you lose all three."

Cosmiel said, "I already said no twice, politely."

"I appreciate how you conduct yourself with civility, unlike some." Satan crushed the sphere between his hands, sending it back to Hell in a spray of sparks. "If you change your mind before Anna changes hers, let me know. I may still feel generous."

Satan flashed back to Hell.

Chapter Twenty-Five

Cosmiel followed.

He didn't give himself the chance to second guess. His soul had been raked over by Satrinah, and therefore he could emulate her power signature enough that when Satan lassoed her, Cosmiel injected himself into her binding and got dragged along. Right through the walls of Hell. Right into Satan's own secure area.

Cosmiel battened down his terror because no matter what happened next, he needed to stay quiet. If Satan caught him, he wasn't escaping. For that matter, Cosmiel wasn't sure how he'd get out regardless. He hadn't left part of himself anywhere else.

You said the gates of Hell would never prevail, Cosmiel prayed as quietly as he could. *Now would be a good time to show me the permeable places.*

In the thick dark, Cosmiel remained discorporated and paid attention to everything but himself. He focused not on the danger, but on the inhabitants of Satan's chamber. Based on the signatures, there were three Seraphim, two Cherubim, and the globular soul of Linus Ellington.

Satrinah said, "I knew they wouldn't go for a deal."

"He didn't want a deal in the first place." Moloch's voice was shaken, as if he'd gotten beaten but still needed to stand and deliver a report. "He wants a show of superiority to throw them off their game."

"When I require someone to speak for me," Satan said, "it will not be you. Since you started, however, go ahead. Tell me everything else I'm thinking."

Satrinah said, "I know you're thinking you can handle the remaining siblings better than we can, and I also know you won't believe me when I tell you that's a mistake. Losing the woman was no fault of ours. She had outside help at the last moment. We'd gotten her past the point of selecting a token and all the way to uncapping her pen before the enemy took her."

"It doesn't matter how close she came if she isn't ours," Satan said. "She might as well have deleted the contract on the first reading if she wasn't going to sign. At least then you'd have spent time on the other two, one of whom you haven't even approached."

The room reeked of brimstone. Cosmiel allowed that to permeate himself as well. The more he stank like the stones of Hell, the less likely he was to get noticed. No one ever noticed the stones.

From across the darkness, the second Cherub spoke. "Hand that one to me. I'll have him signed in an hour."

Moloch said, "We have a plan."

The second Cherub, who must be Belior, said, "It's a lousy plan."

Satan said, "The enslaved angels had their intergenerational evil expert in the room, and you'll note she said nothing, which means she was observing everything. The longer you take to bind a soul, the more you risk losing them."

Moloch said, "They went in front of the throne and demanded eleven extra days. Our original plan allotted the woman two, and at the end of two, she would have signed. Longer than two gave them a chance to shore up her allies."

Satrinah said, "We did account for allies in revising our plans, but the outside interference is the reason she lost her courage."

Sparks flew from the opposite end of the room, the only light Cosmiel had seen so far. It was Linus Ellington's soul, its spherical prison once again flooded with fire. It seethed within its globe like a sparkler, sputtering and throwing out painful light. The soul must have been screaming, but no sound escaped.

Satrinah said, "Linus is bound to me. You witnessed the

strength of that tie and how he nurtures it, even now. If you hand over the contract to Belior, he may close the deal, but he'll do it in a ham-fisted way that loses the contractee's loyalty. What I have from Linus Ellington is loyalty in perpetuity. He depended on me in ways even he didn't understand."

Belior said, "And which you don't understand."

Satrinah snorted. "Nor do I wish to understand. Moloch was the technician who showed me how to seal him, tighter and tighter. His suggestions were surgical. He knew how to give and then take back just enough that we had a perfect cycle of dependency and control, and Linus instilled that same dynamic in his children and grandchildren."

Belior said, "While this sounds good in theory, you lost his granddaughter, and you also lost his wife."

Moloch said, "We set up power structures within the family relationships that none of them questioned."

Belior said, "Why all the effort? Offer them the thing they'd never refuse, and then give it over when they sign."

Satrinah said, "As it stood, I could have kept Linus Ellington in hand even if I took everything away from him. Your contracts for power and wealth are easily broken once the contractee lives long enough for power and wealth to lose their appeal. Your contracted souls then search for meaning and whine to our enemies until our enemies take them back. Toward the end, Linus Ellington ceded his power because it had to be funneled through his granddaughter, but he still loved *me*. Even while dying, he encouraged her to sign."

Satan shot fire into the sphere again, and the soul undulated within its confines like a gas giant constructed of pain. "I noted how you used this man's ties to inject thoughts into the targets' minds after he was dead."

Satrinah said, "Hellfire hasn't diminished his attachment to me. That's how I plan to reel in the next generation."

Feathers rustled as Satan shifted position. The globular fire kept undulating, and Cosmiel watched with hypnotic horror. The fires leaned in one direction. All of them pointed toward Satrinah's voice.

Satan said, "Explain further."

"We're implementing the same push-pull that Moloch used with Linus Ellington. You yourself have discouraged deals because when the creatures are face-to-face with losing their souls, almost all of them will decide it's not worth it, and some will revert fully to the other side."

Satan said, "I do prefer the subtle approach."

"I don't mind saying Belior has had the best success with a traditional bargain. Moloch modified Belior and Asmodeus's technique in a way I find brilliant." That was high praise, coming from a Cherub. "Moloch's insights into Linus Ellington snared him at the beginning. We initially offered the success of his company because he couldn't face the humiliation of bankruptcy, but afterward, the field was wide open to claim the rest of his attachments."

A shifting sound as Satan leaned forward. "Continue."

"Humans see little value in trading eternity for material comfort, and only a trifle more value in trading eternity for power. Moloch offered Linus Ellington a ready supply of emotional fulfillment. He showed me how to enflame his pride and ultimately seduce his desire to be appeased by everyone around him. Linus Ellington wanted to be the god, and he wanted worshippers. I gave him the means of becoming their idol."

Belior said, "You buttered him up?"

"I did no such thing. I withheld praise at all cost." Satrinah sounded as though she were grinning. "I'd lambaste him for his mistakes, and I would threaten to leave—and then I'd lavish him with rewards for no reason. I made our approval seem always just within reach, and he kept dancing on the end of my string. He in turn attached chains to everyone who wanted his love, and those, I will point out, are the strong attachments he's still holding. To me and to the grandchildren alike."

Moloch said, "It wasn't that hard to do. I could show Belior how to manage it. What it did require was time and observation."

Belior huffed. "No, thank you. As we can see, it didn't work."

Satrinah said, "Plowing onto the scene like a bulldozer is going to lose the remaining two. They've been primed to accept the contracts in the way we're offering them, and we prepared in advance for every defense on the part of the enemy. More than that, we were counting on their defenses. Do note that until they smuggled in an outsider, every one of their efforts only strengthened our hold."

Cosmiel fought to keep from reacting. Just listen. Watch the lights in the sphere.

Moloch said, "All our method requires is establishing familiar patterns of behavior that keep the offspring locked into specific roles with their providers, each of them hoping for a relationship the provider very nearly but never actually gives. I do have experience with convincing parents to sacrifice their children for their own benefit. It doesn't have to be tossing their firstborn into the fire. Give them enough insight and they'll establish emotional control over their offspring like a leash, but they'll never turn that insight on themselves."

A momentary attention passed over Cosmiel, but then it flickered out.

Satrinah continued, "The enemy forces are accustomed to Belior's strategy. We banked on having their intergenerational evil expert involved, and therefore incorporated her defensive strategies into our offensive strategy. As soon as you switch to a more standard offer, you will lock in all three siblings for the other side. I strongly advise we continue with the current approach."

Belior chuckled. "Of course you'd say that."

Satan drummed his fingers on the table. "How would you describe your current approach?"

Good question. Cosmiel again struggled to keep himself nonreactive.

Moloch said, "In the past, Belior has offered one product or service in exchange for another product, dealing on a contractual basis. Our deal with the Ellingtons is relational. Call it a covenant."

Cosmiel's shock was dwarfed by the way Satan's energy flared. "Tell me more."

"With Linus Ellington, we never asked for his soul. We asked for his loyalty in exchange for our assistance. As he moved forward in life, he willingly gave us his soul. We then shaped his relationships with his offspring, and subsequently with their offspring, to incentivize them to first be loyal to him and later to transfer their loyalty to us. We will become the surrogates that provide them everything Linus Ellington withheld. Your deals exchange goods. Our deals exchange persons."

Cosmiel wanted nothing more than to escape. He needed whatever information they were divulging, but the icy discussion—measured instructions on conducting psychological abuse, emotional negligence, and malignant parenting—made him long to run. Run straight back to the Throne of God and beg. Beg for Jesus to return to the world and end it now. Beg for God to put a stop to this mockery of fatherhood.

Satrinah added, "We built contingencies into our approach to the other two, just in case the woman turned us down. I assure you, her refusal will secure the actor for our side. The politician will soon follow. Once we have both, she will re-initiate negotiations on her own."

Cosmiel went even colder.

Moloch said, "Moreover, when she comes to us, it won't be with an eye toward her own benefit. She'll believe she needs us. We can offer her next to nothing."

Satrinah said, "If she doesn't come to us, we will tempt her to suicide and remove her from the dynamic."

Cosmiel's heart burned. By contrast, Satan kept his voice low and smooth. "You've thought this through."

Satrinah huffed. "Of course."

Again that fleeting attention focused on Cosmiel. Much as he wanted to blast his way out of the stink and the darkness, he relaxed further. Momentarily he realized the attention's source was the sphere.

Cosmiel bore Satrinah's signature. Detecting that faint resonance, Linus Ellington's soul had fixated on him. Was, in fact, tugging Cosmiel toward him.

Fighting the tug might draw attention, so Cosmiel allowed it to happen.

Satan said, "Answer me this: if your hold on Linus Ellington was covenantal in nature, why didn't you have him convince his heirs to sign themselves over before his death?"

Excellent question.

Moloch said, "He refused."

Belior sounded disgusted. "You allowed a *refusal* from a soul you owned?"

Moloch said, "We saw no benefit in pressing the matter. The heirs will be ours, and the delay gave us more time to prepare."

Belior started to speak, then stopped. Cosmiel couldn't tell what had stopped him. Maybe Asmodeus through their bond.

After a brief silence, Satan said, "I've decided. I'll allow you to continue, but my patience is not infinite. I want the second one, the one you already offered a deal, signed in the next day. I want reports on everything he does, at least every hour."

Satrinah said, "You'll have him. Even if we do nothing at all, he'll sign on his own without additional encouragement."

Head reeling, Cosmiel had come near the sphere but braced himself along the edge of the desk. When he stopped, the sphere rocked toward him.

A flash of light, and Satan again filled the sphere with flame.

Belior said, "Can I toss that thing into the Lake of Fire? It's annoying, and it's paying attention to us."

"We require it," Satrinah said. "I'll be taking it with me when we leave."

Satan added, "But since you're offering yourself as a participant, Belior, you have any number of assets within the extended circles of the remaining targets. Put them at Satrinah's service for the duration of this assignment."

Irritation flared from Belior, but he only said, "Agreed."

The soul inside the sphere was still tugging Cosmiel, so he flowed toward it again. All the globular bits of light were near him at the edge of the sphere.

Satan said, "How sweet, Satrinah. It loves you."

Cosmiel steeled himself to reach for the hungry soul within the sphere.

In response, Linus Ellington pulled Cosmiel inside.

The world went silent, and the brimstone stench ebbed. Even so, light had returned: light from the hellfire coursing over what was left of Linus Ellington's immortal soul.

The soul surrounded Cosmiel, who recoiled from its touch.

The soul realized he wasn't Satrinah, but no matter. The soul began pulling off whatever bits of Satrinah's power that it could, nibbling them away like a shrimp picking meat shreds off the corpse of a whale. Cosmiel stayed as still as possible, disgusted.

Satan sent fire into the sphere. The soul howled in electric agony, projecting betrayal and loneliness.

It still longed for Satrinah. After all this—even knowing she'd used him—Linus Ellington still craved her. Frozen in that moment of longing, he focused his desires on her and only on her. She'd gutted him, and reflexively he reached for her to make him whole. He cried out for her, and if the only thing he could get was the residue of her wrath on an angel she'd injured days earlier, he would take those crumbs.

Cosmiel tried not to cringe as the soul scoured over him. He remained in the sphere and hated every time Satan injected fire into the trapped soul. Cosmiel wanted to pray, but he also didn't dare project anything, so instead he focused inward. He tried to dwell on the idea of peace. What peace meant to God. What peace meant to Cosmiel. What it meant that the soul trapped inside this sphere would never again experience peace.

But for that matter, when had Cosmiel last experienced peace?

Eventually he realized the fire hadn't filled the sphere for a while. Linus Ellington's soul had finished with him and was pressed against the opposite side. It was glowing...with warmth? With tenderness? Then, after a moment longer, threads began spreading from the sphere.

Those threads—Linus Ellington's attachments.

They rayed out in multiple directions. Not just the attachments to Sid, Forrest, and Anna, but others as well. Many went in the same direction, but not all. The strongest one would be to Satrinah, but the second strongest would be Sid's, and it pointed away from the others.

Satrinah was tugging and pulling them, sending information as though they were wires. In the heart of the sphere, Linus Ellington's soul grew brilliant, and it offered energy to assist.

That the attachments headed in different directions meant Satrinah had carried the sphere to the plane of creation. Cosmiel gathered himself to leave, then took another look at Linus Ellington.

Satrinah was using him, and Linus was urgent. Urgent to keep being hers.

Nauseated, Cosmiel flashed away.

Chapter Twenty-Six

Mid-afternoon, Tuesday. Anna walked Fifth Avenue in her long rain jacket, holding a coffee that would keep her awake tonight when really, she ought to be asleep. She'd craved something warm, though. Something familiar.

Up until now, the only familiar thing was her work, and now it was gone. One board meeting, one no confidence vote, one stark removal. One former CEO.

Really what she wished she had was a therapist. Or really anyone who might be able to decipher all this. Instead she had a life full of broken promises, and now she also had a text from Sid saying, "You're an idiot," as well as one from Forrest saying, "I didn't think that could happen."

It hadn't been a question when she rejected the contract. Certainty had filled her last night that if she rejected it, she'd lose everything her grandfather had set her up to achieve.

It hadn't taken long.

Uncertain what to do in Manhattan in the middle of the day, Anna had texted Yolanda that she wouldn't be home for dinner, so she could end her day whenever she wanted. A silent apartment was for the best right now. Looking Yolanda in the face would mean having to voice her failure. Her shame.

Instead, Anna meandered through the drizzle. She tried going through one of the boutiques, but shopping didn't appeal. She likewise didn't bother buying a $5 umbrella from the vendors with their folding tables. How would she get money? She'd have her inheritance, and there would be her severance package, but then what?

At 50th and 5th, Anna stopped in front of Saint Patrick's Cathedral. Did she dare? She'd been on the verge of a deal with the devil. She hadn't even been inside a church since Ryan got baptized. Before that, it had been Gavin's baptism, and before that, her wedding. She was divorced. The holy people wouldn't let her in the door.

Well, God, do your worst, she half-thought, half-prayed. *I already got my head lopped off today, metaphorically speaking. I might as well go scorched earth and then figure out what to do afterward.*

The cathedral was as impressive as ever. The white marble, the towering arches, the echoes that blurred into one another as tourists walked through. With so much motion, it wasn't a place to pray, and that made visiting easier. Anna could be just another tourist. She could act like any random visitor at the gift shop to pick up a present for her housekeeper. She shoved a twenty into the donation box, then walked up the side past all the mini altars tucked into the alcoves.

Votive candles stood in cups of blue glass. Anna used to come in here with Grandma to light a candle. Her parents' funeral had been...here? Or had it been uptown at Saint Ignatius Loyola? Grandma used to give Anna a quarter to slide into the slot, then touch a stick to the wick of a nearly-consumed candle and pass the flame to a fresh one. After that, Anna was supposed to close her eyes and ask God for something. How much of a prayer could you get answered for twenty-five cents?

That question actually came from Grandfather, but Grandma had replied, "We donate a million dollars every year to charities. Let the children have their fun."

She stared at the statue of Jesus Christ positioned over a forest fire of candles. *Do you have a price sheet?* She had a five in her wallet, so she pushed the bill into the slot, then pulled a stick from a cubic sandbox to light a candle. *I'm the opposite of everything you want someone to be. I admit that. But yesterday I did the right thing, and today I got the consequences of it. Now I'm not sure what to do. Sid thinks I'm an idiot, by the way. I'm not sure he's wrong. Grandfather would definitely say I'm an idiot. I couldn't handle it alone.*

She walked through the rest of the church, stopping briefly at the front to look at the altar and its ornate carvings.

What was she doing here? She should be working right now. Would be, in fact, except that Pilaster no longer wanted her.

God doesn't care about people. That's what religion always gets wrong. Once again, those were Grandfather's words, delivered twenty years ago over dinner when Sid mentioned a religious festival in the news. *The whole system is based on death. Other things have to die in order for you to survive. Does that sound like a world made by a deity that cared about everyone? Believe in God if you want,* Grandfather had added, *but it's not like any god knows about you or would care if it did.*

Grandfather had encountered some entity that did know about him. Why would a preternatural creature have cared about Linus Ellington? What aspect of Grandfather had caught its fancy, that genii or demon with a sigil for a signature, and then held its fancy for sixty years? Why would it be fond enough of one man to straighten the road before his business and then renew that offer with his grandchildren? That would be like her caring about the dreams of one of the gourami in her fishtank. She made sure they were fed and had clean water, but would anyone care about their friendships or their imaginings?

If God didn't care about a young man with a failing business, it made even less sense for a spirit to care. At least in theory, an omnipotent God would have the power to spend on insignificant hobbies. An angel or an alien wouldn't have any reason to notice either the creatures living on this planet or their economies. One company, in its failure or its success, would add nothing to them.

At the front, Anna stopped in front of a wooden statue of an angel, kneeling as it held a book.

Did angels read? What would they read if they did?

Two nights ago, she'd read *Where the Red Fern Grows*. What if a pair of angels had sat at her side the way Sid and Forrest used to sit, listening to her telling a story about coonhounds?

That image made more sense to her than an angel (or a fallen angel) caring about a profit and loss sheet. At least if you read to an angel, the angel got some entertainment for its trouble.

She craned back her neck last of all to regard the crucifix, that garish moment when a man claiming to be God died in agony. Grandfather was right: that made no sense because you don't exchange something valuable for something that isn't valuable. A human life isn't worth much in comparison to a deity's. Likewise, her grandfather's loyalty (or hers) wouldn't have been valuable in comparison to the valuation of Pilaster at the time of Linus Ellington's death.

She thought toward the cross, *I did the right thing, and I got crushed for it. Where were you when the board met this morning? Hanging here in a pretty church? Thanks for nothing.*

Chapter Twenty-Seven

Jezaryah monitored every emotional vibration sounding through Forrest, but he couldn't dampen the undercurrent of frustration. Forrest had worked all morning answering calls and coordinating with his campaign manager, meeting with professional fundraisers and reviewing documents, and with every decision, that frustration mounted.

He was meeting a reporter for lunch and a lobbyist for dinner. In between that, he was looking online at articles about the upheaval at Pilaster, as well as scanning the group chat messages between Anna and Sid.

Frustration. Isolation.

In Heaven, Jezaryah used to play cello. Not for performances, but just because he enjoyed the sound. The setup was such a clever mimicry of the human tenor vocalization, only without a human voice box anywhere in sight. When he'd first learned it four centuries ago, however, he'd kept encountering one note that made the instrument growl.

He'd brought the cello to Jesus, since the cello was wood and Jesus was a carpenter. "Why is it making a sympathetic vibration? Is that a subharmonic?"

Jesus said, "That's called a wolf tone," and explained how to tame the lone wolf.

Forrest's soul reminded Jezaryah of that wolf tone, vibrating like an unwanted bonus beneath the vibrations that were good and proper to the instrument.

Cosmiel stayed beside them the whole day. His first action had been to try undoing the snares they'd built up among the siblings, but those were knotted in deep. Auriel was exploring alternatives, and in the meantime, Jezaryah tried to level out Forrest's emotions.

Forrest called Anna briefly, but she hadn't wanted to talk. "We're in this together," he assured her. That snare was embedded like barbed wire around a tree trunk with the bark swollen over it. "You can count on that. It's always been us against the world."

Anna said, "What am I even good for if I'm not part of the company? I've worked for Pilaster since I got out of college."

Forrest said, "Take the rest of the day to yourself. Tomorrow, you start networking. Between you and me and Sid, we have three phone books full of powerful people. All those people know other people. We'll find you a soft place to land. Three months from now, you're going to be glad this happened."

Jezaryah had read an article over Forrest's shoulder years ago that recommended one month of job search for every ten thousand per year an executive expected to earn. Three months was more than a little optimistic.

Dinnertime. The wolf tones increased in intensity. Sid texted Forrest that he might make his contract contingent on Anna getting her job back. That only increased the wolf tone.

Isolation. That's what Jezaryah was detecting. Not just frustration, but the sting of being ignored. Once again, one Ellington had been forgotten.

In the lobby of a steakhouse, a man in his sixties approached. "Forrest Ellington? I'm Jack Kenner."

The man had no guardian angel.

Jezaryah and Cosmiel both armored up. Every guardian angel in the area was watching, hands on their swords.

As Forrest shook his hand, Jezaryah sent a static shock through him, but Forrest masked his reaction. "Have we met?"

"I'm here in place of Karl Morrison, of the Alliance for Sustainable Greenery. He was unavoidably detained, so I took his place." Kenner gestured toward the dining room. "Let's have a seat, and I can tell you more about our work."

It was either a human in thrall to a demon or a demon in human form. As they went to their table, Jezaryah sent to Cosmiel, *Have you figured out what we're dealing with?*

Cosmiel sent, *Not yet.*

Sophiel's sigil wasn't repelling him. If it was a demon, he must be either a strong one or else under duress.

Reaching into Forrest's heart, Jezaryah made him queasy. He made the ambient noise more annoying. *If it's not the person you're supposed to be talking to, staying is a waste of time. Anna might need to talk.*

Forrest glanced at the door, then checked his phone.

Kenner said, "It's a shame about your sister."

Forrest looked up. "You heard about that?"

Kenner opened his hands. "It's a shock that the Ellington dynasty could get dethroned so quickly, but they do say your family is cursed."

"*They* say a lot of ridiculous things." Forrest checked the menu, and Jezaryah again filled him with annoyance. *This is a waste of time,* he prompted as though Forrest himself were thinking it. *This isn't the person I need to be talking to.*

Kenner said, "Never mind. We have a lot to talk about. I recommend the daily specials, by the way."

Forrest gave a tight smile as the waiter approached. "Do you eat here often?"

"I've been through here before."

The waiter recited the specials, and Forrest picked one. Jezaryah tightened his grip on Forrest's shoulders. Little chance of extricating him now.

Kenner began with a well-rehearsed spiel about his organization's advocacy work, and Jezaryah diverted Forrest's attention to other things. Did he recognize that individual in the corner? What was that spice in the soup?

Over the entrée, however, Kenner said, "Do you know why Pilaster voted out your sister?"

Forrest concentrated on cutting his steak. "Not because of the Ellington Curse."

"On the contrary, it was her rejection of the Ellington Curse."

Forrest looked up, his face bland but his attention riveted to Kenner.

Kenner said, "Last night, she declined an offer that was of longstanding benefit to the company. It stands to reason they had to replace her."

Forrest said, "What agreement would that have been?"

Kenner chuckled as he reached for his glass. "We're both men of intelligence, so I would appreciate if you please refrain from lying to me, and likewise, I will not lie to you. But to be clear, I know she refused to continue an agreement initially offered to the company founder."

Forrest said nothing, which Jezaryah would have to admit was better than lying.

Kenner handed his phone across the table. "You will recognize that signature. I understand these agreements. They're not terribly uncommon."

Satrinah's sigil filled the screen. Cosmiel flinched, and Jezaryah again seeded dread into Forrest.

Forrest passed back the phone. "My sister handles her own life. While I'm sad to see her removed as the CEO, she made what she thought was the best decision."

"I'm sure she thought it was, but naturally, the company would think otherwise."

Forrest chuckled. "The chief officers had no clue about the backstory. My grandfather was respected but disliked, and I'm sure they resented him installing a thirty-something woman into his office. My sister was a remnant of the old guard."

Kenner said, "If she had signed, her job would have been protected."

Forrest opened his hands. "The board of directors would still have resented my grandfather, and again, it's not as if any one of them could have known whether Anna signed or rejected the agreement."

Kenner shook his head. "You're not respecting my intelligence the way I asked. The parties with whom she made the agreement would have taken action to secure her position. They would have humiliated her key enemies and cowed the rest." Kenner set down his utensils and leaned into the table. "Forrest Ellington, I have been empowered to make you the same offer."

Jezaryah tried to fill Forrest with unease, but it bounced away as Forrest concentrated on Kenner's words.

"The offering party extends its apologies for the delay, but they very much desired to hold a conversation in person rather than through third parties."

Forrest returned to eating his steak. "You yourself are a third party. Also, I'm amused by your insistence that they could have confounded Pilaster's board of directors, but they can't figure out the postal system."

That nonchalance was a performance even Sid would have been proud of. Forrest's heart was pounding, and his pupils had dilated.

"A letter or a SignAgree email or even a phone call—they're all so impersonal. The offering parties asked me to arrange a face-to-face meeting."

Forrest swallowed a bite of steak. "A face-to-face meeting with what I am told is an entity without faces."

"Or rather, with many faces."

Forrest waved a hand. "I understand the legal ruling that corporations are people, but what we're talking about has no faces. This offering party—individual or corporate—is smoke. They knew how to reach me. They chose not to."

Jezaryah had expected this response from Forrest, but he couldn't mold it into rejection. It vibrated like the wolf tone. It was hunger.

Forrest continued, "And how did you manage to become an agent for the offering party?"

Kenner's smile was cold. "I received a similar offer, and I saw its advantages."

Forrest recoiled.

"I did say the arrangement wasn't terribly uncommon." Kenner shrugged. "I wasn't given the honor of an in-person discussion. Neither was your grandfather."

Helpless, Jezaryah looked to Cosmiel. Cosmiel took a shot with a flaming arrow of his own: sarcasm.

Forrest smirked. "You aren't exactly a billboard for the fame and success that follows on such an agreement."

Abruptly Cosmiel changed gears and reinforced the sense of dread Jezaryah had tried. Again, it bounced.

Kenner raised his eyebrows. "Don't limit a deal's potential benefits to money, power, and name recognition. I negotiated for something far more important, and they've upheld their end of the bargain."

Forrest said, "And you're upholding yours? For some things, the price is too high."

Kenner gestured with a hand. "Prices. What are you handing over, and to whom? You would sign a lease on a car without a second thought if you needed a car. You paid quite a high price for a home in Bethesda where you live less than half the time. You make monthly payments to the electric company and your cell phone provider, never once negotiating the price."

Forrest raised his eyebrows. "I'm not locked into an eternal cell phone plan."

"You're locked into an eternal agreement no matter what you decide." Kenner's stare drilled into Forrest. "If you believe in fairy tales like the story of Faust, then either side is demanding a permanent commitment. After looking at the world with my eyes wide open, I decided the other side was promising less and delivering less."

Forrest returned to his steak. "That I have a hard time believing."

Cosmiel reached through Forrest's heart and sent a jolt outward, directly toward Julia. Jezaryah warmed with wonder. He should have thought of that himself.

Kenner huffed. "One party has better public relations, nothing more. That gives them a better marketing budget, more platforms, and more opportunity to shape the narrative. To my mind, their press releases have too many inconsistencies, and their spokesmen are too unreliable. I'm sure you feel that way too. I've eyeballed your career. You aren't a militant atheist, but you've never committed to anything other than a vague Christianesque understanding of values and standards. Enough to secure votes, but not enough to commit you to any stance in particular."

Forrest tilted his head. "Since we're talking about public relations, I'm sure you understand why someone in my position might keep his opinions private."

"I absolutely do, but I'm also sure that someone who held exclusively Christian beliefs would be acting on them." Kenner sat back from his plate. "Also for your information, America has a two-party system, but not the whole of creation. My agreement is with a different party than your grandfather's."

That drew Forrest up short. Not Jezaryah. He'd figured this agent was Belior's.

Forrest's phone buzzed with an incoming text, and Jezaryah pushed him to look at it. "It's my wife," Forrest said. "Hold on."

Julia had texted, "I know this is ridiculous, but I just got really anxious about you. Is everything okay?"

Forrest texted back, "I'm at dinner with an environmental lobbyist. Everything's fine except my cholesterol."

Her reply appeared immediately: "Okay. I know this is silly, but please be careful."

After sending, "I will," Forrest put his phone back in his pocket.

Kenner seemed amused. "I'm not privy to the terms of your offer, but since it's a continuation of a previous contract, yours would most likely follow the same format: career guidance and protection, immediate access to a technician who can resolve any problems you encounter, and services extended to any children you may have."

Forrest said, "What were the terms of your contract?"

Kenner smiled coldly. "One of my terms is a nondisclosure agreement, but I am allowed to say the other party's terms have been fulfilled to the letter."

Jezaryah pushed the thought of Julia into Forrest's mind. *This contract is the thing she was scared of.*

Forrest said, "Could they protect my wife as well?"

Jezaryah's feathers flared. How could that have backfired?

"Of course." Kenner seemed surprised he'd asked. "Since you're interested in specifics, I'll arrange for you to speak directly to the offering agent tomorrow." When Forrest hesitated, Kenner added, "I have to stress, not everyone gets a face-to-face encounter. They must really want you."

Forrest finished his steak. The wolf tones had abated, and the frustration was diminished.

Jezaryah didn't look to Cosmiel. Instead, he dove into Forrest's heart.

Forgotten again, Jezaryah input. *This is coming right after Anna refused them. Second choice. Last resort.*

The wolf tone barely thrummed any longer. But that had to be the key: Satrinah and Moloch had delayed offering to Forrest because Forrest was the forgotten sibling. Grandfather never included Forrest. Anna got the company, and Sid got everything else. Forrest got no attention, no love, no accolades, no scolding. He'd gotten no offer from the devil himself—until now.

Satrinah wanted Forrest to do what he'd always done: redouble his efforts to prove himself. If his straight A report card won nothing more than a lackluster, "Good job," then next semester he'd try to get all A pluses so maybe then he'd get praise.

Meanwhile, every effort had served only to irritate Linus more because it flew in the face of the narrative he wanted. Linus wanted Sid to succeed, so although he'd say the right things about Forrest's achievements, his eyes would betray his true feelings. His tone of voice. His short responses. He'd become a master of punishing Forrest's successes without ever punishing him.

Jezaryah tried to twist Forrest's desire into resentment. As a guardian, you weren't supposed to do that. You were supposed to diminish resentment and encourage peace, but centuries with Special Ops had shown Jezaryah there was a time for everything. Including a time for making people bitter.

Forrest straightened his napkin on his lap. "I'm not sure why your so-called offering agent would even be interested in me, other than the way my sister turned you down flat. Family curse and family dynasty aside, I do trust Anna's judgment. She's an excellent CEO and a conscientious sister." He gave a tight smile. "I'm done with this part of the conversation. If you want to discuss sustainable metropolitan green spaces, I'm listening. Otherwise, I consider our business concluded."

Kenner was about to speak, then stopped. Jezaryah didn't have to reach out to trace Kenner's attachment: Belior would be feeding him information with a tie as strong as Jezaryah's to Forrest. Instead, Kenner dutifully changed the subject to urban environmentalism, and at the end of the dinner, he handed Forrest his business card. "I'm always available to answer questions."

With a measured blankness, Forrest took the card.

Jezaryah's heart fell. Forrest was testing whether the enemy would reach out again after being rejected. His grandfather would have failed.

The enemy would not.

Chapter Twenty-Eight

Auriel couldn't focus, and she needed to.

Everything they were doing was just...leading the siblings to Satan? Satrinah had not only predicted everything Auriel would do, but also built it into her strategy?

Just as unfocused as Auriel, Sid was pacing his apartment, sometimes texting Forrest, sometimes texting his agent. Angry, he brewed a cup of coffee and then forgot it on the countertop. When he returned to it, cold, he flung the mug into the sink. Indri made sure it didn't break, but coffee spattered up the wall.

Auriel had already apologized to Indri five different times, but Auriel wasn't even sure how their defensive tactics were tying into the enemy's plans. *Botany,* Auriel thought to God. *Although maybe then all the trees would rot.*

Sid stalked back to his recliner with a digital copy of the script he'd be filming this afternoon.

For her own part, Indri was praying hard while undoing the protections they'd already installed. The snares weren't coming out easy. The reason the snares functioned in the first place was how natural each of those thoughts felt to the siblings.

Only now... The snares were just leashes for Moloch to yank them forward?

Auriel sent to Cosmiel, *We're removing the snares, but we need something else.*

He replied, *Suggestions?*

His voice in her mind sounded thinner than onion skin and twice as brittle. Auriel sent, *We could re-do the snares with something different.*

The thought bubbles had stopped Anna once. They'd leave those in place.

Cosmiel sent, *What does Indri think?*

Indri was holding herself together with nothing but prayer and desperation. Asking her opinion now would push her into a panic, and her panic would feed Sid's anger.

Anger...or frustration? Or was it helplessness?

Auriel got right in front of Sid and stared in his eyes while he read his script. She rested her hands on his heart, then slowed everything about herself while gauging all the levels of his body chemicals.

Very high stress levels. Lots of cortisol. Oddly, oxytocin was high. His adrenal glands were pumping out everything they could like a fire hose.

Father, is he offended? Auriel sat back just as Sid got to his feet and started practicing an exchange from the script.

Indri slipped into his abandoned seat like a cat. In calmer days, Indri would act opposite Sid during his practices. They could play out the scene together even though Sid had no idea she was doing it.

The longer Auriel watched, the more she decided she was right: Sid was offended that Anna had turned down the offer.

Talk to me again about the contract being covenantal, Auriel sent to Cosmiel. *Exactly how did Moloch explain it?*

That instead of Linus Ellington's soul, they asked for his loyalty. They then reshaped his relationships in order to make his heirs loyal to him, with the intention that thereafter, their loyalty would transfer to Satrinah. She said they wouldn't even need to offer anything. Moloch bragged that he's no stranger to getting parents to sacrifice their children.

Auriel tucked up her knees and wings, then covered her face in her hands.

Cosmiel added, *I never considered how our enemies might be programming the grandchildren with the family dynamics. This is my fault.*

I'm not letting you take responsibility for this. We had no reason to assume Satrinah was trying to improve on Belior's process. It's been the same since the beginning: they offered material gain in exchange for spiritual loss, and it worked because it formalized a decision the humans were consistently making anyhow.

Sid paused mid-recitation to re-read a section. "Did the script writers ever *hear* a human conversation?" he shouted at nothing, then backed up several lines to re-take the offending dialogue.

Auriel sent, *Moloch's demonstrating a degree of emotional intelligence we never saw from Asmodeus, way beyond anything I'd have believed Satrinah would have adapted her methods to. He took a straightforward operation and turned it into a series of interlocking snares where struggling against one only succeeds in tightening the rest.*

Sid stopped to text an angry message to the director. He then retook the line the way he wanted to and continued with the scene as written.

A golden child, a scapegoat, and a forgotten child. Auriel frowned as Sid performed. He was fantastic. Everything he was acting, she believed he felt it at the moment. Even though his heart was outraged, his voice and carriage were heartbroken. *Linus forced them all to earn his approval by doing his bidding. The children learned never to break out of their assigned roles because doing so risked his wrath and loss of affection. When Sid succeeded, Linus praised him. When the other two succeeded, he shifted the goalposts to ensure it became natural and normal to strive but never achieve. Those two never questioned his established truth, that love is a thing you earn. Sid's established truth is that love is a conditional thing, and once lost, is lost forever.*

Cosmiel sighed. *Good analysis. So for new snares, should we reassure them they're worthy individuals no matter what they do?*

They would never believe it. She could hear Cosmiel negating his own thought even as he sent it, so she maintained silence.

How to convince them they had value...when they were already powerful individuals who "had it all"?

If they didn't believe they had value just by virtue of being human, what were they doing instead to convince themselves their lives had value?

Auriel sent, *Linus was shameless in making love a commodity. Forrest especially was trained to believe he didn't deserve love without hard effort, so he expects to give everything just to get a few crumbs. That actually helps him as a politician because he'll put anything on the table in a negotiation. Sid, on the other hand* —

In the middle of a line, Sid tossed his tablet aside, snatched up his phone, and dialed Anna.

Indri put her hands on his shoulder, and Auriel got to her feet. She couldn't detect a demonic presence, but Satrinah and Moloch had made it clear they could pull Sid's strings from a thousand miles away. According to Cosmiel, they didn't need to pull his strings at all.

Auriel didn't hear when Anna answered, but she knew when Sid said, "Are you out of the office now? Still wandering Fifth Avenue feeling like an idiot for chucking everything Grandfather gave you?"

That was definitely offense.

Sid's eyes were bright. He was emotional from practicing a breakup scene, and he'd keyed his voice in just the right way to provoke a reaction from Anna. "How could you not have known they'd yank everything back the split second you refused?"

Anna might have been trying to explain herself, but Auriel didn't tune up her hearing to catch it. Whatever Anna said didn't matter if Sid wouldn't listen. Instead Auriel paid attention to Sid's soul and the connections attached to him. She rested her hand on him and did a trace even though she knew what she'd find.

Indeed, she encountered a very thick, very focused evil intent. From the other end, Auriel felt laughter. They weren't trying to hide what they were doing. So secure in their victory, they wanted Auriel to try stopping them because her failure would be funny.

Auriel delved deeper into Sid's soul. Indri exclaimed, "Please don't. They hurt you with Forrest."

So what if Moloch hurt Auriel? Her pain would end. If they hurt Sid, they could hurt him eternally.

Auriel followed that evil chain until she found Sid's attachments, and there she encountered the same series of bonds as within Forrest—except the attachment to his sister was burning.

She'd been wrong to say he felt offended. No, he felt betrayed. Anna had betrayed their grandfather, and he couldn't countenance it. Changing your role meant challenging the family structure. All along, Sid's role in the family was to be the protected one, the favored one, the one who never got hurt.

For Sid to remain the Golden Child, he had to obey. He had to keep their grandfather happy by keeping the others in line. Even his interventions on their behalf had served only to lock them into their expected roles.

Anna's rebellion was a threat. Whenever Sid had stood up for her, he'd risked his position, and now she'd backed out.

Indri's energy coursed through Sid, trying to calm him. He rejected calm. "You destroyed everything he worked for!" Sid was shouting. "His entire lifetime! He sacrificed and gave everything to that company, and you tossed it aside like a pair of worn-out sneakers!"

There weren't even flaming arrows in him. Satrinah wasn't pulling the strings. She'd claimed Sid would come to them within twenty-four hours even if she did nothing, and here he was, rushing toward her. Satrinah had built either eventuality into her plan. Either Anna would accept, and Sid wouldn't allow himself to be outdone, or Anna would deny, and Sid would take corrective action to put the family back to rights.

"You betrayed him! You didn't just lose your job. You destroyed his entire legacy!"

On the other end, Anna must be in tears. She'd been crushed when the board of directors voted her out. She'd turned to Sid and to Forrest for comfort but gotten none. Now this. Now the venom.

"You're just like Grandma!" Sid went for the kill. "You were waiting for the old man to die so you could discard him. What about everything he did for you? What about the employees who were counting on you to take care of them? What about your own children? You divorced your husband so you could serve the company. Now what do you have left?"

The snare of "All we have is each other" burned like a noose around his soul, and around hers as well.

Anything Auriel tried had no effect. His grandmother's disapproval? She was weak. His brother's needs? Sid's own eternity? None of it mattered. His sister's betrayal had exposed the family to peril. All the siblings had was each other. To save the family—what of the family remained—Sid had to reject her. Forever.

He hung up the phone. Auriel dropped to the floor, gasping, wings limp. Indri had her arms around Sid, her heart pleading with his. She had nothing left but pleas.

The phone rang in his hand. Auriel knew who it would be.

"Hell, yes," Sid said into the phone. "Unlike my sister, I'm good with your contract."

Indri fell to her knees. Sid's soul blackened up. Something shot from his soul and skittered across the floor: Sophiel's sigil.

As the room itself went dark around the angels, Auriel wrapped Indri in her wings. Satrinah and Moloch strode in to take possession of the area.

Moloch kicked the sigil back toward Auriel. "Take your toy."

Satrinah said with a hand-wave, "Are you two still here?" She turned toward Sid and spoke in a crisp voice. "Have you chosen a token to represent our agreement?"

Unable to see her, able to hear her only through the phone, Sid said, "I have." At the shelf with his family photos, he lifted his grandfather's pocket watch and popped it open. "I've identified the perfect token for a lifelong union."

Indri covered her face with her hands, and Auriel flashed her into Heaven.

Chapter Twenty-Nine

Anna texted Eric from the street. "Are you and Sharon both home?"

It was nine thirty and the boys would be asleep, but Eric sometimes worked late.

He texted, "We are. Why?"

She replied as the doorman let her into the building, "Can I stop by? I need to talk to you both."

His reply appeared at the same time as the elevator. "I suppose."

He let her into the apartment, wary. She hung her dripping coat on the rack as Sharon came up behind him. "Are you all right?" Sharon asked.

Thanks for the reminder that she looked awful.

Eric said, "Is it about the boys?"

"Somewhat." As he led her to the kitchen, she said, "I'm sorry for everything I said to you, and all the terrible things I threatened to do. We've worked hard to keep things stable for the boys, but I let myself get crazed."

Their coldness toward Anna wasn't undeserved, but it still stung. Sharon watched her with caution. "It did sound out of character when Eric told me. Would you like some tea?"

Anna nodded. Sharon put on the kettle, then sat beside Eric, across the table from her.

Anna said, "The board of directors fired me today."

Eric straightened. "What?"

Wide-eyed, Sharon said, "But your grandfather founded the company!"

Anna shook her head. "They could have fired *him* if they'd wanted. We're publicly traded now, and we no longer have a controlling share."

Eric said, "I thought part of the contract we were talking about meant you'd stay in control of Pilaster."

Anna said, "I declined the contract last night, and this morning, that was their response."

Sharon turned to Eric. "Is that legal?"

Eric snorted. "Yeah, the party who drafted the contract wasn't interested in the American legal system."

Anna rolled her eyes. "But they were generous enough that we could interpret the contract through the laws of the State of New York." She glanced at Sharon. "Didn't he tell you about the contract?"

Sharon shook her head.

Eric huffed. "It's a mess. I'm glad you declined," he added to Anna.

Anna rested her head in her hands, massaging her temples. "Except it affects the boys. I'll get my severance package, but over the long term, we may need to re-negotiate the child support payments, and I'm not sure what the living conditions will be."

Eric raised a hand. "Please. Rejecting it was the right decision. You and I can file a joint emergency injunction tomorrow stating that we anticipate the child support will become a problem after this month. After which, we can re-evaluate."

Anna looked up. "I can make the next few payments, but I don't know what happens after that."

Sharon said, "We'll work something out."

Eric looked strained. "You just went through something awful, and there's no reason to stress over the child support. We can float things for a while if necessary."

Anna stared at the table top. "I was awful to you when you picked up the boys. You were right. My grandfather was a terrible human being. I was turning into him."

Eric looked aside. "I shouldn't have said that."

"I needed to hear it." She shuddered. "Sid went off the deep end at me. He says I betrayed my family. He says I destroyed everything our grandfather ever worked for."

Eric said, "Maybe he should vent that anger at the board of directors. How about the chairman who was supposed to be working with you and instead set you up for failure?"

"Or the CFO? I saw proof that he mishandled the merger to make me look bad."

Sharon said, "Can't you present that proof to the board of directors? Shouldn't that have been a firing offense? You could bring it to the papers."

Anna said, "Unfortunately, I wasn't going to be given the proof unless I signed the contract. Which I didn't."

Eric said, "Walk away from this situation with your head high. You did the right thing."

Anna bit her lip. "Well, other than betraying my family and wrecking the lives of thousands of employees and torching my grandfather's legacy."

Eric said, "Sid will calm down. He wasn't thinking. Also, Pilaster Group isn't going to disappear without an Ellington in the C suite. All those employees will keep being employed."

The water boiled in the kettle, and Sharon got up to take care of it. "Is lemon-raspberry tea okay?"

A sleepy-eyed Gavin appeared in the doorway, and when he saw Anna, he beamed. "Mommy!"

He rushed to climb into her lap. "You shouldn't still be awake." Anna kissed his forehead, then nuzzled him. His hair smelled of sandalwood shampoo, and he fit perfectly into her arms. "I'm sorry I was so grumpy when you left."

Gavin hugged her. "Daddy says grumpy days are when we need to get more sleep."

"Daddy is very smart. I'll try to get to bed earlier tonight." She hugged Gavin. "I'm also not going to be staying late at my job anymore."

Sitting up straighter, Gavin beamed. "Can we do lots of board games?"

She squeezed him as Sharon set the tea in front of her. "Absolutely. We can play board games every night you're with me."

11:59. Jezaryah stared at the clock, eyes dull, wings tucked high and knees to his chest.

If he killed the power, the clock wouldn't tick over to midnight. It wouldn't become his final day with Forrest. He could sit in an endless pre-midnight, holding the universe in a pause between the exhale of one breath and the inhale of the next, preserving Forrest from a decision and a loss and an eternity apart.

Jezaryah closed his eyes so he didn't have to see it happen. When he opened them, it would be tomorrow.

He tried to pray, but prayer wouldn't emerge past the knot in his heart. Instead he presented that knotted heart to the Holy Spirit and knew the Spirit would decode the need. Then the Spirit could take that rope, swollen with sea water, and cut it loose to bring to the Father. Maybe the Spirit would find words Jezaryah didn't even understand.

Yaron knelt at Julia's side of the bed, gazing into her soul and guarding her dreams. Jezaryah ought to do that as well, but everything felt too final. If he had just this one day, he ought to use every second of it. Except—

Except. Right.

If he didn't cherish every last second, if he gave up now, then he was accepting Cosmiel's verdict that Forrest was hopeless. Not what Cosmiel *said*. Cosmiel was good about saying there was always hope, but he'd been acting as if there wasn't hope. Cosmiel did all the right things and took all the right actions, but with an expectation of failure. Was Cosmiel actually comfortable with loss, or did he just have such long experience that he knew when to budget his efforts?

Cosmiel should just have handed over this doomed assignment to some upstart team lead who hadn't yet concluded that some souls weren't worth his time. Maybe less expertise and more risk-taking would have won the war.

That thought wasn't fair. It wasn't fair to Cosmiel, who had dived into Hell twice already trying to find a rescue for Forrest. But Cosmiel's conviction of their eventual loss also wasn't fair to Jezaryah and Forrest, who were about to start their last day together.

Jezaryah didn't *know* it would be the last day. He only had to treat it as such. He should walk into it like a gladiator, since the only certain thing about today was that it would bring a fight. A fight without weapons. A fight waged with feelings and ideas and dreams.

So frustrating not to be able to do more when Jezaryah had stood before God and sworn to do everything.

He opened his eyes. 12:01. They were committed.

Jezaryah tried again to pray, and again the prayers wouldn't leave his heart. God would have to enter him to get them, then stay inside to answer.

The Guard shivered as Auriel flashed into the room, and momentarily her energy coursed through it as she checked the perimeter. Everything was safe for now. Ever since Sophiel had given his sigil, and then after Satan had gotten involved, the minor demons had stayed far from Forrest. The sigils' power had degraded, but even so, no demon was going to mess up Satrinah's sterile field. They'd get no credit for Satrinah's success, and if she failed, she'd blame their interference—and then they'd get tortured. Every last one of them had found something else to do.

Speaking of distancing oneself, Jezaryah needed to have a conversation. He sought out Yaron's eyes in the dark, and when their gazes finally met, Jezaryah projected unease. "I can't advise you to encourage Julia to stay with Forrest if he accepts."

Yaron shuddered. "It didn't hurt Cecilia's soul that she stayed with Linus."

Jezaryah's brow furrowed. "It could have so easily."

Auriel turned away from her work. "On the contrary, Linus's contract saved her."

Jezaryah's feathers flared. Settling herself at the head of the bed, Auriel stroked Forrest's hair. Humans could be so peaceful when they slept, and on his worst days, Jezaryah envied that. Although angels could sleep, usually sleep meant the angel needed to heal. An angel in healing wasn't an angel at peace. Humans got that respite every night, and in doing so, gave respite to their guardians.

Forrest, though, wore tension on his face even now. It didn't ebb under Auriel's touch, and Jezaryah fought the urge to push her out of the way to try easing it himself.

Well, for that matter, he ought to ease his own.

Auriel studied Forrest with eyes that looked deeper than his skin. "Cecilia married Linus knowing she was the trophy wife, ten years younger and the only child from a high-society family. She knew he'd previously discarded an engagement with a working-class woman. She had no interest whatsoever in God or the spiritual life. But then her oldest son died."

Jezaryah's wings raised. Auriel shook her head. "Yes, I'm revealing information about a person's private state of soul, but let me finish. Cecilia had figured out even before marriage that Linus had sold his soul. She found it funny. He was rich, and she was beautiful. It was a game." Jezaryah projected anger, and Auriel clenched her hands. "Because of her complicity in the agreement, the enemy believed Cecilia was their property. After their first son died, she began awakening. That's when she rejected Satan and embraced God."

Jezaryah blew off a flash of light. "How could she reject Satan but remain in a living situation where every luxury was a gift of Satan?"

Auriel sighed. "I don't understand it either, but through God's mercy, it was enough. She spent every day of the rest of her life praying for Linus's salvation. Every single day. She was on the cusp of leaving Linus when the second son died, only then Linus claimed the three grandchildren."

Jezaryah stared out the window. "If she'd left him and taken them—"

"If she'd taken them, Satrinah would have told him to get them back. He had the money and the means, and Cecilia would no longer have been able to intervene."

Jezaryah closed his eyes.

Auriel told Yaron, "Geron, Eloricel, and I had long talks about how Cecilia could intervene on behalf of the children." Jezaryah had been part of these discussions. "She was like us, a soldier working behind enemy lines. Linus recognized this, and he turned the children against her. Even so, she prayed for them every day. She hoped to outlive him so she could undo the damage, but then she didn't get the chance."

Moloch and Satrinah hadn't required permission from God to harm Cecilia's body. Her death only required Cecilia to delay visiting a doctor because she had gotten too used to denying the things she felt. For all that she'd prayed about Linus's salvation, she herself had been enchained by the gaslighting and manipulation. When faced with her body's signals versus her husband's mockery, she'd doubted her senses. Cecilia's early death was considered part of the Ellington curse.

Yaron rested a hand on Jezaryah. "Now you're the one working behind enemy lines."

Auriel sighed. "You're right on the front line. My point is, Cecilia wouldn't have embraced God if she hadn't so keenly felt the risk of losing Linus."

Yaron murmured, "Was there never any love?"

"Cecilia loved him." Auriel swallowed hard. "Linus found Cecilia advantageous."

Maybe picking up Jezaryah's swirling emotions, Forrest shifted in his sleep and extended a hand to Julia.

Auriel ran her fingers through her hair. "We need a defense for tomorrow. Forrest must still have something in his heart to brace him against closing the deal."

Did Auriel think Jezaryah hadn't already wracked his mind for anything they could use to defend? Anything at all?

Auriel turned to him. "That's not what I meant."

Jezaryah lowered his eyes. "I'm sorry."

"Don't apologize. You're doing the most amazing job, and Forrest could not possibly have had a better guardian angel." She extended a wing to his, and Jezaryah relaxed. "I keep thinking back to when Satrinah attacked me inside Forrest's heart. What did she want me to avoid?"

Jezaryah moved close to Forrest's head and rested a hand on him, trying to ease the lines of strain on his face. If only he could relax him. If only he could let him know he was loved. If only he could show Forrest the value of what he was trading away. "Most people set the price too low," Forrest had said, not seeing how he was doing exactly the same.

Auriel drifted to the windows. "Cosmiel says these three view indifference as love and love as weakness." Nice of Cosmiel to have put that much thought into the matter. "I'm going one step further. They view conviction as ridiculous, and goodness as negotiable."

Wings sagging, Yaron sighed. "Then it's over. If nothing is non-negotiable, then the only thing that matters is the benefit to Forrest. Their side is offering far more obvious benefits than ours, and they're registering as the greater threat if they're denied."

At that moment, even Auriel couldn't mask the hopelessness rolling off her heart.

Jezaryah covered Forrest with his wings, and he closed his eyes. *God, please, help me.* Finally, a prayer. A real prayer had gotten past the tension. *Give me something to help him, and if there's nothing that can help him, then at least give me the courage to love him right until the end.*

Chapter Thirty

Yolanda sat across the kitchen table from Anna in silence.

"I'll keep you onboard for as long as I can." Anna wrapped her hands around her coffee mug. "If you think it's in your best interest to find another position right away, then I'll write you the best recommendation I can to get you started."

Yolanda waved her off. "I'm not worried about that. Yes, I'd like to keep my job, but I didn't think they'd boot you out so soon. The old man's barely in the ground."

Anna had asked her admin to give a prepared statement to any reporter who'd wanted it, and she'd spent time this morning skimming all the New York papers to see how they viewed her ouster. "The old man's barely in the ground" might as well have come from the *Post*, whereas the *Times* had run an editorial about female CEOs and predatory boards of directors, using Anna Ellington as an example of the glass cliff phenomenon.

Anna said, "Anyway, that's why I didn't bother heading to the office today. If they don't want my work, then they can handle my transition without me at their endless meetings."

Yolanda got up from the table. "Well, you'll be needing to network and find a different company to operate, or maybe write a book about how to deal with stuffed suits." She paused in front of the counter, then turned. "Two nights ago, I was really scared for you. I started praying like crazy. I called my mother and told her, something's wrong with Anna Ellington. She said she'd pray for you too. I guess it didn't work."

Two nights ago, Anna had nearly signed the contract. "I think it did work. But maybe ask her to pray again that I find another job."

Her cell phone rang, and it was the attorney handling Grandfather's estate. "What's up, Lisa?"

Lisa said, "We have a major situation. Do you have half an hour to talk?"

"At your hourly rate, aim for fifteen minutes." Anna took the call into her office. "Is this about me leaving Pilaster?"

"What? No, I didn't even know you'd done that, although I wish you hadn't. Sid got an attorney and is challenging the will."

Anna's vision whited out.

Facing the enormous desk her grandfather had insisted she move from his home to hers, Anna felt again like a little girl called on the carpet over a small infraction, a dark figure repeating that none of this was hers. It never would be hers.

Anna whispered, "On what grounds?"

"Well, if you've left Pilaster, some of this make more sense. He's challenging on the grounds that you aren't fit to execute the will. He wants you removed as executor, and he wants you disinherited."

Anna said, "Last night, he called me. He was outraged, but I didn't think he'd do this."

Challenging the will was more than outrage. He'd had time to decide, to contact an attorney, and get the attorney to send a letter to her attorney before seven o'clock in the morning California time. That wasn't impulsive.

About to take a seat at her desk, Anna stopped. Instead she sat in a leather chair facing the desk. She'd faced into the desk more often than she'd faced away from it.

Your grandmother and I are taking you in because it's the right thing to do, but I expect you to do the right thing, too.

Lisa said, "I'll draft a response to his attorney, but first I need to know if you want to fight it. Sid claims he has a document in which your grandfather laid out steps you should follow that aren't being followed.

Anna went cold all the way to her core.

A sudden emotional turnaround.

Secret documentation.

An opening salvo.

Sid had been offered the same deal she had. On the verge of signing it, Anna had threatened Eric and her children with fifteen years of court battles over nothing at all. She'd branded Yolanda as her betrayer. The very act of considering the contract had distorted her opinion of her closest allies. And now Sid...

There was only one conclusion. Anna's eyes burned. "Yes, I want to fight it."

"Good. This should be straightforward, but I'll reach out to Forrest to make sure he's also onboard. The fact that Sid initially signed papers saying he had no interest in contesting the will means we have a decent shot at defeating him, but he'll be able to tie up the estate for a couple of years."

Anna closed her eyes. *I wish it would stop.*

What if she'd been born into a family that lived in a Brooklyn apartment and took the subway to work every day? What if she'd gone to public school and worn her cousin's hand-me-down sweaters and used the same backpack for three years running? What if she'd worked her way through community college and then been delighted to get an admin position in the Pilaster sales department? Would she have been happy when the new young CEO came in and boosted her salary? Would she have been upset to hear about the upheaval in the C suites? Or would she have set her take-out coffee on her desk and said, "Whatever. It's not as if my work changes"?

Except Anna did care about her job. She was born to do this. She'd grown up with wealth she couldn't possibly have deserved. Grandfather always said none of them deserved it because they hadn't worked for it. He'd even said that to his wife.

If Anna lost her inheritance, well, she had never deserved that either. It wasn't her money to own. If Sid claimed all the cash the same way he'd claimed all the affection and all the attention, then Sid was no doubt taking Grandfather's approval all the way to the bank.

Grandfather would have wanted it this way. Anna had defied Grandfather's dying wish. If she deserved anything at all, she deserved to get cut off from him.

She said to Lisa, "Update me after you hear from Forrest."

Lisa said, "I don't have to tell you this, but don't talk to Sid. Don't block him because we'll want any evidence he's stupid enough to send you, but don't take his calls. Save all his voicemails and any other correspondence, and if there's anything in writing from him about the will, send it to me."

Anna's phone beeped with an incoming call, so she said, "Will do," and got off the call with Lisa in time to get the other one.

It was Frederick from the law firm that handled Anna's everyday issues. He led off with, "Please tell me you haven't signed a termination agreement from Pilaster."

Anna said, "Nothing yet. I'd have run it by you."

He sighed. "Good. They sent me paperwork this morning asking you to forego your severance package."

Anna sat up. "Why?"

"They're claiming you were fired for cause, which of course is ridiculous. With your permission, I'll send back a letter that singes their collective eyebrows and sets out any number of legal threats if they attempt to withhold your payout."

"Go ahead." She tried to calm herself. "Why would they do that?"

"Whoever has a vendetta against you isn't content unless they can also destroy you. Either that, or they're cheap. I've seen it before." Frederick didn't sound worried. Of course not: he was getting paid regardless. "They may tie up your money for a while if they insist on being stubborn." He sighed. "Your employment contract wasn't the best to begin with. They felt entitled to take advantage of you because of your grandfather."

As opposed to, you know, having any kind of gratitude toward their founder.

"Don't put a down payment on a Martha's Vineyard mansion," Frederick added. "This kind of action can go both ways. They may be rattling their sabers, or they may actually have some reason both for the firing and for contesting the severance package."

By the time Anna hung up, she was actively fighting the urge to start shouting. Except that would be unprofessional. You don't shout at people. You do what Grandfather did, and glower like an angry idol on its altar until everyone around you begins the rituals of appeasement.

Anna had sacrificed her family in favor of her job. Then she'd sacrificed her job in favor of nothing at all.

By the time this was over, her grandfather's invisible allies would leave her in the gutter with no career prospects and no family.

If I ever want to work again, I should ask if I can still sign that contract. She could beg Sid to contact them. She could re-open negotiations.

Those demons would have her back on Pilaster's throne in five hours. Sid would drop his suit, and the board of directors would be on their knees fearing for their futures, just as they'd have been for her grandfather.

She bit her lip. How good would it feel to stride back into those offices and clean house? She'd sandblast the C-suite so it sparkled, and then her brand-new allies would rearrange the world so she'd end up with a set of executives who were absolutely loyal. If Grandfather had been an idol on an altar, she could be a queen reigning over an international empire.

No, think of the boys.

Her own thoughts jolted her back to herself. Her sons. Signing to save her own life was only kicking the can down the road. In forty years, Gavin or Ryan would face the same no-win scenario she was facing.

Worse, what if the Ellington curse continued the same way it had before? What the demons killed Ryan and Gavin the way they'd killed her father and her uncle? The contract would pass to her grandchildren instead. These entities—? They could hold the threads of her sons' lives in their hands and snip them off. Her sons could die if she signed. Her grandchildren could be orphans.

People laughed about the Ellington curse, but that's how the world should work: parents *should* sacrifice for their children, not sacrifice their children to save themselves.

At least her grandfather hadn't done that. He'd signed his contract before he even knew her grandmother. Although...there was that nebulous woman, some woman before Grandma.

Regardless, Anna wasn't her grandfather. If her children's peace and safety required her destitution, then that's what it required.

Destitution...or perhaps her absence. How could someone as messed up as Anna ever be a good mother? What example did she have? Her iron-clad grandfather? Her enabling grandmother?

I should die now. My kids would be better off without a mother.

Eyes closed, Anna fought tears. Sharon was good with the boys. Eric and Sharon would take over seamlessly, and the kids' lives would be smoother without having to split parenting time.

Die now, and then...silence. Cessation. No stress about her job or her inheritance or whether people were laughing at the curse. No brother in the teeth of a demon. No nothing.

It sounded peaceful. She could walk away from this shattered life straight into nothing.

If she died now, she'd miss Gavin's kindergarten graduation.

Again, she jolted free of her entangled thoughts.

That was dumb, but—well, Gavin needed her. Ryan needed her, too. They didn't deserve to grow up with the knowledge that their mother had checked out of her life because she'd lost a job. Gavin was so proud whenever she showed up at his events. He'd want her at his kindergarten graduation. The boys would never know about the contract unless their father told them, but why would he? Instead they'd assume a single professional setback—or any setback—was a reason to lose hope.

In twenty years, when Gavin lost his job, or when Ryan failed a college class, did she want them to check out of life, too? She would want to tell them that giving up wasn't an option, even if they had to give up on one specific dream. In the face of failure, they could find the strength to create themselves over again.

Grandma had kept trying. Grandma had suffered more

"setbacks" than any human being on earth. She'd experienced both her sons dying, then raised her grandchildren and lived the heartbreak of rejection by those same grandchildren. She'd endured a loveless marriage to a financial and emotional abuser. Through all that, she'd kept striving to show her grandkids a light to the path forward.

Grandma had pushed through for decades. That meant Anna could white-knuckle at least through the next week, right?

Maybe Sid would back down. Maybe Forrest could talk sense to him. Maybe Anna's golden parachute would open enough to float her through the gap until her next job, and maybe her sons wouldn't grow up despising her for losing everything.

Everything she had, she'd been given by demons. But maybe her boys could grow up safe from that, too.

She reached for the prayer shawl, thinking of a woman's hands holding two needles in a Brooklyn apartment, knitting two stitches together and yarning over. Yarn in one continuous strand, looping into itself to create a half-circle of fabric. So many myths used yarn-craft as a metaphor for life itself, except Anna had no idea what would happen once this part of her life finished casting off.

Chapter Thirty-One

In the Divine Temple, Cosmiel refused to make his request until he got an invitation to the inner sanctum. He didn't want to do this in front of the choirs the way he'd done with the shawl. He wasn't even going to make his request here, not among other angels, not with watchers, not among the pure ones. He'd stopped considering himself pure two thousand years ago, after he started regularly annexing demonic techniques for defending souls on the brink of damnation. Some impurities shouldn't be voiced among the other angels. What he wanted wasn't sinful, but it might cause scandal.

Maybe he'd get a private audience with God, and maybe not, but he wouldn't proceed unless no one could overhear. To be honest with himself—and Cosmiel was always honest with himself—he didn't even want God to overhear it. Cosmiel was not only about to cross the line—he was about to race over it like a quarterback with a football tucked under his arm and two seconds left in the fourth quarter.

One of the Temple angels appeared before Cosmiel, draped in white robes and with mahogany eyes that glimmered in wonder. How long had it been since Cosmiel had the luxury of wonder? How long since he'd felt intoxicated by God's purity and absorbed in the marvels of eternity?

He arose to follow the angel. Not today, that was for sure. Likely not tomorrow, either. In fact, best to cross off the rest of the year.

Two angels held censers at the entrance of the inner sanctum, and Cosmiel passed through a cloud of incense composed of the prayers of the saints. It had a gorgeous smell and created a nebula in the air, bright sparks against his black hole of a heart.

In the inner sanctum, he processed as deep as he could. God's heart beat here. Here Cosmiel should be encountering God face to Face, and instead Cosmiel wanted to hide his eyes. His instincts screamed to drop to his knees with his arms crossed over his chest and his wings tight to his back. Instead he remained standing because as much as he longed to adore, he couldn't risk losing himself here. Not with all three Ellington siblings on the line.

They were going to fall. They'd always been certain to fall, but Cosmiel still had to try.

Cosmiel crossed his arms over his chest and stood with his eyes lowered. God remained silent, and Cosmiel tightened his wings against his back. *I'm sorry.* He kept thinking it over and over. *I'm sorry. I'm sorry to do this, only I don't know what else I can do.*

God let him wait until he was ready. God always did. This time it felt worse.

Finally, Cosmiel gathered himself. "Father, I need your permission to work a miracle, or something that seems like a miracle."

"Tell me."

Cosmiel looked up to find himself meeting the eyes of Christ.

Tell me, said the Holy Spirit inside Cosmiel's heart.

God had always known what Cosmiel was going to ask, what he wanted, why he wanted it. Cosmiel burned with frustration and reflexively offered it up for Forrest, whose own frustration was driving him into Satan's arms.

"Tell me what action you want to take," said the Father.

Cosmiel shuddered. "I won't do it without Your permission. My current assignment is beyond my limits. Leading my team to the best of my ability has only dead-ended them. It's my fault, and three human souls are going to pay for my mistakes."

Jesus said, "In what way?"

Cosmiel shook his head. "I directed all three guardians in how to give their charges the best fighting chance they could. Instead, we've lost Sid. We're on the cusp of losing Forrest, and if we lose him, then we'll lose Anna too. Anna just burst the last two of her thought bubbles, and now she's exposed. If they can't tempt Anna into a new contract, they're going to push her to take her own life."

Jesus said, "Would it surprise you that Auriel has already been to me and claimed responsibility?"

Cosmiel's head jerked up. "She's wrong. I'm the one spearheading the defense. The failure lies on my shoulders, and mine alone."

You may want to examine that conviction, the Holy Spirit prompted.

Jesus said, "Are you implying I would punish three human souls because of your well-intentioned mistakes?"

Cosmiel stepped back.

Jesus said, "You never had a desire to harm Anna, Sid, or Forrest."

That was a statement, not a question.

The Holy Spirit added, *Where do you feel you've fallen short?*

"In the results." Cosmiel turned his head aside. "I'm asking for authority to intervene hard. If you give me permission, I can undercut every method our enemies have of contracting with Forrest. I want to approach him myself, immediately, in human form, and give him something important enough that he'll come onboard with us."

Jesus frowned. "I don't buy their souls from them."

Cosmiel clenched his hands. "But with your permission, I will. I'm willing to do whatever Forrest wants in order to keep him with you."

Jesus shook His head. Inside, the Holy Spirit grieved at the suggestion.

Cosmiel looked into the face of the Father. "Please! I'll trade for Forrest's soul—and for Anna's too—just to keep them safe. I'll show them proof that you love them. They believe gifts are love and love is weakness. Let me give them gifts in your name so they'll recognize how much you love them."

God remained silent. That was a refusal.

Cosmiel's shoulders sagged, and his wings dropped.

The Holy Spirit moved in his heart. *Don't I love them as much as you do?*

"More," Cosmiel whispered.

Jesus said, "And I love them, too."

"Enough to die for them." Cosmiel looked up. "I don't understand why I can't follow your lead. Let me give them something they can perceive, even at cost of myself. If I can jumpstart their understanding, they'll accept the gift of faith. Then they'll love you. Once they love you, they'll see how everything the enemy offers is valueless."

The Holy Spirit added, *Is that love? Or would that be indebtedness?*

Cosmiel said, "To them, there's no difference. They're broken."

The Holy Spirit's sadness meant Cosmiel's plan would only break them further.

His wings flared, and he looked from Jesus to the Father and back again. "How would it break them to know they're loved?"

Jesus said, "You said yourself they have a distorted paradigm for love. Playing into that distortion perpetuates the misunderstanding. I love them for who they are. If we lead off with gifts and favors, then what happens when they want to show me they love me, too?"

The Holy Spirit said, *If they don't first know who they are, they can't offer themselves. They're willing to sign away their souls because they believe those souls have no value.*

Cosmiel urged, "Let me show them their value. I'll step into that role, and I'll lead them to you."

Jesus said, "I paid for their souls. They can claim that at any time."

That felt final. The Holy Spirit was likewise inflexible, and Cosmiel didn't raise his eyes to the Father for a threefold confirmation.

Cosmiel said, "The enemy has promised to reach out to Forrest today. Can I please keep the enemy away from him beyond twenty-four hours?"

Jesus said, "A longer silence isn't going to change the outcome. Think of how long he waited on his grandfather for approval, and even past death, he still craves that approval."

Cosmiel would walk out of here and head back to Auriel. The first thing he'd say was that she had no cause to accept responsibility for the three siblings' damnation. She had in every way acted honorably, and she'd never flagged in her efforts. If Special Ops managed to hold even one sibling, it would be to her credit.

Cosmiel folded his arms. "Can I give Forrest a vision of his grandfather in Hell?"

Jesus said, "You know the answer."

Yes, but as with all lost causes, he'd had to follow through.

There was nothing else, nothing palatable. Paul had written to the Romans that he could even wish himself lost if it meant others were saved, but Cosmiel couldn't bring himself that far. He'd seen what had happened when a guardian had gone that route to get his charge into Heaven.

The Holy Spirit swirled around and through Cosmiel until the angel's eyes burned. This was the hard limit. God's commitment to a soul's free will meant that while demons engaged in wholesale temptation, the angels couldn't. They could tempt a young man to volunteer in a soup kitchen because his crush also volunteered there, but they couldn't tempt him to accept salvation. If they did that, then the human soul was accepting the temptation rather than God. Whatever the soul had been tempted with became its idol, and afterward the soul was in a worse place than at the start.

God had chosen to make them in His own image. God wasn't going to pervert that image in order to compel their love.

But why couldn't the angels at least lock away the most destructive choices? Human parents gave their children controlled ways to fail. They let their child brush by a hot stove so they'd avoid sticking their fingers into an open flame.

Cosmiel clenched his hands and tried not to sound petulant. "What can I do?"

Jesus said, "You can keep offering each of your assignments the best alternative, and you can pray for them to keep receiving the grace to accept it. You can refuse to give up hope."

In other words, nothing extra.

Cosmiel said, "Indri. Can you please comfort her? Indri doesn't deserve to suffer."

The Holy Spirit warmed Cosmiel's heart. *Of course. Always.*

Filled with frustration, Cosmiel bowed his head. "Thank you for hearing me."

He didn't want to say thank you. He wanted to keep fighting, but as always, he recognized a lost cause. It was just, sometimes, sometimes he wished some causes would come his way that weren't already the equivalent of a burning munitions factory.

Jesus said, "Before you go, I have a gift for you."

Cosmiel's heart recoiled, but he didn't snap a question about why it was okay for Jesus to give Cosmiel a gift when Cosmiel couldn't give Forrest a gift. It was a truism among the angels that you never refuse a gift from God. Instead, Cosmiel put out his hands, and Jesus filled them with four opals.

They thrummed against his palm. Cosmiel's chest tightened because each of these stones was a feeling. Specifically, the knowledge and experience of how God felt about you.

Gazing into them, Cosmiel fought dread. *This isn't a gift.*

He choked out, "Thank you."

Jesus said, "They're for whomever needs them."

Cosmiel tucked them into his heart, but he double-walled the Guard, taking no chance of setting off one of these little bombs within himself. "I'll do my best."

Jesus rested a hand on Cosmiel's forehead, a blessing. "Your competency was never in question."

Chapter Thirty-Two

When Cosmiel flashed to Auriel, he expected to find her at Forrest's side. Instead, he arrived in Auriel's garden where she prayed among the tall flowers, eyes closed and senses withdrawn. By turns she radiated urgency, demands, desperation, and hopelessness.

She can't go on this way, Cosmiel prayed, settling down to face her. *Please strengthen her.*

In this layer of Heaven, Auriel's gardens spread out in every direction, bordered by grassland. Birds darted overhead, and still higher, the clouds drifted. Seedheads waved in the wind, and the two angels were isolated from everyone.

They needed to be with Forrest. Her retreat meant she'd run out of strength.

When Auriel opened her eyes, Cosmiel extended his wingtips to hers.

Auriel didn't meet them. "I should have believed you. You said there was no hope."

"You didn't hold back. At no moment have you withheld help from the siblings."

"As of an hour ago, Anna was considering either new negotiations on a contract or maybe suicide. Sid's already signed. In the next few hours, Satrinah will approach Forrest, and he'll be signed." Auriel tucked her head to her knees. "I don't want to hate, but I hate what the enemy does to human souls. I hate how they take every good and noble thing about the human heart and weaponize it against them. I hate how the humans accept what Satan's offering as if it's the best possible good, and then I hate that we can't raise the curtain and show them what they're setting aside."

Cosmiel shuddered. Wasn't that what he'd just asked permission to do?

Auriel gestured to the garden. "I should have stuck with botany."

"You're a great botanist. I would regret losing you, though." He offered a smile. "Would you be happy doing just botany? You'd get bored."

She blinked hard. "Try me."

Cosmiel's heart broke. "You need time off."

"I'll get it after. These are the critical hours."

Cosmiel bit his lip. "Then it's critical to have angels at the top of their game."

Auriel shook her head. "I'm not going to crumble. Until the minute they're in Hell, I'm sticking to the assignment."

Cosmiel reached past the doubled Guard into his heart. "Then I have a gift for you." As he placed an opal onto her palm, he added, "Or rather, God has a gift for you."

The moment it came in contact with her, she gasped. Trembling, she met his eyes.

He assured her, "I received three more, along with the instruction to decide who needs them."

Auriel cradled the nugget, and then she did the thing Cosmiel wouldn't have been brave enough to do: she accepted it into her soul.

Her body shimmered like mother of pearl, and her face transformed with light.

Praying and aching, Cosmiel sat with Auriel while she accepted God's gift of feeling exactly how He saw her. He'd be revealing to Auriel all His particular care for her, His concerns, His pride in her work, His joy in her brilliance. She glowed with delight as He refilled her heart and strengthened her from the inside out.

When God spoke to you, He didn't use the name everyone else used. That 'el' at the end of so many angel names meant "of God." Speaking to you Himself, God would alter it to "shêli" or simply "li," meaning, "of mine." *Auri'li*, He'd say. It was the best sound in the world, when God used your pet name. Auriel needed to hear it. Needed to hear it over and over.

This was good for her. Auriel needed a dose of God's perspective, not simply to know she was loved. He'd let her feel the way He noticed all the little details she'd covered to help the people under her protection, and the extra things she'd done to comfort the guardians while keeping them fully involved in the fight. God appreciated her efforts, and He'd be letting her experience that appreciation.

Cosmiel retreated into himself while Auriel relaxed into God's heart. His initial thought that this wasn't a gift had been unkind. It was exactly the gift Auriel needed.

Auriel herself had been a guardian, so she knew, intimately knew, the pressures and the anxieties. She'd watched intergenerational evil play out in the lives of too many humans adjacent to her own, so when she'd returned to Special Ops afterward, she'd volunteered for those assignments. Surely God approved of her selfless advocacy for guardians, and He would reflect it back so she could see it.

Plus, she's an excellent botanist, Cosmiel told God. *I really don't want to lose her to the herb gardens of the world.*

In Cosmiel's heart, God smiled.

When Cosmiel returned to himself, he found Auriel with her knees tucked to her chest and her wings cupped around herself—but not tight. Sparkles glinted in her champagne-toned eyes.

Thank you, he prayed.

Auriel sat straighter. "We have a couple of hours, and Jezaryah needs anything we can give him to fight with."

Cosmiel said, "I have three more gems like that one."

Auriel rested her chin on her forearms. "Noted. Thinking out loud, everything we've done to now has worked in our enemies' favor."

Cosmiel said, "Except for the thought bubbles."

"Those helped, but at the rate we're going, I have to assume even the thought bubbles might bolster Satrinah's offer." Her eyes narrowed. "A month ago, if you presented this situation hypothetically, I'd have suggested we give each of the guardians one gem and let them deploy it in their charge's heart at a time when the charge is most vulnerable to despair."

Cosmiel recoiled. "You're saying you wouldn't do that now?"

"As of now, I am second-guessing everything I know about intergenerational evil, on the grounds that everything I know has been undermined by enemies who know even more. Granted, they invented intergenerational evil, but Satrinah's innovation represents a radical change in the terms of engagement." She pursed her lips. "God gave these to you, so I have to assume they're of help to Anna and Forrest. How best to use them?"

Cosmiel prompted, "Keep thinking out loud. If we'd had these gems from the start, when would you have recommended deploying one in Anna's heart?"

"The first time she came near to doing it and then backed off." Auriel hadn't hesitated. "We'd have wanted her to come to the realization that she'd almost rejected God's love."

Cosmiel said, "Knowing what we know now, how would she have responded?"

"Badly." Auriel ran her fingers over a flower stem. "They've been told by academics and clergy that God loves them, but by the same token, they were told, and believe, their grandfather loved them."

Cosmiel's nose wrinkled. "Ah. You're saying their very definition is wrong."

"Experiencing real love leaves all three of them feeling suspicious. Consider Anna's relationship with Eric, where he loved her and she distanced herself in order to keep soliciting approval from her grandfather. Forrest married a cold woman who's self-absorbed. He provides for her while she remains emotionally out of reach, and I have to assume he's most comfortable keeping it that way. Sid hasn't had a long-term romantic attachment in years. Genuine love is threatening to all three. The closest they've come to experiencing love is what they have with each other, but instead of love, they've branded that as loyalty."

Cosmiel said, "Hence Sid's volcanic response to Anna's rejection of the contract. She was disloyal."

"Exactly. Now, take Anna on the night she nearly signed, and inject her with an understanding of how much God loves her. Her first response would be denial. Her second would be humiliation, and then the third would be mistrust. She would attempt to ease the cognitive dissonance by re-embracing her grandfather's transactional-but-familiar version of love, and she'd do it with an immediate signature."

Cosmiel frowned. "And yet God gave us these as gifts for them."

"Did He specify these were gifts for the siblings?" Auriel's eyes tightened. "Or are they just gifts?"

Cosmiel shrugged. "Given what I was praying, I assumed they were for our use in converting the siblings."

"I would have assumed that too, but we need to be circumspect. What had you asked Him?"

Cosmiel flinched. "He refused, so it doesn't matter. He said the gems were for whomever needed them."

Auriel glanced aside, smiling with the afterglow of her prayer. "Thank you for deciding I needed one. I agree with your instincts. On the assumption that they're for Anna, Sid, and Forrest, we should give one each to Turmiel, Indri, and Jezaryah."

Cosmiel handed her the Guarded packet of gemstones. "Do that now, and then join me. I'll be with Jezaryah. Maybe some last-ditch defense will present itself."

There had to be something, or else God wouldn't have given Cosmiel the gems. Or maybe the same way one gem was for Auriel, the remaining gems were intended for three heartbroken guardian angels. Angels needed Him too.

Auriel said, "One last caution. Anna was sure her grandfather is in Heaven and at peace. She still hasn't questioned that. I assume the same is true for Forrest. If we deploy these in the humans' hearts too soon, will they assume they can act as selfishly as they want without distorting their relationship with the Divine?"

Cosmiel said, "Let me turn it around. Would they work harder to please God if they assume God is silent because love is silent?"

"I refuse to turn their image of God into an abuser like their grandfather." Auriel got to her feet. "Appeal to them as if God were their grandfather, and God will get their blind obedience. That would be thorough and performative, and they'd always hold back." Auriel's eyes darkened. "When they model love on their grandfather, they think love is demanding and absent. When they think of their grandmother, they frame love as weakness. I have no idea how to tackle that, but with the countdown clock measuring in minutes, we're going to have to."

Auriel hadn't even voiced to Cosmiel her fear of what would happen if they used one of those gems on Sid. In his current state, God's perception of him would be...well, mixed.

Auriel had never sinned. She had no idea how it would feel to face God having made a knowing choice to act against Him. To look Him in the eyes and be conscious of her own filth...it wasn't something she ever wanted to happen.

Cosmiel had handed over all three gems without question. He shouldn't do that, except that he'd worked with her for so long that he trusted her judgment.

It went both ways. A thousand years ago, Cosmiel had given an order that Auriel couldn't see as anything other than disastrous. Carrying it out was going to cause her pain and lead to defeat—and she knew it. He knew it, too. She would have doubted anyone else, but Cosmiel she'd followed without hesitation. The assignment had worked out. Her defeat had been a part of an overall victory because she trusted him.

Still, should *she* have these gems? When Auriel had visited the inner sanctuary, God hadn't given her anything beyond reassurance. Cosmiel was her boss, though. Maybe it was more fitting to give them to him, and God never fussed about efficiency.

If anything, when it came to winning souls, God seemed to love inefficiency. One at a time, He met them where they were, courted them, worked with their idiosyncrasies, and then invited them to draw closer.

Auriel approached Turmiel with a gem. "I have no instructions as to its use." Eyes lowered, she sighed. "Pray and discern."

She tried delivering a gem to Indri, only to find Indri in the company of the angelic grief support ministers. They maintained a twilight sanctuary in the heavenly hills, the ministers quiet in their drab uniforms as they moved among the bereaved guardians. Geron sat at Indri's side, arms around her as she cried and prayed.

Indri hadn't fully lost Sid, but Auriel understood why she'd come here. To all intents, Satrinah had become Sid's guardian. Indri needed to grieve what was, and then she could do what Geron had done and retire to decades of prayer.

The ministering angels confirmed that Indri hadn't left a state of prayer for hours. Auriel would not disturb her. Why would she? Indri might in theory be able to flaming-arrow a gem into Sid's heart, but what then? Leave Sid in despair?

No, best to wait with that flaming arrow nocked. If Sid ever reached the point of thinking, "Now neither side wants me," that would be the time to shoot. Auriel wasn't sure of anything right now, but of that she felt closest to certain.

Still holding Indri's gem, Auriel flashed to Jezaryah. She'd saved him for last because here the stakes were highest, and here she'd remain. Cosmiel was already with him, and he double-checked the Guard surrounding Forrest's office while she handed it over.

Jezaryah tucked the opal into his heart, then pivoted to stare through two walls at the waiting room. His feathers flared, and he breathed, "Oh, this is bad."

Chapter Thirty-Three

Jezaryah's armor flashed into place, but he didn't form up his sword. There was nothing to fight. Forrest had given permission to the demons—permission to talk, permission to offer gifts, and permission to appear in person.

But why that *person?* Jezaryah prayed.

Satrinah was in a body, and that body looked just like Linus Ellington.

Forrest's congressional intern knocked on the door to bring him a coffee. "A visitor arrived to see you. He's not on the schedule, but he says you're expecting him." The young man looked unconcerned. "Your eleven-thirty appointment just rescheduled for tomorrow, so you have some time if you want me to send him in."

Forrest's adrenaline spiked—and not from the warm ceramic of a coffee cup against his palms. A lifetime of deferred promises was coming to roost. In every direction, Forrest could see one thing: recognition.

Jezaryah saw only one thing: loss.

Forrest prompted, "What's his name?"

Momentarily confused, the intern said, "Um—I forgot to ask."

Of course not. Satrinah's glamour had blinded the young man enough that he didn't think about the details Satrinah wanted not to give. The young man wouldn't make the connection that their guest looked like Linus Ellington from thirty years ago. He likely wouldn't ever think of this encounter again.

If anything, all this made Forrest even more eager. "Sure, send him in."

Auriel urged Jezaryah, *Creep him out. Make him feel offended. Say they're disrespecting his grandfather.*

Cosmiel offered no advice. Of course not—he'd already given up.

The intern escorted Satrinah-as-Linus into the office, and Forrest stood, his face a well-practiced blankness.

Jezaryah shot Forrest full of outrage that drained away like rainwater into a leeching field.

Linus Ellington's clone crossed the room to shake Forrest's hand. Satrinah said, "I appreciate the opportunity of a face-to-face meeting."

Her voice was Ellington's. She was even mimicking his mannerisms.

Jezaryah probed her, and her eyes flashed at him as she smiled. She wasn't carrying Linus Ellington's soul but rather running Linus's connection to Forrest right through her heart. Linus-in-Hell must be luxuriating in the attention, and she was playing him like a mandolin. Worse, Satrinah was using that same attachment to play Forrest like a mandolin. With a tight smile, she was withholding approval, the same way Linus would have. She was going to draw Forrest out and tempt him to win her over.

Forrest gave a professional, "Thank you for coming. Would you care to sit? Coffee?"

Instead of going to the desk, Satrinah took her place on a couch near the window, and Forrest sat on a leather chair facing her. Demons hated wearing bodies, but Satrinah must have practiced every one of Linus Ellington's mannerisms, even his slight hesitation due to knee pain. By moving to a pair of couches rather than to the desk, she'd maneuvered Forrest into a familiar position. For pity's sake, the seats were even at the same angles they'd been at in the family home.

Jezaryah pushed again for outrage. How dare they use his grandfather's visage? Instead, Forrest was dazzled. "How are you doing this?"

Satrinah inclined her head. "I nurtured your grandfather's career for sixty years. He thrived under me. This," and she gestured to herself, "is a testament to how I remember him at his best."

This was the Linus Ellington who had opened his door to three newly orphaned grandchildren, ushering them inside and then bestowing a cold glare on his wife as she fussed over Sid with his runny nose. Linus Ellington at this age had been the unquestioned emperor of his world, lord of his manor, and a cold substitute for Forrest's own father.

Jezaryah's eyes burned. Forrest had been so small, so hungry for reassurance. Everything he'd wanted, his grandfather could have provided. Could have, if he'd chosen to.

Forrest breathed, "It's exact."

"If it weren't, you'd have presumed my offer a plot by your political enemies—who, I might add, are about to become my political enemies." She copied Linus Ellington's inflection, but added an even sharper edge. With the skill of a lifelong abuser, she'd even managed in that single sentence to blame Forrest for his reasonable skepticism. "I've already secured for Sid the role he believes will cement his career. In the coming weeks, I will take similar steps to secure your re-election. Tell me, Congressman Ellington, what will settle your heart to believe I am what I say?"

She made it sound like the only reasonable objection was verifying her identity, and Forrest was falling for it. His soul was opaquing before Jezaryah's eyes. Cosmiel tried to lower the ambient temperature, but nothing changed. Of course not. He'd done it for Anna, so their enemies were prepared. Primed for failure, Cosmiel hadn't come up with a backup.

Satrinah raised a gold ring to the light: Linus Ellington's wedding band. "And here is a token for you, to represent our union to one another."

Jezaryah tried to shoot Forrest full of disgust, and Forrest paled. "He was buried wearing this."

"Why waste the eternal symbol of his heart underground? His soul is no longer in that body." Satrinah sounded as clinical as

Linus Ellington ever had. "You were present at the coffin's sealing, and you saw it buried. You know there's no means of procuring this ring other than my being who I say I am." Satrinah forced a cold smile. "Don't render my efforts for nothing. Accept this ring as proof of my identity, as well as proof of my commitment."

Obligation. Guilt. The threat that Forrest wasn't appreciative enough. Satrinah was a master, and they were nothing but amateurs.

Jezaryah exclaimed, "Can she do that? The token comes from the human, not from the demon."

Satrinah glanced at them, laughter dancing in her eyes.

Auriel said, "Forrest's token is a separate matter. They can give him anything they want."

Desperate, Jezaryah tried again to disgust Forrest. *That was on his dead body.*

Forrest shifted the ring in the light and looked at the inscription on the inside of the ring. *Eternally mine.* "I'm already married," he offered with an unnerved laugh.

Satrinah said, "I will look after your wife as well as you. Everything matters to me, Forrest. I see how hard you've worked to make a good life for her."

That hadn't been his objection—but, well, now it was. Satrinah kept pivoting, forcing him to fight the wrong battles.

On the other hand, Forrest was a politician, and Jezaryah flagged that thought. Anyone who won't directly answer a question has a reason not to answer it.

The price is too high. Jezaryah reached past Forrest's emotions and into his professional skills. *What isn't being said here? If it's just an agreement, why is it as binding as a marriage?*

Forrest knew about spin. He knew about not getting locked into a stand forever.

Satrinah's eyes narrowed. "You doubt me, Forrest?"

The bond to Linus was engaged in its highest gear, turning hard. Doubt was ingratitude. Doubt would get punished. In the face of that stare, saying yes was the only way out. Say yes, and don't expect more.

She said, "Don't question that I would uphold my end of the deal the same way I did for your grandfather, and the same way I have done for Sid. As for you, I'm asking so little." Her eyes glinted, but she wasn't using glamour on him. For this deal to take, he had to be one hundred percent willing.

Jezaryah couldn't keep Forrest's deliberations in the logical zone, so instead he shifted into pure emotion. *I'm not good enough. They'll see I can't uphold my end of the bargain.*

Concern shuddered through Forrest, but not enough. It was like jumping as hard as you could on the Brooklyn Bridge and expecting it to collapse.

They'll see who I really am.

This was always Forrest's fear: that Grandfather had recognized him as a failure, even as a child, and that's why he'd embraced Sid and rejected Forrest.

This creature will control me the way Grandfather did, and they'll hate me for being so weak.

This was everything Forrest had feared. Everything. A guardian shouldn't use that private information against his own charge, but now?

Once they see me—knowing who I am—they'll reject me too.

Jezaryah sent electricity through all the pain of Grandfather's rejection. He evoked as much of the grief and bewilderment as he could, and he left it churning in Forrest's heart. It might break Forrest, but Jezaryah could work with brokenness. He couldn't work with damnation.

Then, up from the base of Forrest's soul, Jezaryah experienced a recollection of his childhood. Because Satrinah too had slipped into Forrest's heart, leering, tugging at the strings of Linus Ellington's soul and bringing Forrest to heel. She'd gotten in her hook and fished up a memory.

Forrest as a little boy had stood at Grandfather's desk. He wasn't supposed to be there, but he'd snuck in. Now he was touching things. Uncapping the pens. Opening the boxes. Finding all the drawers locked. Grandfather had surprised him by walking in.

Forrest, terrified. Grandfather, accusatory. Was his grandson a thief? Forrest, backing away. No, no, no.

Except, yes. He'd opened the cigar box and found the change, and he'd kept the only nickel in the box.

He'd escaped without Grandfather knowing. But now Forrest burned because he'd lied. Always, always, always, he'd never been good enough.

Grandfather had punished Anna for the missing nickel. He said it was a special coin. They were all special coins. The next night, Forrest snuck back into the office and put it back in the box, but there was already another nickel in there. No, two. Maybe Anna had put one in. Maybe Grandma Cecilia had done it. Unsure what to do, he'd left his as well. He was a thief. A little thief who'd let his sister take the blame.

When Grandfather had told him about investments, he'd told Forrest every week, when he got his allowance, to "invest" some back in that horrible box. Every week, Forrest had done it. He'd never told the other two why. They'd thought he liked doing it.

As Satrinah brought up the memory of the cigar box, Forrest shuddered with the weight of a debt he could never repay. The weight of a home and an education and an entrance ramp to his career.

As a last resort, Jezaryah turned Forrest's thoughts to Anna. He couldn't abandon her.

Forrest met Satrinah's eyes. "Can you protect my sister, too?"

They were all in this together.

Forrest agreed to the bargain, and at that moment, Jezaryah was cut off.

Chapter Thirty-Four

Forrest's soul ejected Jezaryah like the opposite end of a magnet, and Cosmiel lunged to catch him. Sophiel's sigil shot past them both and cracked down the middle when it hit the floor.

No. Blast it, no. Sid, gone. Forrest, gone. Was Anna next, and all three would topple like dominos?

Moloch coalesced behind the material forms of Forrest and Satrinah. "You can leave now. Your interference is finished."

Nauseated, Cosmiel tried to shield Jezaryah from Moloch, but the guardian pushed to his feet, wings flared.

With her sword drawn, Auriel got between them. The angels had no right to be here now. There was no protection. If Moloch struck, he'd take down all three.

Satrinah smiled with Linus's trademark restraint. "I gave the ring to you as a seal. To finalize our agreement, I require a seal from you as well."

Forrest gazed into his grandfather's eyes. "What kind of seal?"

Jezaryah urged, "It's too much. Whatever she's asking, it's too much."

Cosmiel sent, *We have to leave.*

Jezaryah sent back anger.

"The choice is yours." Satrinah looked right into Forrest's eyes with the same expression his grandfather had whenever he'd noticed Forrest long enough to disapprove of him. "Choose something that represents everything I'm offering to you. It doesn't have to be grand. You don't even have to hand it over to me. The token just needs to be something you can touch, and it should have meaning."

Forrest looked at his grandfather's wedding ring, then glanced at the ring on his own finger.

Jezaryah breathed, "It's at home. The thing you want is at home."

The guardian had nothing left. Nothing but seconds unless this ploy worked, in which case he had nothing but minutes.

Satrinah prompted, "Your ring is important to you. Make that your token."

Jezaryah replied, "That ring already signifies a bond."

Shaking his head, Forrest looked again at his hand. "I have my grandmother's ring at home. It's the mate of this ring, so that can be my token for you."

Satrinah's eyes flashed, and Forrest flinched. Even so, she couldn't object. The human had to choose the token. Irritated, she said, "Get it now."

Forrest glanced at his desk.

"Your work can wait. I will ensure your work can wait." Satrinah stood. "Go home and retrieve the token. All you need to do is touch it to seal our agreement." She recovered her equilibrium and again put on Linus's smile. "I'm so pleased, Forrest."

Jezaryah's heart blazed, but Cosmiel's crumpled at the same time. For decades, Linus Ellington had withheld all of this when he could have given it as easily as Satrinah lied about giving it now.

Forrest handed back the ring, but Satrinah demurred. "Keep it. It's fitting to preserve the two rings together."

Although Jezaryah was shaking, Forrest's hands were steady as he put the ring in his pocket. Then he offered a hand to Satrinah. "Thank you. Here's to a long and fruitful partnership."

It was finished. Cosmiel flashed Jezaryah from the room back into Heaven, but an outraged Jezaryah anchored himself to creation. His grip wrenched the space around them, and with a dizzying lurch, Cosmiel got yanked back from Heaven with the equivalent of angelic whiplash. They crashed into creation in Washington DC's National Cathedral.

Jezaryah drew his sword on Cosmiel and blasted him to the far wall. "It isn't finished!"

Cosmiel spread his wings and raised both hands. "He's signed! You can't go back."

"It's not done until Forrest hands over the token." Jezaryah's sword threw sparks, as did his eyes. "It's going to take half an hour to drive to Bethesda. I can still reach him a little."

Auriel appeared, radiating surprise that they were still in creation. Colors streamed across the ceiling, the light distorting as where it hit the glass and then distorting again when it kaleidoscoped across the opposite wall.

Jezaryah was crazed. Cosmiel's heart bled. "Half an hour isn't going to make a difference."

"I'm not giving up!" Jezaryah strode toward Cosmiel, sword ready. "You gave up from the start because we were fighting a hopeless war, but I'm not giving up."

In the face of the flames shooting off Jezaryah, Cosmiel said, "I'm not 'giving up'. Look at what happened. We've lost."

Every angel in the cathedral was staring. Praying. Their eyes gleamed in the stained light.

"It's not sealed!" Jezaryah's wings spread. "We haven't lost until it's sealed. I'll convince him not to seal it."

Auriel's eyes were downcast, her hands clenched, her wings sagging. Cosmiel lowered his voice. "There is no reasonable hope."

From the heart of the flames, Jezaryah's eyes fogged, as if tears were boiling as soon as they hit his cheeks. "I don't need reasonable hope. I need any hope."

Cosmiel clenched his fists. "He'll reach the token in thirty minutes. What do you think you can do?"

Jezaryah choked out, "I can love him. For thirty more minutes, I can love him."

Cold despite the flames, Cosmiel locked his gaze with Jezaryah's.

Urgent, Jezaryah turned to Auriel. "Can't you have Anna reach out to him? Maybe she'll talk sense."

Cosmiel said, "How's that going to work?" Jezaryah mustn't turn his ire on Auriel. Have him lash out at Cosmiel—that was acceptable. Not her. "Rejecting the deal puts Forrest into the same two-on-one position he was in before. He's in the favored category now! The minute Anna talks to him, he's going to think she's dragging him back into the mire."

Why couldn't Jezaryah see that? Rather than letting Anna pull him free, Forrest would yank her in again.

Pivoting back, Jezaryah stared through Cosmiel. Stared at the failure and the impotence. Now he was tallying one more failure into the column. But they'd both known it was hopeless from the start.

Cosmiel stepped toward him. "We need to fall back and come up with a long-term plan. As of now, our focus switches from how to help Forrest to how we can best help you."

Stone-faced, Jezaryah extended a hand. On it lay the opal gem.

Of course Jezaryah would need reassurance now. "That's a good idea. Use it."

Jezaryah pushed it up against Cosmiel's heart.

Cosmiel backed away. "On yourself."

"Auriel told me to pick how to use it. I'm picking you. Now." Heat rippled off Jezaryah, stinging Cosmiel's face. "You gave up before you started, and now you're surrendering before it's over."

Eye to eye, they stared.

Jezaryah said, "Even if it's for a half hour, I don't want you in charge any longer. You're burnt out. I won't lose Forrest because of you. If you refuse, I'm going back in without support. I still have authority."

Sophiel appeared alongside Auriel, his eyes jet black.

Recoiling from the gem, Cosmiel raised his hands. "This is unreasonable. If you want to pursue Forrest, we need to concentrate on Forrest."

Jezaryah's eyes narrowed. "You're blocking me. You're declaring no hope when it's not finished. You've said there's always hope. *Now* is part of *always*."

Behind him, Auriel said, "There's still a chance until it's sealed."

Sophiel said, "You're spent, Cosmiel. I'll take over."

No. You don't hand over a project in critical failure. You don't give someone else a cause for grief to get yourself off the hook. Not when you'd recognized a lost cause from the first minute.

Auriel said, "Seconded. You need to stand down."

Jezaryah said, "Thirded."

"Stop." Cosmiel looked at Sophiel. "You can't take over. I'm your commanding officer."

"We have rules about standing down for a reason, and if you'll recall," Sophiel said in a very low tone so the other angels in the cathedral wouldn't hear, "we set up that rule because the operative who needs to step down will never do so willingly."

Cosmiel closed his eyes. The ultimate failure.

Auriel said, "If you take the gem, you can stay on the job. You had me take it. It will energize you."

Cosmiel clenched his fists. "There's only one per sibling."

Jezaryah said, "I'm choosing you for Forrest's."

There was no good way out. They wouldn't let him move forward.

On the other hand, a lost cause was already lost. If Cosmiel refused and got furloughed, Forrest was just as lost. If it were all on Jezaryah, then Jezaryah would feel as if he'd failed his charge that much more.

It was better for Jezaryah to blame Cosmiel for all eternity, rather than himself.

There's always hope. Cosmiel had said that too often, and he hadn't believed it.

He always made every sacrifice he could for his team. He had to shield them again.

He let down his barriers and absorbed the gem into his heart.

Chapter Thirty-Five

Cosmiel kept his eyes on the kaleidoscope lights overhead until the gem took him fully out of himself and into the presence of God.

Then, nothing.

Cringing away from his own awareness, Cosmiel waited for the overwhelming judgment and rejection. He kept his eyes on the wall that absorbed the warped wavelengths of light, light that had traveled ninety-two million miles in perfection before hitting the earth and getting stripped of its purity. There it crashed to a stop, splaying out for everyone to see the distorted image of its former beauty.

Still nothing.

Time wasn't passing. That was to say, real time wasn't passing. Part of Cosmiel could sense the cathedral with its echoing stone, the tourists in the narthex, two people at prayer before the altar, and security guards at their stations. Frozen in time, the same way Forrest was frozen in his role and Sid was frozen in his will.

The world around Cosmiel wasn't moving, and neither was God moving within him.

Dread built inside.

It hadn't been like this for Auriel. She'd told Cosmiel to take the gem because she'd drawn strength from knowing what God saw in her. God had reflected back at her all her single-heartedness and earnestness. God had lavished on her praise for all her hidden sacrifices and all her devotion. She'd expected the same for

Cosmiel, but it wouldn't be the same.

Instead God was about to show Cosmiel all his failures. Every time he'd undershot the mark, or overshot it, and some other soul had paid the price...? Every loss, every time he'd been unable to shield his own team from the backlash of the difficult work they were doing? Every way Cosmiel had tainted his own soul? God was readying the scorecard.

That God hadn't shown it yet was a mercy. He was waiting for Cosmiel to brace himself so the revelation wouldn't destroy him. The moment this session concluded, Cosmiel was going to have to wall off God's disappointment in its own airtight compartment so he could function for the next half hour until Forrest was beyond help.

After that, Cosmiel could fall apart. But no, at that point they'd have to shore up Anna or else she'd reach back out to Satrinah on her own. But afterward. After that. Then Cosmiel could try to deal with God's disappointment.

Cosmiel steeled himself and waited.

Not a second had ticked by in Creation. Jezaryah stood with his palm against Cosmiel's chest, that gem only barely dissolved, flames rigid in their dance around his wings.

Auriel wore naked concern in her eyes. Sophiel looked grief-stricken. Of them all, Sophiel suspected best what Cosmiel was about to endure.

Maybe it was better this way, for the open secret between Cosmiel and God to finally be admitted. Together, God and Cosmiel could acknowledge that Cosmiel knew God was disappointed in what he'd done with his life, and maybe Cosmiel would be less tense with Him.

Likewise, it would have been better for Forrest just to accept that his grandfather never loved him. It would have been better for Anna to accept that she was her grandfather's scapegoat. It would have been better for Sid to realize his grandfather didn't love him either, only loving the image of Linus that Linus had projected onto Sid.

Accept where you are, and then you can make better decisions.

It was the basis of the "oh no" checklist.

The frozen cathedral, the light on the walls, the ornate tile, the columns stretching toward the ceiling and meeting overhead like tree branches. The brilliant love of God and the purity of Cosmiel's friends before him. The hot desperation on Jezaryah. The steely darkness of Cosmiel's own heart. All these converged like a symphony with one dissonant tone drawing attention. Even so, Cosmiel felt that one wrong note needed to be there, if only to highlight the purity of the whole.

God was waiting for him. Waiting for...permission?

That was why God hadn't overwhelmed him yet. In all these decisions the humans made, God ensured them a moment of freedom. Cosmiel had been coerced into accepting the gem. If he denied consent right now, God would return Cosmiel to time, and the others wouldn't realize what hadn't happened. They'd consider Cosmiel strengthened for the final battle, and he'd go forward.

If Cosmiel wasn't approaching on his own, then God wanted him to wait until he fully consented.

Except Cosmiel would never be "ready" to face up to everything he'd done to his soul. He'd said it was the service of God, but how could God be served by someone cherry-picking the tactics of their enemies and bleaching them into techniques free of their evil taint? Other than the taint of their conception, that was.

Cosmiel would never willingly sin. Over time, though, by playing so close to fields rioting with flowers of sin, he'd gotten covered with its pollen and saturated with its scent.

He could, in this moment, choose not to have this conversation with God. God would not be any poorer for the lack of encounter, and Cosmiel's assignment would remain his.

Except he kept coming back to that angelic truism: you never turn down a gift from God. God wouldn't have offered Cosmiel a gift that would hurt him. Well, not permanently. It might hurt in the short term—hurt intensely. Over the long term, though, maybe Cosmiel needed to stop denying the obvious.

There was a mosaic of Isaiah's seraphim in the cathedral, their six wings covering themselves as they beheld God Almighty. Two wings covered their feet, two wings covered their hands, and two wings covered their faces. For three thousand years, Cosmiel had felt that image to his core, only he didn't have enough wings to cover everything. God could see right through his flared feathers.

Well, then. Spread the wings. Uncover it all. Let God render judgment on what He had made, on what Cosmiel had ruined.

Stillness.

The cathedral was gone and all awareness of it, only God's spirit looking into Cosmiel's. They were everywhere, and they weren't. This wasn't God's inner sanctum. This was God's heart itself, not located in Heaven or in creation because it stood over and above it all, but within and through it as well.

Responding to his urge to cover up, Cosmiel's wings twitched. God deserved better, but this was all Cosmiel had to offer.

That was all God was asking for, though.

Cosmiel pushed back against the thought.

He was still resisting.

Well, shouldn't he resist? It was fitting for God to love holy and beautiful angels like Auriel and Jezaryah. Unreserved with their love, they offered God one hundred percent of the best of themselves at every turn. Always intent on serving Him, they followed God's law and cared for the poor and the weak and the grieving and the exposed. They set themselves on the line without counting the cost.

And Cosmiel...didn't?

No, Cosmiel was the one dabbling with the edges of evil. He was the one who failed. He always tried to take the blow so his charges wouldn't get hurt, but hurt overcame them anyhow. He was a rock wall standing against the tide, and every time, the waves splashed over the stones.

To be fair, though, retaining walls weren't to prevent water from getting through. They were to prevent the current from eroding the shore. Civilization was built on the ground retained by those walls.

And? And then what?

The wall is doing what it's supposed to do.

Not good enough. Cosmiel's heart blazed hard. Not good enough. He'd never been good enough, but he'd stepped into a role where everyone had to be more than enough. What audacity of spirit had caused him to think he'd be able to take on problems too great for the army? What reprehensible pride danced in his heart that could beguile amazing angels like Auriel and Sophiel away from their own vocations and into this merry-go-round of futility? Then, worse, to copycat their enemy's tactics and wash them into something resembling whiteness so Cosmiel could stain his squad's souls even worse than Satan would have dared?

Wrong. Cosmiel had no power to stain another angel's soul.

Well, okay. But Cosmiel had the power to hand his operatives the tools to stain their own souls.

This wasn't about their souls. God had already met with Auriel about her soul, and she'd emerged energized and pleased. This was about Cosmiel's soul and how God encountered Cosmiel.

Cosmiel closed his eyes, shuddering. An apology. Two apologies.

Maybe, just maybe, Cosmiel should yield the floor to God and let God speak to his heart. Now. In this moment which was also eternity, from God who saw Cosmiel as he'd been made and also saw Cosmiel in the midst of every decision that had helped him become fully himself.

Fully himself wasn't a good thing. Cosmiel always had the harshest losses.

Agreed. Because Cosmiel was one of God's most dedicated angels.

Cosmiel crumbled, and then he saw himself as God saw him. Yes, as a rock wall holding back erosion from the shoreline. God saw him putting himself in front of his team to shield them. God saw Cosmiel pushing harder and further in the defense of every living soul. God saw him wearing himself to tatters trying to keep others covered. God saw him purifying the tactics of the enemy which, in the end, were only tools, and tools could be used for different ends.

Cosmiel thought of Jesus, eating with public sinners, entering their houses and their conversations, but never being stained by their sins. Jesus, purifying those people's hearts because at no point had He said, "This table is too stained for me to sit at," or, "This house has seen too much evil for me to enter its doorway." He'd touched filth without getting filthy, lepers without getting leprosy, and death without eternally dying. He'd walked into Hell and remained the soul of Heaven.

You're doing what I did, Cosmi'li.

Cosmiel pushed it all out there, every moment he flinched to remember. Get it all over with now, and don't leave anything in reserve for God to condemn later. One at a time, though, he felt God's approval and God's encouragement. Some situations might have been handled differently, or better, but at no point had Cosmiel wanted anything other than to serve, to save, to protect, and to safeguard.

In all those places where Cosmiel was most ashamed, God loved him the most. God loved him hardest in the broken places. In all the areas of failure, God saw his greatest successes.

Moreover—no, don't object, let God finish—moreover, all those failures weren't failures. Cosmiel had never controlled the outcome of a human soul's choice. What he'd done in every case— in every single case—was win the humans a clear field in which to exercise their free will. And that? That, My sweet son of My own creation, was success.

Cosmiel went to his knees, covered his face in his hands, then covered his face and feet with his wings.

He wasn't worthy of this kind of love. No one was. But he wanted to be.

God had called Cosmiel one of his most dedicated angels. God was not a liar. Had God ever given upon him? No. Then Cosmiel had to do for Forrest what God had done for him. It was time to get back to the field.

Forrest needed hope, and there was always hope.

Cosmiel came back to himself seeing the stained-glass lights adorning the cathedral walls.

The colors weren't there. They were artifacts, but they didn't really exist. The light was God's. The colors were the souls He was pushing that light through. The opposite wall where the light sprayed out was also to some extent God. It was beautiful.

And Cosmiel was clean.

Cosmiel turned to the three of them. "We have half an hour. Auriel, go to Anna. Anything you can get from her, you do it. But first of all, secure her. If Turmiel thinks it's best to gem her, do it." He turned to Sophiel. "I need you to gum up traffic. Give Jezaryah as many extra minutes as you can. Once you've locked up the Beltway, I want prayer support. Anyone you can ask for prayers, anyone we've ever prayed for, anyone who might have a reason to pray for us? Get them praying. Any human who's ever cared about Forrest or Julia—hit them hard and rally their prayers."

Sophiel vanished.

"Michael," Cosmiel called into thin air, "I need five soldiers who aren't afraid of Moloch. Assign them to Jezaryah." He turned to Jezaryah. "Go back to Forrest as close and for as long as you can. Encourage him to hold back about choosing the token, and worry him about what's become of Sid."

Auriel held up the fourth gem. Cosmiel nodded. "Yes, give that to him. Jezaryah, I'd suggest waiting, but trust your judgment."

It had been Jezaryah's judgment that got Cosmiel to use the gem, after all. And he'd been right. He'd been right about a lot of things.

Five soldiers appeared in full gear. Jezaryah said to Cosmiel, "Am I going back alone? What are you going to do?"

Cosmiel opened his palm and created a very weak copy of

himself, no more than a breath puffed into a Guard. He handed that to Jezaryah for safekeeping along with the gem. "I'm going to Hell."

Chapter Thirty-Six

Wrapped in her shawl while drinking tea, Anna listened to Yolanda working in the kitchen.

Grief felt surprisingly new. Unexpectedly so. Her parents had died, after all. Her grandmother had died. So had her grandfather. After all that, she'd have told any reporter that she understood grief. Now she knew.

Rather, now she *felt*.

As a child, had she grieved? Or had she pulled herself together to take care of her brothers? Had she obeyed her grandfather's adjuring her to be mature and not snivel over things she couldn't change?

At her grandmother's death, had she not stood stoic at her grandfather's side, presenting herself to the world as the up-and-coming CEO of Pilaster Group? He'd never cried, so neither had she. He'd solemnly accepted condolences, so she'd learned to perform.

She'd repeated that performance at his death.

Sid, though—Sid she loved, and Sid was lost.

Forrest hadn't texted her after talking to the lawyer. She was losing him too.

They'd always been in this together, and now they weren't.

For the first time, this was grief. Losing her brother, maybe losing her other brother, and losing them both to something permanent. With no job to distract her—and that's what it had been, a distraction from every good thing in her life that she should have been nurturing—and her boys with their father for the week, Anna had space to feel emotions she'd never allowed herself the luxury of experiencing in full.

Luxury? No, her previous life was the luxury, the life where she could shove every uncomfortable feeling to the side so she could care about an organization that didn't care about her. This feeling was torture, and she wasn't allowing it into her life as much as she had no means of diverting it.

She'd never deserved Sid's or Forrest's love to begin with. That they'd withdrawn it shouldn't surprise her.

Everywhere Anna looked was pain. Everywhere she went, she carried a weight in her throat and in her gut. It pushed her into the couch and kept her there. Tonight, it would close her eyes with its pressure and then keep her awake with its grinding.

Was this the rest of her life? Every day to have her heart sliced open anew on the jagged wreckage of her relationships? If so, she'd be better off dead. One quick pain versus decades of hard labor in solitary confinement.

Anna took her tea into the office and locked the door. There she opened the photo albums to the pictures of her childhood. Her parents. Had her father known about his father's deal with the devil? Had her mother?

Fingers clenched in the shawl, Anna wondered again about her grandmother, and whether she'd ever unlocked that secret drawer and found a contract more binding than wedding vows.

Anna straightened. There was a second tiny key. She'd found only one hidden drawer.

With the day gaping wide before her, Anna took herself on a guided tour of the desk. The second anonymous key didn't fit the compartment that had held the contract. There must be another. She looked in the drawer opposite, but nothing.

From there she pulled out everything that could be pulled out, emptied every drawer she could empty, and where possible removed the drawers themselves. What a beautiful antique, so well-constructed to safeguard its secrets through the centuries.

Her grandfather had kept the moving parts lubricated and the finish at a high shine. Using a flashlight, Anna examined every panel and divider, searching for pieces that were too thick or joins that didn't feel solid.

Maybe the second secret drawer was like her grandfather's love for the grandchildren. Maybe the key was for a lock that had never been installed, a compartment untouched in all of time.

She started replacing drawers, and as one of them slid back into place, it made the wrong sound.

Breath catching, Anna pulled the drawer back out and shook it. Something felt loose. She had a culprit.

Ten minutes later, she'd identified a partition that was two boards pressed together. She slid out the back half of the board to reveal a minuscule keyhole, into which fitted the second of the tiny keys. She had to drip in lock oil to force it open, but once the lock clicked, out slipped the second half of the partition. The partition gone, she was able to pull up the drawer's false bottom.

Beneath that she found a ring. A diamond solitaire.

What on earth...?

The engagement ring was slender, the stone almost a chip—not even a quarter carat. Her own engagement ring had larger stones in the side channels.

She swiveled it in the light. Unscratched, unworn. Inside the gold band was a date.

The date drew her up short. Grandfather's contract was dated May 10th. The date on this ring was March of the same year. Both dates were five years before he'd married Grandma, and Grandma had a large and glittery engagement ring with a matching wedding band, the one passed on to Forrest. That ring had dwarfed Grandma's tiny hands.

Which, speaking of size, this ring would have been too large for Grandma's finger.

Grandfather really had proposed to another woman.

Amidst the disassembled desk, Anna ignored the clock, blew off the scheduled transition meetings over at Pilaster (what would they do, fire her again?) and went searching online. Eventually in a newspaper archive of her grandfather and grandmother's engagement, she found an answer:

Grandfather had indeed been engaged before. Briefly, said the papers, making it sound scandalous.

It wasn't scandalous, of course. Moreover, as the ring remained in Grandfather's possession, he mustn't have been the one who'd called it off. Why would a woman fall in love with a man in poverty only to break it off once he attained wealth?

In the hallway, the clock tolled off noon.

Anna exclaimed, "Oh!" and dropped the ring back into the drawer.

This was Grandfather's token.

If she'd been forced to guess his token, she'd have guessed this desk, but no. He'd picked the ring. The woman would stay with him, and he'd own his bride, and therefore the ring would remain his.

Except then he'd fallen out of love with the woman, or she'd fallen out of love with him. His wealth—no, his contract—had changed him. The man she'd fallen in love with no longer existed, and the relationship had dissolved.

Anna had been correct that there was no compartment for love in Grandfather's heart. When the woman returned the ring, or when he demanded it back, he'd locked the last vestiges of real love in the desk. Years later, when he'd scored his trophy wife, he'd bought her a trophy ring.

The demons had given Grandfather success. Grandfather had given them his heart.

On the brink of her own agreement, Anna had been about to do the same. Sid had actually done it—*oh, Sid*—and Forrest...?

Anna couldn't leave the ring in the drawer. She didn't even want to donate it, but how do you get rid of a diamond when the diamond's very indestructibility was the reason it represented eternity?

Where was her grandfather spending eternity? If you sold your soul, didn't you have to go to Hell? Was he really being tortured forever and ever?

Grandfather wasn't that bad. He hadn't killed people. He hadn't been a terrible businessman, either. Sure, some of his employees were underpaid, but when she'd pointed it out, he hadn't objected to her raising salaries. Under his auspices, Pilaster had donated millions to hospitals and museums. An Ivy League college featured the Linus Ellington chair in their history department. Was generosity the sign of a man going to Hell?

So? Anna thought to God. *Did you set his soul on fire because of a paperwork technicality while kids are getting lifesaving surgeries in a hospital downtown?*

She pulled the prayer shawl tighter around her shoulders, staring hard at the ring in the drawer. None of Christianity made sense. Not if a generous man could go to Hell. Not if God could get strung up on a crucifix like in that midtown church. Not if souls spent centuries under relentless torture while preachers claimed God was love.

Anna tightened her eyes. *Jesus Christ, Son of God, do you love me?*

Here she was, a woman with everything dead set against her as far as the Christians were concerned. She'd lost everything in her life and should chuck out the rest as well. She'd not only profited personally from a deal with the devil but had considered signing a deal of her own. Every single asset in her life came from Satan: her education, her connections, her career, her investments, her trust fund, and her golden parachute.

Jesus Christ, Son of God, do you love me? Was this how God paid back the people He supposedly loved? By letting petty corporate drones conspire with one another until they destroyed a family legacy? By rewarding the criminals and punishing the people who did the right thing?

Did she really want to know the answer to this?

Yes, I do, she thought. *Jesus Christ, Son of God—do you love me?*

She burst into tears.

The sobs came from nowhere and from everywhere, from deep in her gut and all over her skin. Everything about her came to mind. She saw herself as bruised, saw herself neglected but struggling. She was a tiny sidewalk flower fighting up through the seam between curb and asphalt, stepped over by millions but drilling to get its roots into the world, struggling to put forth its fragile beauty in a city full of downcast eyes.

She was loved, but love wasn't favors and networking and tax-deductible donations trumpeted on bronze plaques. That was a transaction, and she wasn't a product.

She was a child, a child who was herself clenching two smaller children's hands, tears burning behind her eyes, listening to a lean man lecturing about responsibility and obligation. She was a child searching for warmth and finding rules. She was a child. She was a child.

She was a child of God.

With her face buried in the prayer shawl, she struggled to cry quietly. She'd always been unlovable. Unwanted. Unworthy.

No, not unlovable. Anna's grandmother had loved her with patience and fortitude. In all things, Cecilia had never been weak. She'd ended every day exhausted and then awoke the next day to face her husband's thousand mockeries while shielding the three grandchildren entrusted to her care. Anna had never recognized it then. She'd never acknowledged love. For years, Grandma had waited for her to open her eyes.

God had been waiting for her, too.

Every day, Anna had gotten up and gone to work, and God had smoothed the way and waited. Anna had conscientiously rotted out every relationship in her life while God had slowed the decay but respected her decisions. Anna had ended every day just as numb to love as she'd begun it, and God had bided time for the next day when maybe she would open her eyes.

Anna had never been unloved. All along, love had been there, but she'd never opened herself up to it.

The tears kept coming, and the shawl absorbed them all. Even across town, someone loved Anna who knew nothing about her.

God knew about her, though. God knew the obligation and guilt that kept her tied to a role she'd assumed had to be hers, and here she remained with choices before her and an important decision. Unfettered, who did she want to be? Would she choose the path of love? Would she give without expectation of return?

Would she allow God to love her?

The tears trickled to a stop. Anna huddled over herself, gasping through the lacework of the shawl. God loved her. Anna had thought Satan had given her everything she'd ever had, but from the first minutes, God had given even more. God had given her life, and He'd given her a soul that could make decisions. She could decide to do more than just pull back her hand from the devil. She could choose to reach forward and put her hand in God's.

I'm sorry, she prayed. *I'm so sorry.*

It was all right. She was here now. All those uncaring moments, they could wash away. She was loved. She was cherished and treasured, and God wanted so much more for her. She'd denied love and been denied it for so long, but that past denial didn't need to define her.

The warmth still clung to her, and she looked again at the ring in the drawer. Grandfather hadn't just discarded his bride. He'd discarded love itself. In the end, that had been the deal. Wherever he spent eternity, it was the place he had chosen.

But for Anna, love had been this close all along.

Tell Forrest.

Anna needed to tell Forrest. He needed to know what their grandfather had given up for success. Forrest should be glad he hadn't heard yet from their enemies.

Given the choice between love and success, maybe Forrest would choose love. She reached for her phone.

Chapter Thirty-Seven

When Cosmiel left Anna, she'd been sitting on her couch with a mug of tea, draped in a shawl on the outside and despair on the inside.

He'd nearly stayed. Nearly. Turmiel had Anna in hand, though, and while God might not condemn Cosmiel's next actions, Cosmiel would never order anyone else to do what he was about to.

He'd had Turmiel bring up Anna's connection with her grandfather, and with that in his grip, he'd tugged himself along the length of it.

This was the path into Hell that Cosmiel had promised himself never to follow again. *And here I am,* he told God, *breaking promises.*

For the best reasons, God replied. *I won't hold you to a rash promise you made to yourself.*

On the other hand, if you didn't keep promises to yourself, you were giving others a signal that you didn't value yourself enough to keep your word. Not a good look. To be fair, though, he was going to Hell—which also wasn't the best look.

The Cherub Gabriel had discovered this method back during the Triduum, with Jesus newly crucified and the Archangels of the Presence gathered together with the intention of breaking Him out of Sheol. Which failed. Cosmiel joked in later years that Michael should have summoned Special Ops because they'd have succeeded. Except Gabriel had indeed gotten all the way inside the walls of Sheol before being rebuffed by Christ Himself.

Back then, Belior had revealed the way demons contacted the dead. The demons would detect a filament of connection stretching through a crack in Sheol's stone, then use a human soul to communicate through that hair-thin wire. Gabriel had modified the demons' technique to follow that connection through the crack.

Hell's walls had fissures like Sheol's, but connections didn't ray out. Souls in Hell were there, generally speaking, because they didn't care enough about others to have formed such long-lasting connections. Now, though? Linus Ellington's soul was trapped in a cage, and the cage was in Hell, and his connection to the grandchildren was what Satrinah was using to reel them in. She'd nurtured and strengthened those connections. Cosmiel could follow them like an interstate.

Satrinah was running Forrest's connection right through her heart, so that wasn't a viable route. Moloch and Satrinah together owned Sid's. That left Anna's.

Back at the time of the crucifixion, Gabriel had initially used this mechanism to probe through Sheol's walls before realizing it was possible to tug oneself forward via the thread. The thread would do the navigation. The walls had pressed in close and hot, and the stone had struggled to collapse on itself, but love is stronger than death.

So is the urge to control.

With Anna's soul stretching toward her grandfather, and Linus's reaching back toward her, Cosmiel could discorporate and tug himself along that razor wire right to Linus Ellington's hot and cramped heart.

It worked. It was efficient.

It hurt like blazes, this three-ply cord with its first ply forged of jealousy and possessiveness. Around that one wrapped Anna's longing for acceptance as the sharpest strand of the three. Linus's third ply was coercive and rigid, using obligation to create an unbreakable bond.

With every inch forward, Cosmiel felt Anna's obligation toward her grandfather. Her wordless fear of what he might do. Her instinctual urge to placate him so she could secure her brothers' safety. Every time he slid along its sharpness, Cosmiel felt again the grandfather's iron-cold heart. His calculation. His urge to be the one and only important figure to people who would never be important to him.

Linus alone stood at the center of his heart, and he wanted it to be the same for Anna. For Sid. For Forrest. For Cecilia. For Satrinah. He'd be their idol, and they'd be his people.

The frustrated desires stung like shrapnel. The guilt burned. The shame—unbelievable. The lost potential—unfathomable. This was the worst route into Hell.

Hell resented the intrusion and pushed back at Cosmiel. The deeper he went, the tighter Hell squeezed around him, and he had to spread himself thinner. After the halfway point, though, Hell started squeezing him forward rather than pushing him back. Once that began happening, like a mountaineer rappelling from a high point, Cosmiel used the connection to guide him toward the target. Not smoothly, but using less effort, he fell forward toward the tug of Linus Ellington's self-centeredness.

A snap on the cord brought Cosmiel to a stop. He pushed back into motion, but before him and behind him, the connection was thinning out.

Anna.

The central ply of the cord crumbled, and Cosmiel pushed forward as fast as he dared. He couldn't chance getting wedged into Hell's cavernous walls, but likewise, he couldn't push too hard or that disintegrating connection would snap. Anna's heart was evaporating out of the link. She was trying to tap into her grandfather's love for her and simultaneously recognizing there was none. In response, she was pulling back all her obligation. With no obligation toward a dead man—cold in life, cold in death —she could shed her guilt. With no more guilt—no more fear. As the seconds passed, she withdrew from the relationship, and Linus Ellington's control slipped. His coercion had nothing to grasp. The only thing remaining was his demand for her duty, and she was rejecting it.

No, no, no! Not now, not before Cosmiel got all the way inside. Yes, do it, but he needed another minute—

The connection snapped, and the mocking stones pinned Cosmiel in the dark.

Blast. *This is a good thing,* Cosmiel tried to pray—although clamped in place by Hell, prayer wasn't the easiest thing to do. *This means a good thing happened, but I wish it hadn't happened right now.*

Reduced to inching forward, Cosmiel guessed his way through the fissure based on other threads running alongside. Two of these would be Sid's and Forrest's, but identifying them would take time he didn't have. Forrest would have a maximum of forty minutes from getting into his car to reaching the token. Cosmiel had wasted five minutes arguing with Jezaryah. He'd spent even more time getting this far.

At least it meant Anna was safe, but criminy, the rest of the fight wasn't supposed to happen this way.

Stilling himself, Cosmiel concentrated until he could sense the residue of the Linus-Anna cord clinging to him. His technique for penetrating a Guard—would it work with a soul?

There wasn't enough of Anna's residue to do anything. Whenever Cosmiel tried to gather it, it evaporated. This was worse than collecting silt in the aftermath of Sheol's destruction. At least that stuff clung to itself.

Cosmiel kept inching forward, but this progress wouldn't reach Linus in time to help Forrest. Think. What assets did he have?

Well, he had plenty of Hell material around him. He had motivation. He was covered in the destroyed remnants of Linus Ellington's control over Anna.

Ah. Then Cosmiel did have something.

Human souls naturally bonded with what they loved. Somewhere in this mess of connections was Linus Ellington's connection to Sid and his connection to Forrest. But what Linus Ellington had valued, always and above all, was himself.

Cosmiel gathered the Linus-generated debris of Linus's

connection to Anna, and because the one Linus loved best was himself, those fragments did cling to one another. Cosmiel twisted them and encouraged them until they extended themselves toward the rest of Linus Ellington's heart. Had Linus loved the control he could have over others? And had Satrinah used that to control Linus? Likewise, Cosmiel could use Linus to control Linus.

Cosmiel wound his heart into the gathered bits of Linus, taking Anna's place. He yielded control as if allowing a fellow operative to possess him, and by doing so, let Linus reel him in like a fish.

The loathing and superiority burned like red-hot wire, but Linus pulled Cosmiel through the fissures, through Hell itself, through Satrinah's Guards, and then right through the barrier of Satrinah's spherical prison.

He'd arrived. Where, he wasn't sure. But he'd reached Linus.

Unflinching, Cosmiel let Linus grasp him with his hungry rage. There was none of Satrinah's power on Cosmiel now, and none of Anna's heart left either. The only thing Linus would recognize about Cosmiel was the debris of Linus's own soul. Perhaps that had been the case all along. Other humans were puppets into which he could insert his hands, the same way Linus had eventually become a hollowed-out puppet for Satrinah to insert hers. If he'd ever loved anything about another person, it had been the ways they became extensions of himself.

Three hard connections extended now from Linus. Satrinah, Sid, and Forrest.

Forrest's single slight chance rested in breaking the connection between him and Linus. Anna had broken hers from her side, but Forrest would never do so willingly. Not on the cusp of receiving the approval he'd craved for ages. If this monstrosity broke, it had to break here.

Also, it had to break cleanly. The moment Satrinah sensed Cosmiel's interference, she'd flood power back down the connection and fry him from the inside out. With Jezaryah rightly occupied with Forrest, Cosmiel would have no one to drag him to safety. Whatever he attempted was one-and-done, and afterward he'd just have to suffer the consequences.

We did acknowledge I never take the easy jobs, Cosmiel prayed. *Please help me give Forrest at least one clear-eyed moment without their interference. Please bless my efforts.*

Linus's soul kept wrapping around itself, struggling to become the center of its own universe. Always it grasped on the fragments of those connections, tugging them, trying to consume them.

They emerged so strongly from within soul. Like the cables on a suspension bridge, the connections braced themselves against themselves, at full extension and with no slack whatsoever. There wasn't even the beginning of a place to break them.

Longing. Wanting. Devouring. It was the opposite of love. God loved and released His children. Linus wanted to consume them.

Linus Ellington wouldn't have created Hell, that's for sure. He'd have forced and coerced until every soul was frozen on its knees with compulsory adoration in its throat and terrified praise in its eyes.

He'd have taken and gnawed and never given. He'd have surrounded himself with mirrors and reflected his own light back at himself, dazzled and delighted by the illumination.

Linus tugged at the leftover connection with Anna.

Cosmiel nearly released it because it had done its job by getting him inside Linus's prison shell. Just before it slipped free, though, he clasped it hard and pivoted so Linus couldn't re-absorb it.

Instead, Cosmiel spread the remnants of that connection along the cord leading to Forrest, filling them with a thought: *Of what use is Forrest?* No, that was too complicated. A damned soul didn't think in depth. It had to be primal. *Useless.* Cosmiel thought of his own history with himself and tied those thoughts into Forrest's connection. *Failure. Disappointment.* This wasn't enough. *Waste of resources.* Cosmiel had used his own failure to break out of Hell, but now Cosmiel could see and reject all the sensations. He wasn't any of these things. Forrest wasn't either. Those thoughts about a soul made in God's image were evil. Devaluing someone because they weren't of use—even himself—it wasn't love. It was never love.

Never loved him. Cosmiel tied his old thoughts into the

attachment to Forrest. *Useless. Hated. Burdensome. Distraction.*

That last thought brought Linus to the edge of his cage, all his focus on Forrest like a laser.

Cosmiel realized then, there was no connection to Cecilia.

There wasn't even a tendril waving unmoored in her direction. There never had been.

Cosmiel built on that. *Competition.*

Linus burned even harder at Forrest.

Was that it? Was that the key? Was that why Linus had refused to have the grandchildren sign while he was still alive?

Competition, Cosmiel sent again. *Forrest wants to be better than you.*

Outrage from Linus.

Cosmiel sent, *Forrest is taking Satrinah.*

Jealousy surged from Linus's burning soul, traveling up the connection. Cosmiel pressed against the side of the sphere, projecting images of Satrinah courting Forrest. Oh yes, Satrinah was going to feel that rage. Mid-seduction, she'd sense it and come running.

Cosmiel urged Linus, *Forrest is seducing Satrinah.*

Linus burned even brighter, a fusion reaction of ego and outrage. *Mine. Mine!*

Cosmiel urged, *Sid already took her! Now Forrest will too!*

Linus was nothing but fire now. *She's mine!*

Cosmiel added, *She'll want them more than you!*

Exploding into Hell, Satrinah detonated Linus Ellington's sphere with fire that engulfed every corner of the room like a shriek, blasting Cosmiel backward into the rocks.

Satrinah grasped Linus Ellington's soul in her hands. Darkness dripped from her like crude oil.

Stunned, Cosmiel struggled to raise his head. They were in the lab area. Satrinah's quarters.

Mine! Linus continued roaring in his personal hell where he sat on his throne. White hot, his connection to Forrest should have been visible like a supernova across entire galaxies, but it was just this one chamber and its one set of walls. That connection glared on Satrinah's outraged expression. *You are mine, and I won't let him have you!*

Linus detonated his connections to Forrest and to Sid, and darkness took the lab.

Chapter Thirty-Eight

As much as Jezaryah wanted Forrest to avoid anger in his heart, today he praised every vehicle that stood between Forrest and his home in a gated community in Bethesda. Every car inching forward was a blessing. Every brake light that turned red was a gift.

Jezaryah wasn't even watching the traffic. He should. If Forrest died in this condition, he'd be Satrinah's forever. Satrinah was seeking more than just one more soul in the Accounts Receivable column, though. She wanted to own a politician for life, and potentially his children. This was the safest Forrest ever would be in Beltway traffic.

The clock turned to noon. A message popped up on Forrest's phone even though he'd turned off notifications before the drive. Sid. "Congrats on joining the right team."

Forrest grinned, and the phone went dark.

Worse than the helplessness was Jezaryah's sense of Satrinah co-inhabiting Forrest's awareness. She'd wrapped his grandfather's connection around his heart like a leash, and whenever she twitched it, she could change Forrest's thoughts and affect his mood. She was angry at the traffic, too; he rode close to the bumper of the next car, hitting the gas whenever he could rather than idling up to a glide and drifting down again.

Michael's soldiers stuck close, but there wasn't much for them to do. They had authority to defend Jezaryah, but they couldn't peel the demon pair off Forrest.

Moloch mused aloud, "The Special Ops angel—is he here in defiance of his superior officer?"

As a guardian, Jezaryah didn't have a superior officer except God. They knew that.

Satrinah said, "If he wants to stay with the human, he can do so forever by transferring his loyalty to us."

As if.

Moloch snorted. "I don't want him."

Satrinah said, "You're being ungenerous. We have what he wants. Humans aren't the only souls who can make a deal."

That smear of Jezaryah was aimed at the Archangel soldiers, which was an odd comfort: Satrinah wouldn't bother staining Jezaryah's reputation if he truly had no chance of turning Forrest.

Even so, in the next moment, Satrinah's thoughts again twitched through Forrest's head, and with a dull nausea, Jezaryah felt her impulse burning as a combination of fear and self-consciousness. Jezaryah tried to quell the command, but then Satrinah blended it with worry about angels as voyeurs, and then fear about angels as interfering thieves who would snatch the agreement out of Forrest's hands. Forrest said out loud, "No. No soldiers. Leave."

With that, Satrinah had undercut the Archangels' authority. They remained anyhow, but with only authority over the other drivers. They couldn't do anything to or for Forrest.

Jezaryah wasn't a soldier, and also, Forrest couldn't eject his own guardian angel. With just enough authority to stay near, but not enough to take action, Jezaryah struggled to keep whatever handhold he had on his charge's heart. *I love you.* He buried the feeling deep because Satrinah and Moloch's mockery was already too much to bear. *I love you, and you're throwing away everything over a man who never loved you.*

Auriel's voice came to Jezaryah: *Anna's secure. Make sure Forrest checks his phone.*

Satrinah hadn't let Anna's texts through the way she had Sid's. Whatever Anna had sent, it would have to wait.

Don't let them block Anna's texts, he sent to one of the soldiers.

An Archangel replied that Satrinah had tried to block messages from Anna's phone, but they'd ensured the messages arrived.

All well and good. Now Forrest needed to read them.

Forrest pulled off the highway. He was ten minutes from home, eleven minutes from touching the ring. Jezaryah had made no headway.

Also, now that he wasn't in traffic, the Archangels weren't able to stay near. The streets were oddly deserted. Well, odd for Bethesda. Not odd to an angel who realized two demons had rearranged the traffic patterns. How much power did that take? But then again, they were also tapping into Belior's authority, and Belior commanded Hell's army.

Jezaryah reached out to Julia's guardian angel. *Please try again.*

Yaron replied, *She's not going to call him. She feels ridiculous that she was so worried yesterday.*

Blast. A shot fired too soon. Julie was as over-conscious of her own pride as Linus ever had been.

The whole time that Forrest navigated toward his gated subdivision, Jezaryah prayed harder. *Please, save him. Save him. Save him.*

Mid-prayer, memories flooded Jezaryah. Forrest as a child reading in bed with Anna and Sid. The three kids watching television. Forrest with his hand in his grandmother's, walking to a shop in the garment district to pick up his school uniform. Forrest graduating *Summa cum Laude*. Forrest phoning home after his election, elated and eager. *We won,* he'd told his grandfather, to which Linus Ellington had replied, *We did it.*

Forrest pulled up at a stop light. Five minutes to home.

Jezaryah projected deep into Forrest's heart as though Forrest were the one thinking it, *Is this why Grandfather said, 'We did it'? Grandfather was never working alone. Yet he always expected me to go it alone.*

Forrest took a sudden breath, and it felt freer.

Jezaryah picked up his head. No longer the tightness around Forrest's soul like a python at full squeeze.

Free.

Satrinah flared with rage, and she vanished.

The connection to Linus—it was broken.

Satrinah fired bolt after bolt of lighting into Linus Ellington's soul, venting a rage so hot and so deep it could have no words— unloading an eternity of fury into one man, one little human.

Trapped, Cosmiel struggled to hands and knees. His wings wouldn't work, and his head spun. Linus was screaming. Screaming. Screaming.

Cosmiel collapsed like a rag doll. He needed God but couldn't pray. Sound rang in his head. *Get up.* He couldn't defend himself. She'd pour out her rage on Linus and then tear Cosmiel apart— and that was good because every second she stayed in Hell was one more second she wasn't bedazzling Forrest.

Wrath erupted from her with an intensity that dwarfed any Seraph's, punching a thousand holes in Linus Ellington's soul while Cosmiel stared through tears, a long, long minute spent at the heart of a nuclear furnace. This was the fruit of his interference.

His fault, except Linus had long since consented to have anything done to him that was Satrinah's whim to do.

Satrinah flung Linus into the wall—whatever was left of him. She'd re-destroy him at her leisure for all eternity, whenever she remembered him. He'd reconstitute over time, but for now, there wasn't enough of him left to savage.

Cosmiel pushed to sitting, hoping not to wobble. "I'm next?"

Her eyes narrowed. "You wish you were next. I have work to do, and you haven't changed a thing. You've only caused him pain."

He'd changed any number of seconds while she was here and not there. "*You* caused him pain."

"What I've caused him isn't the first hint of pain. He'll gaze back on this moment and rejoice in my generosity." She fixed her attention on Cosmiel, something he felt rather than saw. "You can remain to witness it, or not. I'm too busy to amuse myself with you."

Cosmiel said, "You do love playing with your toys," but she'd flashed away. Cosmiel dropped to the floor.

Silence. Solitude. Also, imprisonment.

Well, then. Time to break out of Hell. Again.

"Oh no" checklist, step one: feel your shame. Except, oddly, there wasn't any.

Step two: *God, please help me get out of this. You're probably tired of the same prayer from me all the time, but as You can see, I'm not very good at my job.*

Step three: assess the mess. Not terrible for once. He'd achieved his primary goal. It was just that he was too dizzy and weak to use his escape hatch.

Step four: his new objective was getting back to Forrest.

Step five: he could still use his previous plan, but he needed to recover his strength.

Step six: Enacting the plan would be a problem. There weren't ready sources of healing in Hell.

When the first fragment of strength returned, Cosmiel dragged himself toward Linus. In agony, the soul quivered without enough cohesion even to whimper. Satrinah had brought him close to cindered.

Cosmiel breathed coolness over the remnants of the soul, soothing it. Linus was damned, but he was still human, and Cosmiel was still an angel.

Easy. At first it flinched from his touch, but finally it stilled. There was no rescuing this, but at least there was now. For this minute, Linus could be calm. Could be quiet.

With the soul's pain relieved somewhat, Cosmiel readied himself again for prayer.

Except Linus Ellington was focusing. It projected a question, a need. Cosmiel extended a hand, and the soul reached back.

Satrinah?

Cosmiel thought back, *It's okay. She's gone.*

Sadness flooded from the soul. Grief. He wanted her to come back. He missed her. Longed for her.

Cosmiel sat back on his heels, wings drooping. Linus had chosen his idol.

Doing what Cosmiel's angelic nature demanded had restored some of his strength, though. He extended his heart until he could detect the wispy duplicate of himself within Jezaryah. Even so, he didn't have enough strength to wink out this part of himself. He'd have to try activating his other self, that way Jezaryah would detect Cosmiel and the message he needed to send.

While waiting, emotions kept sublimating off the human soul on the stones. It didn't grieve about losing the three grandchildren whose bonds were now broken. Instead, Linus Ellington grieved over Satrinah.

Moloch tried again to wrench Jezaryah out of position, but as long as Jezaryah concentrated and remained discorporated, he didn't budge. This was a good sign: Moloch hadn't cared about the guardian's presence until Linus dropped the connection to Forrest.

That had to be Cosmiel's doing. Cosmiel, who'd said nothing more could be done.

Jezaryah tried to quell the anger. Anger wouldn't help Forrest, and Cosmiel was making it right. Only Forrest mattered now.

Jezaryah burrowed deeper into his charge's heart. With some breathing room, he could instill doubt. Instead of Grandma's ring as the token, wouldn't it make more sense to choose that nickel? It was still in the cigar box. Even Anna had known the box was important to Forrest.

Another thought: What if Forrest chose the wrong token? Would Satrinah revoke her offer?

The gate guard waved Forrest through, screening for intruders but welcoming in one of Satan's top demons.

Jezaryah fed more doubts into Forrest's mind. *What if Julie is home? What will she think if I'm carrying someone else's wedding ring?* And then, *Should I be wearing Grandfather's ring? Should I hide it and never look at it again? Or would they find that offensive?*

Off-balance, Forrest might second-guess the biggest decision of his life. Might un-make it.

Satrinah returned, engulfed in flame but otherwise silent. On the instant, Moloch stopped trying to pry Jezaryah away from Forrest.

Instead came a different tug at Forrest's heart: his connection to Sid.

Every time. Every time Jezaryah thought they might get a break, Satrinah switched to a backup plan that was just as deadly as the first. Special Ops would dig in a trench against the oncoming army and then watch the bombers fly overhead. Decades of preparation hadn't been enough to fortify Forrest against one pair of demons and a tangle of puppet strings.

Auriel sent, *Status?*

Jezaryah bundled his frustration and Linus's dropped connection and the tugging via Sid's, then sent it to her.

Auriel replied, *Acknowledged. Can you break that bond?*

Jezaryah sent a negation. Forrest and Sid were comrades in arms. They didn't call it love, the way they owned one another's hearts; but love it was, nevertheless.

Cosmiel's sphere made itself noticed in Jezaryah's soul, and he focused on it.

Cosmiel's voice was so weak it couldn't be understood as words, but Jezaryah thought Cosmiel might want Jezaryah to possess him.

Except...that wasn't permission, was it? Possession would be an awful thing to do to someone without consent. Although possession wouldn't work if Cosmiel didn't consent.

Cosmiel pushed the question again. Jezaryah steeled himself to hold tight to Forrest, then commanded Cosmiel's soul to yield to his.

The moment he did so, he felt the lingering hint of a desire: the moment before he'd stopped wanting anything, Cosmiel had wanted Jezaryah to give an order.

Come to me, Jezaryah demanded. *All of you. Now.*

Chapter Thirty-Nine

Cosmiel obeyed Jezaryah's order as though he'd given it himself. Which, in this state, he had. Jezaryah's used his own strength to pull Cosmiel back together in Creation. A moment after, Jezaryah accessed Cosmiel's most recent memories. Approval swept through him (them?) followed by renewed determination.

At the same time, Cosmiel found himself knowing they'd arrived in Bethesda, and that Satrinah was manipulating Forrest using Sid's connection.

Jezaryah had access to Cosmiel's power. Well, should have had access to it. There wasn't much. *You're weak,* Jezaryah thought to himself (to Cosmiel?), *so regain your strength while I'm in charge.*

Cosmiel had no will to do otherwise. Jezaryah had wanted him off the case before, and now he could keep it that way until the end.

Guilt flickered through Cosmiel, followed by an apology. Jezaryah wasn't sure who was apologizing to whom, or if the apology and the forgiveness came from both of them.

Satrinah slipped her spiritual fingers into Forrest, reminding him of Sid securing that career-defining role in a guaranteed blockbuster. That role would seat Sid on Hollywood's throne, and that was all due to Sid's contract.

Burning with desperation, Jezaryah seeded a counter-feeling in Forrest's mind: derision because Sid would achieve stardom without Sid doing the work. That thought fizzled away.

Satrinah picked up on Jezaryah's urgency, though, and amplified it. She twisted the fraternal bond and lit it up with a little rivalry. Sid wasn't the only one who could reap career-defining benefits. Why should Sid outstrip him again? Forrest's contract would ensure he won his next election. And the one after. A politician's career lasted longer than an actor's.

Cosmiel thought to Jezaryah, *Tug back.*

Forrest pulled into his driveway and pushed the button to raise the garage door. Jezaryah didn't try jamming the remote. Instead he released his possession of Cosmiel just enough that they could communicate.

Sid's still alive, Cosmiel urged. *The fraternal relationship can change. Tug back on that connection.*

Jezaryah flooded Forrest's heart with grief as he pulled into the empty two-car garage. *Since signing, Sid's different. Ten days ago, he'd have contested the will if he was named the only heir. Now he's suing to make sure that's the case.*

Jezaryah's longing spilled into Forrest: longing for Sid to be like he'd been before. Longing for Anna to be safe.

Forrest responded by narrowing his eyes. Once he completed the deal, he and Sid would be on the same side again. Then they could protect Anna.

Blast. That wall was too high to vault, too smooth to scale.

Auriel had wanted Forrest to check his phone, though. *I should see if Sid texted again.*

Forrest shut off the engine and pulled his phone from the mount. *Check your messages,* Jezaryah urged. *Ask Sid about his token.*

Forrest opened the door, then stopped. Drawing power from Cosmiel, Jezaryah injected fear into the Sid-Forrest connection. *What was Sid's token?*

Satrinah was hissing threats, but Jezaryah had every right to be here. Wrapped into and around Forrest's heart, Jezaryah renewed the worry that Forrest would choose the wrong token, and then his preternatural partner would prefer Sid. Again.

Meanwhile, Cosmiel glowed with warmth at the tactic. Jezaryah was good at his job. It was only because of Jezaryah that they'd come so close to success.

Jezaryah caught that sensation and dismissed it.

A click of the phone, and Forrest's lock screen filled with messages and a photo from Anna. Sid's reply was among them, and Forrest went right for Sid's.

"Congrats on joining the right team," Sid had sent when Forrest had gotten into his car. After that came another message. "I can't believe you got a personal visit. I need to re-negotiate."

Forrest frowned.

Cosmiel told Forrest, *Reply now. That can't stand.*

Forrest texted, "For once I got recognized. Why do you need to take it away?"

Jezaryah breathed on the discontentment. *What if I don't handle the contract right?*

Cosmiel added, *What if I do handle it right, only they prefer Sid anyhow?*

Jezaryah built on the paranoia. Practically speaking, Sid had no reason to tell Forrest the truth. If Sid was making their respective agreements a competition, why wouldn't he undermine Forrest's?

Again Jezaryah strummed on the mistrust. Sid was always taking, taking, taking. Grandfather's injustice benefitted him. Now Forrest was the favored one. For once, Forrest should be the golden child. Sid couldn't stand that.

Forrest clicked off his phone and stepped out of the car.

Anna's messages, Cosmiel sent. *Is she in danger? Does she need you to negotiate for her right now?*

They needed those messages viewed, so Jezaryah leaned into the jealousy.

Forrest woke his phone again, but before he went to Anna's messages, Sid interrupted with a text. "Don't be so sensitive."

Jezaryah didn't even need to encourage the jealousy. Forrest replied, "Yeah, don't be so sensitive, like all the times I was too sensitive because our grandfather didn't remember I existed."

Their connection was aglow with offense.

That was when Satrinah noticed Cosmiel, and Moloch attacked because Cosmiel had no right to be there. Cosmiel held on tight, encouraging Jezaryah to open all the channels between the brothers. Nothing held back.

Sid: "How dare you insult our grandfather! Everything we have is because of him."

Forrest: "Despite himself. I at least see him for who he was."

With the connection to Linus gone, Jezaryah could fill that empty space and keep it cold. Grandfather had never loved Forrest, and it hadn't been Forrest's fault.

Sid texted, "Quit campaigning. Just get the token and seal it already."

That message felt like Satrinah trying to close the deal. Meanwhile Moloch was working Cosmiel loose, and by pulling on Cosmiel, he might also yank out Jezaryah.

Forrest raised the phone and dictated, "Who exactly are you to tell me what to do?"

Cosmiel sent to Auriel, *Forrest's got his phone in his hand right now. Anna needs to text him!*

That thought was separate enough from Jezaryah for Moloch to rip him out like a rubber mat off a bathtub.

Cosmiel slammed back into his subtle body, materializing with sword in hand. He spun with the momentum to plunge his blade into Moloch's side. The demon erupted in flame and dashed Cosmiel shoulder-first into the cement floor.

Stay with him! Cosmiel ordered Jezaryah. Standard protocol. Guard the target. Let your fellow operative take the fall.

A text came in from Anna. "I'm scared. Talk to me when you can."

Forrest walked into the house, frowning at his phone.

Cosmiel shot toward Forrest, then braced himself against Moloch's approach. He couldn't Guard the house. He couldn't stop that endless drag on Forrest's soul because Forrest had given the demons permission. Cosmiel couldn't stop an enraged Seraph. But even so. Even so—

With his wings spread and his sword drawn, Moloch blasted

Cosmiel back into the garage.

Satrinah flashed into the hallway ahead of Forrest. "You're wasting time! Get the ring! Now!"

Blind to both the demons and the angels, Forrest lowered his phone. That Sid-Forrest connection was stronger than an anchor cable.

Cosmiel raised his head. *Jezaryah! The connection to Anna!*

Jezaryah's heart lit up in surprise. It wasn't just Sid who had a live connection to Forrest.

Pull it! Light it up!

Cosmiel didn't wait. He dove right through Moloch's flames, calling to Auriel as well. Anna's connection was live. It was live, and Forrest yearned to protect his sister.

Moreover, was Cosmiel detecting a prayer? Was Anna praying for Forrest?

Anna, Cosmiel sent into Forrest's heart. *Anna. Anna.*

Forrest paused in the entry of the bedroom. He clicked on Anna's messages, then scrolled back to the beginning.

Moloch pinned Cosmiel to the floor, but instead of struggling, Cosmiel opened his heart to Jezaryah so the guardian could access to his strength.

Jezaryah grasped the Forrest-Anna connection. Into it, he gushed all the love he had for Forrest. All the love since Forrest's first moments and every day they'd spent together since. That wave of nostalgia and desperation stopped Forrest in place, and he read Anna's texts without moving.

Anna had texted, "I found an engagement ring in a secret drawer in Grandfather's desk, like the contract. I think this was his token."

She'd sent a photograph of a diamond solitaire on the antique wood.

"I don't remember if I told you this, but if you make an agreement with them, they ask for a token. It's got to be something that represents everything to you."

"Grandfather offered them this. But it wasn't Grandma's. It was to another woman. I searched online, and her name was Catherine

Morrow."

Jezaryah's heart bled into the Forrest-Anna connection. He'd stopped vibrating it, and instead he warmed it with his soul.

"The date engraved on the ring is two months before Grandfather's contract date. Four months later, she said he'd changed. They broke up."

Satrinah was telegraphing demands down the line from Sid, and Moloch was filling the home with spiritual fire, but Forrest couldn't sense them over the tie to Anna—Anna, the only unconditional love left in his life.

"I never knew any of this, but it shows I was right to say no. You're lucky they didn't make you an offer. Grandfather didn't just give up a woman. He gave up his ability to love."

Then, "Sid made the same deal, and the same thing is happening. The way he turned on us is scary."

Forrest looked away from his phone, toward the bedroom closet, then back to the phone.

Jezaryah was in tears. Spent, broken, and emptied out. Whether or not this worked, the guardian needed a long, long reprieve afterward. They all did.

Anna had texted, "I love you. I know we don't do this, but I love you. I love Sid, too, and I'm afraid we've lost him."

And with that, Forrest reached the final message: "I'm scared. Talk to me when you can."

A new text arrived from Sid. "Have you done it yet? Or are you being an idiot like our sister?"

Forrest leaned against the wall, lowered the hand with the phone, and closed his eyes.

Cosmiel flashed to Forrest's side and spread his wings around the man. Forrest's heart was less opaque than before. The hidden trap door had been theirs all along, like Hezekiah's tunnel beneath Jerusalem. Forrest's downfall would have hurt Anna, but instead Anna's faithfulness could be his channel to salvation.

Deep in Forrest's heart, at the base of every connection to everyone and everything, Jezaryah detonated the final gem.

Forrest's soul resonated with a gold glow, and he gasped.

"Stop that!" Satrinah reached for Forrest, but that swirling light created a perimeter that left her howling. She tried again, but the light and the holiness scorched her. Moloch snatched her back and held her, wings covering her crackling form while his eyes bored into the only human in the room.

Forrest clenched his hands. Breath by breath, the minute ticked by. The next one started. He squeezed his eyes shut.

Auriel appeared alongside Cosmiel. Sophiel arrived, armored. Next, Geron with his shadowed eyes. Eloricel, her hands clasped. Indri, her sword raised.

Cosmiel wrapped his wings around Forrest. As the light ebbed, he breathed into Forrest's heart, *We're all in this together.*

Forrest kept his eyes screwed shut. His breathing grew more punctuated.

Ask Christ to break your bonds, Jezaryah begged. *He sees you. He sees every part of you, and He loves you.*

Shaking, Satrinah pushed away from Moloch. "The token. Now."

Trembling, Forrest stepped out of the angel's embrace and walked into the bedroom. He pulled down the cigar box from the closet shelf. Set it on the dresser. Withdrew the velvet box with Grandma's wedding ring.

He flipped the lid so he could see the gold band with all those diamond chips in the channels. With his other hand, he grasped his grandfather's ring and held it alongside.

Satrinah said, "By rights, you are mine. You can make something of your life. Everyone will see you and know your value."

In a thought barely a whisper, Cosmiel sent, *Don't give up your ability to be loved.*

Forrest tucked Grandfather's ring against his palm, extended a finger toward Cecilia's ring in the box, and then snapped down the lid.

No token. No deal.

Cosmiel dropped to his knees, face in his hands. Auriel wrapped around him, warm. Jezaryah clung to Forrest as if he'd collapse.

Forrest whispered, "I reject you. I reject your agreement, and all your works, and all your empty promises."

Despite the burns all over herself, Satrinah's wings flared for a fight, but Sophiel stepped forward with his sword drawn. Moloch seized Satrinah and flashed her from the room.

Forrest raised his phone, and he pushed the button to dial his sister.

Thank you, Cosmiel prayed, eyes closed, heart wide open. *Thank you for giving us everything we needed. Thank you for giving Forrest a clear moment to decide.*

Anna answered her phone on the first ring. "Forrest?"

"It's me." Forrest's breathy voice wavered. "Something weird just happened, and I need to talk to you."

Chapter Forty

At the entrance of the Special Ops headquarters, Cosmiel raised his wings. "What do you mean the password's changed?"

He didn't turn his head to glance at Sophiel. Cosmiel's second would be standing at his back with arms folded, a self-satisfied smirk plastered across his face. Both gate guards were pointedly not looking at Sophiel because if they did, they'd end up laughing.

"Sorry, sir. New security protocol." That was from the guard who looked less likely to break down in laughter. Even when they weren't on assignment, his operatives were great at trading off cues and playing to one another's strengths. The second guard was a feather's breadth from losing composure. "If you don't know the password, you'll have to break in."

Cosmiel exclaimed, "This is a terrible protocol!" which finally did in the second guard, and the second guard's laughter undermined the first one's composure.

By contrast, Sophiel sounded thoughtful and collected. "How will you handle this interesting development?"

"Easily." Cosmiel vanished, taking one of his secret backdoor mechanisms directly into his office.

Should he have this? No. Did he have it because he'd predicted Sophiel's perfidy? Yes. You don't stay long in a job like this if you aren't one step ahead of your own subordinates while they're trying to get one step ahead of you.

At his window, Cosmiel stared at the expanse of Heaven. His

view faced the sunrise, and the morning washed through him. Clouds picked up the light and refracted it in every direction, but not the same as stained-glass light on a cathedral wall. This time, it was pure light and pure vapor. Longing surged within him.

At his back, Sophiel said, "You need time."

"You're not supposed to create secret entrances into my office." Cosmiel forced a smile. "I'm pretty sure that's insubordination."

"Demote me when you get back from furlough, but put me in charge until then."

"And give you time to install more backdoors?" Cosmiel turned to him. "There's that situation in Bengaluru."

Sophiel waved a hand. "We're on it."

"And the school over in Mithymna. That's about to reach a crisis point."

"I've been there every morning this week." Sophiel drew closer to him. "Do I need to bring in Auriel to back me up, or will you believe me for once?"

Anna. Forrest. Sid. Cosmiel's world had been everything Ellington for two weeks, and now every iota of that exhaustion flowed through him, along with a yearning for peace.

Days at prayer. Mornings at the Divine Liturgy. Evenings at concerts. Blessed silence in the depth of night. Silence and stars.

Except he had to check on the team protecting the Ukrainian politicians. And there was the multinational corporation working on that advanced navigation satellite system. Each of those situations required attention or else it wouldn't have landed in the lap of Special Ops. Luxuriating in silence and prayer was a ridiculous self-indulgence.

For that matter, he needed to present himself back before God to report the end of this assignment. He hadn't done that for so long.

The Holy Spirit nudged Cosmiel. What had he said to Auriel?

"You need time off."

Yes, and then?

Auriel had replied, *"I'll get it after. These are the critical hours."*

What had been Cosmiel's response?

"Then it's critical to have angels at the top of their game to assist."

Sophiel folded his arms, eyebrows raised.

Cosmiel's shoulders sagged. "I do believe you. But I don't even know how to be quiet with myself anymore."

Sophiel joined him at the window, wing to wing. "Do I have your permission to furlough you right now?"

Cosmiel forced a chuckle. "You're going to do it either way."

"Actually, no. But if that's permission, then I'm going ahead." Sophiel put a hand on his shoulder, and suddenly the office was Guarded.

Cosmiel laughed. "Wait, what?"

"You are now under house arrest." Sophiel's eyes sparkled. "Special Ops is in open rebellion, and your charming but treacherous second in command has seized power."

Cosmiel folded his arms and narrowed his eyes. "Oh, do go on."

"You'll have to break out of this room, at which point we'll admit defeat in the face of your cunning superiority." Sophiel gestured to the table at the room's center, on which appeared three boxes. "I'm sure leaving these curious items won't at all assist you in your attempt to escape."

Cosmiel rubbed his chin. "Along with a perfectly-ordinary-looking pocket-knife? I do believe I've seen this movie."

"Oh, likely a dozen times. Break out of the room, and you're free to go back to work." Sophiel hugged him. "You've earned some time off. Don't hurry. Also, if there's anything you want, ask for room service. I'll keep things under control until you're back."

Sophiel vanished.

Cosmiel laid a hand on the wall, and it shed outraged sparks at the contact. He'd chosen a clever second in command. Sophiel had sealed the office with several interlocking Guards that used changing, pulsing frequencies, all of which were attuned to Cosmiel.

Cosmiel had a backdoor for this, too. He could be out of the room in a heartbeat.

On the table were three packages. Cosmiel opened the first and found the puzzle created for him by the Cherubim, the one that existed in six dimensions and would require four riddles and a multi-spatial algorithm to solve. He could knock that out in two days, and he sensed that once he did so, it would reward him with a key. No doubt the other two packages contained similar. Or maybe he had to solve them in the right order. Maybe solving all three would let him out, but maybe Sophiel had taken a straightforward sequence of problems and turned them into a series of interlocking snares, where each solution would increase the difficulty of the ones remaining.

Sophiel knew Cosmiel would never gear down for three entire days. Instead, here was a challenge to keep him occupied—an "active rest" furlough.

Cosmiel prayed, *Sophiel created a meta-puzzle, just for me.*

The Holy Spirit replied, *And he had quite a lot of fun doing it.*

That leaves me no choice. If Sophiel took this much joy in assembling Cosmiel's trap, it would be rude to solve it too quickly.

Instead of getting started, Cosmiel took advantage of "room service" to summon his personal library. He couldn't send anything back out again, but now there was plenty to read with his free time.

He left the puzzle on the table and carried a book to the window. While the lights continued changing color against the sky, Cosmiel opened to a page he'd last been reading fifty years ago.

Free time. A free moment to decide. Cosmiel closed his eyes and prayed. *Thank you. Thank you for my team, and thank you for all those moments.*

Epilogue

"Jump!" Anna held up her arms to Ryan. "I've got you, sweetie!"

Standing at the edge of the pool, Ryan bit his lip. Gavin was splashing in his floatie right at Anna's side, but the waves kept dragging him away. She tugged him back. The lifeguards at the indoor waterpark were strict about families staying together, and she was only one person.

Ryan got to the edge, crouched to jump, then backed off again. He really wasn't ready for this yet, was he? "Sit on the edge," she said, then said, "Whee!" as she lifted him in a pretend jump. Both boys were wearing life vests, but now she positioned a secondary floatation device under Ryan's arms.

Ryan whispered, "Sorry, Mommy."

She kissed his forehead. "I'm sorry I asked you to do something that scared you. If you want to try again, you let me know. For now, we can swim."

For three hours, they'd gone down the slides and bounced in the wave pool and gotten showered on the splash pad. If Ryan had expended all his bravery, that was understandable.

Gavin urged, "Let's swim to the deep end!"

Anna grabbed a pool noodle and guided the boys, using a modified sidestroke so she had her eyes on both of them all the time. Their assortment of floaties kept them up even as the water lurched with the action of so many other swimmers.

Life is like this, she prayed. *We could drown.*

She felt her attention drawn to how she was guiding Ryan and

Gavin. How she stayed near them, and how they were held safe by the devices and her guidance. There were lifeguards on the side, like guardian angels ready to help. Over time, as Anna kept training her sons, they'd begin to swim on their own. That was how they learned, and that was what God was doing in Anna's spiritual life as well.

Thank you, she prayed.

All the same, Gavin's lips were turning blue. "How about we go back to the room?" Anna ushered them to the steps. "After you're dried off, we can order hot chocolate and maybe watch a movie."

The suggestion of hot chocolate restored life to both boys. In a family locker suite, she peeled them out of their swimsuits and back into dry clothes, then left them in the open area so she could change into workout pants and a loose shirt, both brandishing logos. Before losing her job, she hadn't even remembered she owned clothes to relax in. These had come as a long ago Christmas gift from Sid, still with the tags attached.

Sid.

Closing her eyes, she sighed. *Please, God.* She didn't have anything more eloquent. She'd have to come up with a beautiful prayer at some point, something able to wring God's heart. She'd probably be praying for a thing that wouldn't happen before the end of Sid's life—and statistically speaking, she should outlive him. For now, the only prayer she'd ever been able to come up with was clumsy and awkward. *Please.*

The boys were laughing on the other side of the curtain, so she hurried a brush through her hair before they destroyed everything. They were good boys, but exhausted and excited as they were, the slightest thing might trigger a tantrum. Hot chocolate was most likely a mistake, but she'd promised.

Ryan and Gavin were bouncing on the bench. "Get down!" she exclaimed, but they were still giggling. "Time to put your shoes on." She should ask for room service, but maybe they needed to blow off more steam by taking a trip to the lobby.

While they wiggled into their sneakers, she checked her phone. Forrest had texted. "I don't want to bug you on vacation, but Lisa called. Sid is still being a jerk about the will, but we've got a settlement offer. She says it's not too bad."

Anna sighed.

Forrest added, "I know you and Sid can keep paying lawyers for a hundred years, but I'm ready to close this chapter."

If it lasted a hundred years, she did have the money. A few nasty letters from her personal lawyer, plus the threat of going public, had pulled the ripcord on Anna's "golden parachute." For Forrest's sake, though, and just to get Sid off the defensive, she'd probably accept Lisa's proposed settlement. Sid had already inherited the worst of Grandfather's legacy.

Anna told the boys, "Put the towels in the bin." While they shoved three hotel towels into it as though it were the gullet of a twenty-foot anaconda, she sent, "I'm not averse to settling if it gives us a chance to open communication with him."

Forrest replied immediately. "I've given up hope."

Something tickled in the back of her mind. Anna texted, "There's always hope."

With the boys shod, she ushered them into the hallway, but then Ryan wanted to be carried.

"I'm not used to this." She shifted him on her hip. "I need to get in better shape if I'm going to keep up with you two."

Gavin bumped up against her and hugged her waist. "But I like it better now."

Now. The last two months had consisted of Anna networking during her solo weeks and then finding activities with the boys during her parenting time. They'd hit every museum in New York City (and the Transit Museum over and over so the boys could climb through the antique subway cars). They'd driven to every destination she could think of and spent overnights in drafty cabins or plush hotel rooms. They'd gone to movies, and story time at the library, and even a Broadway play.

Except somehow the boys didn't need field trips and destinations to have a great time. They'd had just as much fun at a furniture store picking out a new desk to replace her grandfather's.

Whatever job she landed, it would not involve seventy-five hour weeks. She might start freelance consulting and bundle her working hours into her non-parenting weeks. For that matter, she might invest her golden parachute, start up a charity foundation, and live a tightly budgeted life off the interest and an annual salary of one dollar. For the time being, she'd make a full-time job out of her hours with her boys.

At the hotel cafe, Ryan and Gavin begged for donuts, but she told them no, just the hot chocolate. They were, to no one's surprise, devastated and certain to starve—until they beheld someone carrying a to-go hot chocolate topped with a mountain of whipped cream. In wonderment they stared, all thoughts of donuts in the past.

"I want whipped cream," Ryan whispered.

Still a CEO at heart, Anna knew how to negotiate. "Do you promise not to fight about taking a bath?"

Ryan nodded solemnly, urgently. Gavin said, "Me too!"

Anna said, "How about this? We go upstairs with the hot chocolate, and we watch a movie." Either the sugar would have worn off by the end of the movie, or else both boys would have passed out. "Then you each get a bath before dinner."

Even though he was excited about hot chocolate, Ryan looked strung out. He slipped his hand into hers. "Hot chocolate and a movie."

In the middle of ordering two (small) hot chocolates with whipped cream, plus an herbal tea for herself, Anna got interrupted by a shriek. Jumping in place and nearly yanking her arm from its socket, Ryan pointed to a fruit cup in the display case. "Can I have one? They gave us a fruit cup at school, and I loved it!"

Gavin nodded. "I love fruit cups!"

Fruit salad in a clear plastic cup was bright and colorful and probably as much sugar as the donut she'd already refused. Anna, however, was tired of being the mean mommy. "And two of the fruit cups," she said. The teenager behind the counter looked amused. She couldn't be the only mother who got badgered into extra treats, could she? Why else would they set the fruit cups at eye level to a preschooler?

The guy handed each boy a fruit cup and a packet of plastic silverware. Gavin grabbed a wad of napkins. Holding his fruit cup in both hands, Ryan bounced. "Calm down, little man." Anna shook her head as she took the drink holder, then added to the cashier, "You can see how badly they need more sugar."

Ryan leaped down the hallway like a kangaroo. Surely this was not an overtired child. He'd eat half his fruit and all the whipped cream, and then he'd lie unconscious in bed for three hours. They'd have dinner and go back to the pool. Both boys would sleep like rocks, and tomorrow they could do it all over again.

Right in front of the elevator, Ryan made a huge leap, tripped—and fell right onto his fruit cup.

He screamed, and Anna rushed to him. Some of the fruit was on the floor, and juice had gotten on his shirt. She balanced their drink tray on a little table and tried to comfort him, but he kept crying because of his lost fruit.

The elevator door opened, and a woman in jeans and a copper-colored top stepped out. "Oh no!" She crouched beside Anna and righted the cup with as much of the fruit in it as she could. Then she set it beside the drinks and used Gavin's napkins to clean the floor.

"You don't have to," Anna protested while Ryan sobbed into her shoulder.

The young woman met Anna's gaze, her eyes a sky blue that was startlingly out of place against her beige skin and black hair. She seemed friendly. "It's no problem. You look so stressed right now with the kids."

Anna rocked Ryan until his sobs subsided to hiccups. The kid was beyond overtired. Gavin kept patting Ryan's shoulder and saying, "It's okay. We cleaned it up."

When Ryan wouldn't detach from Anna, the stranger said, "I can be an extra pair of hands. You carry him, and I'll carry your drinks."

Gavin pushed the button for the elevator. Anna got to her feet, hefting Ryan up with her. "Thank you. You're like a guardian angel."

The woman gave a startled laugh as they stepped into the elevator. "You do have a guardian angel, and he loves you."

Anna huffed. "My guardian angel should be fed up with me after everything I've put him through. Gavin, push three."

For the first time, the woman seemed off-balance. "Well, no matter what happened in the past, there's more joy in heaven over one person turning her life around than over the lives of ninety-nine perfect people."

Anna side-eyed her. "Have you ever met a perfect person?"

The woman's eyes crinkled. "I'm going to decline to answer that."

Anna laughed out loud. "You must have gone to the same public relations school I did! Well, I'm not perfect, and my guardian angel deserves a medal of honor."

At the door to their suite, Anna set Ryan down so she could use the key card. Gavin went in with the fruit cups, and Anna took back their drinks from the woman. "What was your name?"

The woman said, "Turmiel."

Anna paused. "*Turmiel.* I like it."

The woman looked a little more pleased than Anna would have expected. "I'm glad you like it."

As she turned to leave, Anna said, "Thank you so much for your help."

Turmiel fiddled with the edge of her braid. "My pleasure. We're all in this together."

In the room, while the boys set up their snacks at the table in the sitting area, she went to stand by the window. Ryan would need a new shirt before they watched the movie. She ought to text the swimming photos to Eric and Sharon. Actually, she could send a photo right now of both boys ascending their mountain range of whipped cream.

Instead she gazed at the horizon. A guardian angel...? She hadn't thought about that before. If demons could take an interest in her, it made sense that an angel might as well.

Thank you, Anna prayed. *Thank you for angels, and thank you for saving me. Thank you for protecting Forrest. Please help Sid.*

She closed her eyes. *That woman was right. We're all in this together.*

The boys called her back to the table. "I have an idea," she said as she took a seat. "What if, instead of a movie, we cuddle in bed, and I read you a story?"

Thank you!

Thank you so much for reading about Special Ops! I had an inordinate amount of fun writing this book, and I hope you enjoyed it as well.

Special Ops wasn't originally "a thing" in the Seven Archangels saga—at least not until I rewrote *The Wrong Enemy* from its first published form, and Miriael ended up talking about his background. I thought, "That sounds interesting." After that, Miriael showed up in the novelette, *Once Only,* when Special Ops got involved in rescuing a baby.

Once I saw an actual Special Op, I wanted so much to give these guys their own story. I'd never written about a Power before, so I came up with Cosmiel. In *Sacred Cups,* Belior tells Gabriel about demon-to-human contracts, concluding with, "And now I own a family." Voila! That was the rest of everything I needed.

I'd like to thank everyone who helped me with plot-storming and early reading, and especially Karina Fabian for her insights and for her help with the title. Thank you to Charlotte Volnek, who came out of retirement to create the cover, and to Michaela DeToma for her proofreading skills.

Please consider leaving a review for the book at Amazon or Goodreads. Reviews really help so much, and they don't have to be complex. Just a star rating and a couple of sentences to say how you felt.

I keep a mailing list at http://eepurl.com/dEJjI1 where I share stories about my weird life as well as recommendations for books

I've enjoyed or patterns I've knit. When I knit the shawl that was the model for Anna's prayer shawl, I posted a photo there first. (Newsletter subscribers learned, for example, that the pattern's name is *Wavedeck*.) It's only once a week, and I'd love to see you there.

Thank you again for reading, and I hope we meet again soon!

Did you know there are five other full-length novels in the **Seven Archangels Saga**? Did you know there's also a novelette, **Once Only**?

Well, they're all available on Amazon in Kindle format, and the full-length novels are available in print, as well. Even better, the full-length novels are being released as audiobooks, so check Audible, Overdrive, Hoopla, Chirp, or wherever you pick up your audio. You can ask your public library to pick up a copy, too.

A number of my other books have angels, too. If you want some humor, check out **Honest and for True**. Lee considers New York City her personal playground. She dates for fun, loves her job as an auto mechanic, and can see her guardian angel—a wisecracker with a strange fascination for the Rumours Album. (I love this story. It's so much fun.)

If you want drama, there's **Relic of His Heart**, the story of an angel who's trying to locate a relic stolen from an Italian church at the end of World War II—and the midwife who seriously does not have time for this.

A rosary in one hand. A dagger in the other.

Sister Magdalena never heard of the Catherinite nuns until the day she was faced with her own death sentence.

Rome, 1562. It's the era of the Index of Banned Books and the Roman Inquisition. Kings still burn heretics. The worst threats come from within the Church itself

Only seventeen, Magdalena killed a priest who tried to rape her within the walls of her convent. His powerful family will see her executed, and then they'll destroy her mother and young sister.

Instead, the pope makes an offer. To save her life and protect her family, Magdalena can disappear into a secret religious order, one with a demanding physical regimen to go along with the prayers. She'll pray the psalms and learn to climb walls. She'll sharpen her mind and fine-tune her body. Perfected, she'll infiltrate the Council of Trent.

Magdalena's order slips through cathedrals and palaces at the council, the Pope's silent operatives. They act as bodyguards for the cardinals They gather intelligence. If they find heresy, the penalty is death.

But when one of the pope's own men is named a heretic, Magdalena must decide how far she'll go to protect her church.

Available in ebook and print formats! Assassin nuns doing parkour? Why not pick up a copy and check it out?